Critical acclaim for in
RICHA

Reformed maste
is trapped in a mystery as old as humanity . . .

THE THIEVES OF DARKNESS

"[A] masterpiece. . . . Richard Doetsch handles all the elements of a classic thriller superbly, and his characters are fleshed out and involving. He has earned his seat at the table with other A-list thriller writers."

—*Booklist* (starred review)

"Whip-smart and lightning-paced, *The Thieves of Darkness* left me breathless and awed by the scope and scale of its story. Truly a masterwork by an exploding talent."

—James Rollins, *New York Times*
bestselling author of *Altar of Eden*

Richard Doetsch's breathtaking thriller
THE 13TH HOUR
is "a modern masterpiece of structure and story"*

"Brilliantly conceived, perfectly executed. Fresh, exciting, bristling with originality."

—Steve Berry, *New York Times*
bestselling author of *The Paris Vendetta*

"Daring, original, and perfectly attuned to the pop culture."

—*Providence Journal-Bulletin**

"*Twilight Zone* fans will love the means, mystery fans the method, in this galloping, inventive whodunit."

—*Winnipeg Free Press* (Canada)

"If there ever was a novel that deserves to be read in one sitting, this is it. With a totally original and compelling story line, *The 13th Hour* is one of the best thrillers of the year."

—*Booklist* (starred review)

"Suspending disbelief is worth every moment of Doetsch's thrill ride through time, which tantalizingly reveals the true nature of all the characters involved."

—*Library Journal* (starred review)

"Readers will enjoy the clever razzle-dazzle of a story whose parts fit together like clockwork."

—*Publishers Weekly*

"Explodes out of the box with pace, verve, intrigue, and an ingenious premise—a breathless race to stop a murder that has already taken place."

—Andrew Gross, *New York Times* bestselling author

These titles are also available from Simon & Schuster Audio and as eBooks

THE THIEVES OF HEAVEN

"Enjoyable and suspenseful."

—*Publishers Weekly*

"Devilishly fun and enjoyable—more than that, a thriller rich with inspiration, passion, cleverness, and intelligence told by a superbly gifted writer. A highly ambitious novel, and one that delivers on every count."

—Brian Haig, *New York Times* bestselling author of *The Capitol Game*

"At the heart of this spectacular thriller is a classic love story. Michael St. Pierre will literally move heaven and earth to save the woman he loves."

—Stephen Frey, *New York Times* bestselling author of *Hell's Gate*

THE THIEVES OF FAITH

"Well written, fast paced, great characters, history, secrets, tantalizing plot, what more could a thriller reader ask for? This well-choreographed, globe-trotting adventure will keep you totally engrossed. I loved it."

—Steve Berry

"A spine-tingling thriller. . . . An intriguing adventure from its very first pages through to its electrifying concluding chapters."

—MysteriousReviews.com

RICHARD DOETSCH

THE THIEVES OF DARKNESS

POCKET STAR BOOKS

New York   London   Toronto   Sydney

Pocket Star Books
A Division of Simon & Schuster, Inc.
1230 Avenue of the Americas
New York, NY 10020

This book is a work of fiction. Names, characters, places, and incidents either are products of the author's imagination or are used fictitiously. Any resemblance to actual events or locales or persons, living or dead, is entirely coincidental.

First Pocket Star Books paperback edition March 2011

POCKET STAR BOOKS and colophon are registered trademarks of Simon & Schuster, Inc.

For information about special discounts for bulk purchases, please contact Simon & Schuster Special Sales at 1-866-506-1949 or business@simonandschuster.com.

The Simon & Schuster Speakers Bureau can bring authors to your live event. For more information or to book an event, contact the Simon & Schuster Speakers Bureau at 1-866-248-3049 or visit our website at www.simonspeakers.com.

Cover design by Alan Dingman

Manufactured in the United States of America

10 9 8 7 6 5 4 3 2 1

ISBN 978-1-4165-9897-8
ISBN 978-1-4391-0328-9 (ebook)

For Virginia,
My best friend.
I love you with all my heart.

"The most beautiful thing we can experience is the mysterious."
—ALBERT EINSTEIN

"Myths which are believed in tend to become true."
—GEORGE ORWELL

PROLOGUE
THE AKBIQUESTAN DESERT

Chiron Prison sat atop a large outcropping at three thousand feet with a commanding view of the rust-colored, rock-strewn desert of Akbiquestan, a small breakaway republic north of Pakistan. Fifty miles from any civilization, the three-story stone structure was carved out of the top of the Hersian Plateau, the lone hint of a landmark in an otherwise flat, barren wasteland. At midnight, with its watchtowers illuminated, it looked remarkably like a crown atop a demon.

The legendary penitentiary had been built in 1860 by the British as a prisoner of war camp to hold and execute those who disagreed with the ways of the Empire. Beyond the addition of electricity, not much had changed in 150 years. The sixty-foot-high building was a giant block of granite capped with castlelike battlements and four octagonal guard towers at its corners. Named for Dante's chief guardian of the seventh circle of hell, its reputation far exceeded even Dante's vision. Of late, it sat 30 percent full, with a downsized staff of eighteen guards, men who would likely have been residents if they did not work in the prison. The penal complex was underfunded, and a destination for the type of convict that drew little sympathy from Amnesty

International. A stretch at Chiron was a death sentence, even if a prisoner wasn't technically scheduled for execution. Whether he had been sentenced for five years or thirty, no prisoner ever lived to see parole.

Death came in a variety of ways: execution, either by the electric chair or beheading, depending on the warden's mood; a guard's bullet while trying to escape; murder by a fellow convict; or, as was most often the case, the prisoner's own hand.

There was only one way to get to Chiron, and that was by a hardpack road, six miles long from the desert floor and barely wide enough for a single truck, that meandered up the mountainside.

There had not been an escape from the prison since 1895. If one were lucky enough to somehow breach the three-foot-thick walls, one would be faced with two options: a six-mile run down the access road—which was under the watch of two permanently manned guard towers—followed by a perilous fifty-mile desert journey; or a three-thousand-foot dive off the front cliff, where one could taste the air of freedom for all of twenty-five seconds before being shredded on the razor-sharp rocks at the base. It was one of the few prisons in the world that had no need to be encased within a circumference of razor wire.

Chiron was a destination favored by the world's more corrupt judicial systems, those that wanted to make people disappear. It was a place where no thought was given to the population, where white-collar, blue-collar, and no-collar were thoroughly mixed, with the hoped-for end result that they would wipe each other out.

Simon Bellatori sat within his eight-by-eight cell, on the earthen floor, scheduled for death at 5:00 A.M. He didn't know where the dramatic idea of a dawn execution came from, but he thought the practice inhumane.

It was supposed to have been a simple theft, of a letter from the office of a businessman that had been illegally acquired through auction, a letter of great antiquity written by a Muslim grand vizier to his Christian archbishop brother, a letter never meant to be shared with the world. In the modern world, it was a crime undeserving of a death sentence, but the modern world existed only in dreams within the ancient prison walls.

Simon and his partner were supposed to get in and out and be on time for a late dinner reservation at Damsteeg near Prinsengracht Canal in the old center of Amsterdam by 9:00 P.M. But the best-laid plans of mice and men . . .

Now, as he sat in his cell at Chiron, Simon felt a profound regret for what he had done. Not for the theft or any of the deeds in his past. His remorse was solely for involving his friend, who sat in the neighboring cell, for placing someone he cared about in such danger, for delivering someone who trusted him to death's door in this godforsaken land.

For tomorrow, come dawn, they would be awakened and marched into the neighboring room, where a man in a medieval hood would lay them across a cypress table, shackle their arms behind their backs, secure their prostrate bodies to the enormous block of wood, and, finally, strap their heads down with necks exposed to the world for the last time.

The room of death would fill with spectators. The guards would march the prison population in to witness the event, to fill them with fear, to paralyze them into compliance in hopes of avoiding a similar fate.

Last, and in a ceremonial fashion, the warden would

enter, sit front and center, and glare into the eyes of the condemned, peering into their souls. And with a half-smile, his thoughts no doubt already on breakfast, he would give the signal.

Without further delay, the executioner would grasp a ceremonial saber, raise it high, and with blinding speed, bring it down upon the exposed flesh of their necks, severing their heads from their bodies.

THREE DAYS EARLIER

Michael St. Pierre walked into the high-ceilinged great room of his large ranch-style home in Byram Hills, a small town just an hour's drive from New York City. He threw his mail on the leather couch and poured a set of blueprints from a long cardboard tube onto his pool table. His three Bernese Mountain dogs, Hawk, Raven, and Bear, followed him in and sat at his feet as he unfurled the set of security schematics, smoothing them out upon the green felt surface. He had spent four weeks designing the pin-sized cameras and encrypted video surveillance and alarm system for an art storage facility belonging to a billionaire philanthropist by the name of Shamus Hennicot.

Michael understood full well Hennicot's desire to protect his collection of Monets, Rockwells, and van Goghs, and by applying his expertise, unique perspective, background, and insight to the overall project, he had created a system that rivaled anything used by the CIA in its technological impenetrability.

Michael turned and stared at the large painting hung above his stone fireplace, a painting of a majestic angel with wings spread wide, rising out of a glowing tree, its realistic perspective and warm colors reflective of the Renaissance age. It was a Govier, painted in the late sixteenth century and given to him by a close friend, a friend who had begged him to steal its sister painting and destroy it. The request weighed heavily on Michael, as it had been her dying wish—an unusual request, and one that he had fulfilled.

Michael had been a thief, *had been* being the important words. That was a world he had promised to leave behind. He had made that promise to his wife, and to himself, but circumstances had pulled him back in. Since then, he had pulled a single job for the money to pay for his wife's cancer treatment and had helped his friend Simon on several occasions. But each of the acts had been selfless, performed without remuneration, in service to others, in situations in which he had been forced to make moral compromises.

But that was all in his past now; theft was something he was exceedingly good at, but he was happy to tuck those skills away. He had established a legal business, a security business with a constantly growing clientele, a clientele that was fully aware of his conviction for breaking into an embassy to steal diamonds several years back. Michael was and continued to be hired on the basis of his illicit background and a reputation for quality that he had built up over the years. He was consulted because he could think like those who wished to infiltrate buildings, penetrate computers, lay waste to security systems, and steal Monets, Rockwells, and van Goghs. Michael thought like the opposition, he thought like those whose devious minds were focused on defeating safeguards and slipping into bank vaults. Hiring Michael was like stealing the playbook of the opposing team a week before the big game. You learned where to concentrate your defenses, where to plug up your unseen vulnerabilities. With Michael St. Pierre, you learned how to win.

Michael rolled up the blueprints, tucking them back into the cardboard tube, and left them on the couch with his unopened mail. He headed through the kitchen into the dining room. The table was set for two. The marinated steak was in the fridge and ready for the grill, the wine unopened, the crystal glasses lying in wait. Fresh flowers bloomed on the center of the table.

Michael had finally begun to date after eighteen months of mourning the loss of his wife. Mary had been his center, everything he had lived for. Everyone referred to them collectively as if it were one name: Michael-and-Mary, Mary-and-Michael. He'd never imagined being alone at thirty-eight; he'd never imagined life without her; he'd never imagined the swiftness and evil of cancer. And as the weeks and months slowly crept by, he'd never imagined how he would cope. But over time, with the support of his friends and father, he slowly began to regain hope, pushing aside the tragedy, replacing it with the memory of her smile, embracing the words, "Don't cry because she died, smile because she lived."

So, with his wedding ring off his finger and strung about his neck in memorial, he told his closest friends he was ready. And so were they.

With thick, tousled brown hair, his dark blue eyes sharp and focused, Michael was not the type who would ever lack for female prospects. He had a strong, handsome face that bore the signs of having been through life more than a few times. Just shy of six feet, Michael had remained fit, his body hardened by weights, rock climbing, and swimming. He was proud of the fact that he wore the same size jeans as when he was eighteen; he wasn't going to let himself slip down the drain like so many guys his age.

Paul and Jeannie Busch had him booked four Fridays in a row. Four dinners, four dates of smiles and nods and stories to impress, four uncomfortable "Good nights," and four beyond-awkward kisses. To say he was out of practice was an understatement.

But it was on the fifth date that things became unusual.

To start with, it wasn't a dinner date, or a movie; it wasn't even lunch. It was a game of one-on-one basketball on a Saturday afternoon, a date set up by, of all people, his friend Simon Bellatori. *Father* Simon Bellatori, an unconventional priest who was in charge of the Vatican Archives. Simon was a loner, his job consuming his every waking moment, leaving him with little time for many friends beyond Michael. He and Michael had faced life and death together, participating in each other's quests, sharing each other's pain. They had bonded in the worst of circumstances, which resulted in a relationship closer than family. And so, when Simon had mentioned KC, Michael did not want to hurt Simon's feelings, but he couldn't imagine that a date set up by his reclusive, priestly friend would amount to anything short of mild discomfort.

Michael arrived at the outdoor court behind Byram Hills High School, ball in hand, confident in his game. He had never played in school, hockey being his winter sport, but he had a good shot coupled with some moves that never let him come up short in any street match.

KC was already there shooting baskets as he approached. She moved with the grace of a dancer, her feet silently skirting the ground as she dribbled the ball. Katherine Colleen Ryan was tall—taller than anyone Michael had ever dated. At five-ten, she stood almost eye-to-eye with him. Her hair was blonde, the color of cornsilk, pulled back in a ponytail;

her emerald green eyes were clear and brilliant and filled with life. She was trim and athletic, though entirely feminine. She wore a white Nike T-shirt over dark blue shorts; Michael couldn't help his eyes as they were drawn to her tan, lithe legs, amazed at how long they were. As Michael tried not to stare, he thought of the Valkyries, the Norse goddesses who carried the Viking dead from the battlefield.

"Hi," Michael began, extending his hand in greeting. "I'm Michael."

"KC," she said with a subtle English accent that made her sound almost exotic. She took his hand and shook it with confidence. Michael was unsure if the moisture he felt was from his palm or hers.

They both stood there lost for words, their introduction growing uncomfortable with self-conscious smiles and too many nods. They silently walked onto the court, bounce-passing the ball to each other as if it was a language more easily spoken than words. Michael skipped warming up and threw KC the ball to get the game under way.

The game started off cordial; few words were spoken as KC dribbled the ball. She took the ball out, faked left, faked right, took the shot from beyond the three-point line, and drained it. It was after the first basket—the one Michael let her have—that things started to heat up.

She smiled at him and tossed him the ball, her blonde hair swaying with her every move. Michael nodded and took it out, moved right . . . and KC darted in, stole the ball, drove to the basket, and made the shot.

Michael stared at her as if he were looking at a female Michael Jordan. He didn't feel as if he were playing a girl, he felt as if he were the poor schlub plucked from the stands at an NBA all-star game whose lack of talent was being demonstrated in front of fifteen thousand fans. He was already cursing Simon for putting him in this situation and thinking they were a good fit. Some friend.

Nothing was said as KC and Michael looked at each other, one smiling in triumph, the other in amazement-tinged embarrassment. Michael knew he had to step it up to avoid total humiliation.

Swish. Michael watched her make another basket.

But then Michael regained his game and his dignity. He answered with three straight baskets and the game remained head-to-head for the next half hour. For every one he sank, she sank one in return. The sweat was building, their hearts were pounding. Neither gave quarter. They were like two kids playing for the championship.

"Thirty-eight, thirty-eight," KC said in her English accent.

"Next basket wins?" Michael said through heavy breaths.

KC nodded as she dribbled in, but Michael stole the ball, spun left, took the shot, and . . . missed. KC got the rebound, brought it back, and drove for the basket, but Michael stuffed her, stealing the ball. He brought it back, faked a drive, and from forty feet, with a prayer, nailed it.

"Good game." KC smiled.

"Yeah, good game," Michael said as he leaned over, hands on his knees, catching his breath.

"I thought I had you," KC said as she brushed a few stray blonde hairs from her face.

"There's always tomorrow." Michael laughed, hoping to avoid a rematch.

DINNER WAS AT Valhalla, Paul and Jeannie Busch's restaurant in Byram Hills. They ate in the shadowed back corner, like two teens on the first date of their lives. Though they were both hungry, their steaks sat almost uneaten as they became lost in conversation for over three hours, talking about sports and life.

"Is there a sport you don't play?" Michael asked as he sipped a Coke and leaned on the table.

"None that I wouldn't try," KC said. "Though I kind of prefer my sports faster, a bit more dangerous. The civil ones bore me after a time."

"Dangerous?"

"You know, the edgy ones. That's why I love the United States; it's like an extreme playground. You've got the Colorado River for whitewater rafting, the Rockies for climbing and skiing, California for surfing, Lake Placid for luge and bobsled, Wyoming for horseback and hang gliding."

"An extreme junky." Michael laughed. He had always had an affinity for adrenaline, an addiction that had helped shape his former life. "Bungee jump?"

"I can still feel the sweat on my palms from the first time I did it."

Michael sat there absorbing what she said, her interests, her smile, her personality, understanding why his friend had set them up. "How do you know Simon?"

"I was writing an article about the Vatican a few years back," KC said.

"Journalist?"

"Used to be." She paused. "I was researching religious history. He was quite helpful. How do you know him?"

"We help each other out from time to time." Michael hoped the lie wasn't that obvious. "He's a good friend. One of my closest."

"Mine, too," KC said. "I never blind-date, but he kind of insisted."

"I can't tell you how uncomfortable it is to have your friends picking your dates."

"Makes you feel like you can't do it yourself," KC said in total agreement. She smiled. "What do you do for a living?"

Michael thought on this, speaking about the present with no allusion to his past. "I have a security firm."

"Stocks or safety?"

"Safety." Michael laughed. He could never wear a suit and stare at a computer screen all day. "Home and business security systems." Michael hated lying, but it really wasn't a lie as she had asked in the present tense. "Do you still write?"

"I'm actually a terrible writer. I do consulting for countries in the European Union, guide them in bridging the culture gap between their respective countries. Help them see eye to eye."

"Sounds . . . exciting," Michael said with feigned interest.

"Now you understand why I like jumping off bridges with a rubber band around my ankle." She smirked. "I do get to travel a lot and it allows me to work when I feel like working. And better yet, we Europeans take the month of August off."

"August off? Nice. Growing up, my dad the accountant never took any vacation."

"Neither did my mom," KC said, a tinge of sadness flowing through her voice.

"Siblings?" Michael asked, trying to short-circuit her melancholy.

"Little sister. She's a little financial whiz, Goldman Sachs in London. You?"

"Only child; meant more food for me. Are you and your sister close?"

"As can be," KC said warmly. "She keeps yammering about starting her own company. She has this mantra, 'Thirty million by thirty, three hundred by forty.' It's all she talks about. Money. It's getting kind of annoying. I just wish she'd get on with it instead of talking about it."

"If she ever needs help . . ." Michael dug through his pocket, pulled out his wallet, and extracted an elegant, embossed business card, handing it to her.

"Stephen Kelley?" KC said as she read the card.

"He's a financial guy, we're close, he's in that field if your sister ever needs a hand. Tell her to say she knows me. Just don't call on a Monday."

KC tilted her head. "And what's wrong with Mondays?"

"I usually kick him around the golf course on Sundays cleaning out his pockets. It takes him a few days to recover."

"Thank you." KC smiled, moved by the gesture. She reached across the table and took Michael's hand.

KC AND MICHAEL continued seeing each other over the coming weeks, their frequent dates becoming more interesting: golf at Winged Foot, dinner at Nobu; tennis in Forest Hills, lunch at Shun Lee Palace. Michael even got to pitch to her in Yankee Stadium thanks to his father's connections and the Yanks being on the road. The games were always serious but filled with laughter, jokes, and witty repartee. They played for bragging rights and winner's choice of restaurant. The victories were split down the middle, the games consistently going head-to-head, the loser always chiming in with the optimistic rematch phrase, "There's always tomorrow."

Their growing relationship was like nothing Michael had experienced before; it was as if she was a forever friend.

They would talk for hours about anything and everything and then sometimes just sit quietly, comfortable in each other's presence. He felt a sense of calm with her yet at the same time found her alluring, sexy. She had a sense of humor that was self-mocking and sharp, as if in direct response to a discomfort with her own beauty. Even his wary dogs liked her.

It had been almost a month since they met, one month since he barely beat her in basketball. They had yet to consummate their relationship. She respected his heart, his loss. She knew that some things couldn't be rushed; that intimacy occurred only with comfortable, guilt-free minds.

Michael had made dinner, the marinated steak already on the grill, the table set with fresh flowers, the wine open and airing. As KC walked in, she saw the small box on her plate. It was square, pale blue: Tiffany's. They simply smiled at each other as she opened it.

She withdrew a small silver locket and chain and turned it over, reading the inscription:

There's always tomorrow.

She held it in her hand and felt it touch her heart. It was better than a Christmas or birthday gift, for it was given unselfishly, not because of ritual or expectation; it was given from his heart. As she looked up, she could see behind his eyes: He was giving her far more than a locket.

They never made it to dinner. The steak burned, charred to a blackened crisp.

Michael took KC in his arms. He moved slowly. It was like his first kiss, his first time. It had been so long. But he lost himself in the intimacy, his head swirling, his heart pounding. She held tight to him. Neither could tell where one ended and the other began. Their breathing came in fits and starts. They focused on each other, losing themselves to time, each selflessly forgoing his or her own pleasure to ensure the other's. Michael's hands moved gently along her skin, feeling her goose bumps rise despite their heat. There was a passion to the moment. And Michael realized that they weren't having sex—they were making love.

And as they lay there in the afterglow, they took pleasure in the silence, in knowing that they were safe with each other, that no harm could come to them as long as they were in each other's arms.

The following day the call came: KC had to return to work, a business trip to Paris, the City of Lights, to help mollify the egos and temperaments of the German, French, and Spanish representatives to the Union, who constantly bickered over policy. She would be back in a week's time. She asked for a second chance with his steak, yearning for a home-cooked meal. Michael said it would be marinating and ready. The good-bye was quick, as if it was a common practice, both preferring to look forward to long hellos. And as Michael watched her pull out of the driveway, he smiled. He had found something he thought he had lost forever.

Now, as Michael stared at the dining room table, at the unopened wine and fresh flowers, he wondered how he could have been so foolish. It had been four days since KC said she would be back; there had been no call, no note. He had left her countless messages without response. He felt the fool, opening his heart, sharing his soul, naively thinking he would find love again, so quickly, so easily.

He took solace in the fact that he had loved once and married, that he had been allowed to experience something most never truly feel. So Michael counted his blessings, buried his heart, and erased Katherine Colleen Ryan from his mind.

Michael patted Hawk on the head and had begun to clear the unused plates from the table when there was a knock at the door, stirring him out of the moment. The three dogs spun into a barking frenzy.

Michael walked through the great room, hushing his dogs, and opened the front door. A tall man, trim and fit, stood on the front porch, his eyes sharp and alive, belying his age, his salt-and-pepper hair perfectly groomed. He wore a blue Zegna sport coat and tan slacks with razor-sharp creases; everything about the man was exact and precise, even the angle at which he had parked his Aston Martin.

"Hi, Michael," Stephen Kelley said.

"Hey, Dad," Michael said with surprise.

"Are you alone?" his father asked as he peered into the house.

"Mmmm, you might say that. Come on in. What's up?"

"It's about Simon."

CHAPTER I

The gale-force wind whipped back Michael's hair, buffeting his clothes, rippling his cheeks. His body was prone, his arms and legs extended to control his fall. It had been five seconds since he left the safety of the plane and Michael was already at the terminal free-fall velocity of 120 miles per hour.

Michael glanced at the altimeter on his wrist, watching the numbers fall toward his deployment height of four thousand feet. Though comfortable with skydiving, he was never foolish; he didn't want to deal with that fatal free-fall injury, SDT: sudden deceleration trauma—what some people called hitting the ground.

Michael pulled the rip cord; his chute fluttered out of his para-pack and jerked him to a halt. The parafoil spread above him, capturing the air and guiding it across its air-foils, allowing Michael to control his descent and direction as if he were flying.

Every time he released his chute he said a little prayer and made sure he could easily reach the hook knife that dangled at his side. Though he packed his chute himself, he dreaded becoming entangled, having to cut away his main chute in time to deploy his reserve. He knew it was rarely the novice who was killed skydiving; more often than not, it was the overconfident expert.

He gripped the guidance handles of his parafoil and directed himself toward the far edge of the outcropping. The prison sat upon a ledge that was more akin to a Wyoming mesa than an Akbiquestan mountain. The lights of Chiron Prison were the sole sign of civilization for fifty miles. It was an imposing structure, seeming to grow out of the earth, out of hell itself. There was no barbed wire, razor wire, or fences. Its location and height served that purpose far more effectively. At three thousand feet, surrounded by desert, the prisoners would be imposing their own death if they attempted escape.

The half moon on the cloudless night painted the world blue, softening the sharp rock outcroppings, dyeing the desert so it appeared as comforting as the sea.

Michael landed softly on the far edge of the mesa, a quarter mile from the prison. He immediately pulled in and balled up his chute, removing the chute's container harness and tucking it under a tree. He unclipped the black sack off the front of his chest, knelt on the ground, and opened it.

He removed two 9mm Sig Sauers—oiled and holstered—and affixed them to his body. Michael hated guns; he had never used them until Simon taught him how and even then it was always with great reluctance. He had become proficient only through necessity, and he much preferred his knife. But coming into a prison alone, against a group of armed guards, he had no choice.

He pulled out two small backpacks: BASE jump chutes. Different from the chute he'd just worn, these were designed with a small primer release chute that would be deployed by hand from a low altitude.

He extracted three blocks of C-4. He tucked a timer remote in two of them and stuffed the other block in his pocket. He opened the side pouch and removed a small electrical box, a frequency jammer that would render not only portable radios but all cell phones useless.

Michael had stolen art, he had stolen diamonds, he had stolen keys and golden boxes, but he had never done something like this. Tonight he was stealing his friend back from a death sentence.

Michael worked his way around the perimeter of the prison. There were no guards on patrol, no guards on the battlements, just two teams poised in the north and east three-story towers who were probably more interested in the World Cup soccer match being played on their small TVs.

He looked at the hundred-yard stretch of barren land in front of the prison, his line of sight following the rocky terrain toward the cliff's edge. He confirmed the lack of obstacles and the moon shadow provided by the penitentiary to his rear. If they could survive the ten-second run without being shot, they just might make it.

Michael pulled out a small block of C-4 and buried it at the south base of the prison, the red LED barely glowing through the dirt.

Michael fell back behind the prison and walked a half mile to the power station, the loud whine of its generators echoing off the prison and surrounding terrain. Utility lines and electrical power were still foreign words in this remote section of the country. Chiron's desolate location forced them to generate their own power, using gas-driven generators. The electricity was used to power the prison's minimal lighting, radios, satellite phones, and guard-tower searchlights, which were turned on only in the event of an escape attempt. But first and foremost, the generated electricity ensured the comfort of the warden.

The fuel depot contained two five-thousand-gallon tanks that were filled once every two months by a trucker who was paid triple wages to drive up the narrow mountain pass. He was always paid in advance, since the money in his pocket kept him focused as he drove past the hulking charred remains of his predecessors' fuel trucks that littered the valley below.

Michael carefully affixed a small block of C-4 to the first fuel tank and triple-checked the remote. He crept over to the generator and found the main electrical panel. He picked the lock almost as quickly as if he were using a key. He found the main breaker, and without hesitation, flipped it off. The lights of the prison immediately blinked out. Michael closed the panel, affixed the lock, and fell back into the shadows.

It was five minutes before the flashlights of the guards could be seen, bouncing with their approach. Michael watched as two guards came into view, their cigarettes glowing in the night. He couldn't hear them over the whine of the still-running generators, but watched as they unlocked the panel, flipped the switch, and restored the power.

Michael waited until they were back in the prison, reopened the panel, and, once again, flipped off the lights. This time, the two guards walked fast, the anger about being interrupted once again evident in their stride. Michael quickly worked his way around, directly across from the prison door they exited, and waited as they reset the system once again. Michael watched their return. The lead guard removed the key ring from his waist, opened the door, and disappeared inside, the door slamming shut behind him.

Michael went back to the generator, shut off the power again, and hid within the shadows.

It took them ten minutes to arrive this time, their curses easily audible above the generator's roar. They were so lost in their exasperation they never saw Michael two feet away in the dark.

The bullets passed through and erased the anger from the guards' minds; both were dead before they hit the ground.

Michael quickly holstered his pistol, bent, and stripped them of their guns, keys, and radios. He took the lead guard's jacket and hat, put them on, and headed for the prison.

MICHAEL SLIPPED THE key in the side door of the prison. A sudden chill ran through him; he hated prisons more than anything in life. To him it was like having one foot in hell. He had spent three years at Sing Sing a few years back and still had nightmares.

He shook off the feeling and refocused, opened the door, and stepped into the square, dungeonlike room. A raw smell hung in the air. There were only two pieces of furniture: a table and a chair that sat directly across from each other. The floor was slightly sloped toward the middle, where a lone drain sat, from which dark stains radiated outward toward the furniture. Michael looked more closely at the two pieces. They were both rough-hewn, made of thick heavy wood, and were marred by a pungent dark residue. Michael took two stumbling steps back as he realized they were stained with death. The heavy table bore the scars of countless beheadings, and the electric chair . . . Michael could see the scorch marks on its arms and back.

Michael quickly exited the horrific room and stepped into a hall that he supposed could loosely be called death row. In Michael's mind, death row was a term that encompassed this entire prison. This corridor, though, was designed for those who were next in line. From the little that Michael had seen of Chiron, he thought it might be the least cruel exit.

Michael's quickly gathered intel told of the prison's lack of funds, which manifested itself in the absence of roaming guards. He knew that the prison's operation was two small steps above chaos and the guards' attention to duty would be compromised by bitterness and anger, as their treatment was only slightly better than that of their captives. The idea of a breakout would be met with laughter, and therefore, Michael knew, the last thing they would consider was someone breaking in.

Michael quietly walked down the hall, his ears attuned to sounds and movement. His heart raced as the adrenaline pumped through his veins, but where he usually took pleasure in breaching security, now he found himself filled with trepidation and fear, for he had no idea of Simon's condition. If he was hurt, Michael would have to carry him out; it wouldn't be like some artifact that he could abandon, some piece of art he could drop on the ground to steal back another day.

Michael worked his way down the hall and looked through the small slotted window set in the middle of a heavy, solid wood door. The cell was small, shadow-filled, the smell of human waste acrid in the air. And it was empty. Michael continued down the hall; there were ten such doors, and the first six cells were vacant. He came to the seventh and peered through the small, barred opening. A figure sat on the floor, back to the wall. Michael could barely make out the silhouette.

"Simon?" Michael whispered.

The figure's head jerked up in surprise, cautiously turning. Not a word was said as the shadowed figure rose and approached the door.

As Michael looked through the small opening, he realized this wasn't Simon. The person was shorter, the shoulders less broad. Michael lifted his small penlight, flicked it on, and shone it into the cell. As the dirty hair was cleared from the face, Michael could finally see the eyes staring back. They looked at him with a mix of emotion: fear and anger, shame and rage. Their emerald-green color was muted by circumstance.

Michael's heart plummeted, his mind spun into confusion by the unexpected sight of the woman before him, the woman who sat on death row, the woman he had held in his arms less than two weeks ago.

Michael was left speechless as he stared into KC's eyes.

SIXTY-THREE HOURS EARLIER, KC had stared into the dark recess of a two-by-two-foot wall safe. She stood in the middle of a top-floor office in Amsterdam, the midnight world dark around her. The room was lavishly appointed: Hancock & Moore chairs and tables, antique Persian rugs, priceless Expressionist artwork, the latest electronics.

On her head she wore a small headband, its central pinlight illuminating the open wall safe before her. In her hand she clutched a yellowed letter encased in clear plastic. It was impossibly old, its black handwritten lettering having bled into the paper's creases. Written in Turkish, it was indecipherable to her but for intertwined symbols of Christianity, Judaism, and Islam that appeared in the uppermost corner.

She handed the letter to Simon, who quickly ran it over a portable scanner that was attached to his cell phone, sending the image back to his office in Italy.

KC carefully closed the safe door, careful not to trip the alarm system that she had so expertly overridden fifteen minutes earlier. She rehung the picture over the safe door and straightened out the bric-a-brac and curios that sat on the shelf below.

She had turned to leave when her eyes fell on the painting hanging on the wall nearest the desk. It was called *The Suffering*, by Goetia, a masterpiece painted in 1762, at the height of the artist's career, just after the death of his wife. KC knew it well, probably better than any painting on earth. She had researched its trail of ownership, the artist's biography and mental state, the type of paint used, the canvas it was created upon. She had become an expert in all things Goetia, as *The Suffering* was the first thing she had ever stolen and sold on the black market.

Her mind spun and she stared at Simon.

"What?" Simon said, seeing her concern.

"I stole that painting ten years ago," KC said as her eyes darted around the room. "We've got to get out of here, now."

Simon pulled out a preaddressed and stamped envelope as he ran out of the office. He stuffed the plastic-encased letter inside, raced to the lobby, and shoved it down the mail chute.

KC was already at his side. "Do you think this was a setup?"

Simon stared at her. "Absolutely not, I—"

But before he could finish, the elevator pinged open, its interior lights off. Three guards burst out, while two men remained in the shadows of the dark cab, silently watching as Simon and KC surrendered. And though KC couldn't see their faces, she knew exactly who the shorter man was. It wasn't just his silhouette that confirmed it, it was the change in the air, a feeling of dread she hadn't known since she was a teenager.

BARABAS AZEM AUGURAL, the warden of Chiron, sat in his apartment on the uppermost floor of the prison. It was a twenty-five-hundred-square-foot space whose décor stood in sharp contrast not only to the prison but to the desert kingdom as a whole.

The walls were paneled, covered in art and mirrors; the furnishings were elegant and refined—deep suede couches, wingback chairs upholstered in silk. The view out the large windows was of the desert world, its moonlit sand and rocks rolling to the horizon. The room was cool, in sheer defiance of the weather, but the humidity was already seeping in. Barabas cursed the generator. If it was broken it would take weeks to fix, and he refused to tolerate anything short of his accustomed comfort.

It had been ten minutes since Jamer and Hank had gone to reset the power plant for the third time this evening. He knew he should have done it himself. There was not a soul in this prison above the desert who possessed an ounce of intelligence, himself excluded, of course.

He had risen through the ranks of the Akbiquestan army, achieving the rank of colonel through hard work, bribery, and the elimination of the one general who disapproved of his inhumane tendencies. Barabas had retired

with a full pension and a full bank account courtesy
of his innovative, capitalistic acumen and his ability to
blackmail and strong-arm the people and country he
had sworn to protect. He had accepted the job as warden
for Chiron, as it provided the perfect haven from which
to run his varied enterprises, including "disappearing"
people—some of whom didn't come through the judicial
system—into the bowels of their cells and eventually their
unmarked graves.

Barabas shone his flashlight about his apartment, found
his radio, and thumbed the talk button. "Jamer!" he
shouted. "If you don't get the power back on in the next
thirty seconds, don't bother coming back."

He waited for a reply but nothing came.

"Jamer?" Barabas didn't have a slow build to anger; he
was already fuming. Anyone who didn't snap to, anyone
who crossed him always paid the price. And Jamer would
be paying the highest. But then he recalled the fear in which
his men held him. They knew his lack of hesitation in putting a bullet through the head of an underling and tossing
his body into the valley. They knew his wartime reputation
for slaughtering the innocent for a bottle of vodka. Jamer
was his second in command, and if he wasn't answering, he
wasn't capable of answering.

Barabas went to his closet and quickly dressed in his
fatigues, cursing the two guards the entire time. He grabbed
his pistol, radio, and flashlight and headed out the door.

THE GUARDS HAD been lulled into passivity. The triple
loss of power had clouded their minds to suspicion, all
thinking that the weather had finally taken its toll on the
generator's overused circuits. Most of them actually wel-

comed the dark—no one would be the wiser to their nodding off in the 105-degree heat.

They collectively smiled as they heard Barabas's anger on their radios. Though none of them voiced their opinion, for fear of reprisal, they all internally rejoiced that maybe for once the warden would have to endure the desert heat that they suffered under.

The prisoners were all sleeping, unaware of the situation, as the cells and hallways all lacked lighting and electricity to begin with, the natural light of the sun and moon being the sole source of illumination to the prison blocks as it had been for a century and a half.

It would suit them all just fine, guards and prisoners alike, if the power didn't come back for days. It wasn't as if they needed it. It wasn't as if anyone was going anywhere.

MICHAEL SLIPPED THE guard's key into the lock, ripped open the cell door, and locked eyes with KC. She stared back at him, her face a mask, devoid of emotion. She was dressed in torn black coveralls that weren't standard prison attire; they fit too perfectly. Her face and hands were smudged with dirt and filth. Michael's mind melted to confusion as he looked upon the woman who had left him ten days ago with no contact since. The silence of confusion quickly slipped to anger. KC was too smart, too capable to be here by accident. Michael realized that the month they had spent together was a lie, her deception exceeding all bounds.

Suddenly the guard's radio clipped to Michael's belt emitted a burst of static, and words in an incomprehensible language.

KC looked at Michael and finally broke the moment.

"He said, 'There's been a breach,' something about 'no one gets out alive, shoot on sight.'"

Michael heard the silent prison explode into chaos on the floors above. His focus quickly returning, he tucked his emotions away along with the question of KC's foreign language abilities, and quietly asked, "Where's Simon?"

"Michael?" the voice called from the neighboring cell.

Michael keyed the cell door to the left and tore it open. Simon stood there, at his full six-one, wearing a dark shirt and pants, both of which were shredded, barely clinging to his taut body. He looked more like a soldier than a priest. His rugged face was bruised and bloodied, his jet-black hair matted with sweat, the gray flecks and streaks more pronounced. His calloused knuckles bore the welts of someone who had recently used his hands for something beyond prayer.

Simon said nothing as he looked back at Michael; he knew what he was thinking. He and KC were in this together. Michael wasn't sure who had put whom in danger but now was not the time to sort things out. Michael tossed him one of the guards' pistols. Simon pulled back the slide, ejected the clip, verified everything was working, and readied the gun.

"Let's go."

As the three ran down the corridor, Michael was already thinking how the entire jailbreak had just skidded out of control. Unless he thought quickly, no one would survive.

MICHAEL, SIMON, AND KC slipped through the rear door and into the night. Michael again heard the foreign voice over the guard's radio. He opened his black bag, pulled the frequency jammer, and affixed its magnetized back against the standpipe adjacent to the door. He flipped the switch, watching as the small red lights began to glow and flicker. He checked the guard's radio; white-noise static cried out. The small black box had jammed all radio communication.

Michael reached back into his bag and pulled out the two BASE chutes, handing one to KC. "Do you know how to use one of these things?" Michael asked.

"What do you think?" KC said with no sense of humor.

"Just a yes or no answer," Michael exploded.

"Yes," she snapped.

"Strap it on, then."

"Where are we going?" she asked as she affixed the pack to her back.

Michael pointed to the cliff's edge one hundred yards away, across the wide-open range in front of the prison.

Michael tossed the second chute to Simon. "You know how to—"

Simon held up his hand as he quickly strapped himself into the harness.

Both KC and Simon realized at that moment that Michael's black bag, his bag of tricks, was empty.

"What about you?" KC said as she tucked her long blonde hair inside her shirt.

"Don't worry about me. I'll meet you down there."

"No way." Simon glared at Michael. "Take mine. I'll find another way down."

"I said don't worry about me. I'll get down." Michael pointed at the stretch of land they needed to cross. "On my signal, you both run like hell and dive out as far as you can off that cliff. It's three thousand feet and sheer. Throw your pilot chute after a three count and ride it out into the desert."

"We can't run fifty miles of desert," KC whispered through gritted teeth.

Michael glared at KC. "I thought you liked extreme sports."

Simon and KC looked at the barren wasteland before them, pulled out the small pilot chutes from their BASE packs, and gripped them tightly.

Michael held out his arm, motioning them to wait. He glanced at his watch, watching the seconds tick down, pulled the small remote from his pocket, its high frequency operating above the jammed radio frequencies, and thumbed the switch.

The explosion echoed off the far side of the prison, its roar climbing up into the night. Simon and KC took off in an all-out sprint for the cliff.

Without a word, Michael raced in the opposite direction.

BARABAS STARED AT the open and empty cells of the two Europeans. He knew he should have forgone the ritual morning execution and just shot the man and woman in the head upon their arrival.

He tried his radio but found it a static mess. Not only were the lights out, and all the electricity, but so were all of the handheld radios. Everything electronic was fried. Which was why he was thankful for his good old-fashioned gun. No electronics, simple reliable mechanics. He pulled back the slide, chambered a bullet, and headed through the execution room.

A sudden explosion reverberated through the halls, startling Barabas and notching up his anger tenfold. Without thought he raced past his electric chair and chopping block and headed for the door.

Barabas had been paid fifty thousand dollars to ensure the deaths of the man and woman. He had taken delivery from someone who acted as their judge and jury, a man who paid him a thirty-thousand-dollar bonus above his going rate for such things to ensure Barabas's expeditiousness, discretion, and silence. Barabas had a reputation for efficiency and ruthlessness; he was afraid of nothing and never failed in his dealings. But the judge-and-jury man had raised something in Barabas that he had never felt before: fear. He had heard the saying that everyone is afraid of something. Well, Barabas had found what scared him. If he didn't ensure the death of his two escaped prisoners, there was no doubt that the judge-and-jury man would return to ensure his.

Barabas charged out the back door and looked around. He saw the black box with the blinking lights affixed, tore it off the wall, threw it to the ground, and crushed it under his boot. He flipped the button on his radio and smiled as it sang to life.

"There has been an escape; all guards, shoot to kill."

He looked across the yard at his jeep, his 1972 jeep, his jeep without any electronics to speak of. He hopped into the seat and breathed a sigh of relief as the jeep started right up. He turned on the headlights and jammed down the gas pedal, heading out of the parking lot toward the front of the building.

KC AND SIMON ran across the open ground in front of the prison. Simon was fast, but KC passed him right by. She ran silently, her arms and legs pistoning, a blur in the night. They were enveloped in darkness but could see the bluish outline of the cliff ahead. They held tightly to the small pilot chute in their hands. Simon didn't look back at the prison towers or battlements, but he knew the bullets would be there any second. And though they might not see their running targets, a contingent of rapid-firing guards would very likely strike their mark. Simon had been under fire before but he wasn't sure if KC had ever truly experienced the fear that came with being under a barrage of bullets. She was a good thief, as good as Michael. Their capture was not her fault. They had fallen victim to something neither could have anticipated.

And even though the gunfire could start at any minute, their situation now was preferable to sitting in the prison behind them. They had a chance, a chance given to them by Michael. Simon hoped Michael wasn't sacrificing himself for their survival; he hoped he truly had a way to get off this godforsaken rock.

UTTER CONFUSION RIPPLED through the prison, with guards shouting, stumbling through the dark halls, and calling out to one another. And then, like an infection, the prisoners caught on, aware that one of their comrades in crime had jumped ship. They began shouting, cheering, banging anything they could against their cell walls. It was as if hell had suddenly awakened, crying out, cheering on those who would defy inevitable death.

The guards didn't know which way to turn. They ran to the battlements, peering out into the night, but were blind; they raised their rifles as if they'd somehow catch sight of whoever had slipped their grasp.

SIMON AND KC heard the chaos erupt within the prison walls. Simon chanced a glance over his shoulder and saw the silhouettes and shadows of the guards scurrying about the ramparts and battlements, guns raised. He braced himself for the inevitable fusillade, turned back, and ran harder.

And the gunfire erupted. Bullets hit and skittered on the rocky ground around them. Simon could hear the high-pitched whizzing as the full metal jackets sailed past. The reports of the guns sounded like thunder as they echoed around the mountain.

Ten yards ahead Simon spied the cliff's edge. He turned to KC, saw her focus and speed up. Side by side they came to the edge and without hesitation, without slowing a bit, dove straight out, sailing into the night.

As Michael raced for the woods, he heard the roar from the prison confines, the inmates on the verge of riot. He did not know their crimes, he did not know their hearts, but a sentence in Chiron was certain death. Michael knew his friends did not deserve to die, no matter what they had done. This was not a place for the carrying out of justice, this was a place of death, a place with no regard for guilt or innocence. He hoped that those left behind would find salvation, though it would never be here on this lifeless rock.

Michael ran along in the shadows a quarter mile to where he had hidden his parachute. He hoped his lungs would hold out long enough for him to make it there and all the way to the cliff without exploding. Michael cursed himself, cursed everything around him. He was always a careful guy, but he had opted not to bring the extra, redundant BASE jump chute. He never imagined he would be breaking out two people, let alone that the second would be KC. He struggled to keep his mind focused, the swirl of emotions impeding his every thought, his mind vacillating between love and hate, fear and anger, deception and honesty. He had no idea why KC and Simon were here or what they had done. All he knew was that he wanted answers, all the answers, if they all got out of here.

Michael made it to the tree line and quickly found his discarded chute. He pulled his knife and cut away the main chute line from the harness. He wasted no time, strapping the harness back on his body, praying that the reserve chute was packed right.

Without a moment's thought, he charged back toward the prison.

BARABAS'S JEEP ROUNDED the corner, his headlights falling upon a man in a full-out sprint. It wasn't one of his prisoners; it wasn't the man or the woman. Barabas didn't know who it was, but it was obvious he was responsible for the escape. Barabas aimed his jeep right at the running man, leaned out the doorless side, pointed his gun, and hit the gas.

The headlights drew the guards' attention. They all looked out from the battlements and saw the jeep gaining quickly on the running man, and as if in automatic response, they raised their rifles and began shooting. Gunfire echoed throughout the valley, the trigger-happy guards reveling in the fact that they could take advantage of the moment and enjoy some target practice. What had once been a dull evening filled with no electricity and boredom had suddenly blossomed into excitement as they all smiled and shouted with each pull of the trigger.

Barabas himself took aim at the figure before him, fifty yards ahead. He steadied his gun hand while guiding the jeep and began rapid-firing.

* * *

FEAR TORE THROUGH Michael; he had not expected to be the bull's-eye target of all of the guards, the fifteen-strong contingent rapid-firing at him. The bullets hit the ground behind him as he raced for the cliff. The edge was up ahead, falling off into total darkness. Michael ran harder than he had ever run before, knowing that the effort and pain would prove worthless if he didn't make it.

But the bullets were erupting closer, shattering the ground around him. It would be only seconds before one of the shooters got lucky.

Without breaking stride, Michael reached into his pocket and pulled out the small remote. He thumbed back the cover, hit the red switch . . .

And the night was torn apart. An enormous fireball rose from behind the prison, lighting up the world around it. The fuel tanks, in concert with the C-4, rained destruction upon the generating plant. Even at a distance, Michael could feel the heat of the blast searing the air. The barrage of gunfire fell to silence as the guards instinctively dove for cover.

THIRTY YARDS BACK, Barabas was not deterred. He never even looked in the direction of the fireball. His attention was like that of a hawk on its meal, fixed without distraction upon Michael. He rapid-fired his pistol until it clicked out of bullets. There was no time to reload. He pinned the gas pedal to the floor. He was out of ammo, but that didn't deter him. Ten yards. It would only be seconds before he ran the man down, the man who had destroyed his prison, freed his captives, and ruined his life.

MICHAEL HEARD THE roar of the engine behind him, its pitch climbing as it approached with unabated acceleration.

He could hear the crunching of the ground, the pinging of the pebbles as they hit the undercarriage of the jeep. Michael refused to look back; he refused to look at death. The jumping headlights grew brighter as they played off the cliff's edge only feet away . . .

Michael leaped out into the night. The wind once again poured over his body. Without a pilot chute, he would have to pray that the reserve was packed properly and the deployment was quick. He held tight to the rip cord as he free-fell into darkness.

BARABAS SAW THE abyss too late; his focus had been only on the runner. He slammed on the brakes with both feet, ramming the pedal into the floorboard. The jeep skidded left to right, its inertia determined to sail him out over the edge. He threw the wheel hard left, hoping to avoid the inevitable, but it was too late. His speed was too great for the brakes to overcome; the jeep skidded sideways, finally slipping over the cliff into oblivion.

MICHAEL HEARD THE jeep behind him scrape over the edge. He craned his neck and watched as its headlights fell through the air, tumbling end over end. He turned his body and waited before pulling his chute, afraid of being pulled right into the descent of the two-thousand-pound vehicle that was still behind him, tumbling his way.

Michael turned his body, expanded it as much as he could to create the most drag, slowing his descent. It was only moments before he would be killed by either the falling jeep or an abrupt impact with the ground.

The jeep, as if in slow motion, crept alongside him. Michael briefly saw the driver's fear, saw him clutching the wheel as if it would somehow deliver him from death. And Michael yanked the rip cord.

The chute skittered out of the pack, dragged up into the night by the wind, and the canopy deployed, yanking Michael's body to an almost sudden halt. Michael watched as the lights of the jeep fell away to pinpoints and then a sudden fiery explosion glowed at the foot of the cliff, its orange tendrils reaching up for him. The deep, resonating sound echoed up seconds later.

Michael turned and guided the chute through the plume of rising smoke out into the desert on a northerly heading. He caught his breath as he began drifting. Suddenly, headlights flicked on, illuminating a section of level ground. Michael glided in, coming to an easy landing. KC and Simon were leaning up against a Land Rover.

A tall man, six-four, walked up to Michael, his blond hair a tangle in the night's summer breeze.

"You're always late," Paul Busch said as he wrapped his bearlike arms around Michael, hugging him tight.

CHAPTER 2

At forty-seven stories, Wake Financial was the tallest building in Amsterdam. Built in 2007, it soared above the Amstel River and had an unobstructed view west to the North Sea. It sat just south of the historic district of the Dutch capital with its meandering canals that gave the city its nickname, Venice of the North. The three uppermost floors of the glass structure were occupied by the PV Group. Floor forty-five traded stock and precious metals, floor forty-six bought and sold real estate, and floor forty-seven dealt in the more illicit trades.

The organization was owned and presided over by Philippe Venue. The sixty-two-year-old sat behind an enormous black onyx desk, his thick, gnarled hands stroking a large paperweight, his eyes locked on a dark oil painting that hung upon the near wall. Over two hundred years old, it depicted a sick child in its mother's arms amidst a host of warring gods fighting among the sunlit clouds.

Venue's office was vast, over one thousand square feet. The furnishings were thick and heavy; leather and suede. There were several seating areas, a long cherrywood conference table that sat sixteen, and an enormous fireplace that lay dormant for the summer months but was constantly aflame during the cold Dutch winters. There were book-cases adorned with antiquities, with a heavy representation of Byzantine sculpture and carving; the walls were covered with a host of Renaissance and Expressionist paintings, while Classical Greek and Roman statuary rested upon squat, fluted pedestals. Though some of the art had been procured through auction houses, some had been obtained in a less legitimate fashion. It was similar to the way he collected companies: some through aboveboard monetary transactions, others through more physical confrontations. But whatever the acquisition might be, he orchestrated its obtainment and concluded it here in his palatial office suite, the inner sanctum of a man whose reputation had grown to mythic proportions.

Venue stood six-foot-three and carried the weight of a wrestler. His hair had receded almost to nothingness, and what little he possessed had been gray since he was thirty. His face was thick and gnarled from several broken noses and small scars achieved on the streets of his childhood, the streets that had afforded him an education that could never have been achieved at Yale, Harvard, or Cambridge. He had been handsome in his youth in a rough-and-tumble way, the broken, slightly off-kilter nose giving him character as opposed to hideousness.

He wore a black pinstripe Armani suit, a blue Hermès tie, and black Gucci cap-toe shoes. It was his battle uniform of choice for negotiations, hirings, and firings. He was a man of singular purpose and that purpose was himself. He had amassed a fortune of more than three billion dollars over twenty-five years and had done it with no one standing at his side. There was no room in his life for the foolish demands of family or love, only the drive to gain wealth and power.

At the age of thirty-eight Venue started an investment firm from scratch, basing himself in Amsterdam. It had always been his favorite city, in a beautiful world where laws were lenient and morals lax. He loved the canals and the architecture of old; the brick and stone town houses that lined the picturesque waterways; the four hundred quaint bridges that crossed them. As Amsterdam was one of the few European cities spared bombing during World War II, the old section of the city was able to resist the encroachment of the modern world.

Venue hired experts in stock trading, real estate, and finance, and went about investing judiciously, buying companies for their synergistic capabilities. He installed fifteen security monitors upon the wall near his desk, hooked up to over fifty cameras on the two floors below so as to monitor the productivity of every employee as their images cycled by. Venue would sometimes stare at them for hours, watching the hustle and bustle, the frantic deal-making, all for his sole benefit—a hive of men and women serving to enrich their keeper.

The companies Venue purchased were varied: energy, textiles, pharmaceuticals, entertainment. Once he set his sights on his quarry, he wouldn't relent until he had taken it down, dragging it into his conglomerate. He had a unique style of negotiation, one that could bend the will of even the most difficult seller. While organized crime looked to control drugs and prostitution, he used similar tactics to acquire and control legitimate enterprise, bending people to his will through fear, intimidation, and sometimes even death.

Accusations were only whispered, and bringing charges was never even considered. He had filled officials' pockets with money, graft, and trepidation. He was as feared as the devil and no one thought he could be stopped. But as in all things in life, even the devil has his day.

The markets had turned; vast profits became stunning losses. Real estate prices became depressed, wiping out his highly leveraged equity positions.

Now, as he turned his attention to the images on the wall of monitors, there was hardly any activity beyond a handful of traders trying to shore up his company and a bevy of accountants fabricating books, building illusions to keep the authorities away.

But what troubled him more, beyond the loss of his riches and power, was that *they* had found him. It was only a matter of time before he was revealed to the world for what he truly was and what was left of his fragile empire crumbled around him.

A young man sat before him; he was blond, blue-eyed, and had yet to realize he was actually handsome. He had grown up poor and longed to give something back to his parents, who had sacrificed so much for his education, for his life. Jean-Paul Ducete did his undergraduate work at the Sorbonne and his graduate work at the London School of Economics and was first in his class—both times. Recruited two years earlier for his unnatural intelligence and his insatiable drive to succeed, he worked eighteen-hour days seven days a week for Venue. His apartment, only one block away on Vristed Street, was used solely for sleep. He took all his meals while at work and postponed life and marriage so as to always be on the job. He dedicated himself to Venue and his visions, knowing that this would lead to the beginning of his own fortune, to being able to give back to his family, to being able to create a life of meaning and value.

But fortune is a word with many meanings, and his fortune had changed less than a half hour earlier. The mistake wasn't his, it was made by an underling. It was a simple error that could not have been detected by regulators, an error that was easily corrected without consequence, but an error nonetheless. And in the eyes of someone like Venue there was no room for error, unless it was committed by himself. Venue delivered a two-hour lecture to Jean-Paul, most of it on his own brilliance, his own honesty and integrity, exhaustively expounding on his own genius and how moronic the rest of the world was.

Venue demanded Jean-Paul's resignation and typed up the email announcement to the employees that Jean-Paul had left to pursue other interests.

Venue stood and walked around his desk. Leaning against it, staring down at Jean-Paul, he explained he didn't want to hurt him; he just didn't have room for a single mistake. He stood over him like a father over a son, silently staring down in disappointment at the seated young man.

Then, with a blinding swiftness not natural to a person of sixty-two, Venue grabbed the paperweight and, in a single motion, swung it around, hitting Jean-Paul square in the side of the head. He raised the paperweight again and smashed it down on Jean-Paul's nose, driving the bone back into his brain. Again and again he hit him, the gore exploding about the room. Jean-Paul tried to spin away, but it was useless. He tumbled out of the chair and the old man leaped upon him, pummeling his blond head until it was unrecognizable, his blue eyes swollen shut, what was left of his hair matted red with blood.

Venue finally stood, walked to his private bathroom, and showered. He dressed in a pair of linen pants, a green sport coat, and crocodile loafers. He headed back to his desk, being sure to give a wide berth to Jean-Paul's bloody corpse so as not to stain his clean clothes and shoes. He looked once more at the email announcement of Jean-Paul's resignation and departure from the firm and hit Send.

The phone upon Venue's desk rang. He hit the speakerphone and was greeted by a static-filled voice. "Venue?"

"Well?" Venue said as he leaned back in his chair.

"Barabas is dead," the man said.

"Am I to assume that is not the state of his two latest inmates?"

"They're gone," the man said, as if announcing a death in the family.

"That's what I get for trusting things to corrupt wardens." Venue tried to contain his anger. "What a waste of money, thank you very much."

"Hey, Barabas was your guy," the man shot back. "He did your bidding, not mine."

"If we'd killed them here or at least let the police handle it like I said in the first place—"

"If they were killed in Amsterdam and the bodies traced back to you . . . if they were sent through the court system and it was revealed what they had stolen . . . think about it."

"Don't think you are beyond reproach," Venue said.

"Seems I'm having to clean up more and more of your messes—" the man began.

"And you will continue to do so until I say otherwise," Venue screamed, pounding his fist on the desk, silencing the man. "And how the fuck did they even know we had the letter? How did they know it was in my office? Of all people to know it was in my office . . . What the fuck's going on? The girl and a priest, for Christ's sake, you know what my feelings are on that."

The man on the other end of the phone remained silent but for his steady breathing.

Venue took a moment, allowing his mind to calm. "Speaking of cleanups, I know you're a couple thousand miles away, but you need to send someone to my office for a disposal." He looked at Jean-Paul lying on the floor in a pool of his own blood. "Now do you mind telling me where they escaped to, where they're going?"

"Where do you think? They're coming here."

"I thought they didn't have the letter."

"What does it matter?" the man asked. "We have a copy. I thought you didn't care if they got it."

"That was when I thought they wouldn't survive prison. Before I thought they'd try to beat us to the punch."

"I checked them both myself; they didn't have it."

"Bullshit. They're smarter than you."

"Smarter?" the man's voice was laced with anger.

"Yeah, smarter. They have it and they're going to use it." Venue felt the rage flow through his brain; he wrapped his hand tightly around the paperweight. "What the hell have you been doing? It's been two weeks since I gave you the copy of the letter. You told me it wasn't going to be a problem, that you could break into both places undetected and get me what I want without delay."

"Things like this can't be rushed; it takes time."

"You no longer have the luxury of time. You have to steal the chart before they do."

"Relax, I have a plan."

"What is it?"

"Mmm, no," the man said, trying to take control of the conversation. "Just trust me."

Venue looked at the monitors on his desk, at the images

of empty spaces and crumbling dynasties. He wondered how it was all slipping away. "I don't care what you have to do. I don't care who lives or dies. Kill the priest, kill the girl if you have to, I don't care. I need that chart. My world is falling apart. And if my world collapses, so does yours."

CHAPTER 3

The Range Rover cut across the rutted excuse for a road that bisected the nighttime Akbiquestan desert. Paul Busch pushed the vehicle to eighty, looking to escape this desolate part of the world as fast as he could, thankful for the luxurious suspension that cushioned them against the frequent potholes. At six-four, 225, Busch's oversized frame could hardly be contained by the driver's seat. He resembled a large blond bear, someone who looked more attuned to riding the waves in Hawaii than driving two escaped prisoners and their liberator out of this Eastern desert country. Over the past eighteen months he had gotten himself in shape, running five miles a day, and was proud of the fact that he could once again bench-press his weight. He didn't mind the frequent comments on his ever-improving appearance from his wife, Jeannie, who said he looked like he did back when he was a rookie on the police force, though he couldn't help thinking she was angling for a third child through flattery.

Paul liked to say that he tended bar at Valhalla, though his wife preferred calling him a restaurateur or at least the owner. He had retired after twenty years on the Byram Hills police force and was happy pouring drinks and running what had become a thriving business. What was once a quaint eatery grew into a destination that was sometimes booked a week in advance. The bar, of course, didn't require a reservation and was always filled with a crowd of singles looking for their next conquest.

While the restaurant provided them a comfortable living, he still played the Lotto every week, tucking the lucky sure thing in his back pocket—this in spite of the fact that he had a priceless ruby necklace hidden in the back of his sock drawer. The Russian souvenir from a life-threatening exploit with Michael could be sold for a small fortune, but he decided he'd leave it under the pair of blue argyles for the time being. Busch had found that the anticipation of desires sometimes outweighed their realization. Life was much better when you had what you needed but still held wishes for things yet unattained—it's what kept the drive alive, kept him hoping.

Busch was a contented man, though he still missed his days on the force solving crimes, righting wrongs, burying the arrogant assholes who thought they were above it all. His "the law is the law" attitude had put him in conflict with Michael in the past, particularly when Michael had been his parolee, his charge, his responsibility to ensure he remained rehabilitated and a law-abiding citizen. But it was Michael's unselfish actions in the service of others that made Busch realize that sometimes laws had to be broken for the greater good.

Michael was his best friend, like a younger brother. And like most younger brothers, Michael had a habit of finding trouble—finding it, creating it, solving it—and Paul was often at his side pulling him out of it. And so here he was driving Michael out of trouble—again—the only difference being this time there was a girl involved.

As he looked into the back of the Range Rover, it still hadn't sunk in that KC had been in that prison with Simon. It was a surprise to both him and Michael. Paul had met her twice back in New York. He thought her perfect for Michael: beautiful, intelligent, with a biting sense of humor. He was genuinely happy that his friend was dating, but he never thought he would be dating someone like this.

So Busch was beyond amused as he watched Michael and KC argue and fight like an old married couple. He watched the two of them go at it, trading barbs and accusations, criticisms and self-righteous boasts; there was no doubt in his mind that they were perfect for each other.

"Are you okay?" Michael asked as he saw the bruising and cuts on her arm.

"I'm fine." Though you could see she wasn't. She was banged up, her face smudged, a hint of dried blood ringing her nose.

"Is there something you failed to tell me?" Michael asked, a tinge of condescension in his voice.

"What?" KC snapped. She turned her head, looking out the window.

Michael paused, attempting to calm himself, to purge his veins of the adrenaline that still kept his heart and mind racing, desperately trying not to explode. He continued to look at the back of her head, her blonde hair that was dirt-filled and windblown. He reached out his conciliatory hand, but just as it neared her shoulder—

"What?" KC said, still facing the window, seeming to sense his approach.

Michael pulled his hand back.

"What do you want me to say?" She spun around.

Michael finally boiled over. "A consultant?"

"Look—" KC began.

"You don't work for the European Union." Michael turned to Simon, the moment escalating. "And you . . . with friends like you . . . how the hell can you set us up and not tell me?"

KC turned to Simon, raising her voice, double-teaming him. "How come you didn't tell *me*?"

Simon sat in the passenger seat, the questions hitting both ears. He kept his eyes fixed to the nighttime road ahead, remaining silent, keeping out of the battle.

"How come Simon didn't tell you what?"

KC turned back to Michael, her green eyes growing intense. "Don't start with me. An alarm guy has the know-how and wherewithal to skydive in, penetrate a prison, blow it up, and escape with two people? The reason Simon knows you is the same reason he knows me." She turned back to Simon. "Did you think it was cute to hook us up?"

Simon glanced at Busch, who eyed him, offering no help but a sympathetic tilt of the head as he gripped the steering wheel.

"Okay," KC finally relented, calming down. "So I don't work for the EU and you don't own a security company."

"I actually do own a security company," Michael said defensively. "A legitimate security company where I make a decent, legal living."

"Whatever delusions you live by," KC said as she held up her hands and looked back out the window.

The Range Rover drove through a rusted wire fence and onto a runway. There was no tower, no terminal. The car's headlights, the only illumination, fell on a group of five private planes at the far end of the runway surrounded by eight armed men. They were dressed in light gray pants and shirts; each held a rifle aimed at the high-end vehicle. Busch intermittently flashed the lights in a predetermined signal and the men stood at ease.

He drove the luxury SUV up next to the guards, who opened all four doors. He stepped from the vehicle, nodded, and handed the lead man a roll of cash. Michael, KC, and Simon exited the car and followed behind Busch as he walked toward the largest plane of the grouping and headed up the portable jetway stairs.

KC's eyes went wide as she stared up at the Boeing Business Jet. She turned to Michael with raised eyebrows. "Must be some security company."

CHAPTER 4

The jet climbed into the star-filled sky, heading west toward Rome, its passengers all glad to leave the desert behind. The Boeing Business Jet was state-of-the-art, capable of speeds over 525 miles per hour, with a max altitude of forty-one thousand feet; it was truly capable of world travel. Beyond the spacious seating area it had a fully equipped office, a stateroom, and a lounge.

Simon sat at a mahogany conference table that would have been more at home in a Wall Street boardroom, a medical kit open before him, as he threaded a needle with a black suture. Michael and Busch had pulled out sandwiches and water bottles and sat in large leather recliners, the tan seats equipped with individual phones, media centers, and trays. KC sat directly across from them, downing the first food she had eaten in three days.

Michael was glad to be back in the plane. Though it wasn't his, it still felt like home. Safe and sound. Far from danger and peril in the clear nighttime skies.

"I told the pilot to set a course to take you back to Rome," Michael said to Simon.

Simon looked up at Michael, a question in his eyes.

"Okay," Michael said. "If not Rome . . . where?"

"Istanbul," Simon replied as he threaded the needle through the flesh of his arm. "I need to visit the Vatican Consulate."

"Istanbul," Michael repeated, the moment hanging in the air. He and Busch exchanged a concerned glance.

"It's a beautiful city," Simon added in all seriousness.

"Okay," Michael finally relented with a smile. "Either Rome or Istanbul, we need to stop in Azerbaijan to refuel."

"Azerbaijan?" Busch's voice echoed with concern as he sat forward in his seat.

"Unless you prefer Tehran. But I don't think you'd be as welcome." Michael turned to KC, who hadn't said a word as she polished off two sandwiches and a bottle of water. "Can I get you some more to eat?"

"Thirty-five-million-dollar plane . . ." KC said, more as an accusation than a passing comment. Her face was covered in dirt and grime, her matted blonde hair hanging flat against her face.

"It's not what you think," Michael said.

"Yeah, right," KC said skeptically. "How the hell did you find us?"

"You can thank my father, who, by the way, owns all this," Michael said as he waved his arm, alluding to the food and the plane. "He got a call from the Vatican; they got an anonymous tip that Simon was being held in Chiron." Michael paused, looking back and forth between Simon and KC. "Any idea who Mr. Anonymous might have been or why they would call my dad?"

"Nope." Simon shook his head, not bothering to look up as he stitched a gash on his right forearm.

KC looked at Michael, long, hard, and silent.

Michael didn't press her on what she chose not to reveal;

answers sometimes took patience and time. "At any rate, he received pictures of Simon in handcuffs along with a death notice and a rough diagram of the prison. We pulled some satellite pictures of the area, and presto . . ."

"Your father is rich?" KC asked.

"You might say that, with a capital R-I-C-H," Busch cut in, his eyebrows raised.

"It's not like you think," Michael said in defense. "I'm not some silver-spoon kid."

KC stared, confused. "You said your dad was an accountant and had died a few years back. I distinctly remember you saying, typical middle-class upbringing. You never mentioned this."

"Long story. Abbreviated version: I was adopted," Michael relented. "After my adopted parents died, I met the man who gave me up. We've grown close these past twelve months. He let me borrow his toy—insisted actually."

"Why do I think there is more to the story?" KC said as she stared about the jet.

"There's always more to the story," Michael said, nodding. "But I guess you know that just as well as I do."

KC held Michael's eyes as she changed the subject. "I don't suppose there's somewhere I could get cleaned up."

"Of course."

"Do you think I could use the air phone to call my sister?"

"Use the one in the bedroom, it'll be more private."

Michael stood and led her through the plane, through the living area, past the galley, finally arriving at a master bedroom. Though small, it had a queen-sized bed and was decorated like an old New England inn: white lace curtains and bedspread, oak furnishings. There was a small door that opened into a full bathroom.

"The water pressure's not great on the shower." Michael pointed to a black duffel upon the bed. "There are some clothes in my bag, feel free to take what you want."

KC said nothing as she looked around, unaccustomed to such wealth and convenience.

"And just be sure to dial the country code," Michael said as he pointed to the phone on the wall by the bed.

KC nodded. "Thanks."

The moment dragged on in silence. Alone together for the first time since the rescue, they stared at each other, as uncomfortable as if they had just been introduced. Neither said a word as their faces fought to hide emotion. Michael struggled between the urge to grab her and hold her tight and the urge to just shake her for getting herself into such a mess and for lying to him. They had shared such a degree of intimacy, such a connection, and it all seemed to have been washed away by a tide of deception, leaving them strangers.

Without a word, KC entered the bathroom and closed the door.

Michael turned, walked back through the jet, and sat down at the conference table in front of Simon.

"She's a thief . . . You set me up with a thief."

"A very good thief," Simon said as he finished up his stitches.

The statement cut Michael, in a bit of professional jealousy.

"I've known her for years," Simon continued. "She is the finest of people, Michael. She puts everyone before herself and has experienced much pain; she's alone in the world. She needs to stop for once, put herself first. So I sent her to you; you guys are more similar than you realize."

"What?" Michael shook his head in doubt. "That's ridiculous."

Busch turned toward them. "You're just pissed."

"Damn right, I'm pissed."

"You're pissed because she didn't tell you she was a thief; you're pissed because she hid things from you. Kind of like you did from Mary when she was alive." Busch bowed his head as he offered the admonition. "You never told your wife what you really did for a living until after you were married. And, by the way, when you and KC spent your wonderful month together, at what point did you tell her you were once—or should I say still are—a thief? You're just hating yourself." Busch laughed.

Michael turned to Simon, who tilted his head in agreement.

"You guys are so full of shit," Michael said.

"Oh, quit being pissed at the world," Busch shot back, ribbing his friend. "You're going to let a little thing like this get in the way?"

"What?" Michael tried to hide his nervous laughter. Busch was like a moral barometer and knew Michael better than he knew himself. When Busch had been his parole officer, he had tapped into Michael's heart and mind and never left. They had a brotherly relationship: They could kick the shit out of each other and five minutes later be laughing over a beer about it. As much as it angered Michael, he knew Busch's words to be true.

"She's a female you, Michael," Busch chuckled. "And you just can't handle looking in the mirror."

KC SAT ON the edge of the bed in the stateroom at the rear of the plane, a white towel wrapped around her showered body. Though Michael was right about the pressure, it didn't matter, the hot water washed away the last bits of the nightmare she just escaped from.

"Hello," the female voice said.

KC pressed the air phone to her ear to hear over the ever-present whine of the jet. "Cindy? It's me."

"KC?" Cindy's voice cracked with emotion. "Are you okay? I've been so worried."

"I'm fine," KC said as she looked at a wall mirror, her tired reflection saying otherwise.

"Where are you?"

"In a plane."

"That's not an answer."

"I'm on my way to Istanbul."

"Istanbul?" There was a long pause. "How did you get out of prison?"

"How did you know . . . ?" KC asked in confusion, suddenly sitting up.

"I'll meet you there. I've never been to Istanbul. We can go shopping," Cindy said.

"Shopping?" KC said, completely thrown. "No. I'll be back in London in a few days."

"Why do you need to go to Istanbul so bad? Tell me what's going on. Are you with that guy?"

"Michael?"

"Like there's been any other guy?" Cindy shot back. "Of course, Michael."

"I'm in his father's jet," KC said as she looked about the room, still coming to grips with the luxury she was traveling in.

"He has a jet?" Cindy was impressed, but the tone of her voice suddenly shifted. "KC, I'm glad you're all right, but we need to talk."

"Listen, I'm fine. We'll talk when I get back."

"No, it can't wait. You were in prison, for God's sake, in some desert country."

"How did you know that?" KC demanded.

"I'll tell you when I see you in Istanbul." Cindy's voice echoed with condescension. "And you can explain to me what's going on."

"Do not go to Istanbul," KC shot back, growing angry.

"You're not my mother, KC! Don't talk to me that way."

"You know what, Cindy?" KC could barely contain herself. Her sister knew how to rile her up better than anyone. "I'll call you when I get back." KC slammed down the phone.

MICHAEL HAD FINALLY calmed down. He sat in a leather chair, across from Busch and Simon, sipping a Coke as he stared out the port-side window. The stars filled the night skies as they chased the ever-setting moon into the west.

He was hoping to get a little sleep in. It was more than twenty-two hundred miles to Istanbul, and with a fueling stop in Azerbaijan, the eight-plus-hour travel time would put them in Turkey just when the world was waking up. But he couldn't sleep until he got some questions answered.

He finally turned to Simon. "Do you mind telling me what you were stealing?"

"A letter," Simon said as he zipped up the med kit.

"So the postal police had you sentenced to death?" Busch laughed as he headed back to the galley, his head nearly skimming the ceiling. "Give me a break."

Simon paid him no mind. "It was a letter, a very old letter."

"And the letter said . . ." Busch called out.

Simon looked at Michael; they had been down this road before. It took Simon a moment to gather himself, to phrase the words. "The letter speaks of the location of a sea chart drawn over five hundred years ago and thought lost to time."

"You mean like a treasure map," Busch said dramatically. "You're kidding, right?"

"It's nothing of the sort." Simon shook his head, trying to quell his annoyance. "It's a detailed chart, meticulously painted on animal hide."

Michael was hesitant to ask. "And this chart leads to what?"

"A mountain, somewhere in Asia."

"Of course, where all *sea* charts lead," Busch shouted from the galley.

"Do I want to know what's at the end of this chart?" Michael hated asking.

"Not really." Simon shook his head as he and Michael stared at each other.

"All kidding aside, you got the letter, right?" Busch came back with a tray of food and beer, placing it on the conference table.

"There were complications," Simon said quietly.

Busch shook his head as he took a bite of a sandwich. "Aren't there always?"

"It was almost like they were watching, like they wanted us to steal it."

"Right, and then sentence you to death for it." Busch laughed.

"Who was your unlucky victim?" Michael asked.

"Philippe Venue, a wealthy businessman with the ability to make people disappear with a single phone call."

Michael smiled. "He didn't realize you had friends who, with a single phone call, could find you."

"So, what happened?" Busch said as he grabbed a church key and popped the caps of three Heinekens.

"Basically, KC and I broke in, grabbed the letter from a safe, but before we could get to the ground floor . . ." Simon paused. "Thank God for office building mail slots. I tucked it into an envelope and mailed it to myself in Rome before they grabbed us."

"Simon, no offense, but you got caught," Michael reminded him.

"That's the thing. KC's real good at what she does, she's never been caught. That's what's got her so upset. It's not you, Michael, it's that she thinks she almost got us killed. She thinks we were set up."

"Were you?"

"I don't know."

"But you got the letter," Michael said. "That's good."

"Yeah, I also scanned it. I've got someone translating it now. Venue had it, though, he saw it, no doubt he made copies. He knows where the chart is and I guarantee he's sending someone for it."

"To steal it?" Michael asked.

Simon nodded.

"That's why he had us sent to Chiron. So he could get to the chart first." Simon sipped his beer. He took a moment and leaned back. "We have to steal it before they do."

"What do you mean, *we?*" Busch said as he looked at Michael.

"Relax." Michael turned back to Simon. "So, what are you going to do?"

"I'm going to steal the chart and destroy it."

Michael stared at Simon, a world of conversation flowing between their eyes.

"Michael?" Busch said. "Don't even think about it."

"You know I can't help you," Michael said to Simon. "Paul is right."

"Michael, I'm not asking you to." Simon smiled as he hoisted his beer in toast to Michael. "You saved my life . . . again. I wouldn't ask you or guilt you into this."

"But you're going to steal it anyway?" Michael asked rhetorically.

Simon nodded. Michael understood Simon's determination: He was relentless, and he was not stopped by adversity, police, or prisons.

"What's at the end of this chart, Simon?" Michael asked.

Simon quietly said, "Like I said before, you don't want to know."

"Okay, so *where* is this chart?" Michael asked.

"Istanbul." Simon smiled. "It's a beautiful city."

Busch glared at them. "I don't like this."

Michael turned to Busch and smiled. "We're just dropping him off."

"Actually, you need to drop us both off."

Michael turned and saw KC standing there, cleaned up, her hair once again gleaming, her face as soft as he remembered. She stood in the doorway, her confidence making her appear taller than five-ten. She wore a pair of dark blue sweats and one of Michael's white Oxfords, neither of which had ever looked as good on Michael. Michael's initial anger at her was lost as he stared at her, all thoughts of her deception, of her being in such danger, evaporated; all he could think of was what he had felt ten days ago. She was once again who she was when they had first met, innocent and stunning.

"What do you mean 'us'?" Busch said, seeing Michael was temporarily lost.

"You didn't think Simon was going to do this alone, did you?"

Michael snapped back to the present and glared at her. "No way. You can't do this."

"Don't feel threatened," KC said matter-of-factly.

"Threatened?" Michael shook his head, offended.

"You're threatened that I'm better at this than you."

"What?" Michael couldn't keep the laugh from escaping his lips. "I'm not the one who just got caught with her hand in the cookie jar, who needed to be rescued from a 5:00 A.M. death sentence. I'm sorry, I can't let you—"

"You can't tell me what I can and can't do," KC shot back.

Michael's voice grew louder. "You're on my plane."

"Oh, it's your plane now; I thought it was *dad's*."

Michael was doing everything not to explode. He turned to Busch, whose smile at the situation only managed to stoke him further.

"I'm going to steal this chart, Michael," KC said. "Whether you like it or not."

CHAPTER 5

Katherine Colleen Ryan was fifteen when she stole for the first time. The man was in his forties, single, and living alone in a town house off Trafalgar Square in London. She saw him for five days straight sitting alone in the same seat inside the penny arcade, leering at all of the young girls as they came and went.

It was on a Thursday afternoon that her life changed. She had arrived at the Whistle Down Arcade with two young friends, Lindsey and Bonnie. Each bought a soda, and they were heading to the pinball room to ogle boys when the man approached Bonnie. KC had become used to men staring at her. Her height and appearance were more suggestive of an eighteen- or twenty-year-old. But Bonnie looked her age, she looked innocent and pure with her short dark hair and freckles, so seeing the man approach her made the bile rise in KC's throat. KC pulled her aside and asked her what she was doing, but Bonnie pulled away, telling her to mind her own business. KC and Lindsey watched her take a seat with the man in a corner booth and angrily left her to her stubborn foolishness.

KC and Lindsey spent the afternoon consumed with the social jockeying of teenagers: flirting, laughing, and losing themselves in the moment. When five-thirty rolled around, they found that Bonnie had left without them and each headed home.

KC arrived home to the small apartment off Kentshire, the smell of leftover beef stew hitting her nostrils as soon as she walked through the door. She found her nine-year-old sister, Cindy, on her bed doing homework, her dinner plate on the table next to her. Both girls had learned early on to be self-sufficient. Their mother, Jennifer Ryan, had a nighttime job working for a cleaning company in Langate, mopping floors, cleaning toilets. During the day she worked as a seamstress at the local cleaner down in Piccadilly Circus. She'd had at least two jobs for as long as KC could remember, sacrificing her days and nights to support her two girls. And she had done it alone, the girls' father having died eight years earlier.

It was one of KC's first memories. Not like the blurry, staccato memories from when you are a child. This was one of those first memories where it is all clear: the colors, the smells, the people, and, especially, the emotions. The winter winds howled across the frost-bitten ground of St. Thomas Cemetery in Shrewsbury, England, the swirling snowflakes feeling like shards of glass as they blew against her skin. She stood holding her mother's right hand, Cindy stood holding her left. KC was all of seven. And what she remembered most vividly was the emotion, or really, the lack of emotion. She was told funerals were sad, a time to say good-bye to loved ones, but as KC looked up at her mother, she saw no tears, no sorrow. And though she was only a young child, she knew that something was wrong.

She had seen the man only through a one-inch piece of glass when her mother visited him in prison, and those times were few and far between. He had never even laid eyes on Cindy, who was the product of a conjugal visit.

He had died two hours after escaping prison. The subject of a countywide manhunt, he had made it only a half mile before he was killed. He wasn't shot by the police, detectives, or prison guards; he was killed by Mickey Franks, the man he escaped with, his cellmate from Far Height Prison. They argued and her father lost, a butterfly knife was shoved in his gut, and he was doused in gasoline and set ablaze. He was the victim of fate, KC's mother said, a karmic payback for the pain he had inflicted on them.

As the years went on, KC's mother explained that she had needed to see the man placed in the ground. She wanted to ensure that he was dead and entombed under six feet of worm-filled earth. KC saw such bitter hate, such anger in her mother's eyes for the man that had been their father, the man who showed up for conception and not much else.

AT EIGHT O'CLOCK that evening, KC's friend Bonnie stood at their apartment door sobbing, her shirt torn, her skirt in tatters. KC held her tight as Bonnie told her what the man had done to her. She was afraid to tell her mom, to go to the police. No one would believe a poor young girl; the man's wealth would buy him lies and would condemn her to a reputation as a greedy slut looking to take advantage of the rich. They had both seen it happen too often—the kids who "had" always seemed able to escape situations the kids who "had not" were punished for. KC was sure Bonnie wasn't the well-to-do man's first victim, but they had no proof.

KC dried Bonnie's eyes and walked her home. She asked for the man's address, but Bonnie was reluctant; she knew her friend and didn't want KC to do anything stupid. But

KC had a way of convincing people to see her point of view, of getting them to bend to her will whether she was right or wrong, whether they wanted to or not.

The granite town house was double-wide. Ivy flowed down the façade from the roof parapet five stories up. Polished brass rails and lion-shaped knockers adorned the entrance.

KC slipped in through the unlocked back door and padded across the kitchen, her heart pounding, ready to explode from her chest. That was the first time she could taste the air, see the colors grow a bit brighter, her senses heightened by fear and adrenaline . . . and she liked it.

Once she had made it into the house, though, she didn't know what she would do. She had no plan, no goal in mind. She was just fifteen and angry. She looked around at the display of wealth, at the artwork and statuary, at the silver and crystal. Never had she thought people lived like this, and the fact that the pervert who had assaulted Bonnie lived this way sickened her.

She wanted to hurt him as he had hurt her friend but didn't know how. She thought of vandalism but didn't have the stomach for destruction. Arson was out of the question, and she couldn't even ponder physically harming the man, but she still wanted to cause him pain. And as she walked about the vacant home, staring at how the moneyed people lived, it came to her. He was a man of possessions. He liked his riches, his art, his jewelry . . . and young girls. He liked to possess things, even people, and Bonnie had been just another piece to satisfy his ego lust, his power trip.

She knew exactly how to hurt the man.

She grabbed a pillowcase and filled it with watches and silver, gold bracelets and cuff links. She avoided electronics and hardware, focusing on smaller, tangible pieces of value.

As she headed for the back door, the painting on the wall called to her. It was of two sisters, sitting by a pond. She didn't know what type of painting it was and had never heard of Monet, but for some reason it resonated with her soul. It wasn't large, no more than two by two. She looked at her bag and looked at the painting. And without a second thought she snatched it from the wall.

And all hell broke loose. The alarm screamed as dead bolts slammed home in all of the doors. She raced to the windows only to find them all locked, their seals impossible to break. She was suddenly trapped. A fifteen-year-old girl with a bag of stolen goods in her hand, she would have no explanation, no way of talking herself out of being sent to a girls' home or worse, prison.

Her mind began to race. She tried every door and window to no avail. She soon heard the police siren's whining approach and within moments there was a pounding on the door. She collapsed to the floor, shaking, terrified, the tears streamed down her face. What would her mother say?

And then it came to her. She wasn't sure from where the thought arose, but her mind became suddenly focused and resolute.

She tore her shirt and screamed, she screamed as loud as she could. She threw the bag of valuables into the closet and put the painting back on the wall. The police pounded the door again and KC answered with another scream.

And the door exploded open. Two cops barged into the room to find KC on the floor crying. She cried harder as the woman officer leaned down to her, asking who she was, and she simply answered, "I could never do those things he asked."

"What things?" the woman asked.

And KC said, "Ask Bonnie."

The man was arrested the next day; he had preyed on countless teenagers and was found to possess a cache of child porn in his closet. And no matter how much money he had, it would never buy him out of prison for crimes against children.

KC arrived back at their apartment that night to find her sister sitting with a middle-aged, gray-haired woman. Cindy looked up, her face streaked in tears, and raced into KC's arms, sobs racking her nine-year-old body. KC held her tight, rubbing her back to calm her; she crouched and clutched Cindy to her chest.

"Hey, kiddo," KC said. "It's okay. What's up?"

But as KC stroked the auburn hair out of Cindy's face, as she wiped the tears from her cheeks, she could finally see into her blue eyes. She saw the pain; she saw the suffering that no nine-year-old should ever know.

And KC's world spun. She knew what had happened before the gray-haired woman had uttered a word. Their mother was dead. Jennifer Ryan had "fallen" from the Langate Tower.

Their mother had battled depression for all of her thirty-four years, but it had become acute in the last twelve months. Jennifer Ryan had taken to wearing false smiles under lying eyes, her conversations with her children growing distant and odd. And every night, KC heard her mother's gentle sobs as she lay in bed clutching the Bible. She was a God-fearing woman who never missed Sunday Mass, who lived her life by the Good Book and never would have knowingly condemned her soul by taking her own life. So, as she sat there with Cindy, two sisters suddenly alone in the world, KC knew her mother had finally gone insane.

KC sat on the floor, rocking Cindy in her arms.

"Your sister will have to come with us," the lady said. "We will place her with a family."

"But I'm her family," KC said through her tears. "Her only family."

"I know this is hard—"

"Do you?" KC exploded. "Do you really or is that some line they teach you at Child Services?"

KC stopped herself, reining back her emotions, in a matter of seconds maturing into adulthood. She held tight to Cindy and looked at the older woman. "Imagine that someone you love dies and then you are ripped away from the only other person in the world who cares for you and you're dumped with uncaring strangers. I can take care of her."

"How old are you, child?"

"Nineteen," KC lied. "I work, I can support her," she lied again. Convincingly. She had a knack for it.

The woman looked at the two sisters clutching tight to each other. She looked at the small apartment, the meager furnishings. The three hearts in the room were breaking. "You have no one else? Where is your father?"

KC and Cindy looked at each other. "He's dead," Cindy whispered in shame.

"Please don't take her from me," KC whispered. "I'm all she has."

"I don't want to leave you alone, child."

KC held tight to Cindy. "We're not alone."

The woman packed up her bag and stood; she took a deep breath and looked at KC with sympathetic eyes. "Let me see if I can work something out."

KC stood and walked the woman to the door, closing it behind her. She turned back to her sister and held her tight, their tears merging. No one would separate them. No one would take Cindy away from her.

But as KC stood there, the fear began to creep in. She had no skills, she, too, was still a child, there were no means of support, her words to the woman a desperate, naive plea to keep both of their hearts from further damage. For as much as Cindy needed KC, KC needed Cindy. She loved her sister. Though she was six years her junior, they shared a bond, like identical twins. KC resolved she would find a way. She would put herself aside and be there for her sister.

That was the last time she cried.

THE FOLLOWING NIGHT KC was back in the house on Trafalgar Square. This time she knew better. She grabbed the pillowcase from the closet, still filled with valuables. She once again looked at the painting by Monet upon the wall; she looked at the two sisters holding hands. She went to the kitchen, returned with a knife, and cut it from its frame. She rolled it up, tucked it into the bag, and slipped out the back door.

She went to the pawnshop on Piccadilly. Old Man Rist stood hunched behind the counter, an icon of the run-down neighborhood. She knew him from church, or rather he knew her mother.

"I'm sorry about your loss, child," the man said, his ancient, wrinkled face sincere with emotion.

KC nodded and placed a silver goblet on the counter.

He looked at her with sad, troubled eyes.

"It was my mother's. My sister and I, we need the money."

Rist really did know KC's mother, he knew her well, and he knew that she never had the means to possess such an item. As he looked at the goblet and up into KC's eyes, it broke his heart, for he knew what KC was doing. He gave her a thousand pounds for it, almost its real worth. He couldn't swindle a motherless child.

And so it went for the next three months. Whenever they needed money for food or rent, KC would sell Mr. Rist a piece from the Trafalgar house pillowcase. But throughout that time not once did she consider selling the painting. She hung it on the wall of Cindy's room, above the bed, as a reminder that they were family, they were the sisters who would never stop holding hands.

KC cared for Cindy as if she weren't her sister but her daughter. KC grew up overnight; helping Cindy with her homework, cooking for her, cleaning for her. They had each other and neither would let the other come to harm.

But after three months the bag was empty; it was all gone but for a single piece. KC feared their illusion of security was over. There was nothing left to sell. KC went back to the house on Trafalgar, but it was empty, cleaned out and for sale.

And the panic surged through her again. KC needed money and she needed it by week's end. She sat every night staring at the painting that hung over her sister's bed, thinking of its worth, but she had made a promise. She feared if the painting was sold, their future would be over.

KC walked down to Piccadilly and sold the last piece, the man's watch, to Mr. Rist. Three thousand pounds. Only enough for one more month.

And as she walked from the door, he was standing there. He was shorter than she was: He stood about five-seven, and was a wisp of a man. His hair was jet black, perfectly groomed, his lightly tanned skin accentuated pale, blue eyes.

And though his face was strikingly pure and innocent, he scared her. But then he smiled; it was a warm smile, it carried through his eyes, and it vanquished her fear and concern.

He nodded to her. "Hi."

She looked at him and smiled.

"Mr. Rist is a good man. He would never turn you in."

KC's heart fell. "What do you mean?"

"No, no, no, don't worry. I just meant he cares for you." The man's accent was American. Southern. It had one of those friendly tones, the kind that soothed, the kind that could take the edge off even none-too-friendly words.

KC was speechless. This man knew what she had done, what she was selling.

"Please understand, I mean you no harm. My name is Iblis, I knew your mother. I know what you have gone through. I know you're raising your sister and what you have done; I think it is incredible." The man began to walk slowly down the street. KC fell in step, unsure why. "But to think you can steal to support her. You're fifteen, KC. You're stepping into a deadly world."

KC turned to leave, not sure if she was running from this man or from her situation.

"KC, wait. I just want to help." The man smiled.

KC turned back and looked at him. The warmth of his voice was alluring, it gave her a comfort she hadn't known for three months now. And there was quality to his face: his skin was pure, unmarred by blemish, almost childlike, which imbued it with innocence and inspired trust. But his eyes—she had never seen such pale blue eyes. She thought it silly but they seemed unnatural; they frightened her.

"How?" KC asked, her voice filled with suspicion.

"I want to teach you."

And in a Fagin–Artful Dodger–like way, he did. She was desperate. She had nowhere else to turn. He taught her about locks and cylinders, alarms and safes. He taught her how to case a house. He taught her what to steal and what not to steal. He explained the way the police worked and the intricacies of the law. He showed her how to fence stolen property, its inequities, how stolen goods went for a fraction of their value. He taught her that one well-planned heist could cover her for five, ten years, even life. It was all in the planning. The execution was critical, but the job could be a bust from the start if the planning wasn't thorough.

He differentiated himself from thugs and criminals. He explained his craft as an art, as a field of study, one that had been around since the beginning of time. The true art was in never getting caught. Prisons were filled with the foolish, the unlucky, the desperate and greedy. A craftsman would never have to worry about that downfall if he planned carefully and followed the one rule of thieves: Never trust anyone, not even family.

KC understood him. But what kept her human, what kept her focused, the reason she was doing what she was doing, was her sister. She loved her, and Cindy would be the only person she would ever trust.

KC and Iblis sat in a large apartment, its tables covered with architectural plans and drawings, books and research. KC studied it all, devouring the forbidden knowledge that would allow her to support herself and her sister. Throughout her training, Iblis had given them money, made sure that they were always covered. He came by the apartment often, befriending Cindy, bringing bags of food. Iblis was like the older brother KC never had. After doing all the caring for three months, it felt good to have someone care for her.

"Why are you doing this?" KC asked, turning around in her chair and looking at Iblis, who sat at his computer.

"When I was younger, I prayed for help, I prayed that God would deliver money, a job, a break. You know what I found out? All that praying brought me nothing but false hope. And then one day it dawned on me, it was much easier to steal what I wanted and pray for forgiveness." Iblis paused. "All the praying in the world won't stop you from getting caught. But what I can teach you, I'll be that little answer to your prayers when you're on the job."

"Why?" KC asked.

"I guess to clear my conscience. I'm a troubled man, I've done some bad things, real bad things." Iblis paused; KC could see regret in his light blue eyes. "Everyone, once in a while, no matter how bad we may be, we're all capable of doing some good."

KC's FIRST REAL job, her first real heist, was from a private home. General Hobi Mobatu was an immigrant from Africa who had amassed his wealth by pillaging humanitarian aid that was meant for the innocent, for the sick and dying subjects of his land. He carried his wealth to England, living the high life in his false general's uniform, decorated with medals awarded to and pinned on by himself.

KC had researched Mobatu's purchases; he foolishly bought each work of art with much fanfare, massaging his ego with the accompanying publicity. She reviewed his inventory with Iblis, who helped her select *The Suffering* by Arls Goetia. Painted in 1762, it was from the height of the artist's career, depicting a mother holding her sick child while a celestial war raged above them.

KC waited until the evening that the general was to be

given a human rights award, an award created and paid for by himself. He left his mansion at 6:00 P.M. and by 6:01 KC had already slipped the lock on the back door and disabled the alarm. She wasted no time, heading directly for the sitting room where *The Suffering* hung on the far wall. She disabled the frame alarm, removed the painting, replacing it with a fake, and was out of there by 6:10.

The painting wasn't reported stolen for a month, the result of Mobatu's lack of knowledge about what he owned. The police and private investigators canvassed the area, questioning the locals about whether they had seen anything that warm spring evening. But no one recalled a thing except for one woman who remembered a tall girl in a school uniform and knapsack walking home. The elderly lady tried to continue the conversation, hoping for company, but the police wrote her off and moved on.

The papers and the art world buzzed for weeks with news of the theft, but no trace of *The Suffering* was ever found. The painting had long since been sold to a wealthy European who held it in his private collection. Iblis had shown KC how to move it, how to be paid in untraceable currency, and how to use her ill-gotten gains without raising suspicion.

The job was like her senior thesis, a culmination and demonstration of all she had learned from Iblis. He had never asked for anything in return, which always raised her suspicions, but his sincerity always managed to quell her nerves. And so, with the completion of the job, the money in the bank, he said good-bye.

KC made sure to pay him back all of the money that he had given her; she never wanted to be in his or anyone's debt. And though he fought her on the matter, he reluctantly accepted the funds, seeing the pride and determination in her eyes.

She was his best and only student.

KC WAS AN expert by eighteen. She preferred art to jewels. She hit only the well insured. Her subjects were well researched and deserving of punishment: the greedy businessman who swindled his employees; the rock-and-roll singer who violated young girls and boys, paying off their parents to avoid their pressing charges; people who were always above the law, whose misdeeds never went to trial, whose consciences were unfamiliar with the words *guilt, remorse, or pity*. She seldom did more than two jobs a year, all well planned, well executed, and without a single clue left behind.

KC MISSED OUT on high school, sacrificing her life for her sister's. It was the only way they could stay together; it was the only way she could make the kind of money they would need to survive. And throughout it all she felt a profound guilt for her actions. She'd never intended to be a criminal. It tore her up that no matter how hard she tried she was like the father she never knew, the father who died a criminal. Did he start out like her, eventually becoming the horrible man who left a wife and two daughters to the vagaries of life? She wondered if he had begun as innocent as she; was his heart filled with greed or was he just misguided? And what would time do to her? Would she end up like him, dying in some godforsaken prison or in an alley with a knife in her belly?

She prayed every night for forgiveness for her moral indiscretions, praying that God would understand her motivation.

Cindy never had any idea what her sister did. She was too young when it started, thinking that the money was just there, and as time rolled on KC began to fabricate another life, a fictitious tale of a consultant who worked for the European Union giving tours and consulting with the various nations.

As a result of KC's efforts, Cindy thrived. She grew up in a loving home, excelled in school, wanted for nothing as they moved to a nice small house outside London. And when the time came, Cindy entered Oxford, KC paying her way. KC couldn't have been prouder.

As time moved on and Cindy went off on her own at the age of twenty-three to pursue a career in business, KC was left alone. The house was empty, she had no education, she had no boyfriend—she had sacrificed it all for her sister. She had no other career opportunity, but she had an expertise, a gift that thrilled her, all the while filling her with remorse. But she knew nothing else.

She had no regrets. She had set out to raise her sister, to keep them together, a feat that had seemed impossible at the time, but love has a way of motivating, of creating the drive necessary to prevail. KC had become a thief, an excellent thief who was but a whisper on the wind, an unimagined ghost to Scotland Yard and Interpol.

And of all the things KC was thankful for—for Cindy's success, for the life they created, that she had never been caught—she was thankful for one thing above all: that Cindy never knew how she did it, that Cindy never found out her sister was a thief.

CHAPTER 6

Everyone on the jet was asleep. Everyone except for Simon, who stared out the portside window at the eastern horizon, at the sun slowly rising, painting the sky in pastels of purple and pink. It had been his favorite part of the day since he was sixteen. It was a fresh start, the world beginning anew, a reminder that no matter how dark life might get, nothing could stop the light of a new day.

Simon had grown up within the walls of Vatican City. His mother, a former nun, had been the director in charge of the Vatican Archives, of its history, of its dealings, of its secrets. After enduring a heinous, blasphemous assault at the hands of her estranged husband, she slipped into insanity and took her own life. With his father's subsequent execution, Simon was left alone in the world at the age of sixteen.

He had done a stint in the Italian army, purging his anger while becoming skilled in weapons, hand-to-hand combat, and military strategy. Upon his discharge, he returned to the only family he had known: his mother's friends, the priests and bishops who ran the Holy See, the smallest country in the world. They welcomed him back with the offer of a future. Because of his recently acquired skills and his high degree of intelligence, they proposed he assume his mother's old job as keeper of the Church's vast collection of religious artifacts, of its history, and as the protector of its secrets.

As the plane banked left on its final approach, Simon couldn't help being overwhelmed as he looked down from the jet's window on the city of twenty million, a world that had survived crusades, invasions, kings, and sultans to become a metropolis of unending beauty. The early-morning sky was a brilliant orange that provided the perfect contrast to the skyline of minarets and domes whose tips seemingly reached out to heaven.

Istanbul, Turkey, was the center point of the world, where Europe and Asia come together both literally and figuratively. Since ancient times, whether known as New Rome, the Eastern Roman Empire, Byzantium, or Constantinople, it had been the capital of some of history's greatest kingdoms: Roman, Latin, Byzantine, Ottoman. No other city in the world could claim such a rich, diverse heritage. It had always been the axis of a vibrant culture. It was a world where all met and traded goods, philosophies, women, slaves, and religions; a world where Christian, Muslim, and Jew lived side by side, coexisting long before modern society needed to be preached politically correct tolerance; a world of beauty filled with breathtaking architecture, both ancient and new; a land filled with mystery and intrigue, fortune and glory. It was cosmopolitan and traditional, vibrant and sedate. It was truly a land where East met West, yet, of late, it had played second and third string in global politics, facing extreme opposition when it tried to enter the European Union.

Some of history's greatest houses of worship were within

the city's confines: mosques of unequaled beauty, their towering minarets scratching the sky; cathedrals of impossible grace; breathtaking synagogues of old; palaces whose massive fortifications and elegance had not diminished over centuries.

THE BOEING BUSINESS Jet taxied down the service tarmac of Ataturk Airport, finally coming to a rest in the private plane terminal. Michael, Busch, Simon, and KC walked down the plane's stairs and out into the early-morning light, taking a breath, stretching their legs, letting the sun beat down upon their faces.

A young woman exited the private terminal, pulling a Louis Vuitton roller-luggage behind her, and walked across the tarmac toward the jet. Her hair was auburn, pulled back in a severe bun. She wore a white Chanel business suit and Manolo Blahnik pumps, and looked like a child playing dress-up. There was no question that she was a beautiful girl, she just didn't look old enough to be a customs official.

KC finally caught the eye of the young woman. She halted a moment as her breath caught in her chest, a swirl of emotions running across her face. And then the two women made a beeline for each other, quickly arriving in each other's arms. As they hugged, you could see the relief pour from their bodies.

"What are you doing here?" KC asked, holding her sister tight.

"It's a four-hour flight, how could I stay away?"

"I told you not to come."

"I know."

KC pulled back and looked into her eyes. "But I'm glad you ignored me as usual."

The two women finally turned and walked toward Michael.

"Michael, Simon, Paul," KC said. "This is my sister, Cindy."

Michael held out his hand and shook hers. "It's a pleasure."

Cindy looked at Michael. A broad smile creased her face. "I'm not sure what to say. I've never met one of KC's boyfriends."

Michael uncomfortably smiled and nodded.

"I'm Simon," the priest said in his slight Italian accent as he took her hand. "I've heard much about you."

Cindy nodded.

Michael turned his head toward Busch. "This is Paul Busch."

Cindy took his hand. "It's nice to meet you."

"Likewise." Busch smiled as he towered over the woman, gently holding her hand in his.

Cindy was several inches shorter than KC and her eyes were dark blue, but there was no questioning the overall resemblance. Michael realized that while they might look somewhat alike, they were completely different. KC was tall and lithe, her personality alive and direct. Cindy was refined, cultured. It was as if they had grown up in two different worlds.

Cindy took KC's arm as they walked toward the private air terminal. Michael, Simon, and Busch looked at each other, remaining in place.

KC turned back. "You said the plane needs to go to maintenance before you can fly out, that's what you said."

"Yeah, I said that." Michael smiled.

"So, let's go have breakfast in Istanbul. You never know if and when you'll see this place again."

"I've seen enough already," Busch said as he leaned into Michael. "I'm afraid of seeing any more."

"It's only breakfast; we can't leave until tomorrow anyway," Michael said.

"What? You failed to mention that," Busch said, a tinge of anger in his voice.

"The plane needs maintenance every ten thousand miles. And I'm not willing to find out what happens if it's not cared for, particularly over the Atlantic Ocean."

"Fine, you can explain to Jeannie why I'll be late . . . again."

"Don't worry," Michael said as he walked away. "I'll keep you out of trouble."

"Why did he have to say that?" Busch said as he turned to Simon.

"So, Cindy," Michael said as he caught up to the girls and glanced at KC. "KC mentioned me to you before?"

"She told me you weren't very good at tennis."

"What?" Michael said in complete surprise. "Really?"

A BLACK STRETCH limo drove down Kennedy Caddesi, a wide highway clogged with a sea of honking cars, the drivers all angling, swearing, and waving arms in a universal attempt to curse the near gridlock. Small yellow Fiat taxis swarmed like bees in and out of the traffic jams, far more adept at escaping the madhouse than the stretch limo. The driver pulled a tight maneuver and got off, heading toward the Bazaar Quarter, cutting down the side streets, taking a wide berth around the traffic mess of the Istanbul morning.

The car headed past the Grand Bazaar, through a labyrinth of streets covered by painted vaults with more than four thousand boothlike shops teeming with merchandise, an amazing gathering of merchants that hadn't changed for centuries. Here anything and everything could be found, from gold, silver, and precious jewels to antiques, leather, and fabrics; from clothes to candles, appliances to lingerie.

The limo continued on the narrow cobblestone streets, making its way past the Spice Bazaar, the second-largest bazaar in Istanbul, this one filled with spices of every color and flavor, a rainbow of seasonings such as is found nowhere else on earth. There were herbs, honey, nuts, sweetmeats, a cured beef called pastrima. You could buy toys and plants and choose from a wide variety of exotic aphrodisiacs.

A mixture of cultures, locals and tourists, filled the narrow streets, pouring in and out of the Spice Bazaar like worker bees on a mission.

KC rolled down the window. The smell of food was thick in the air, the sounds of bartering merchants competing with the honking horns. She smiled, absorbing the atmosphere, the culture, and the mayhem.

"Close that," Cindy said nervously.

"Why?" KC asked.

"Just close it," Cindy snapped.

"Is it normally this jammed up?" KC said to the driver as she looked at the gridlock, ignoring Cindy's request.

"There is a large reception at Topkapi Palace Friday evening in celebration of Turkey's full membership in the European Union," the driver said.

Michael looked at Simon but remained silent as they all took notice of the large police presence. They were everywhere, armed, vigilant behind dark sunglasses, a mixture of Turkish police and supplemental private security guards, scanning the crowds, checking the buildings.

"A lot of police," Cindy said. Her eyes darted about,

looking at their surroundings. "That's a good thing, it not only keeps the terrorists away but makes people think twice before doing anything stupid."

"It's mostly for show," the driver said. "But they're keeping a close eye on the mosques and Topkapi. You never know what some nut might do."

Seeing Cindy's unsettled air, Michael leaned toward her and smiled. "What do you do?"

"Actually," Cindy perked up, "I start a new job come Monday."

"What?" KC reeled her attention back from the streets and closed the window. "When were you going to tell me?"

"Sorry, it's not like we talk much," Cindy said without remorse. "As I recall, you've been traveling for six weeks . . . and ended up in jail." Cindy's eyes were on fire.

"What was the matter with Goldman Sachs?" You could hear the disappointment in KC's voice. "You don't get much better than that."

"And what are you going to be doing?" Michael asked softly with genuine interest, hoping to steer the conversation before the moment dissolved to an all-out war between the sisters.

"I'm the CFO," she said, holding her head high.

"I thought you were happy at your old job," KC said, not backing down.

"I've got time to be happy later. It's more money, more diverse hands-on experience. This headhunting group found me, and I couldn't wish for a better job. They came knocking with a pretty attractive financial package plus a chance to be part of an organization with a global reach."

"Did you check them out? I mean, who are they? Goldman is a pretty hard act to follow."

"SQS Capital Partners. They're a finance group. I get to go in to help enhance and improve their assets, work with the principals on formulating new directions. It's a big, stable firm."

"You should have discussed it with me before you made a move, at least gotten my opinion."

"First off, I knew what you would say; you're saying it now. You need to relax." Cindy's voice was thick with sarcasm. And then she looked at her sister more closely, her voice softening. "My career is like putting a puzzle together. I have to gather different pieces, which will eventually form me into a full package so I can have my own company. Remember, thirty million by thirty, three hundred million by forty? Time's ticking."

KC sat there, all eyes upon her, and she realized she might have been overreacting. She finally smiled at Cindy. "If that's what you want to do with Oxford . . . we can talk later. You can explain it to me then."

"I'll explain what I was doing," Cindy said as she tilted her head. "And you can explain to me what you were doing in a prison. And the reason that you needed to come to Istanbul instead of coming home."

The air instantly grew thick. Busch, Simon, and Michael avoided eye contact as silence took over for the next five minutes. The car continued past the growing sea of tourists who swelled the sidewalks, past enormous mosques with towering minarets, past ancient stone walls from the Middles Ages, past sand-colored buildings out of an Ottoman fairy tale.

The limo came to a sudden stop in the middle of the historic section. KC opened her door and, to everyone's surprise, stepped out onto an ancient narrow street. An imposing wall, fifteen feet high, capped with staggered merlons and interrupted by period gates and towers, was just behind her.

KC turned to Michael. "Do you want to take a walk?"

Michael was surprised by the suddenness of the offer.

"KC," Cindy said, "I thought we'd have a chance to talk—"

"We will, I promise. We won't be long."

"If you guys need to catch up . . ." Michael said, deferring to Cindy. "Don't you need to rest?"

"Rest?" KC shot back. "It's all right, if you can't keep up, I can go alone."

CHAPTER 7

Philippe Venue sat in his stone mansion on Van Druer, sipping a cognac on the slate veranda adjacent to his library. Dubbed Azrael Manor, for the sometime archangel, his home was twenty thousand square feet of old-world English style. With no permanent woman in his life, his oversized house was purely masculine: everything was of dark woods, rich mahoganies, deep cherry; the curtains were thick and heavy, divided between forest green and maroon. He possessed a stunning collection of artwork that had been meticulously acquired over the years, a collection far larger than the one he displayed in his office, with over one hundred paintings adorning the walls of his fieldstone home.

He had a staff of twelve, including two chefs, two drivers, and a host of house servants who catered to his every need. The house sat on a rolling piece of land composed of fields and forests, its six hundred acres straddling two townships in suburban Amsterdam.

As he looked out over his estate, over his gardens and pool, past the stables and tennis courts, a fire ignited within him. It was all disappearing. The creditors had already taken his small island in the Caribbean; his 160-

foot yacht, *Crowley*, sat in dry dock, its crew disbanded, its 150,000-gallon gas tanks bone-dry, pending repossession. Azrael Manor and his private jet were owned outright, but as the banks closed in, it wouldn't be long before the liens upon them began. While his current holdings still were great, the rate at which he was losing his fortune was increasing exponentially.

And to compound matters, there were rumblings that an even greater threat was closing in, one that would make the loss of his empire a mere afterthought. Some sins, no matter how old, could never be forgotten; some sins could never be forgiven; some sins brought nothing but condemnation, and God knows, Venue was a man whose numerous sins would have to be paid for.

Venue had floated through his early life with no goal beyond his own immediate gratification. By the age of seventeen, he had been expelled from school for too many fights, had spent time in juvenile hall for armed robbery, and had stolen more cars than he could remember. He blamed it all on the fact that his mom had died when he was five, but he still heard her voice in his sad, troubled head, a convenient excuse to a sympathetic judge that returned him to his alcoholic father.

But his larcenous, violent ways never abated, and on his eighteenth birthday, his father tossed him out, telling him never to come back. He spent the next two years in an ever-escalating one-man crime spree that culminated in murder—but in a serendipitous way, as without the murder he would never have found his calling, he would never have found God.

It had been almost forty years ago. Two lifetimes in jail terms.

Venue had lost fifty thousand pounds on a soccer match: Manchester United let him down once again. He refused to pay up, and when the bookie spread the word of his welching, Venue cut out his tongue and stabbed it into his heart, sending the message to all that no one speaks ill of Philippe Venue.

He became the subject of a nationwide manhunt; it was only a matter of days before he would be caught. Venue had run out of places to turn. He wasn't being hunted just by the police; the underworld had put a contract on his head for killing one of their own. He couldn't hide on either side of the law. He became a man without refuge, a man without a home, and was forced to seek sanctuary.

And he found it, in much the same way as all those who throughout history had sought sanctuary.

He left the country and entered the Church. It wasn't that he had felt the calling, it was the only place left to hide. No one within the seminary questioned his intentions or his background; it was a time before background checks and letters of reference. Those who sought to preach the Word were always welcomed with open arms.

And so he entered St. Augustine's Seminary and became a priest in training, a return to the Christian religion of his youth. One month in, he began to sleep better, his mind calmed, the violent impulses were quelled. After three months he was no longer obsessed with crime or death; the rage that greeted him every day upon waking had disappeared. But the most profound change came at six months. He embraced his faith. He found God in his heart, in his soul, in his every waking breath. Philippe Venue had found his purpose.

His contrition was honest but remained private. He had

yet to reveal his wicked past to his fellow priests and probably never would, as he feared that no matter how much the Church spoke of redemption, how much the Church spoke of forgiveness, he was beyond such things.

As the years went on he embraced his rediscovered faith, becoming a scholar of all things biblical. He absorbed religious history with a fervor, his lust for knowledge extending past the traditional books of the Bible into the more esoteric: the Gospels of Thomas and Enoch, of Judas and Peter and James. He explored the other major religions, wrapping his arms around the similarities of faith: Hinduism, Islam, Buddhism, and Judaism. Religious texts such as the Koran and the Torah became his nighttime reading, which he devoured as others read Grisham or King.

His studies finally brought him to mysticism, that which is hinted at in many religions—Christianity's divine intervention, the holy trinity; Judaism's kabala; Islam's reverence for angels and demons. He immersed himself in the study of witchcraft and druidism. He was fascinated with what people believed, the foundations of belief and blind faith, with religious adherence and sheer devotion.

And then he went deeper. He explored the writings of Dante and the neopaganists. He read of Aleister Crowley, dubbed the wickedest man in the world, of his beliefs and essays, and, in particular, his search in the early twentieth century for the forgotten places of magic and religion. Venue read of the cult of the Golden Dawn, of necromancy and Theistic Satanists, and devil worship. And he found the things of nightmares and of evil, of witchcraft and beasts. As a man who had committed atrocities in his life, he was rarely shocked, but what he found nearly turned his mind. And the more he read the more fascinated he became.

He finally brought these matters to the attention of his brethren, his family within the Church, and shared the mystical world with Father Oswyn.

Francis Oswyn was old-school: He longed for the age of the Latin Mass, for a time when man feared God as opposed to questioning him. He sat at his desk in the seminary and tilted his head, his gray comb-over falling aside as he listened to Venue's words with attention and courtesy. He never once interrupted him, never once looked away. And when Venue finished, Oswyn spoke in a low tone, almost a whisper.

"Can you look into the heart of evil without being consumed by it?" Oswyn asked. "Seductive evil can be disguised by the goal of research, in the form of the quest for knowledge, but sometimes there is knowledge that we shouldn't possess."

"But we are men of God, the most capable to recognize and combat evil," Venue protested.

"I wish it were so." Oswyn nodded. "I have watched our pleas for peace, our prayers for the salvation of man go unanswered. Do they fall upon deaf ears or is evil winning the war for our souls?"

"All the more reason for us to understand it."

"It has become your exclusive fixation, Father. One that has gathered interest and condemnation from those outside our community; even the Vatican has made inquiries about your research."

Venue sat there listening to Oswyn's words, watching his gray eyebrows arch with concern.

"You will discontinue this nonsense, this exploration of darkness, of evil. You have obtained an understanding but your dedication has become an obsession and it is at an end."

"But . . . to understand God's goodness don't we have to understand evil in its darkest forms?" Venue pleaded.

Oswyn would hear nothing further and directed Venue to discontinue his fruitless research and focus his attention on God's greatness and mankind's true need.

For the first time in four years, Venue felt rage. It filled his soul. It was the feeling that had coursed through his body for all of his young life, a feeling that he thought he had abandoned when he entered the Church. But his mind calmed itself. He bowed his head in deference and left the monsignor's office.

Venue had no intention of discontinuing anything. His fascination grew by leaps and bounds; he had become passionate in his pursuit and abandoning his research would have been like abandoning his soul.

So he continued. He became fascinated with the fervor of Aleister Crowley, of his writings and devotion to the occult. He studied the words of Dr. Robert Woodman, a founding member of the Golden Dawn; Blanche Barton, a high priestess of the satanic church; and Madame Blavatksy, a noted mystic who claimed to speak to the dead.

But all the while he continued to embrace his faith, his Church, for it was his home, his family, the air that filled his lungs. His interest did not obviate his faith; rather, it enhanced it. For if there was evil, if darkness and the Devil existed, then surely there was a God and Christ was his savior.

Unlike his brethren of the cloth, Venue had seen evil firsthand on the streets: He had seen it in the hearts and minds of the underworld. He had seen it in his own heart . . . and he had heard the maddening voices in his head. And with himself as the perfect example, he believed that evil could be defeated, darkness could be buried and replaced with light. Voices could be silenced, madness could be cast away. But evil was an equal and opposing force, one that created balance, one that should never be ignored.

THE MORNING SUN was beginning to wash through the stained-glass windows of the chapel, deep reds and purples painting the marble altar as Venue knelt in silent prayer, thankful for his life, for his deliverance.

It was the last prayer to God he would make.

Father Oswyn approached him from behind. He stopped and waited for Venue to turn.

"Father?" Oswyn said, without making eye contact. "Will you please come with me?"

Venue followed him through the church, through the rectory, into a large, intimidating conference room that smelled of incense and leather. Six priests sat around the table. Two chairs sat empty on opposing ends. Venue and Oswyn took their seats in opposition. None of the other six would make eye contact as Venue sat in bewilderment.

Without a word, Oswyn began laying books upon the table—books on witchcraft and the occult, devil worship and druidism.

"*Troubling* is a word that comes to mind, Father," Oswyn began. "So much you hide from us, so much you hide in your heart."

Venue looked about the table, momentarily staring at each of the seven priests who faced him, his eyes finally coming to rest on Oswyn. "So you go through my personal effects and condemn me for my reading?"

"It is what we have found in your heart that troubles us."

"We cannot shut our eyes to the evil that is in this

world, surely you see that," Venue said. "Evil is not defeated through silence. Knowledge is power."

"But we do not seek power." Oswyn paused, the moment hanging in the air. "And that is troubling."

"You condemn me for reading!" Venue exploded. "You all sit here in judgment of me for looking behind the curtain; you are blind to the evil, the darkness in this world."

"We are not blind, Venue." Oswyn pulled out a folder and laid it upon the table. "Father Nolan made some inquiries."

Venue stared at the file; he did not need for it to be opened to know what it contained.

"To say what he found is troubling would be a great understatement."

"The police are here," the eldest priest mumbled, though he did not make eye contact.

"Would you like us to hear your confession?" Nolan's voice quivered in fear.

Venue turned to him, unsure if he should be amused or angered.

"You should know that your crimes, in concert with your outside interests, have brought us to this point. Your actions have left us no choice. Not only are you to be removed from the priesthood, but for the acts you have committed, for the deceptions you have promulgated, for the evil that is in your heart that we fear you shall spread in the Church's name . . . you shall be excommunicated from the Church."

Oswyn's words were like a lightning bolt through his soul. He was being kicked out of the only real family he had known, the one place in his life that he had called home.

And in that instant, Venue's heart turned black. Rage filled his soul. He stared at each of the priests with hate-filled eyes. If the Church didn't want him, if God turned his back on him, there were other places to go. There were alternatives.

Two policemen silently entered the room. Not a word was spoken as they flanked him and led him toward the door. Venue turned back and looked at each of the elderly priests, committing their names and faces to memory. He didn't know how, but he would find a way, he would avenge himself on the men who had destroyed his life.

CHAPTER 8

Michael looked up at an enormous wall fifty yards wide, thirty feet high. Battle-hard and imposing. Two armed guards in military dress flanked the twenty-foot arched entrance. "You've got to be kidding me."

KC smiled a disarming smile.

"This is Topkapi Palace," Michael said.

"Actually, it's a museum; the sultan packed his bags a long, long time ago."

"Tell me this isn't where your chart is."

"Let's just take a look."

"You're really going to go through with this?"

KC raised her eyebrows and walked toward the enormous mouth of an entrance. Michael watched her a moment and reluctantly followed.

"Just pretend it's a game."

"KC, you know better than that," Michael said angrily.

"Humor me?"

Michael was beginning to become annoyed with KC's English accent. Not that he disliked it; in fact, to the contrary, he liked it too much, and it had a tendency to soften his judgment. "After you."

The Imperial Gate to Topkapi Palace was an enormous

granite and carved marble edifice. The archivolt that sat above the twenty-foot entrance was inlaid with exquisite gold Arabic calligraphy and the monograms of Sultans Mehmed II and Abdul Aziz I. The central arch led through a high-domed passage exiting into the first courtyard of the compound, a 190-acre world surrounded by a battle wall over one and a half miles in circumference and capped with imposing toothlike merlons. It was dotted with twenty-seven towers and enveloped a world that had stood still for centuries.

Topkapi Sarayi—meaning "Cannongate Palace"—was once the grandest of all palaces the world had ever known, housing over four thousand people within its walls during the height of the Ottoman Empire. With the fall of the Empire in 1921, it had been converted to a museum by government decree and had opened its doors to the world by the end of the decade.

For strategic reasons, Topkapi was built atop a hill at the tip of a historic peninsula where the waters of Marmara, Bosporus, and the Golden Horn meet on the European side of Istanbul. It was constructed on the site of the Byzantine Acropolis and an ancient monastery at the behest of Sultan Mehmed the Conqueror in 1459. The world's most experienced craftsmen had come from far and wide, using rare materials, with cost considered no object. Completed in 1465, Topkapi was the Ottoman Empire's first step in recapturing the former glory of Constantinople.

With an asymmetric, nonaxial design, Topkapi Palace was far different from European palaces. Though immense, Topkapi was constructed of many smaller interconnected buildings with warmer, more comfortable living spaces, unlike the grand halls and chambers of its European counterparts. The design was not balanced around a central axis but rather grew off in varying tangents in all directions.

The layout was based on a concentric design with four courtyards tucked one within the other, a design from the age of Constantinople that was carried into many of the castle designs of Europe, a design that provided far greater fortification and protection for the ruling monarch. Topkapi's first circle, called the Courtyard of Janissaries, was a giant park that included museums, churches, and tranquil gardens.

Michael and KC walked past the Byzantine-era church, Hagia Eirene. Built in the sixth century, it was one of the few churches not converted to a mosque following the Ottoman conquest of Constantinople. They continued past the stone and marble Imperial Mint and up a wide, open walkway under a canopy of cypress trees.

KC disappeared into a squat brick building and emerged moments later, tickets in hand. She pointed to an ornate Romanesque marble fountain tucked in a corner. "Executioner's fountain. That's where they washed their hands and swords after public beheadings."

Michael looked at her with raised eyebrows, trying to stifle a laugh at her morbid description.

"Big, razor-sharp swords—"

"Let's go."

"—they would stuff the heads with cotton and straw and put them on marble stanchions for display. Kind of like the penalty box, except the penalty was forever."

"Thanks." Michael couldn't help smirking. "You've been here before."

"Three times, actually."

"And you're dragging me here because . . ."

"Not because I enjoy your company." KC smiled. "I need to see two things."

"You've been here three times."

"But that was before we saw the letter."

"What did the letter say?"

"Ah, I knew I could make you curious." KC turned and headed up the stone walkway.

They strolled along a park path that was bordered in trees and came to an enormous gate that looked as if it had been imported from a German castle. Seventy-five-foot turreted octagonal towers sat on either side of the large granite arched entrance. The central structure was capped with merlons, the arched opening looking as if it concealed a drawbridge, all incongruous with the rest of the Ottoman-flavored architecture.

As Michael and KC walked through the arch, under golden Arabic lettering, they were thrust back into the twenty-first century. Before them sat a security detail of guards, scanners, turnstiles, and metal detectors, as if they were entering the White House.

KC presented their tickets with a friendly nod and smile. She and Michael were looked over and motioned through the body scanners.

"I always love this part," KC said.

Michael remained silent.

"What's the matter with you? You, for once, are actually a tourist. Sit back and enjoy it. And lose the puss face, it makes you appear ten years older."

Michael shook his head in futility.

As they entered the formal grounds of Topkapi Palace proper, Michael felt transported back in time. Before him was a world of granite and marble buildings, quiet gardens, enormous porticos, walkways covered in elaborate, tile-laden overhangs supported on detailed marble columns. The roofs of many of the structures were dark earthen blue, a color brought about by the patinated lead covering. Checkered arches of sandy pink marble and white granite accented the buildings and added a taste of the Middle East. Flocks of tourists milled about, enraptured by their surroundings, speaking in hushed tones as if in the presence of gods.

The influence of architects and artisans from such far-off lands as Persia, Rome, Hungary, Albania, and Greece had contributed to the constantly evolving scheme of the palace that was the home of the sultans of the Ottoman Empire. There was no uniformity to the overall design, it was more organic, growing up and out in fits and starts into a host of interconnected buildings that exceeded over seven hundred thousand square feet.

Michael and KC walked in the shade of the Italian cypress, the dark green trees lining the walkway that meandered through what was once considered the garden of paradise. They headed toward the Tower of Justice, the tallest structure of the palace. The high steepled building of marble was capped with a room wrapped in windows from which the sultan could look out upon the breadth of his vast domain. The blue-gray patina of the oxidized lead on the tower could be seen from all of Istanbul and spoke of the sultan's far-reaching power.

A wide, elaborately tiled awning supported by columns of green marble and pink basalt sat directly below the tower. The grand Turkish architectural style of the Divan was something that had been echoed throughout the city and had become one of Turkey's signature styles.

As Michael looked around, he couldn't help being overwhelmed at the minute detail, the intricacy of the smallest tile; the craftsmanship and design was like nothing he had ever seen in all of his world travels.

Michael pulled his eyes from the varied buildings of the second courtyard and turned to KC. "So are you going to tell me where we're going? Where is this so-called chart?"

"You don't think I can do this," KC said with a self-assured smile. "Do you?"

"You have to know your mark better than you know your own reflection in the morning mirror. Look around, KC," Michael said as he subtly pointed to the five guards in their line of sight who walked the grounds. "Without knowing everything about what you're stealing and who you're stealing it from . . . No, I don't think you can do this."

KC looked at her watch and took off in a brisk walk as if she were late for a train. "Let's go."

Michael stood there a moment, confused and amused by her sudden purpose of direction. He finally took off in a jog after her.

They headed across the central courtyard to a short building that spanned the northern edge of the second courtyard. Michael and KC walked under a golden awning and passed through the Gate of Felicity. Constructed in the fifteenth century, the monumental gate was the entrance to the inner, third courtyard of the strictly private and residential areas of the palace. Back in the days of the Empire, no one could pass through it without the authority of the sultan.

The sultan used this gate only for special ceremonies, when he used to sit on his golden throne observing his subjects and officials as they performed their homage and paid him respect.

KC led Michael along the cobblestone path of the third, inner courtyard through more gardens to a long monumental arcade. She made her way along an arched colonnaded portico to a large, elaborately carved dark wood door and, with Michael right behind her, headed into the Topkapi Treasury.

As KC and Michael entered the first salon, they passed a large case containing the medieval armor of Sultan Mustafa III, an iron chain-mail suit encrusted with gold and diamonds, along with an elaborate sword and shield. They passed a second case, containing Korans whose detailed covers were decorated with pearls and jewels and had been for the personal use of the sultans. There was the ebony throne of Sultan Murad IV, inlaid with ivory and mother-of-pearl. Displays of pots and solid jade vases, gold Egyptian candelabra, a 1700s gold water pipe, the diamond-studded walking stick of Abdul-Hamid II, a gift from Kaiser Wilhelm. In the room's central case, holding great interest to a horde of Frenchmen, were dozens of heavily decorated military items.

KC and Michael continued into the second salon, known as the Emerald Room, which contained a glittering display of aigrettes—ornamental headpieces—and pendants decorated with emeralds, diamonds, and other precious gems.

They walked past cases with emerald prayer beads and arrow quivers covered in gold, past an emerald pendant belonging to Sultan Abdul-Hamid I, framed in gold and containing three large emeralds arranged in a triangle, with forty-eight strings of pearls forming a tassel.

KC briefly paused before an elaborate display containing the famous Topkapi Dagger, created in 1747 as a gift to the Persian king Nadir Shah, who was assassinated before the Ottoman emissary crossed the border into Iran. As a result, the sultan retained it and kept it in his collection. The dagger contained three large emeralds in its handle, with an eight-sided emerald at its top that concealed a small watch. Along the hilt were rows of diamonds, while the back of the handle was covered in mother-of-pearl and enamel.

KC checked her watch and continued. Michael was two steps behind as they wended their way through the crowds into the third salon. A room filled with enameled objects, medals, and decorations of state presented to the sultans by foreign monarchs, it contained the golden throne used by the sultans during coronations and religious holidays. A large crowd was gathered around one of the world's most famous jewels, the Spoonmaker's Diamond, an eighty-six-carat, teardrop-shaped gem discovered by a poor fisherman in a rubbish heap and sold to a merchant for three spoons.

As a result of construction and the renovation of the Topkapi library, several of its more important artifacts were on display in the treasury's third salon, including books on Islamic law, theology, and world affairs, Korans of historical significance, and books and charts chronicling the rise and fall of the Ottoman Empire. Written in Turkish, Arabic, and Persian, the works in the Topkapi library were considered an important collection not only by the Muslim world but by the world as a whole.

KC came to an abrupt halt, Michael right on her heels, and slowly turned her eyes to the goal of their brisk, short journey. They had stopped before a large glass case, its contents displayed below a soft yellow light. The object was made of tanned gazelle skin, the markings exquisitely rendered in rich brown, deep red, and black ink. The thirty-six-by-twenty-four-inch, highly detailed chart displayed the west coast of Africa, up to and across the Mediterranean to the Iberian Peninsula, across to the Caribbean and South America, and down to the northern coast of Antarctica. Numerous islands from the Azores to the Canaries to the mythical Antillia filled the sea. The Andes Mountains of Peru were depicted, with the various great rivers of the continent, including the Amazon, the Orinoco, the Magdalena, and the São Francisco, all flowing into the Atlantic.

The chart was in the Portolano style, with lines radiating from center points, a style that guided ships from port to port. Instead of latitude and longitude grids, compass roses were placed at key points with azimuths radiating from them to far-off lands.

Elephants and ostriches, kings and sultans were rendered in detail upon the African continent, while monkeys, cougars, cattle, and wild men danced across South America.

Copious notes scattered the chart, speaking of everything from Christopher Columbus and his discovery of the New World to naked South American natives to sea monsters and land beasts.

The chart was jagged on its rightmost edge, torn down the center of Africa. Aside from this damage, it was well preserved. The case seemed to hold no interest to the tourists who were entranced by the neighboring collections of jewels and daggers.

"Do you know this was drawn by a Turk, Piri Reis, in 1513?"

"And . . . ?" Michael said, knowing she was trying to make a point.

"They had the circumference of the world accurate to

within fifty miles." There was an underlying excitement in KC's voice.

"So did Eratosthenes in 230 B.C.," Michael cracked.

"Look at the bottom," KC said, pointing at the lowermost portion. "See Antarctica?"

"Yeah."

"That is the landmass of Antarctica."

"Yeah . . . I see."

"Antarctica has been covered in ice for almost six thousand years."

"They say it's real cold in the winter down there," Michael joked.

"Modern man had no idea what the landmass looked like until the U.S. Navy ran some satellite imagery in the late 1950s, and you know what they found?" KC was bubbling, all the while ignoring Michael's quips.

"You're going to tell me." Michael enjoyed playing off her.

"That what you see right there," KC pointed at the depiction, "is accurate, real accurate . . . scary accurate."

"So this guy, Piri, dreamed it or what?"

"He said he based his chart on over twenty different sea charts. One came from Christopher Columbus, which is how Piri was able to depict the Caribbean, some from the Portuguese, the Italians, the Chinese, many acquired from his and his uncle's travels, even some said to be from the library of Alexandria."

"So, who gave him the Antarctic one, the Atlanteans?"

KC raised her eyebrows as if to say *who knows?*

"You're kidding, right?"

"I have no idea, haven't really thought much on it." KC laughed. "But it raises the possibility that people have been sailing the seas for a lot longer than the experts have surmised."

"*Expert* is a relative term, a term used way too loosely these days."

"I agree." KC looked back at the chart as if it called to her. "Would you believe this chart was found in a pile of rubble back in '29? It didn't hold much interest to the world until the whole Antarctica thing came up."

Michael studied the chart, impressed with its detail and KC's mythic stories.

"So, what do you think?"

"I think this is a bad idea." Michael laughed.

"Tempted?" KC smiled.

Michael tore his eyes away from the chart and slowly shook his head. "Not in the least."

"But if you were . . . how would you steal the chart?"

Michael loved the planning; it was like cracking a puzzle, deciphering the weaknesses in the building and the security's design. Michael looked around at the tourists who scattered the room, at the guards who stood ramrod-straight at the door.

He finally smiled. "Well, assuming I had the building plans—"

"Which we do."

Michael turned back to the chart, thinking, suddenly realizing. He spoke as if he was in on the joke. "KC, why steal the map when you can just buy a perfect replica in the gift shop or photograph this one?"

KC smiled and nodded. "Because"—she glanced at her watch and turned to leave—"this isn't the half of the map I'm looking for."

* * *

THE LIMO PULLED away from the Vatican Consulate and worked its way back into the Istanbul morning traffic. Cindy and Busch were lost in conversation as Simon unwrapped the large box he'd picked up and pulled out a large leather briefcase that bulged with maps and research. For years he had investigated the Piri Reis chart, researching all of its historical detail. He knew the location of the westerly section, but the easterly section had been lost to myth and conjecture. Through his research he had been able to ascertain its general location within Topkapi Palace, but to find the specific place where it had been concealed, its specific position, he had sought a letter from the grand vizier, a letter that was said to be very specific about where the vizier had secreted the missing chart.

Simon opened the first envelope to find the plastic-encased ancient letter, thankful that it had found its way through the postal service to the Vatican. Attached to it were three two-sided copies, the front of which were Xeroxes, while the rear was an English translation.

"What is that?" Cindy asked, seeing the yellowed, antique letter.

Simon smiled. "Just a bit of research I am doing."

"So, let me ask you . . ." Cindy said.

Simon looked at Busch, hoping he would handle her.

"Are KC and Michael seriously dating or is it just a fling?"

"Well," Busch was momentarily speechless, as not even Michael and KC knew where their relationship stood at this point. "I guess you could say they've been seeing each other for around a month."

"Thank God." Cindy shook her head. "She needs to find someone."

"I don't know about you two," Busch interrupted, "but I'm starving."

"You're always starving," Simon said.

The limo fell silent as Simon examined the translated letter while Busch and Cindy looked out at the city of Istanbul zooming by.

"Can I ask why you and my sister were in jail?" Cindy abruptly asked of Simon.

Simon looked up from his reading. "I think it's best you ask your sister."

"Does it have to do with that?" Cindy asked, pointing at the letter.

"No, it was all a misunderstanding," Simon said, already asking forgiveness for his lie. "I'm sure KC will tell you about it when she gets back."

Cindy's eyes darted between Busch and Simon. Simon could see she was not buying a word of his explanation.

"KC didn't want me to come here," Cindy said in a matter-of-fact tone.

"Then why did you?" Busch asked innocently.

"She just escaped from prison." Cindy stared at Busch. "What would you do?"

Busch nodded in understanding.

"When my perfect sister ends up in jail, besides scaring me, it raises more than a few questions."

Busch grew suddenly uncomfortable as he realized Cindy didn't know her sister very well.

"You aren't going to tell me anything either, are you?"

"I don't think it's my place. It's really between you and KC. I'm sure she'll explain it when she gets back."

Cindy nodded, her charm evaporating as she pulled out and dialed her cell phone.

"Hey, Lara, it's Cindy, I need you to pack up my office and be sure to have the numbers on the Pliant deal before we start at SQS on Monday . . . and I need you to find me a nice hotel in Istanbul. And while you're at it . . ." Cindy became lost in her call.

Relieved by her distraction, Simon took the moment and read the translated letter, taking his time, absorbing every word, but at its conclusion he became confused. He reread it, more slowly this time.

Patriarch Makarije I
Archbishop Makarije Sokolović
Maka

I write this letter, as I fear I will not see the winter. Much has changed since Sultan Murad III has taken power; he is easily influenced by his mother, the Valide Sultan, who has grown powerful and jealous of my dealings. My closest friends, confidants, and allies have perished under mysterious circumstances and if it is Allah's wish to take this old man, then I will embrace death with the promise of paradise awaiting me on the other side.

I grow reflective in my seventies. I miss our home, our childhood where our cares were simple and our troubles few. I find myself dreaming more and more of the thick verdant forests and rolling hills and mountains where we would play unaware of the foulness of man, of the greed, evil, and fear that lurks in so many hearts.

Who could have known the destiny we would follow and the impact we would have upon this troubled world? Our parents instilled in us values and teachings that we have both applied throughout our lives. As the sons of Abraham, we carry much responsibility to our faiths and the faiths of the world. And for men like us, our responsibilities will continue even after we have shed our corporeal beings.

I fear the chart that I showed you on your previous visit, the chart of my deceased friend, Piri Reis, and where it leads. I endeavored to pass it to you last month in hope that you would keep it safe as I had done for over twenty years, but I no longer have a staff I can trust. And while I could not bear to destroy it as its purpose may one day be revealed to wiser men than us, I have hidden it away behind our common father. He was a wise man, a prophet who foresaw the future, whose sons have achieved greatness in the eyes of our common God.

Though our faiths have ridden different roads we are still bound together as the sons of Abraham.

I bid you farewell, my brother, and look forward to our conversations in eternity. I just ask that you delay your journey.

Salaam to you, my brother,

Bajica

Simon had thought the letter would be more exact about the chart's repository, not a puzzle, but as he reread the letter through three times he knew that was what he faced.

And while it frustrated him, he imagined it frustrated Venue and his people even more. Simon had heard through an anonymous tip to his offices that Venue had acquired the letter two weeks earlier from a black market dealer, and though Simon could never confirm the source of the information, it bore out as true, confirmed by the fact that he held the letter in his hand, which he and KC had stolen out from under Venue.

Simon was confident that Venue had not figured out the letter's meaning or the exact location where the chart was held, for if he had he would already be en route east, not sitting in his office in Amsterdam.

For Simon knew that knowing where the chart would lead was Venue's last, most desperate hope and, as far as the world was concerned, the last place on earth someone like Venue should ever be allowed to enter.

MICHAEL AND KC walked out of the Treasury, past the library, past some construction cones and equipment, and back through the Gate of Felicity toward a group that stood under the grand tiled awning of the Divan. KC suddenly took Michael's hand and walked up to a man in a blue hat.

"Hi," KC said with a smile. "Charlie and Elaine Sullivan. Sorry we're late."

Michael looked at KC, trying not to laugh, feeling completely duped.

"Good morning, my name is Hamer." He was dressed in a white shirt and linen pants, wire-rim glasses perched on a long nose, his dark mustache working overtime to de-emphasize its size. He couldn't have been more than twenty-two, probably a student, from Bilkent University in Ankara, working toward a doctorate.

Michael looked around at the small tour group of Europeans and Americans.

"It's the nickel tour," KC whispered in his ear.

Michael couldn't help laughing. "Mr. and Mrs.?"

KC looked at Michael and smiled. "Only in your dreams."

Michael smirked as he shook his head. "Nickel tour of what?"

Hamer led the way, the group of twelve moving as if psychically linked. Hamer came to a heavy pair of black doors, set into the marble of the Divan. He grasped the thick, ancient ring that stood in as a handle and yanked open the doors, holding them ajar for the group to enter.

"When girls passed through this doorway, the Gate of Carts, and entered the harem for the first time," Hamer said as he looked over his shoulder, "they were told that once they passed through, it would be the last time they tasted the outside world. Of course, we will waive that rule for you ladies today."

Hamer's joke brought laughter from the six men on the tour.

"We're taking a tour of the harem?" Michael said as he leaned into KC's ear.

"I knew you'd be excited," KC joked.

Michael and KC took up a position to the rear of the group as they walked en masse down a long corridor, listening to the guide's polished speech.

"Harem. The single word conjures up a host of images in the Western world. A place of naked women in Turkish baths engaged in orgiastic relations with the sultan. A collection of women whose sole purpose is the sexual pleasure of their owner. In fact, the harem was the section of the palace that housed the sultan's family and was known as the seraglio. While it was filled with hundreds of concubines, the most beautiful women in the kingdom, it was far more formal than you could imagine. It was a world unto itself, with a stratified hierarchy, schooling, love, intrigue, and even death.

"The imperial harem of Topkapi contained several combined households. The sultan's mother, known as the Valide Sultan, was the most powerful woman in the empire, holding control over the harem, advising her son, and sometimes even acting in his stead. The sultan's favorite concubines, called kadins, were considered the equivalent of wives. By law the sultan was permitted to have only four. The harem also housed the sultanas, the daughters of the sultan, and their households. There was a contingent of slave girls, odalisques, who served the needs of the harem. And, as you have surmised, a vast collection of concubines, whose ages ranged between seventeen and twenty-three years, with their sole function to entertain the sultan in his bedchamber. But to dispel a myth, there was no sexual free-for-all, no multiple partners in the same night. These women, these concubines, were not only beautiful but educated and refined under the strict tutelage of the harem schools.

"Most of the girls were kidnapped or purchased either out of slavery or from their peasant parents. They were usually between the ages of seven and fifteen when they arrived and came from beyond the confines of the Ottoman Empire. While some girls were found within the sultan's lands, many came from afar, with a heavy representation of Europeans. Georgians, Germans, and Hungarians were brought to the court for only one purpose, to serve the sultan. And while their nationalities were varied, they all possessed the common denominator of extraordinary beauty.

"They were schooled in the arts, poetry, how to play instruments such as the harp, and singing. They were taught how to speak and read Turkish, the ceremonies and customs of the harem and the Empire. They learned sewing and embroidery, and the art of erotic pleasure—"

"I never heard those words used in the same sentence before," an obnoxious, heavyset American cut in.

Hamer ignored the man's remark. "But most of all, the

women that came into the harem were nearly all Christian and they were all forcibly converted to the Islamic faith.

"On average there would be over four hundred concubines in the harem, but their numbers would sometimes swell to more than a thousand. A concubine would only have relations with the sultan once unless she possessed a great skill or became a favorite of the ruler. If she did not become pregnant or a favorite, she would be gifted to viziers—the sultan's advisors—generals, or other dignitaries, and VIPs.

"The harem contains over four hundred rooms, all of which are exquisitely decorated with elaborate tiles and/or paintings of uniquely rendered designs . . ."

The tour guide continued talking as they walked along, but Michael and KC did not pay much attention as they meandered through a labyrinth of corridors, past hundreds of rooms. There were sleeping quarters, large bathhouses, pools, spacious gardens, fountains, endless corridors, and apartments for the sultanas, the kadins, and the Valide Sultan. There were dozens of rooms for the acemis, the young student girls, and open-air courtyards and balconies. Every room, every wall was adorned with extraordinary and intricate art—mosaics, paintings, calligraphy, countless masterpieces.

Michael and KC were both looking about as if studying for an exam, taking in the surroundings, memorizing the halls and doorways, capturing it all as they walked.

"The harem was divided into three sections," Hamer continued. "The actual harem, where the concubines, acemis, odalisques, and other women roamed; the sultan's private rooms, where he would visit and be entertained by the women; and the barracks for the black eunuchs, the guards of the harem.

"According to Muslim tradition, no man could cast his eyes on another man's harem, thus someone less than a man was required to watch over the imperial harem. Eunuchs, as a result of castration, were considered a nonthreat to the sanctity of the harem, as they could not be tempted by the women of the harem, and thus were considered unquestionably loyal to the sultan.

"Eunuchs tended to be male prisoners of war or slaves, castrated before puberty and condemned to a life of servitude. At the height of the Ottoman Empire, as many as seven hundred eunuchs served within the seraglio.

"White eunuchs came from the conquered Christian areas of Georgia, Armenia, Hungary, Slovenia, and Germany. Black eunuchs were captured or gifted from Egypt, the Sudan, and the upper Nile, and transported to markets in Mecca, Medina, Istanbul, and the Mediterranean. All eunuchs were castrated en route to the markets by Egyptian Christians or Jews, as Islam prohibited the practice of castration but not the use of castrated slaves.

"White eunuchs served in the administrative functions and did not interact with the concubines. The black eunuchs, who unlike the white eunuchs had their entire genitalia removed, served the women of the harem directly either as servants of the kadin wives or the daughters of the sultan, as guards of the concubines, or as the master and overseer of the concubines.

"The chief black eunuch, called the Kizlar Agha, was the third-highest-ranking officer of the Empire, after the sultan and the grand vizier. He was the commander of the halberdiers in the position of pasha, the equivalent of a general. He had unlimited access to the sultan, and was the private messenger between the sultan and the grand vizier.

"Every evening, the Kizlar Agha led the selected concubine to the sultan's bedchamber. His duties were to ensure the protection of the women, to purchase the concubines for the harem, and to oversee the promotion of the women and eunuchs. He acted as a witness for the sultan's marriage and birth ceremonies and arranged all the royal ceremonial events, such as circumcision parties, weddings, and gatherings. He delivered sentences to harem women accused of crimes, and was responsible for taking the guilty women to the executioner, who would place them into sacks and drown them in the Bosporus.

"While the black eunuchs protected the concubines from outsiders with true devotion, willing to give their lives, intrigue, betrayal, and rifts were more than common in the harem. The women desperately wanted to become kadins and would conspire against one another to reduce competition. It was considered the highest honor for a concubine to become pregnant with a son who had the potential to one day become sultan, thereby making the mother of the child the Valide Sultan, the most powerful woman in the Empire. As a result, there was intense competition and jealousy, which led to various dangers up to and including murder perpetrated by the concubines themselves. There were many occasions where a concubine would be found dead or never found at all.

"These deaths were ominous and left many of the women feeling unsafe in their palace cage. There was one devastating tragedy under Sultan Ibrahim I, when his lover, Sechir Para, told him that one of his concubines was secretly meeting with a man outside the palace. Ibrahim went insane with jealousy and had his chief eunuch torture several concubines to discover the identity of the mysterious girl. No one revealed the traitor, so Ibrahim had every single one of his harem women—a number thought to be at least 250—tied to weighted sacks and thrown into the Bosporus. Only one of the concubines survived, saved by a French ship. The Valide Sultan, Ibrahim's mother, became so enraged with jealousy of Sechir Para's power that after the drownings she had her strangled in the middle of the night by her chief eunuch."

The crowd fell into silence as the romanticism of harem life was slowly stripped away.

Hamer led his charges down a long flight of stairs and descended into a large room of blue and white tile. Marble water basins were anchored to the walls with a golden spigot protruding above each. There were large marble tubs in each of the four corners of the spacious room and a host of marble benches.

"This was the hamam of the harem, what you would call a steam bath and the Europeans bastardized into the phrase Turkish baths. They were very important in everyday life, thought to cleanse not only the body but the mind and soul. They were a place where a woman could free her mind of the troubles in her life."

In the center of the floor was a large grated drain, three feet square, made of polished brass. It sat flush with the marble floor, its latticework providing one-inch holes for the drainage of the steam bath's waters.

Hamer started back up the stairs as he continued talking about the hamam, its history, and its perceived medicinal benefits, but neither KC nor Michael was listening. They both stood over the drain. KC pulled a coin from her pocket, dropped it, and waited to hear it hit bottom. Three seconds later there was a splash.

"Shit," KC said upon hearing the water. "There's a cistern down there."

"So . . ."

"I hate working in water."

"That's where you need to go?"

"This place is not the room as it was hundreds of years ago; it has been prettified and restored. The Piri Reis chart you saw in that case in the Treasury was found down here in a pile of rubble, but what they found was only half of the chart. The chart was actually torn in two, the other half hidden away down below us almost five hundred years ago.

"There were passages underneath the palace used to smuggle concubines in and out. They were controlled by the black eunuchs who had the command of the harem in their hands. There used to be hidden stairs in here but they've long since disintegrated and their access has been sealed up."

"Excuse me, Mr. and Mrs. Sullivan." Hamer's voice startled KC and Michael. They turned to find him looking at his watch and pointing up the stairs.

"Sorry," KC said as she and Michael hustled up and out of the hamam. They rejoined the tour group but again stayed in the rear.

"Can I ask you a question?"

"Of course," Michael said with a smile.

"Why did you do it?"

"Do what?" Michael asked, genuinely confused.

"Steal. Why did you do it?"

Michael hated that word, *steal.* He hated the words *thief* and *criminal.* They were words used in court, in prison. He thought about her question, he thought about why, but he couldn't answer her. The conversation was too personal; Michael thought it more intimate than sex. He had never bared his soul to anyone; he had never even discussed why he was a thief with his deceased wife, Mary. No one knew the whys of Michael. So he answered in the best way he knew how. "Why did you?"

KC looked at Michael, hating questions answered with questions, but if one is to be trusted one must learn to trust. "My sister."

"Your sister made you do it?" Michael joked.

KC smiled. "In a way. Our mother died. I was fifteen. We had no money." KC paused as she ran events through her mind. "Sometimes in life we are forced to do things for the ones we love, for the ones we care about, no matter how distasteful they may be."

Michael nodded.

"They were going to separate us, stick her with a foster family." Sadness crept into her voice. "She was only nine. And it was the only way I could think of to make enough money for us to survive."

"You raised her?"

KC nodded and Michael felt awful. It was a whole new side of her, one that he hadn't expected—a child forced to raise a child, forced to find her way in the world.

"I became her mother, her friend. I had to help her with her homework. Imagine, I left school, stopped learning the ABCs in order to work, and I had to help her with math, her foreign-language homework. But it worked out. As the years went by, whatever she was studying, I ended up learning. I speak four languages and I'm pretty good with trigonometric functions, I just don't have the diploma."

"And you never got caught?"

"No." KC shook her head. "I did only a few jobs a year. High-end. Art and jewelry. Things that could easily be moved."

Michael bowed his head as they continued walking.

"And you know," KC continued, "I hated myself every time. I was scared to death that I would be caught, thrown in jail, that Cindy would be thrown out on the street. But the thing that scared me the most, what woke me in the middle of the night, was that she might find out what I was doing. I had become a criminal. Everything I preached to her about right and wrong, honesty and integrity, I was violating. I had painted a picture of what was wrong in the world to her, and you know what? It was me. I was what I didn't want her to become. I wanted her educated, in the best job. I wanted security for her. And in order for her to achieve that, I had to put my sense of morals aside and do what I had to do."

Michael could see the pain in her eyes. He understood her better than she knew—her sacrifice of her childhood, giving up her life to make another life better.

"Sometimes we are forced to do difficult things," Michael said, "horrible things for the ones we love. And we can't let our actions, no matter how deplorable we may find them, erase the nobility of our intentions." Michael stopped and turned to her. "Your sister is beyond lucky, and the fact that you raised her from a child when you were not much more than a child yourself . . ."

Michael didn't need to continue. He understood, and he no longer judged.

"I started out . . ." Michael almost laughed, hoping to break the melancholy moment. "I helped out a friend with some school stuff. Sneaking around our high school, stealing some things. Nothing like raising a sister, but, I hate to admit it, I enjoyed it."

KC laughed. "You did it for fun?"

"Well, yes . . . no." He paused. "Yes, at first. I would get this feeling, this rush of adrenaline."

KC grinned. "I know the feeling."

"It was kind of like a drug. It felt good but you felt guilty at the same time."

She smiled and nodded.

"I never stole anything that would hurt someone," Michael continued. "Always things that were insured or from people who I had no doubt deserved it. I never had evil intentions. I kind of left it all behind after I got caught a few years back." Michael was not going to go into the fact that he got caught as a result of saving a woman's life. "Ever since, my hand has been forced."

"Is that what Simon did, force your hand?" KC asked.

"No, not at all. If anything I forced his. You?"

"We had similar intentions and goals."

"How many times have you helped out Simon?" Michael was curious.

KC smiled, not wanting to confess too much more. "Let's just say we've helped each other from time to time."

"And you need to help him again?"

KC looked away. "I promised him, Michael."

"I know you did," Michael said with understanding. He wanted to reach out, to touch her, to let her know how he felt. "Simon's a big boy, he can figure this out himself."

KC stood there lost in thought.

"Why don't you fly back with us in the morning?"

"I made a promise, Michael," KC said as she looked up into Michael's eyes.

"Just think about it," Michael said with a smile. "Don't say anything, just think about it."

CHAPTER 9

Simon, Busch, and Cindy were just finishing up a breakfast in a small sidewalk café adjacent to the Four Seasons Hotel.

"How long have you known KC?" Cindy said to Busch and Simon, the late-morning sun accenting her auburn hair.

"My God, it must be going on thirty days now," Busch joked as he finished off his second cup of strong Turkish coffee.

"Please ignore him, he can't help himself," Simon said in his Italian accent. "KC and I have been friends for five years. We were both vacationing in Austria. You were at Oxford when she and I met."

"You know me that well?"

"KC speaks of you with pride; you're practically all she speaks of. I'm glad to finally be able to put a face to the legend."

"Legend?" Cindy repeated in embarrassment.

"By the way, the new job, CFO, sounds exciting, congratulations," Simon said.

"Thank you," Cindy said with a sincere nod.

Simon had met KC five years ago; they had both been

visiting a small auction house in Bristledorf, Austria. Simon was there in hope of reacquiring *The Birth*—a painting stolen from a Catholic church in Berlin during World War II—while KC said she was just a tourist passing through.

They had both stood in admiration of the Renaissance work depicting the Nativity. Painted by the renowned artist Isidore De Maria, it had recently been put up for auction by Reiner Matis, a wealthy industrialist who was in the waning years of his life. Until 1945, Matis was known as Captain Heinrich Hund, the chief attaché of Hermann Goering, and the officer in charge of Goering's collection of art stolen from the homes, churches, and museums that the Nazi war machine had trampled on.

At the end of the war, and with Goering's suicide, Hund disappeared from the world along with several pieces of art. Heinrich Hund's alias and past were known by only two people: his wife and the tall, dark-haired Italian who stood before the painting.

Simon and KC had struck up a conversation about the piece, about the oil painting's true origin in commission for the Vatican. They ended up talking for hours about the canvas's journey, about the war, the Church, and life. Simon explained he was there to prevent Hund/Matis from profiting from the stolen piece but had been unsuccessful in convincing the auction house to halt the bidding process, as it stood to earn 5 percent of the minimum $25 million price tag.

That night, much to Simon's surprise, the piece known as *The Birth* disappeared. The theft never hit the news, was never mentioned in the papers. Matis had survived sixty-plus years without his former life being revealed; he wasn't about to be exposed now over a piece of art that he never truly loved.

The following day, Simon returned to his office in the Vatican to find an art tube with a simple note:

Forgive me father for I have sinned,
With warmest regard, KC

Thus, through a selfless, illegal act, an unconventional friendship was born, one that had grown over the years into a bond as close as family. KC had opened up about her life, her sister, about her past and her deeds. Simon was not sure if she was telling him in confession, in confidence, or in friendship. He never judged her, understanding her path in life had been thrust upon her. He expressed none of his views, and he offered no spiritual guidance or admonition. He merely listened and answered her questions about life.

"So if you know everything about me," Cindy said, sipping her coffee, "then you must know everything about KC."

"The important things."

"Like why she was in jail with you?" Cindy said with a smile, trying to coax him.

"Now," Simon said with grin, "I'm a much better friend than that."

"She can be so secretive," Cindy said.

"What else does she have besides her secrets?"

"What do you mean?"

"Well, we all have secrets, things we prefer to keep to ourselves out of embarrassment, shame, pride, or fear. And sometimes we keep secrets in order to protect others, protect the ones we love. So, besides her secrets, what does KC have?"

"What do you mean?"

"Do you date?"

"Of course," Cindy said

"You're passionate about your career," Simon added. "You have a full life. What does KC have besides you?"

"I know what you're saying," Cindy said. "But she never seemed to have any goals in life."

Simon paused as he leaned forward in his chair, his arms resting on the table top.

"Oh, boy," Busch said as he adjusted his large body in the small wrought-iron chair. "Here we go."

Simon glared at his friend before turning back to Cindy.

"Are you sure?" Simon asked.

Cindy didn't answer.

"She already achieved her goal in life, Cindy." Simon smiled. "It was you. Raising you, seeing you educated, seeing you prepared for the world. She talks of you with such pride—Oxford, Goldman Sachs. I'm sure once she understands your new job she'll be bragging about this latest achievement."

"You care for her so much." Cindy paused, thinking on his words. "I never realized she had such a good friend. Why didn't you date her?"

Busch laughed.

"She's more suited for Michael."

"That, and Simon has a vow to keep." Busch laughed.

Cindy looked at the tall, ruggedly handsome Italian as Busch's comment took a moment to register. "You're a priest?"

CHAPTER 10

Michael and KC walked through the large arched marble doorway into the lobby of the Four Seasons Hotel, lost in conversation, their laughter filling the air. The five-star hotel sat in the shadows of the Blue Mosque and Hagia Sophia just two blocks from Topkapi in the Sultanahmet district, the heart of old Istanbul. The hundred-year-old building had been modernized from its prior use while maintaining its Turkish neoclassic exterior. The three-story, yellow-gold structure framed a lush, landscaped courtyard, combining the modern world with a historic Middle Eastern feel, harking back to the days when Istanbul was the cosmopolitan center of the world.

As Michael looked around the large marble lobby, at the high ceiling, at the small anterooms, he couldn't help the feeling of déjà vu. It wasn't the décor, the rattan and wicker furnishings, the desert colors and Persian rugs. It wasn't the open Eastern feeling of the building or the international guests who meandered about. It was the building itself. There was an air about it, something familiar.

Michael and KC stepped into the cage-style elevator, the bellman closing the gate behind them. They rode up to the fourth floor, talking of sports and travel, of their desire to run with the bulls in Pamplona, climb the Swiss Alps in summer. Michael was filled with a mix of emotions such as he had never felt. KC attracted him, she angered him, she was alluring but made him wary. His fury about the revelation of her being a thief was dissipating, replaced with fear, fear that she wasn't capable of what she was about to undertake. Fear that she would slip away in the bowels of Topkapi Palace never to be seen again.

They exited the elevator and heard Busch's laughter, following his voice down the hall to an open door. The Occidental Presidential Suite was over thirteen hundred square feet, with white marble floors and exquisite maroon rugs. The cathedral-ceilinged home away from home was the finest in the hotel. The living room's dark wood furnishings centered on a large fireplace. Earth-tone colors, accented in burgundy and blue, gave the old-world Turkish theme an Oriental flavor. There was a full kitchen and dining room, an oversized bar stocked high and wide. Three pieces of luggage sat at the foot of the sweeping marble staircase that led to two large second-floor bedrooms, each with an oversized bathroom, and a small second-floor office.

Oversized floor-to-ceiling arched windows and three large balconies provided picture-perfect views of the world-famous mosque, Hagia Sophia, the Topkapi Palace, and the surrounding ancient metropolis, completing a setting of old-world Ottoman luxury.

Busch and Cindy were having drinks at the bar. Busch smiled as he saw his friend, as he saw his eyes. He hadn't seen him this happy in forever.

"I got us a room," Busch said with a Cheshire grin.

"I thought you weren't keen on staying," Michael said. "Where?"

"Down the hall." Busch's smile managed to grow. "Despite the cost, I think it's worth it."

Michael stared at his friend, waiting for the joke.

"You want to know why I'm smiling?"

Michael nodded. "It would be nice."

"Look around," Busch said. "Look at the windows, the doors. Do you feel it? I know you've got a sense for these things . . . these kinds of places."

Michael slowly turned, taking in the exquisite room, its marble foyer, the high ceilings. He had felt it downstairs but wasn't sure . . . "What am I missing?"

"This place, this five-star hotel, used to be a prison." Busch burst out laughing.

Michael found no humor in the moment. He had felt it in the lobby, in the halls. It sat heavy in his stomach. "You think that's funny?"

KC smiled. "Hey, this is far better than my last accommodations."

"Go ahead and joke." Michael shook his head as he walked to the bar and poured himself a scotch.

Simon sat at the dining room table reading a manuscript, his beat-up, overflowing brown satchel open before him. He looked up at Michael. "Well, how was the date?"

"It wasn't a date," Michael said. "She was just showing me the sights."

"The sights?" Simon said with a knowing eye.

"What sights?" Cindy asked.

Simon and Busch looked at KC and Michael with small smiles.

"What's going on?" Cindy reacted to their looks.

"We just went for a walk."

"Really?" Cindy glared at KC. "Because it seems everyone is clued in to what's going on except me."

"We went for walk . . . that's it," KC said. The tinge of anger in her voice ended the questioning.

The room fell quiet as the sisters looked at each other.

"Why don't we let them catch up?" Busch said as he stood. "If you think this room is nice, wait till you see the water views from ours."

"And who's paying for the views?" Michael said as he sipped his drink.

"I figured you would, as a sign of appreciation for dragging me halfway around the world . . . again."

Michael, Simon, and Busch gathered themselves and headed for the door.

Michael turned back to KC. "We're flying out first thing. I really think you should be on the plane with us."

"What time do you want to have dinner?" KC said, ignoring his question.

Michael shook his head in frustration and walked out.

"We'll see you around six," Busch said, covering for his friend.

As the door closed, leaving the two sisters alone, Cindy's face changed. All pretension evaporated and the real emotion poured forth. "I don't understand how you ended up in prison."

"It's complicated." Though the room was huge, KC felt as if the walls were closing in.

"You were arrested, KC." Confusion rippled Cindy's face. "You were sentenced to die. Nobody's sentenced to die that quick."

"How do you know that?" KC asked, genuinely shocked. She had never mentioned anything about being sentenced to die, she had merely told Cindy she had been mistakenly arrested but that it had all worked out.

"You're changing the subject."

"Cindy, how did you know that?"

"Someone called, told me you were in an Akbiquestan prison, awaiting execution."

"It's important you tell me, who called?"

"I don't know, goddammit," Cindy exploded. "Someone calls in the middle of the night, tells me this, and hangs up. I call and call and call and I can't find you. No one has seen you in over a month. When you finally do get in touch, you confirm the prison thing but lie about the rest."

"I told you to stay in London," KC said.

"Are you kidding? Don't change the subject. You almost died."

"But I didn't."

"What's going on?"

"It's not your concern."

"You're not my mother, KC."

Cindy's words cut her to the bone.

Cindy walked over to her luggage, which sat by the stairs and opened the large Louis Vuitton suitcase. She pulled out a cardboard tube, walked back to KC, and laid it on the table. In a ceremonious fashion, she took a seat. "I need to ask you a question and I need you to tell me the truth."

KC stared at her younger sister. She was no longer the child that she had protected, that she had raised. She was a woman on equal ground. So KC relented. "Fair enough."

Cindy opened the tube and withdrew the painting, carefully rolling it out on the table. KC tried to hide her emotions as she looked at the familiar piece of art, hoping her thundering heart wasn't audible.

"You gave me this when we were kids, right after Mom died, said it was to remind me that we will always have each other, that no matter what happens, we'll always be sisters." She paused. "Where did you get it?"

KC stared at the painting, the painting that had hung above her sister's bed. The Monet of the two girls holding hands. And her heart fell. "You don't understand—"

"I do understand," Cindy said as she looked upon KC with condemning eyes.

"It's not what you think."

"Tell me you didn't steal it. Look me in the eye and tell me."

KC just stared at her.

"Do you think I'm stupid? When are you going to stop treating me like some sheltered child? You're my sister, not my mother." Cindy turned away, wiping tears from her eyes, gathering her wits. She finally turned back. "And by the way, I've known that was a Monet since I was fifteen."

KC looked at her sister. The moment that she had long dreaded had arrived. She could no longer avoid it, she could no longer hide behind fictitious tales and false achievements. She couldn't run from the truth and had only one option.

KC took a deep breath, sat down, and told Cindy. She told her everything. Everything she had stolen, everything she had given up to make a life for her sister. She told her about the what and the where, she told her how she and Simon ended up in prison, she bared her soul to her sister in hopes that she would understand the sacrifices she had made throughout her life so Cindy could have a future.

Cindy sat there in shock, the shame evident on her face,

refusing to look KC in the eye. It was several minutes as she absorbed what her sister had done. "And why are you here now?"

KC couldn't speak.

"To steal something?" Cindy was getting angry. She glared at KC. "You and your boyfriend?"

"He's not my boyfriend."

"You giggled with him, KC. You've never giggled in your life."

"No. He's leaving here tomorrow morning as soon as his plane clears maintenance."

"So, *you* are going to steal something. Tell me what it is."

"Cindy—"

"Our whole life is a lie," Cindy screamed. "You told me that you busted your ass like Mom, you told me you worked two, three jobs to raise me. I suppose the whole consulting thing is bullshit, too. What else have you lied about? What about our mother and father? Is their history all a convenient tale to make you look like the self-sacrificing sister?"

"You know what happened to Mom. And Dad, you were there when he was buried. He was as bad as they come; he deserved nothing less than what he got."

"How can you judge him, when you're just as bad?" Cindy yelled back.

"Cindy, he killed people. He abandoned us. He lived his life for himself. Are you telling me you have more empathy for someone you never even met than for me? I did what I did for you."

"Don't lay that guilt trip on me."

"It's not a guilt trip." KC's voice was thick with pleading emotion. "It's the facts."

"How can I believe anything you say?"

And as KC looked at her younger sister she knew her to be right. She had lied to her their whole lives. She was a criminal just as her father had been and now had lost the trust of the only person who loved her.

"Let's get on a plane tonight, go back to London," Cindy finally said, offering an olive branch.

"I can't."

"Why?"

"Don't make me say it."

"Say it. You're living a lie. Creating some convenient piece of fiction to live behind, all in an effort to forget what you truly are. You're nothing but a criminal."

"I have to steal a document from a museum," KC shouted back, regretting the words before they even left her lips. She had never verbalized what she did in such a way, and it filled her with shame.

It was Cindy's turn to be stunned; she had never thought she would ever hear her sister say anything like that. "Why? You don't need to support me anymore. Let me help, let me support you for a change. KC, there are plenty of legal ways to make money."

"It's not for money."

"Everything is for money one way or another. It's what brings power, it's what brings love, it's what keeps us alive. It's all about money, KC, it's just some people don't get it."

KC paused, gathering her wits. "With all the things I tried to teach you, how can you think that?"

"Don't you even dare talk to me about morals or values." Cindy slid her chair back and stood, looking down at her sister. "KC, you will get caught. You've tasted jail once already; don't tell me you like it? You've already been sentenced to die. I don't imagine you'll escape the reaper a second time."

"It's so much more complicated than you think."

"It's not. If you need it so bad, get someone else. Get Simon to do it, he seems to be your partner. He was in prison with you. I'm sure he has the skills."

"Absolutely not." KC picked up her cell phone. "It's time for you to go back to London."

"I'm not going anywhere. Stop acting like you gave birth to me. I make my own decisions. I made my life. I've got the real job and what are you? You're nothing more than a thief."

The rage built in KC's eyes. It was a slow, pent-up resentment for giving up her life at the age of fifteen, for forgoing her teenage years, sacrificing everything for her sister. And it finally crested as she burst out of her chair. "Maybe I should have let them take you when you were a kid, stick you in a home. Gone off and had my own life instead of giving it up for you." KC stomped across the room, ripped open the door to find Simon standing there, and stormed right past him.

"You all right?" Simon called out as he watched KC disappear down the hotel hallway and around the corner.

He turned and saw Cindy standing there.

"You guys all right?" Simon asked.

Cindy said nothing.

"I just need to grab my bag," Simon said as he pointed to the brown satchel on the table. "You sure you're all right?"

But Cindy said nothing, ignoring Simon, not even looking at him. She walked up the stairs to her bedroom and slammed the door.

CHAPTER II

B usch stood on the balcony of the Oriental Suite of the Four Seasons, staring out over the Sea of Marmara and the Princess Islands. As he turned and looked across the Bosporus to the far shore, he realized he was standing in the only city in the world that sat on two continents, at a juncture of worlds that came together in a city with a culturally amalgamated history unlike that of any other place in either ancient or modern times. This was a world that could not be farther from his hometown of Byram Hills. He was in a city that had been the capital of the world long before Europeans had discovered his little neck of the woods.

Michael walked down a flight of mahogany stairs, showered and dressed in blue jeans and an Armani blazer. "Some view, huh?"

"It's amazing the places I go to save your ass."

"The plane will be ready at 6:00 A.M., unless you feel like hanging around."

"Jeannie is already pissed. I'm seeing the world without her, and if I see much more of it, you're going to end up with a permanent roommate."

Michael smiled. He had a tendency to forget how easy

it was to travel when you're not tethered to the world, to a family, to the ones you love. Paul had never once hesitated in helping Michael, no matter how long it took or how far away from his wife and kids it carried him. He was the truest of friends.

Since his wife died, Michael had forgotten what it was like to live your life for others, to put aside your own wants and needs every single day for the ones you love. He envied Paul and the life he had, hoping that one day he, too, would have a tether to hold him back.

There was a quiet knock at the door, taking Michael by surprise. Michael looked at his watch, walked across the large living room, and opened the door.

KC walked in and right past Michael without a word. She walked to the window and stared out at the water.

Busch, still standing on the balcony, turned and saw her distress. Exchanging glances with Michael, he walked in off the terrace and headed up the stairs. "I need to shower to make this stinky body perfect again," Busch said before disappearing into the bedroom.

Michael looked at KC framed in the window. "Are you okay?"

KC continued to stare out at the water, the moment dragging on. "Do you have room on the plane?"

"Of course," Michael said slowly, hearing the stress in her voice.

"I'm done," KC said, more to herself than to him.

Michael approached her slowly from behind. He placed his hand on her shoulder. "What happened?"

"She knows." KC was lost in her own world. "She knows everything."

Michael knew she meant only one person, the only

family she had. And Michael knew too well how KC felt, the shame, the anger when those you love find out you're a criminal. "I'm sorry."

"All these years, I've lied . . . lived behind illusions, fooling myself that what I was doing wasn't harming anyone."

They both stood there in silence, watching the boats with their wide open sails make their way down the Bosporus to the Sea of Marmara.

"Sometimes in protecting the ones we love, we hurt them. We don't mean to but it happens nonetheless. In time, though . . ." Michael paused. "It's a lot for her to process. She'll come around."

"You didn't see her eyes. It was disappointment. It was shame. She compared me to my father."

As KC finally turned around, Michael could see her pain.

"My father was without a soul. He robbed people, killed people without thought. He was a criminal, Michael, he was as bad as they come."

"Maybe, KC," Michael said. "But that's not you."

"No, Michael. That is me. And what hurts the most, what's ripping my heart in two is Cindy's right, I'm just like him."

Michael placed his hand on KC's shoulder and looked deep into her eyes. "No, KC. She's not right. You're not like your father. You raised your sister. You did what you did to care for her. She hasn't put the pieces together yet but she wouldn't be where she is in life if you hadn't been there for her. You're not a killer, you're not your father."

"Michael, I did it to raise her. I stole things to support her. I can justify that. But the last five years . . . I never stopped. I was doing it for me. Even when I helped Simon, I always thought I was on some crusade, a way to prove that I was doing good by doing bad."

Michael continued to look at her, his compassion never wavering, but he knew what she meant. She had chosen to steal just as he had, and no matter how careful you were, it always caught up with you.

"I can't do it anymore."

"Good for you."

"I have to tell Simon. He's going to be upset."

"No, he won't. Simon's a big boy."

KC turned back and stared out at the passing boats. "Michael, what am I going to do?"

Michael could hear her heart breaking over the shame she had caused her sister. She was lost, knowing that the life, the only life, she had known for fifteen years was at an end. "You need to talk to her."

"I can't," she said, as if trying to convince herself.

"Yes, you can. You have to."

"I don't have to do anything," she shot back, her defenses up, hoping to escape the inevitable.

"Yeah," Michael said softly, "you do. I'll get her."

"Don't you dare."

Michael walked out of the suite and down the hall to the Occidental Suite. KC came running behind him, pissed. "Do me a favor, stay out of this."

Michael looked at her. "Now you want me to stay out of it? After coming to me and unloading your baggage, you want me to shut up?" Michael knocked on the door in defiance.

KC stared, her eyes answering in the affirmative, telling him to leave.

"Not happening." Michael shook his head. "You don't

give up the ones you love that easy. You walk through that door right now and start talking to her. Then, maybe, I'll leave."

Michael knocked again.

KC checked her pockets. "I don't have my key."

"Listen, she's going to be upset. Nothing can change that."

"I don't have my key." KC was frustrated, and her hands shook as she searched her pockets. "I walked out in a huff before."

"The two of you are going to have to talk this out," Michael said.

"And what gives you the right to start giving me advice?" KC snapped at Michael.

"Because," Michael said calmly, understanding her frustration, "I've been there." Michael knocked again. "When we hide ourselves from the people we love, it's a sign of distrust. She's your sister. She'll work through it."

KC stared at Michael a moment, then turned and glared at the door, raising her fist and pounding it. "Cindy, open the goddamn door."

But there was no answer.

"Maybe—" Michael stopped. The world slowed as he and KC looked at each other and realized . . .

Michael raised his leg and kicked the door in.

As THE DOOR exploded open, Michael saw it. All over the floor, staining the white marble tiles.

Blood, fresh, pooled and streaked across the floor as if painted on with a mop. Michael ran into the other room, charged up the stairs, emerging moments later on the landing, looking at the empty suite. No one there.

KC came in behind Michael and saw the carnage. While she remained silent, her mind screamed in terror. She frantically ran through the suite but found no one. Michael and KC looked at each other; rage filled their eyes before slowly slipping to sorrow and desperation.

"Who did this?" Michael looked at KC as if she knew exactly what he was talking about.

"I . . . I don't know." KC leaned down and looked at the blood. Her breathing quickened, as fear robbed her face of color.

They both looked around, scanning the room, falling into a state of mind where the senses grow acute, where everything holds a clue. As they looked about, they both saw it at the same time: the open tray to the DVD player.

Michael closed the tray and pushed the button on the DVD player. He flipped on the seventy-two-inch plasma TV and was greeted with the image of Simon lying on his back unconscious on the white marble floor where Michael now stood. The camera panned up to the tear-streaked face of Cindy, her desperate look filling the large screen as her unsteady breathing poured from the surround-sound speakers. KC ripped back her hand as she realized she was leaning on the chair that Cindy had been crying in moments earlier.

"KC." The voice filled the room; it was deep and, surprisingly, had a southern American accent. "I'm so glad you made it out of Chiron alive. I had even money on your escaping. Impressive. The playboy boyfriend with the fancy jet, nice touch."

The camera panned around and fell on the image of the videographer. His face was tan and childlike, his eyes an abnormal ghostly blue under perfect black eyebrows. The camera held on him and then, ever so slowly, a smile rose on the man's face. It was a forced smile, lacking warmth, the eyes mirroring none of the facial expression's intent. The camera finally panned back and became a wide shot, holding the image of both Simon and Cindy.

The man walked into the frame and looked at Cindy, who sat weeping and trembling in her seat. "She's grown into quite a woman. She's beautiful, KC, and from what I understand, successful and well educated. You must be very proud. Your mother couldn't have done half the job that you did.

"I hate myself for what I have to do." The man continued to look at Cindy. He reached out and ran his hand lightly over her auburn hair. "But sometimes in life, we are forced to do things some would consider distasteful . . . immoral . . . illegal. I'm sure you understand this more than most.

"You'll steal Selim's staff, the Caduceus, as you and Simon were planning, except you'll do it alone."

"Caduceus? What?" Michael looked to KC with confusion, but KC's eyes remained glued to the image of her crying sister.

"Don't bother with the chart," the man said. "That's mine. Always was mine. My challenge, my map. My little contest of skills." The voice seemed omnipotent, like that of a narrator in the ether. The man removed his hand from Cindy's head. His eyes suddenly focused on the camera, as if they were looking right out of the TV into KC's eyes. "I want to make this crystal-clear. Do not go near the map. It is mine to steal."

The man's demeanor finally loosened and his forced, haunting smile returned. "Who knew that we would work together again? Partners, I guess." The deep voice shook the room. "You'll deliver the rod, the sultan's staff, to me Friday at one o'clock in front of the Blue Mosque."

The man walked over to Simon and crouched next to his unconscious form. He looked a moment at their friend and the small pool of blood that oozed from his head. "I'll field-dress his wounds, but that is as far as I'll go. His blood loss is considerable, as I'm sure you can see. Hopefully, infection won't set in. If it does, I'd say he may last three, four days without treatment."

The man walked back to Cindy, who looked at the camera with pleading eyes. He stood behind her and placed his hands on her shoulders, causing her to wince and quiver.

"And, KC, you know me, you know what I'm capable of, what I like to do. I like you, KC." The man paused for emphasis. He once again stroked his hand down the side of Cindy's head. "I love you as if you were my own flesh and blood but I have no qualms about taking everything you hold near and dear in this life away.

"You've got three days to get the rod. And remember, stay away from my map."

The screen held on the image of Simon lying upon the marble, his chest rising in shallow breaths, on Cindy who sat there, her bloodshot eyes unfocused and desperate, tears marring her perfect makeup. The man reached around and touched her under the chin, gently lifting her face closer to the screen. He smiled one last smile and the screen fell to black.

Michael and KC both stood there, the silence echoing in the room, each looking at the bloodied floor, the empty chair.

"His name is Iblis," KC said softly without pulling her eyes from the blank TV screen.

Michael said nothing, trying to process everything that had just happened.

"He's as dangerous and psychotic as they come." KC remained transfixed by the TV screen as if looking away would break her in two. "He's a thief, Michael. Far better than me . . ."

"How do you know?"

KC sat, the moment dragging on until she finally turned and looked at Michael. Her eyes filled with anguish and defeat. "He was my teacher."

CHAPTER 12

Iblis was not his birth name. He had chosen the Arabic name for its intimidation factor. He was actually born in Kentucky, the son of a jockey. His mother was half Greek, half Turkish, which, her husband explained, resulted in her conflicted personality. Knowing Iblis's career, his depraved mind, most would assume he came from a troubled home, a broken home, that he was an orphan, maybe, lashing out at the world for life's unfairness. But he, in fact, couldn't have come from a more stable, loving family.

Christopher Miller, Sr., who preferred to be called Rusty—a nickname attributed to the fiery red hair of his youth—was a traditionalist, a man who believed in the right to bear arms and to know how to use those weapons. He taught his son, Chris, Jr., how to shoot at the tender age of seven. Young Chris could hit a soup can at fifty yards by the age of eight and was marksman caliber by ten. Rusty taught him how to hunt and live off the land. He taught him the worth of knives and their usefulness in the wilderness, for skinning and preparing food, as weapons, as tools. Rusty taught his son how to survive and how the lessons of self-reliance and survival would apply throughout his life, whether in the woods or the jungle of the city.

Nuray Miller was a raven-haired beauty, her crystal-blue eyes and tan skin echoed in the face of her son. While Rusty trained Chris in the more physical and brutal means of survival, she taught him about the more subtle ones. She schooled him about people, about social graces, about getting what you want through gentle persuasion and implied consequences. She showed him how to move about in the different worlds that people live in, as she had done so well as the daughter of a Greek Orthodox shipping executive and a Turkish Muslim mother. She understood the subtleties of diplomacy, knew how to see the different points of view and subsequently gain the trust of all. These were lessons she imparted to Chris, and they allowed him to overcome the awkward appearance he acquired in teenhood, one that was more appropriate to a terrorist than to a kid from Kentucky. He was slight, with jet-black hair; his baby-faced beauty gave him an almost feminine appearance. He walked like a nervous dog, quick and choppy, and had an unnaturally deep voice for such a wisp of a teenager.

When Chris was thirteen, they relocated to Brooklyn, New York, where his father worked at the nearby Belmont racetrack in Elmont. And that's where things had spun out of control. He was the outsider with the funny accent, the funny voice, and the too-pretty appearance; the kid who was laughed at for his small size and looks. He spent sixth grade alone, friendless, and the object of general derision. He never told his parents of his troubles at school. He never mentioned how he was picked on, how he was punched for fun to see how long it took for his skin to bruise.

He was an outsider and, as is often the case, the outsiders came together. They were the ones who didn't fit in, the unpopular, the different, the ones who realized there was strength in numbers. Chris found friends with the rough-and-tumble crowd, the ones who would use their numbers, their fists, and eventually their weapons to intimidate. Chris became a god among their group of twelve, teaching them how to shoot, how to take care of their guns, how to use a knife, skills that the eleven Brooklynites embraced. Chris taught them the power of perceived threat and the sway it held over others, how it was so much more effective in persuasion than the actual physical carry-through.

Their group of twelve grew in notoriety, became a gang that ruled the streets. They took what they wanted from whomever they wanted. They grew in arrogance and their power of intimidation, feeling that they owned the world and there was no one who could stop them.

It was on a Thursday night, Chris was all of fifteen. They had knocked over a few merchants for pocket change and thrills but had decided to move up in the world. Several stood lookout in the streets, while others took up position in the alley. Chris slipped through the small window, his waiflike size affording him easy access. The knife at his waist, the gun in the small of his back made him feel invincible. He hustled through the store, grabbing necklaces and watches, earrings and bracelets; he loved the moment, the thrill of breaking the law, of violating someone's inner sanctum. The alarm blared but it made no difference, he was on his way out in less than a minute.

But as he slipped through the window, landing in the alley, he found himself alone looking down the barrel of a police-issue .38-caliber semiautomatic. His friends, his gang, his outsiders were gone. The cop was alone, holding the gun two-fisted, the drop of sweat along his right temple revealing his rookie status. The young cop was taken aback by the thief's youthful appearance as he barked at Chris to put his hands in the air . . .

And that's when the words of Chris's father rang in Chris's ear. This was why he had taught him how to shoot, how to skin, how to stay alive. Whether in the woods or the jungles of the city, his father had taught him how to survive.

Chris dropped his bag of jewels, drawing the cop's eye, distracting him. The cop hesitated for the briefest of moments and before he knew it, he was dead, the knife driven up through his neck, exiting out the back. It was twisted violently, severing the carotid artery, continuing through the spine, practically detaching the head from the body.

Chris looked around, unfazed by the carnage he had wrought; he stared down at the corpse of the young cop as if detached from humanity. He was intrigued by the way the lifeless body twitched. He looked up to find that his gang had scattered, all diving back to their families, back to where it was safe, leaving him alone to face the repercussions of his actions.

The police arrived three days later, running down leads, acting on tips, and wanted to speak to Chris. Nuray, in her charming, convincing way, invited the police in and explained that her son was at the racetrack with her husband. She made them coffee, insisting there must be some confusion and said they could wait. But they excused themselves and headed straight for Belmont. She went upstairs, packed a bag, and woke Chris. They headed straight for Canada, where she gave him money, stuck him on a plane to Turkey, and told him he could never come back. He stayed with her relatives for all of a week before realizing how much he hated the country. He headed for London; they spoke English there, and if he was going to make his way in the world, he would at least need to understand the language of those he was robbing.

He had just stepped off the train, looking younger than his sixteen years, when the gun was jammed in his back. The man led him to an alley, held the gun to his head, and demanded his money. Chris emerged from the alley moments later. The blood had been minimal. The punk who had tried to rob and assault him had been carrying five thousand in cash. It was a start.

He lived in boarding rooms and flophouses. He worked the streets, developing a reputation. Learning a craft. It was trial and error. Pickpocketing, mugging, small-time robbery. He was quick and deceptively strong for his size. He worked out, ran, and studied various martial arts, honing his body like an athlete to survive the dangerous world he chose to live in.

He worked his way up: jewelry stores, art galleries, high-end homes. He was polishing his craft. He educated himself, reading voraciously on gemology, on art history and technique. He became an expert on value. He learned from the auction houses, both the legal ones such as Sotheby's and Christie's and the invisible ones such as Killian McShane's, which not only traded in black market art and jewelry but were also known for placing orders.

Unlike the other thieves of London, Chris knew no limit. He would set his sights on something, no matter how difficult, and would inevitably succeed. He moved about the continent, stealing a Renoir in Stockholm, a Degas in Amsterdam, three Fermete charcoal sketches from the Louvre.

And throughout it all he developed one additional skill: killing. He was quite good at it, an expert, in fact. Other than a blood-riddled crime scene, he left not a trace of evidence that could implicate him. Whether through the use of a gun or his more preferred method, the blade of his knife, he felt no compunction at ending a life. Neither man, woman, nor child held sway over him or could still his hand. If they were in the way, they would be eliminated.

Chris had actually, on occasion, hired himself out on contract kills. It was a challenge he set himself, to see if he could plan a killing and carry it out without leaving a trace of evidence. Sometimes he did it up close with a knife, sometimes half a mile away with a sniper rifle.

And his slight, angelic appearance, which he had faced such derision for as a child, became his ally, the perfect mask to present to an unsuspecting world, a pure façade that allowed a monster to stand among the innocent.

By the age of twenty-one he had become the most respected and feared man on the street. No one knew his name, no one knew a thing about him other than the fact that his wrath should be avoided at all costs.

He eventually settled in a flat off of Piccadilly Circus. He loved the night life, the neon, the vibrance that permeated the air. It was where he based himself, out of the three-bedroom apartment. And as the years went on, he bought himself a house in Istanbul, a grand summer house that overlooked the water. It was the land of his mother's birth, and while she and his father died before he ever saw them again, he felt connected to her. He learned her language, he learned her culture.

So at the age of twenty-one he left behind the mundane name Chris Miller, and embracing the culture that he had once shunned, he chose his new name. It was one word, as his father was known as Rusty and his mother was known as Nuray. He would be known only as Iblis. He had found it to be most fitting, a name that would instill fear, for it was the Arabic word for the Devil.

CHAPTER 13

Busch scrubbed the marble back to white, stuffing the now-crimson bath towels into a large garbage bag, which he would dispose of later. He fought back the nausea as he cleaned up Simon's blood, trying not to dwell on his friend's pain and suffering. Busch couldn't seem to shake the image from his mind; it was as if he were still on the force, witnessing the horrific violation of an innocent, except that the victim was one of his closest friends. Busch scrubbed harder, as if to erase the images from his mind as much as the blood from the floor. But as was so often the case with Busch, his emotions eventually ran to anger and rage; whoever had done this to his friend would face his wrath.

"How the hell did they get out of here so fast?" Michael said, shaking Busch out of his anger.

"We're not in Kansas anymore," Busch said. "Different rules. I'm sure a back-door, no-questions-asked exit doesn't cost more than a few dollars."

Michael knew they couldn't call the police. It would all come pointing back at them. Michael and KC were both thieves, there was no record of their coming into the country, and who knew what bells and whistles would be going off if Michael's name were run through Interpol.

Michael looked out toward the balcony, out toward KC, who hadn't said a word in the last fifteen minutes. Michael had had enough of the silence and walked outside. "You need to tell me what's going on."

KC looked at Michael but remained silent.

"Simon only spoke of stealing a chart," Michael continued. "Neither of you ever mentioned any artifact. Anything else on your illegal shopping list?"

"I don't know what it is," KC said, her eyes still staring out at the lights shining upon the enormous dome of Hagia Sophia. "Simon said he was going to get it himself."

Michael could see it in her eyes, he could hear it in her voice. She wasn't telling him the whole story and there was no time for games. "KC, I need to know what you guys were doing, I need to know everything."

"I told you everything," KC said, looking away.

Michael tried to hold himself back but his emotions got the better of him. "What the hell is the Caduceus? You were planning two thefts. Were you going to tell me? Jesus, KC, what else are you lying about?"

"Lying?" KC spun back on Michael, her eyes wide. "Lying? My sister was kidnapped."

"That's right, and unless you start telling me the truth—everything—it's going to be pretty damn hard to get her and Simon back."

"I don't want your help." KC stood.

"I really don't care," Michael said, glaring at her.

"Stay out of it." KC roughly brushed past him.

"Not a chance." Michael was right on her heels.

KC raced through the living room, past Busch, ripped open the door, and slammed it behind her.

Busch looked at Michael. "Nice going."

"Fuck you."

BUSCH WALKED INTO his suite at the Four Seasons Hotel and out onto the balcony to find KC sitting on a wicker chair, staring at nothing. She looked up at his large frame filling the doorway, her eyes distant, pain-filled.

"I see someone besides Michael knows how to get into rooms without a key."

KC just stared out beyond the water, unamused by Busch's attempt at levity.

"KC." Busch gently took a seat in front of her. "Michael's not working against you. He's been in your shoes. It's pretty sad to say, but he has been through this before. He knows what it's like to hold someone's life in your hands."

"I can handle this myself."

"Can you?" Busch said gently, his deep voice at a whisper. "Can you stay focused, knowing the life of the one you love hangs on your success? I'm sure you're good at what you do, I don't doubt that. But you can't do this alone. You can turn your back on Michael but don't turn your back on his help."

"This is my fault," KC said abruptly. "I'll fix it."

"You know, a few years back, I knew someone whose wife was dying. He would have done anything to save her." Busch paused. "He ran off alone and tried. And you know, as much as he wanted to save her, he made things worse, far worse than you can imagine. He was real reluctant to accept anyone's help. I had to practically tie him up but he finally accepted it. Now that same guy, Michael, is trying to help you.

"Together, we can get them back and put things right." Busch looked out at the water, amazed at what he was saying. He was trying to convince someone to go ahead and commit a crime, something that he never would have done a few years back when he was on the force. But he knew the stakes, he knew the pain and guilt KC was feeling. "Trust me and trust Michael."

KC finally turned to Busch and saw Michael come through the hallway door into the suite. He carried Simon's briefcase, which was about to burst at its seams.

KC looked across the distance at Michael, the moment hanging in the air. Michael held tight to the case as he walked into the living room. Busch looked between the two of them, waiting, hoping . . .

KC finally stood up.

"It's a staff, a rod, really, about two feet long." KC came in off the porch. "Entwined with two snakes, teeth bared at each other. It is covered in jewels with ruby eyes, teeth of silver. There's a drawing of it in Simon's case."

Busch stood in the balcony doorway and winked knowingly at Michael.

Michael opened Simon's case and removed the reams of documents, spreading them on the large coffee table. KC took a seat on the couch before Michael as they exchanged a glance of truce. She thumbed through the papers and pulled out a reproduction of a painting of a heavyset man, his round face covered in a dark beard, dressed in long maroon and blue robes over a white and gold shirt. Upon his head was a large white turban, a green tassel capped in pearls and diamonds in the center of the headpiece. He lounged upon a sea of green pillows as a cadre of subjects stood before him. In his right hand was clutched a staff while his left hand was raised palm down before his people.

Attached to the painting was a photograph, an enlargement of the staff, its detail revealing a bejeweled dark rod, two snakes coiled up the shaft, their bodies adorned with precious gems. At the crown of the staff, the two snakes faced each other, jaws wide, ready to strike, their silver teeth glinting and deadly.

As Michael stared at the object his mind itched; he had seen the staff before and on more than one occasion.

"Look familiar?" KC asked.

Michael nodded.

"The Rod of Asclepius looks similar to this; a single snake coiling up a wooden staff. Asclepius was the son of Apollo and the god of healing, and his staff became the symbol of the American Medical Association and the World Health Organization, and is on the doors of most ambulances."

Michael picked up the picture, examining it up close.

"It more closely resembles the Caduceus," KC continued. "An ancient astrological symbol of commerce carried by the Greek god Hermes. He was the messenger between the gods and man, and, among other things, conducted the dead to the afterlife. And, ready for this? He was the protector of merchants, liars, and thieves."

"Great, that's what we need to hear," Busch said.

"In Greek myths, Hermes was the only god besides Hades and Persephone who could enter and leave the underworld without interference."

"Don't even go down that road. Mystic mumbo jumbo . . ." Busch scolded.

KC continued, "Hermes's herald staff is usually depicted

with entwined snakes rising up the rod with two wings attached to the upper section behind two opposing snake heads. Oddly enough, many medical organizations, your surgeon general, and the U.S. Army and Navy Medical Corps, erroneously use it as their symbol, not realizing its contradiction."

"Figures," Busch said with a heavy exhalation. "You're not implying that this rod is some myth; please tell me you're not saying that."

KC shook her head and came close to smiling. "No, it's an artifact, modeled after the Caduceus. It's priceless."

"What its significance is doesn't concern me," Michael said to Busch. He turned back to KC. "Where is it?"

KC again dug through the papers and pulled out an ancient sketch of a man who was anything but what Michael expected. This man was tall, with a close-cropped beard, and there was no question of the man's Eastern European origins. Michael had expected someone darker, like an Arab or North African, forgetting that then, as now, the city they stood in was a true crossroads of the world.

"Sokollu Mehmet Pasha was a grand vizier, a man of great power and connections. He was Serbian, taken from his family as a child, as the Ottoman sultans did in many of the Christian lands they conquered. He was raised and educated by the Empire, quickly rising through the military ranks. He had previously served not only as head of the imperial guard but as the high admiral of the imperial fleet, where he became a close friend of Piri Reis, also an admiral in the Ottoman navy—*Reis* actually means *admiral* in Turkish.

"Before Piri Reis was publicly beheaded in Egypt in 1555, he entrusted to Mehmet two items: the second half of the world map that he compiled in 1513, and this rod, which had been given to Piri years earlier by his uncle, Kemal, who asked him to use his wisdom to determine the two artifacts' fate and whether man would ever be worthy to understand their significance.

"The rod was the sole piece of treasure that Kemal had kept from a ship he had captured in the Indian Ocean many years earlier. Mehmet kept the rod and Piri's chart in two different areas of his private estate, taking years to ponder the fate of the two objects.

"Several years later Selim II ascended the throne. He was the son of Suleiman the Magnificent, one of the greatest leaders of the sixteenth century. It was under Suleiman's reign that the Ottoman Empire became a world leader and reached its golden age. He led his armies in the conquests of Rhodes, Belgrade, most of the Middle East, and northern Africa. The Ottoman navy dominated the seas. With Admiral Piri Reis at the helm, they controlled the Mediterranean, the Red Sea, and the Persian Gulf. Suleiman was considered a great statesman, military leader, and ruler, one who was fair and just.

"But his son, Selim II, was far different. He had no interest in the military and abandoned much of his rule to his grand vizier, Mehmet, so he could indulge his more decadent interests. Selim was sultan from 1566 to 1574 and nothing like his father. As good as his father was, as much as his father accomplished for his kingdom and people, Selim did the opposite. He stayed in the harem, always drunk, never paying any mind to his subjects, the Empire, the world.

"Selim was an egotistical drunk who fancied himself like the Egyptian pharaohs of old, though he refused to wear the Uraeus crown of the pharaohs, those crowns with the single snake poised to strike. While visiting Mehmet's home, Selim saw the rod, took one look at it, and snatched it away, fascinated by the intricate serpent design. He carried the Caduceus like a scepter as a symbol of his power, holding out the dual snake heads as a warning.

"Now, Mehmet was considered one of the greatest viziers the Empire had ever known. He had been the grand vizier to Suleiman and continued his role under Selim. He actually led the kingdom much as Suleiman did due to Selim's lack of interest. Mehmet was considered a brilliant leader in politics and warfare who thought far ahead, beyond where other men could. As to the rod, he had a promise to keep to his friend Piri; he knew he would get it back and dispose of it, he just had to bide his time."

"What's the significance of the rod to Simon, why does he want it so bad?" Busch interjected.

"Simon never said—"

"I don't care about that right now," Michael interrupted with anger in his voice. "What happened to the rod?"

"Mehmet had tried on many an occasion to get the sultan to part with it, telling him stories that it might carry a curse, that it would bring pain and suffering, that it was beneath him to rely on a scepter like some Western European dandy ruler, but the drunken sultan barely listened to his chief advisor. Mehmet's words went unheeded.

"Upon Selim's death, Mehmet realized that through the sultan's help he would actually be able to carry out Piri's wish. As grand vizier, Mehmet was in charge of the sultan's burial arrangements and worked to have a tomb built for the sultan, a tomb that took three years to construct."

"Are you saying . . . ?" Busch said, hoping the answer wasn't what he expected.

"The rod is buried with the body of Sultan Selim II."

"So let me get this straight. You go through this big elaborate story to tell me that we're grave robbing?" Busch said. "This is bullshit. I don't know about you, but I've got a big problem with disturbing the dead."

"Where's his grave?" Michael asked, ignoring Busch.

"It's a tomb, actually," KC said as she stood up and walked toward the door of the hotel room. She stopped and turned back. "Well, are you coming?"

Michael and Busch followed her out the door, reluctant and confused. They walked down the hall to KC's suite and followed her through the living room, out onto her balcony.

The three looked out on the old city, at Topkapi Palace, at the surrounding neighborhood alive with locals and tourists, and finally at the enormous building that filled their view to the left. It was a tremendous central domed structure from the age of Byzantium, its basilica design climbing 150 feet in the air. Wrapped in hundreds of arched windows and smaller domes, it looked like a great church lost to history, but the two-hundred-foot minarets that stood at the four corners left no doubt that they were looking at one of the world's finest mosques.

"You're kidding," Busch said. "The tomb's in there?"

"Actually . . ." KC pointed to three small domed buildings on the southeast of the main structure. "Selim's tomb has its own building in the center there."

CHAPTER 14

The smell of almonds and honey filled the air as Venue stirred his custom blend of tea. There were no servants here, no secretaries, employees, or accountants.

The town house, on the Prince's Canal in Amsterdam, was a brick residence whose existence he shared with no one. Its ownership hidden under a labyrinth of corporations and aliases, it was his sanctuary, a place to hide if his world collapsed, a place where he stored over five million in euros, five million in diamonds, and a cache of weapons. There was a fallout shelter, built during the year he experienced extreme paranoia. Filled with six months' worth of food and water, it lay ready in the event he needed to appear to have fallen off the face of the planet. There was a server backup of all of his corporate computer files that sat behind an impenetrable firewall along with hard copies of his leverage files: a set of documents that would lay waste not only to his competitors but also to his employees. It was what he affectionately called his fear file, the file that people hoped never was revealed to their loved ones, the police, or the government.

He pulled out the first file: It was on one of his attorneys, Ray Jaspers, an integral part of his organization who had helped him in achieving his fortune. While the file contained a detailed curriculum vitae it was also filled with information on his predilection for gambling and teenage girls, along with a list of mob debts from his days in America. Venue picked up the next file. It was on a man he considered his right hand, a man who had yet to fail Venue in any task, a man in whose hands Venue's future rested. As he read through the three-inch-thick accounting of criminal activities, of robberies and murders, he smiled. Venue was a man said to be devoid of emotion, but if he had a warm place in his heart it would be for someone like Iblis.

Twenty years ago, Venue had just begun to build his empire and was seeking out those who would compose the foundation of his organization, the integral pieces he would need if he were to achieve his goals. There were CFOs and accountants, tax experts and lawyers, and then there were those whose talents weren't acquired in universities, whose skill sets were not the norm in the corporate world. Venue's business plan, one that he had formulated during the years of his incarceration, required laws to be broken, tasks he was qualified for but could no longer be directly related to.

First a street thug, then a priest, before finally finding his calling in the world of business: In the three years since Venue had left prison, his investment firm had made over twenty million pounds. He had honed his deal-making skills, applying lessons learned from the street: pressure, intimidation, threats, and blackmail. He exploited the weaknesses of his competitors, finding the most vulnerable to prey on. He'd been looking for a kindred spirit with whom he could speak and operate in the vernacular of the street.

And so it was that twenty years earlier Venue had found himself in the corner booth of a run-down pub in Brighton, the howling winter winds off the English Channel penetrating the ill-fitting windows and doors. He looked out of place among the blue-collar locals, dressed in a three-piece charcoal pinstripe suit, hand tailored in London. He sipped a dark ale from a smudged, chipped glass as he tuned out the loud bar rail crowd who were celebrating the end of their day.

The young man took a seat in the booth across from him. He was thin, no more than five feet seven inches, and was dwarfed by Venue's six-foot-three frame.

"Hello, Chris," Venue said.

The skinny young man sat there, his childlike face showing no emotion as his identity was revealed.

"I know you prefer the name Iblis. I'm not really concerned with what you call yourself: Christopher Miller, Nuray Miller's son, offspring of Rusty, or just plain old Iblis. Names are easily shed, but a man can never shed his true skin."

"Tell me why I shouldn't kill you right here," Iblis said, unintimidated by the large man before him.

"Two reasons, really," Venue said confidently, not a hint of fear in his voice. "First, I'm twenty years your senior. I can show you how to raise your game to the next level. You can run around the streets all you want, steal from this museum, that museum, or you can raise the bar and commit jobs that could net you tens, even hundreds of millions."

"And the second reason?"

"I need a partner."

A mousy blonde waitress, her cheeks red from the seaside breezes, placed two pints before them and quickly left.

Iblis laughed as he sipped his ale.

"I've been like you," Venue continued. "I've done the

things you have done; I've even served time, which you have been fortunate enough to avoid. But I can't do the things I used to do anymore. I have an image to uphold."

"I know what you do, how you do it. Wearing a suit just makes you a well-dressed criminal," Iblis said. "If you disappeared, I doubt there's anyone who would shed a tear. In fact, I could probably sell your head for a pretty good price." Iblis laid a long hunting knife on the table. "I could kill you right here."

"So you said. But don't you think that if I'm wise enough to learn your real name, learn about your family, about the jobs you pulled, I would be smart enough to prevent that? Don't you think that before I had you come to see me I would have ensured my safety and planned for your demise?"

Iblis sat there silently.

"Not to worry; if I planned to kill you, you'd already be dead."

Iblis tilted his head and smiled in respect. "What would this partnership entail?"

Venue placed his briefcase on the sticky, notched table between them. "I would need you several times a year, primarily to steal corporate documents, information on my competitors or those I'm looking to acquire."

"Not a lot of challenge to that."

"No, but the reward is great. From time to time there may be some pieces of art; I do have an affinity for certain works, particularly ones that hold religious significance."

"Ah, a spiritual man," Iblis said.

"You don't know the half of it."

"I take it that the bag is on the table for a reason." Iblis nodded to the briefcase.

"Occasions may arise when I need you to perform more serious acts, acts whose effects are permanent."

"Killing?" Iblis leaned in.

Venue arched his brow in silent concurrence.

"I'll pay five million dollars per year. Your time is your own, to do with as you wish, except when I need you, and when those moments arise I would expect you to drop whatever you might be doing to be at my beck and call. In addition, I will pay a bonus fee per job depending on its nature."

Iblis sat there, his mind spinning. Venue could see it.

"You obviously already have a job in mind," Iblis said as he pointed to the case.

"As a matter of fact," Venue said, letting the moment hang in the air, "I do."

FATHER FRANCIS OSWYN walked out of the market in Penzance and placed the armful of groceries in the back of his Ford Taurus. He slid into the driver's seat and drove the five blocks to the seaside retreat that had been donated to the Church by a successful accountant by the name of Miles O'Banion who had died childless two years earlier.

The whitewashed house had been built in the late fifties in hopes of a large family, with each of the six bedrooms overlooking the English Channel. But O'Banion's wife had died in childbirth, along with their son, and he never remarried, dedicating his time to his job, the Church, and God. The house, filled with old English furniture, thick couches, and black walnut walls and floors, became a summertime center of entertainment and merriment, its celebrants overflowing the wide porches that wrapped the home. Its celebrations lasting from May Day to September 1, with a guest list that included every local parishioner, whether friend or foe. But since O'Banion's passing the home had grown quiet. The parties stopped, and the merriment was replaced with quiet prayer.

Oswyn had come to relish the allure of the wintertime sea, the huge swells, the dramatic difference from trough to crest, the enormous waves crashing on the beach with a rhythmic pounding that lulled him to sleep at night.

While most had fled the seaside community in search of warmth and life in the city, Oswyn built a roaring fire in the stone fireplace, grabbed the latest Stephen King novel, and found himself close to peace. He had been trying to finish the book for two weeks now only to suffer constant interruption, but now that he had arrived at the O'Banion house, he finally would get through the last two chapters and be able to start that Robert Masello novel his sister had raved about.

It was a moonless night, the house dark and serene, as Oswyn took a seat in the large wingback chair by the hearth and turned on the adjacent floor lamp. He angled his body toward the warmth of the flame, listened to the crashing surf in the distance, and cracked open the book.

Leaning back in the armchair, he never saw the man approach from the shadows—the man who had waited patiently for two hours under the cloak of darkness.

A strong hand grabbed the crown of Oswyn's head and forced his body forward in the chair. And just as suddenly the priest's body went limp, his arms falling to his side as his book crashed to the floor. His head fell forward at an unnatural angle, his chin upon his chest. He never felt the thin blade as it entered the back of his neck, slipping between his uppermost cervical vertebrae to sever his spinal cord.

With the loss of his nervous system, his diaphragm failed, his breathing ceased. And as the last bit of air that Oswyn would ever hold in his lungs escaped, he found the frame of mind to embrace his faith and utter a single prayer of contrition.

Suffocation came slowly but accelerated with a vengeance; though his body could no longer feel, his head felt as if it would explode. Darkness swept in from the corners of his eyes; white pin lights, like shooting stars, darted along the blackness as it consumed him. And as Francis Oswyn's soul prepared to escape its corporeal binds, the last thought that danced in his head was not of his sister, or his long-dead parents, or his Church, or friends. Oswyn's last thought dwelled on the fact that he would never know how that damn Stephen King novel ended.

WITHIN THREE MONTHS the six other priests on Venue's list were dead. There was nothing left behind, no fingerprints, no witnesses. The authorities found no evidence in any of the slayings, as the country and Europe grew rife with rumor that a serial killer was targeting priests. Theories abounded—everything from Protestant retribution to the devil himself pulling the plug. But after seven victims, the killings stopped, and the investigation inevitably became a cold case.

IBLIS SAT IN Venue's brand-new office in Amsterdam on the fourth floor overlooking the Emperor's Canal. The large bald man's company and reputation had grown dramatically over the six months since they first met, with more than thirty employees filling the offices and cubicles, grinding out millions for their boss.

Venue slid a wire confirmation across the desk to Iblis. "Seven million. Don't spend it all in one place."

"I'm going to get myself a large summer place in Istanbul," Iblis said with a smile.

"Different," Venue said. "I'm more partial to the Italian Riviera, myself."

"We each have our favorite flavors."

"If you do go down there, perhaps you could locate something for me."

"What would that be?"

"A sea chart, more of a rumor really. I only have bits and pieces on it."

"You mean a map?"

"Some people might call it that."

"Which leads to . . . ?"

"Not entirely sure. It's not a priority at the moment, more of a pastime, a curiosity. Like I said, I only have bits and pieces."

"Well, when you want me to put those bits and pieces together . . ." Iblis rose from his chair. "Call me."

"One other thing before you go." Venue stood, walked over to the TV in the center bookcase, and hit the VCR. "I think we make a good team, but I want to make sure you understand that I own the team."

Iblis looked at him, confused, as the video began to play. And as it did, rage washed over his face.

The video showed various images of Iblis: stalking his priestly victims, entering the house in Penzance. Some of the images were still photographs, many of the shots in green nightscope, each leaving no question of Iblis's identity.

"I always find it best to deal in fear." Venue looked down on Iblis through his cold, emotionless eyes and walked over to him, physically towering over his employee. "From my perspective, it is the best motivator, particularly when the fear is for one's survival."

"Why would you do this?" Iblis said, his breaths coming like a racehorse's. "I did your job without question. Killed the men you wanted killed."

"I want to make sure we have an understanding."

"What is that?" Iblis did everything he could to stop himself from snatching the knife from his pocket and slitting Venue's throat.

"That you will remain loyal."

"You don't buy loyalty with fear," Iblis whispered through a clenched jaw.

"And yet I believe I just bought you." Venue smiled. "You see, we are two sides of the same coin. Do you think for a moment that I don't know you have taken your own safeguards against me? Do you think that I am foolish enough to think that you have not kept evidence that would implicate me in the murder-for-hire scheme involving the seven priests who destroyed my life?"

Iblis stood there without a word.

"You do not have to admit things, but I want you to know that I have had twenty more years of experience in bending the wills of men; I know breaking points and limits and I play a damn good game of chicken. You should be aware that I never lose. So we understand, just so we are clear, I believe we have a very fruitful future together, one that we'll both benefit from."

Venue walked to his desk and picked up a manila envelope; he opened it and held the documents before Iblis. "Look familiar?"

Iblis stared at the thick file; it was his intel on the

priests, their movements, their likes and dislikes, provided to him through his own research and with the assistance of Venue. There were several photographs of Venue and a thoroughly compiled stack of notes inexorably tying Venue to his priestly past and the seven dead men who had excommunicated him.

Iblis's pupils enlarged to the point that his eyes were almost pure black with only an aura of ghostly blue; his heart thundered in the veins of his ears, throbbing as the fear made its way from his heart to his soul.

"There is not a thing in this world I cannot get my hands on, be it power, money, or flesh. If I can reach into a Zurich-Pronish safe-deposit box in Switzerland and pull these papers, imagine what I could do if I was upset."

Iblis could no longer mask his fear. It was the first time he had felt it since he'd been a child. This man Venue could literally reach through walls to get what he wanted.

"As I said, I would expect nothing less," Venue commented as he held up the papers. "And I don't hold it against you; it was prudent, and the smart thing to do when protecting oneself. In fact, if you hadn't done something along these lines I probably would have had you killed for being too naive and ill-equipped to function in my employ.

"We've established our lack of trust in each other, we each understand the other's ability to kill. I just want you to understand that now that you work for me, it is for life. I will pay you most handsomely, I will respect your judgment and seek your advice. But I hope that it is perfectly clear that I have the power and the reach to end your life if and when I so choose."

CHAPTER 15

Michael, Busch, and KC were back in Michael's hotel suite, trays of food scattered on the floor as they looked through Simon's voluminous stack of documents on Topkapi, the mysterious rod of Selim II, and Hagia Sophia.

Busch was already through his third hamburger, choosing to avoid the preferred local flavors of goat cheese and seasoned lamb.

"KC," Michael said, "I know we've been warned off the chart, but you still need to tell me what you know. If we're going to get Cindy back, if we're going to get to Simon in time, you need to tell me everything."

KC nodded. Michael could see the pain in her eyes, the difficulty focusing, but then he watched as she pulled her thoughts together. She took a sip from her water bottle, tied her long blonde hair up into a ponytail, and turned to Michael and Busch.

"The first maps were not of cities or countries, they were of the heavens," KC said, "maps of the stars found on the walls of the Lascaux caves in southern France. Man has always looked for guidance, whether through words or charts. Some consider the Bible to be like a map that will lead one to heaven, so, too, the Koran and the Torah. Spiritual maps for the soul.

"To this day, maps are some of the most plagiarized documents on earth, it being common practice to lift information from earlier charts. When pirates captured a ship, the first things they went for, the things of greatest value, far greater than a treasure or gold, were the charts. They could lead them to parts of the world unknown and make them rulers of the sea.

"Maps were the first thing traded when ships came to port. The highest of prices was paid for maps and charts, as they would unlock the mysteries of the sea, and not just destinations but the location of deadly coral reefs, bottom-wrecking rocks, and deadly shallows and shorelines. The Piri Reis map is an amalgam drawn from who knows how many maps.

"Kemal Reis, Piri's uncle, was a corsair. It is believed that much of the information contained in his nephew's map came from the maps and charts he plundered while sailing the seas."

"Plundered?" Busch laughed. "Who was he? Errol Flynn?"

"Corsairs were pirates, they plundered," KC said as if that were obvious.

Busch's laughter fell away. "I thought *Reis* meant *admiral*."

"Who better to make the admiral of your fleet than a man who knows the seas like the lips of his wife? The Ottoman Empire, like many other countries—Spain, England, France—allowed corsairs like Kemal to act as privateers in the name of the crown, permitting them to keep a large portion of the bounty they captured while disrupting the supply lines of their enemies.

"So, being a very good corsair, Kemal plundered many a chart, and from these and certain charts within Piri's possession, some from the Alexandria library, some from the Byzantine library, he created his own map. But the thing is, Piri Reis's chart in Topkapi, the one that was rediscovered in the palace in 1929, is only a portion of Piri's original chart. The interesting thing about the Piri Reis chart is that it is not the complete sea chart, it is actually only half of the whole."

"And . . . ?" Busch urged KC on.

"His chart was a labor of love, not drawn for money, commission, or by sultan's decree but out of sheer passion for mapmaking. He drew from charts new, old, ancient, and, some say, even mythical. Rendered on an enormous African gazelle hide, it was the most complete chart of its time; in fact, it had no equal for over a century. It mapped the oceans from the Atlantic to the Indian out to the Pacific. He detailed the mountain ranges of the Andes, the Himalayas, the major rivers of the world, and footnoted the entire document with historical and legendary details. There were representations of holy sites and places of darkness, animals of history and myth, people of culture and of the wild. It was a masterpiece of historic significance that had started out as a self-indulgent challenge.

"But upon seeing what he had wrought, upon realizing that such a codex would unlock the uncharted seas and rivers and reveal things that isolated cultures had hidden away as sacred to those whose only desire was to conquer, Piri tore his map in two.

"He gave the western section to Sultan Suleiman I in 1517 as a gift. Though torn down the center of Africa, its eastern half said to be destroyed, it was considered a gift of no equal and was held up as an example of the Ottoman Empire's dominance of both the lands and seas of the world.

"Piri held on to the other half, but in his later years, fearing he would die and it would fall into the wrong hands, he entrusted the eastern section, the Asian section, to his friend the grand vizier, Mehmet.

"As I mentioned to Michael earlier, the vast majority of those within the harem and many of the sultan's viziers arrived in Constantinople as prisoners or slaves captured from Christian lands. Upon arrival in the palace, they were forced to convert to Islam, and while they all learned the Koran and participated in the holy practice, that does not mean they abandoned the religious beliefs within their hearts. Imagine if you were imprisoned and told to convert to a foreign religion: Would you do it willingly, would you embrace the new faith and abandon everything that you had been taught? This created a secret Christian solidarity between several eunuchs, concubines, and viziers.

"In order to help ease and acclimate certain concubines and eunuchs, the chief black eunuch, a Kizlar Agha by the name of Attawa, with the help of Mehmet, had a chapel constructed in the bowels of the harem, one that could be accessed by the eunuchs' secret tunnels and passages in and out of the palace. It was an act of extreme subterfuge, one that, if found out, would be punished by death, but one that the true believers in their faith felt worth the risk. It was a small chapel with an altar and catered to the Christians and Jews who had been torn not only from their families and homes but from their faith. It was tucked away along the edge of a cistern that lay beneath the second and third inner circles of Topkapi, a remnant from Byzantine times.

"With the death of Sultan Selim II, Mehmet's advancing age, and the inevitable changing of the chief eunuch, Mehmet and Attawa decided it was time to seal up their small chapel, erasing it from existence, and what better place to hide something than a room that would no longer exist."

"Why would Piri tear up his greatest masterpiece?" Busch asked. "What didn't he want found?"

"I have no idea. Whatever it was, though, it scared Simon, and Simon's a man whom I've yet to see fearful of anything."

"Honestly," Michael said, "I really don't care why the map was torn in two or what it leads to. It is the best bargaining chip to get your sister and Simon back."

"Michael," KC said, "as much as I agree with you, Iblis is beyond dangerous."

"And we're not?" Busch asked, his voice growing rough, his brow furrowed.

KC paused. "Not like him."

Michael looked at KC, his heart skipping as he saw her eyes. She was truly afraid of this man, this teacher of the illicit, clandestine arts who had betrayed her in the worst sense. He saw her pain for her kidnapped sister, fearing for her life.

"KC," Michael said softly, "he thinks it's only you. He has no idea who I am, who Busch is, and even less idea that I could steal this chart right out from under his nose."

"He may have stolen the chart already."

"He was here a few hours ago, he's dealing with tucking away Simon and your sister. If he could just go in and grab it, he wouldn't have warned you off so forcefully."

"Michael, if we steal it, he'll kill her; I don't know if I can take that chance," KC said.

"KC, think about it. Is it the only copy, the only means of finding what they're looking for?"

KC nodded. "Simon said it's the only one."

"That's why we have to get it before he does. That chart is everything; it's your leverage. They won't risk losing it. I promise you, Cindy's not going to die if you have the chart, you know that and I know that. Which means we have no time to waste. If he's as good a thief as you say, he's already planned everything. And if he has, I've got to get to it before he does."

"What are you saying, Michael?"

"I'll steal the map," Michael said as he sat up a little straighter.

"Why did I know you were going to say that?" Busch leaned back in his chair.

"I can't let you do that," KC said with pain in her voice.

"Yeah, KC, you can, but you're going to have to get the rod on your own at the same time; can you do that?"

"You don't understand what he will do to her. He'll make her suffer—"

Michael slowly put his hands up.

"As hard as this sounds, I need you to put your sister out of your mind. Same goes for Simon. They're both alive, we know that. If we dwell on them, we'll all lose focus and end up dead."

KC took a deep breath and nodded. "Fine, but I call the shots."

"Not a chance," Michael shot back.

"It's my sister."

"That's right," Michael said. "My head is clearer on this."

"You've been out of the game too long," KC argued.

"Actually, that's not entirely true," Busch interjected.

"I thought you—you said you bowed out of this stuff years ago."

"He said that?" Busch cut in, stifling a laugh.

"Look, we'll work as a team," Michael said. "Leave it at that. You get the rod, I'll get the chart."

"I'll get the chart," KC argued.

"No way. If this Iblis is as dangerous as you say and you run into him underneath Topkapi . . ."

KC reluctantly nodded.

"Do you think you can handle stealing the rod yourself?" Michael said.

"Are you kidding me? Worry about yourself." KC sounded genuinely pissed.

"Ouch," Busch said, trying not to laugh.

"But we have to move quickly, within sixty hours at most, and do both thefts at the same time."

"And if one of you gets caught?"

"We won't," Michael and KC said in unison.

"Great," Busch said. "You guys even answer the same."

"If Iblis expects you to steal that rod within three days, he's going for the map before then," Michael said.

"How do you know?"

"Once you steal the rod, security is going to go through the roof. What would you do?"

KC nodded in agreement.

"Tell me about Iblis. What kind of thief is he?"

"The kind who has no qualms about running a knife through your neck and watching you bleed out."

"That's just terrific," Busch said.

"He's also paranoid."

"So he's got his eye on you?"

"I guarantee he's watching this hotel right now," KC said.

"Then tomorrow morning, we need to make him think

that I'm leaving the country." Michael turned to Busch. "You've got to find us another hotel."

"Are you kidding?" Busch said.

Michael didn't need to answer; he knew Busch would understand that KC had to appear to be on her own.

KC stood up. "Simon's the one who really knows Hagia Sophia."

"Put him out of your mind and we'll get this thing done." Michael looked up into KC's green eyes and spoke to her heart. "I promise."

Busch thumbed through his stack of papers and pulled out a map of the former mosque.

KC shook her head at the proffered floor plan, looked at her watch, and headed for the door. "It's already three-thirty, I'm sick of reading anyway."

"You going to Hagia Sophia?"

"Where else would I be going?" KC snapped.

"I'll meet you in the lobby in five minutes; we can walk."

"I thought Iblis was watching the place," Busch pointed out.

"I hope he is," Michael answered. "If he sees us taking a walk over to Hagia Sophia, that's just fine. He'll think she's getting the lay of the land."

"But that's what she will be doing," Busch pointed out.

"And he'll think she's staying away from his precious chart, and following his directions."

"Five minutes," KC repeated. Without looking their way, she walked out the door.

And as soon as it clicked shut . . .

Busch stared at Michael.

Michael had seen the look before. It was Busch's look of angry disappointment, one that Michael first saw when

Busch was his parole officer, a look he gave Michael when he found out Michael had broken his parole, broken his promises.

"It's Simon, for Christ's sake." Michael barely contained himself.

"I know it's Simon," Busch shot back. "He's my friend, too. But he plays with fire. And what are you supposed to do, bail his ass out every time? You just saved his life twenty-four hours ago. Now he's in trouble again. And I'm going to tell you what's going to happen: You're going to end up dead."

"You know me better than that. But you know what? Simon will be dead if we don't help him. And are you forgetting about KC's sister? They have her, too. She's got nothing to do with this and her life's on the line. How do you justify that? Huh?"

"Michael, I have a map. It's a big map. It's on the wall in my basement. It's filled with pushpins of all the places I've gone with you, all the places I never thought I would visit, all the places we almost died in. I don't want to be adding any more pushpins. And you know what? When I die I want to die at home, or at least in my own country."

"Take the plane," Michael said in all sincerity. "I'm not asking you to help. Please go home to your family. You've done enough already."

"That's bullshit and you know it. You expect me to fly home and what, fly back when I have to save your ass? I can't tell you how sick I am of this. I face more danger with you than I did in my entire career on the police force."

"Paul, I can't let KC do this alone."

"Tell me something, who is first and foremost in your mind right now? Simon, KC's sister . . . or KC?"

Michael said nothing.

"Are you doing this for her? To impress her, protect her, what?"

"It's Simon," Michael said through clenched teeth.

"I know it's Simon," Busch said calmly. "I know you wouldn't let him come to harm, or KC's sister, so please don't take this the wrong way." Busch paused as if he were about to announce a tragedy. "How well do you know KC?"

"What? What's that supposed to mean?" Michael was instantly pissed.

"I said, don't take it the wrong way, dammit. You met her, what, a month ago? Now you're ready to put your life on the line for her. I'm just saying, she's a thief. Present company excluded, I'm not much for trusting thieves, even if they're women . . ." Busch paused, thinking. "Especially if they're women."

Michael stared at Busch, trying not to hear his words, but they were seeping in.

"We don't know jack shit about her past, we just met her cute little sister, and now we're rushing off to save her. I'm not saying something stinks, but . . ."

"So, what? You think she's setting me up? You think this is some plan of hers to get my help?" Michael tried to contain himself. "Even if I didn't trust KC, I'd still be doing this for Simon. How many times has he saved our asses?"

"Need I remind you it's usually Simon who lures us into the mess that gets our asses in trouble in the first place?"

"I'm not bailing on him."

"I didn't say anything about bailing," Busch relented, backing off. "I'm just saying, can you check your heart at the door on this one?"

"It's not . . ." Michael paused. He knew full well what Busch meant. Busch was his best friend. He knew him even better than he knew himself. "I can't let someone else's life slip through my fingers. I can't go through that again, Paul."

"Do you love her?"

Michael took a deep breath. Thinking, considering. "I don't know. But she made me feel again. And I'm not ready to give that up."

"I understand. But you're playing in a world that's foreign, that's very different from anywhere you've been before. This is Istanbul. You did your thing in the U.S., Europe, Russia, but not here. They think different, they act different, they speak different . . . but . . ."

"But what?" Michael prompted his friend to finish.

"But I'll bet they kill just the same."

CHAPTER 16

Michael and KC walked out the lobby door of the Four Seasons Hotel and headed up the street. They never turned back to see the yellow Fiat that sat near the far curb, its dark-haired driver watching their every move. And he in turn never saw the large, blond American watching him. Busch hung back in the shadows of the hotel lobby; it provided a perfect vantage point as he peered through the telephoto lens of his digital camera.

The driver sat high in the seat, his head almost touching the ceiling. Busch smiled to himself, realizing the man had jacked his car seat up as high as possible to give the world an artificial impression of his stature.

The man's brown hair hung long in his face; he occasionally flipped it back with his right hand. Busch could see his innocent façade, an appearance quite contrary to his soul. His emotionless eyes remained fixed on Michael and KC while he spoke to two passengers who sat in the car with him. They were larger, a counter to Iblis's small size, their eyes fixed on the same target.

Busch clicked off pictures of them all, captured the license plate and a wide shot of the car. He knew from his days of stakeouts and police work how often the people doing the watching never realized they, in turn, were being watched.

As Michael and KC vanished around a corner, Iblis started his car and pulled from the curb. Busch hung back as the car drove right past the lobby, the tiny man never aware of his presence.

Busch committed Iblis's face to memory, thinking all the while of Simon bleeding and unconscious on the white marble floor of the hotel suite, of the pools of blood that he had sopped up with the bath towels.

Busch couldn't wait to drive his fist through Iblis's skull for hurting his friend.

HUNDREDS OF STAINED-GLASS windows filtered the late sun's rays into a host of rainbows that scattered onto the floor of an enormous nave that was almost two hundred feet long—a wide-open space that swallowed up the three hundred tourists, making them seem like a gathering of ants on a football field.

Michael and KC walked briskly across the marble floor, their eyes wandering up 180 feet to the crown of the dome of Hagia Sophia.

One of the most incredible buildings in history, Hagia Sophia was the fourth-largest cathedral in the world after St. Paul's in London, the Duomo in Milan, and St. Peter's in Rome. Incredibly, it had been constructed more than one thousand years earlier than its closest rival.

The 102-foot-diameter crown of Hagia Sophia seemed weightless as it sat upon the unbroken arcade of forty arched windows, which helped flood the colorful interior with the late-afternoon light.

Hagia Sophia had been the religious center of the Orthodox Byzantine Empire for nearly one thousand years. For centuries it contained a large collection of Christianity's most holy relics, including a stone from the tomb of Jesus, articles belonging to the Virgin Mary, the burial shroud of Jesus, and bones of several saints, all of which had been sent to churches throughout the West when Constantinople was raided during the Fourth Crusade in 1204.

The walls were sheathed with green and white marble that was flecked with purple porphyry and richly decorated with golden mosaics depicting Jesus, the Virgin Mary, saints, emperors, and empresses.

After an eight-week siege, on May 29, 1453, Sultan Mehmed II led the one-hundred-thousand-strong force of Ottoman Turks into Constantinople and conquered the city, bringing an end to the millennium-spanning Byzantine Empire and ushering in the Ottoman Empire's golden age of conquest and expansion.

While the sultan ordered his forces to stay their hand against the Byzantine Church of the Holy Apostles so that he might install his own patriarch and better deal with his Christian subjects, he ordered the immediate conversion of Hagia Sophia into a mosque. The bells, altar, and sacrificial vessels were taken away, and many of the Christian mosaics were eventually plastered over. A mihrab, minbar, and four minarets were constructed over time. It remained as a mosque until 1935, when it was converted into a museum by the Republic of Turkey.

Michael and KC walked out the rear of the building, down a long path, and headed straight for the center of three buildings that sat on the southwest side of the museum. The mausoleum of Selim II was a square structure, wrapped around an octangular upper story that was capped by a mottled lead dome. The cut-stone building was paved in marble panels and sat between the mausoleums of Selim's son, Murad III, and his grandson, Mehmed III.

A portico with a center dome and barrel vaults over the side bays sat before the entryway. Two guards stood lazily on either side of the entrance, speaking in hushed tones as the tourists shuffled through the wide-open doors.

The interior was well-lit by two tiers of latticed windows that circled the building, a third row of windows on the dome's drum, and eight windows on the dome itself. The interior red dome was decorated with colored ornamental designs of blue and gold and sat on red and white arches supported by pale marble columns.

A blue band wrapped the eight-sided interior between the upper and lower windows, providing a break between the atmosphere of the deceased below and heaven in the dome above. The band was inscribed with white Arabic calligraphy that conveyed a sense of consecration of the deceased.

The late afternoon's diminishing crowd cycled through the building like automatons past forty-four green-shrouded coffins of varying sizes. The coffins holding males were demarked with white turbans that sat on small extensions protruding from the heads of the caskets. In addition to the large sarcophagus of Selim II, there were less grand coffins for his wife, five sons, and three daughters, as well as twenty-one grandsons and thirteen granddaughters—their three-foot coffins creating a solemn hush among the passing tourists.

There were no displays of art on the walls other than the fixed tile designs, though the walls were priceless in and of themselves. The guards remained outside, lost in their conversation, only occasionally looking in at the revolving crowd.

"How sure are you that the rod is in the coffin?" Michael asked.

"Pretty sure," KC responded.

"That's a ridiculous answer," Michael whispered in an angry tone. "Are you sure or not?"

KC tried to hold in her anger. "Simon said it was there, his notes say it was there. That is the best estimate I have."

"So you're not sure unless we open this thing up right here, right now?"

"Be my guest," KC challenged.

As Michael walked by the sultan's tomb, he quickly snagged the edge of the green shroud upon Selim's sarcophagus, pulling it partially off to reveal the marble tomb beneath. The tourists reacted in shock with subtle gasps, while KC's eyes grew wide in surprise. Michael quickly appeared embarrassed, giving the impression that it had been an accident. He reached back and adjusted the shroud, smoothing it in place before anyone was the wiser.

But Michael had seen what he needed to see. The top of the tomb was seamed, meaning the lid could be lifted, though he estimated it to weigh in excess of twelve hundred pounds.

"How the hell am I going to lift that off?" KC whispered.

Michael paused a moment and smiled. "All that time at the gym . . ."

"Very funny."

"It's going to be a little harder than we expected," Michael said.

"Gee." KC shook her head, mocking him. "You think?"

Michael smiled. "Only when I have to."

KC turned and headed out the door, unable to mask her anger. "Well, you better start thinking, 'cause we're pretty much screwed."

CHAPTER 17

Cindy stared at the enormous steel door, willing it to open, but after thirty seconds, she knew it was nothing but wishful thinking. She sipped from a cold bottle of Fiji water as she turned and took in her surroundings. The room was twenty by twenty. A blue Persian rug filled the space, its rich pile caressing her feet as she walked about without her shoes on. There was a plasma TV on the wall, a kitchenette in the corner, its fridge and cabinet stocked with food and drink. The dark wood walls and heavy mahogany and leather furniture combined to give the impression of a London gentlemen's club.

And then there was the cot along the rear wall. Simon lay unconscious upon it, his head wrapped tightly in white gauze and bandage. He had yet to wake up.

Iblis had uttered only a simple statement as his men led her and carried Simon down. "Your life and your friend's life are in the hands of your sister. Pray for her success." And he left, closing the door, sealing them in this windowless room.

She didn't know what to make of Iblis. It had been so many years since she had seen him, a man who had frequented their house when she was young, who took them out to dinner and acted like a long-lost uncle. He brought presents at Christmas and birthdays and seemed very close to KC. And now, after all this time, he showed up only to kidnap her and Simon.

But even now, she was overwhelmed by emotions beyond fear. Her anger toward KC was something she had never felt toward anyone in her life. KC had lived a life of lies; she was a criminal in every sense of the word. She had deceived Cindy about everything, creating the deepest sense of betrayal she had ever felt, far worse than a lie; it was a deception on the grandest scale. The one person whom she loved, whom she trusted, had lied to her with her every waking breath.

And what if the world were to find out? What if her new boss were to learn that her perfect sister, her hero, the one she had bragged about to everyone she met, was a thief? That her Oxford education had been paid for with the proceeds—the *loot*—from some art heist? She would not only be out of a job but probably out of her career as the business world learned her sister, her *hero*, had abandoned the nine-to-five world in favor of grand larceny.

KC had resided on a pedestal. As far as Cindy had been concerned, she could do no wrong. She was her sister, her mother, her mentor, and yet, all the while, she was off robbing people, stealing who knew what to line her pockets. Her claim that it was all for their survival was crap. She could have done millions of jobs, yet she chose the easy way, the shortcut. And if it was all for their own good, why was she still doing it? KC's lies knew no bounds. KC no longer supported her, she no longer needed to pay for tuition, and yet less than a week ago she had been in prison for God knew what, a prison she broke out of. Who was this woman she called her sister?

But worst of all, if KC had lied about this, what else in their life was a lie? Her entire existence was brought into question.

Cindy had led her life by playing by the rules. She worked hard, went to the best schools, applied herself at work. She wasn't perfect, she knew that too well; she had lied on occasion, even cheated on a test or two in order to maintain her GPA, but she rationalized it in the way that she always did: the means were justified by her goal, a goal created out of her desire never to endure the poverty her mother had endured. She would never work as a maid, a seamstress, she would never want for money. If she worked eighteen-hour days, it was to achieve wealth, not a sweaty existence in a two-bedroom apartment, unable to afford anything beyond the basics of life. Though Cindy had loved her mother, she didn't want to be like her.

But as she sat in this confined space, assessing her life, she questioned it all. Were there other ways to achieve success, other definitions of success beyond money and career achievement? What about love and children and all the storybook guidelines of real happiness? Was her thinking at the moment truly rational or was it brought on by the fear of death?

She looked at Simon, walked over, sat at his bedside, and checked his pulse. It was still strong, though the wound on his head looked bad. A bruise had begun to work its way down the right side of his face along his cheek and eye. She adjusted the ice pack, propping it against his head with the pillow.

She was filled with anger—at Iblis, at KC. She and Simon were here because of them, because of the illegal games they played, the illicit worlds they lived in.

She rose from the bed and walked to the steel door. She had seen vault doors before, in banks, in movies, but always from the outside. She looked at the brushed-steel barrier between her and freedom; there was no handle, no emergency release. There was no phone in the room, no intercom. Iblis's men had taken her cell phone, not that it would have worked through the metal casing. There was no means or opportunity for communication.

She turned back to the door and, not out of fear, not out of panic, but out of rage at Iblis and KC, she pounded on it with both hands. Her emotions poured forth, and tears of anger flowed down her cheeks as she screamed out in frustration, "Open this goddamned door!"

She wasn't ready to die.

CHAPTER 18

The summer sun was setting, painting the earth-tone structures of Istanbul with firelike colors, the odor of scorched lamb wafting in through the open windows from the street vendors in the world below.

Michael sat on the floor of his hotel suite, Simon's satchel in his lap. It was filled with research and maps that the Vatican had sent from his personal stores. Michael thumbed through the vast information on the Topkapi Museum, its contents and history, its security and government records.

The architectural drawings were detailed, depicting the ever-expanding palace, a structure that had been added to over the centuries. The lower floors were filled with mechanical rooms, offices, and storage rooms. There were passages through aqueducts, misplaced rooms, long-forgotten tunnels for whisking harem girls into and out of the palace. Designed by the eunuchs, they were a long-held secret that had fallen from memory.

Michael had read the letter that KC and Simon had stolen in Amsterdam, unsure of its meaning; he looked at the religious symbols of Christianity, Judaism, and Islam in the uppermost corners, which Simon had circled in red ink, unsure of their significance.

Busch and KC sat on the couch rereading what they had already absorbed. KC had made detailed notes of Selim's mausoleum, of the details of the interior not noted in brochures and tourist maps. She and Michael were lost in their own worlds, planning, thinking, devising. The three of them had spent the last three hours reading every piece of paper, making notes, absorbing it all, waiting before comparing conclusions so as not to influence the interpretation of the information. Through their independent review, they hoped things that were missed by one would be found by another.

It was after eight when Michael finally looked up from his stack of documents, stood, and stretched. He took several documents, including a copy of the grand vizier's letter, from his reams of papers and tucked them in his pocket. "You guys feel like getting out of here?"

Busch put down his papers and finished off the last sip from his bottle of beer. "Thank God. I don't know about you but I was hungry an hour ago."

"I really wasn't thinking about food." Michael smiled as he opened the door.

KC finally stood, the emotional exhaustion etched in her face.

"Where are we going now?" KC asked.

"What do you say we go break into a palace?"

MICHAEL AND KC walked through the lobby of the hotel and out to the waiting limo, its rear door open for them. Michael looked around for Busch, but he was nowhere to be seen.

"Think he's in the bar?" KC asked.

Michael shook his head. "Get in the car, I'll go check upstairs."

KC stepped into the black stretch as Michael headed back inside.

"Michael?" KC called out.

Michael turned back.

"Lets go, we're wasting time."

Michael looked at her, annoyed. He wasn't leaving his friend behind; he needed him and he wasn't about to be bossed around by an impatient KC. But then the front passenger window rolled down.

"Quit screwing around," a voice called.

Michael ducked his head into the car to find Busch at the wheel.

"You owe me two hundred bucks," Busch said.

Michael climbed in and closed the door.

"I don't need some unfamiliar driver knowing our every move. Told him I need the car for some no-questions-asked frivolity," Busch said as he put the car in Drive.

"Frivolity? I didn't know you knew what that meant."

"Give me a break. I figured hookers sounded better than theft." Busch pulled out into the heavy traffic, the limo like a lumbering aircraft carrier next to the zipping yellow taxis and local drivers. Horns blared, shaking fists emerged from car windows. Busch ignored the Turkish swearing as he glanced at the GPS displaying the Istanbul Ataturk Airport, gripped the wheel, and hit the accelerator. "I can't promise we'll get there in one piece, but at least we will get there."

THE YELLOW FIAT was like a bee among the swarm, lost and indistinguishable from its brethren. It remained five cars back from the enormous black limo, riding the steady flow of traffic along the road that ran parallel to the waters of the Bosporus.

Iblis hated himself for manipulating KC to do his bidding, using his black-hearted techniques on the one person he respected in this world. He had looked upon her as if she were his flesh and blood. She was intelligent, quick-witted, fearless. From the moment they had met, he had felt a connection. He had spent countless days, weeks, and months shaping her, molding her, imparting knowledge that he had come by through bad experiences, trial and error, police pursuits, and desperation. Of all his accomplishments, legal, ill-gotten, or otherwise, KC was his greatest achievement, the one person who filled him with pride.

Iblis reached into his breast pocket and pulled out the dog-eared photograph, propping it up on the dash. He glanced at the young woman as he had done so often, at her blonde hair, her green eyes that mirrored the smile on her face. The picture was ten years old, taken on a sun-filled day in Essex before she knew the truth about him, before KC finally glimpsed his heart.

When Iblis had found her in Venue's office less than a week ago, he wasn't consumed with anger, rage, or any sense of betrayal. He was filled with a sentiment his heart rarely knew, a feeling of affection and warmth at seeing her for the first time in a decade; he was filled with pride, for she was doing what he had taught her, what he had schooled her in so many years earlier. And she was doing exactly what he wanted her to do.

He had channeled news of Venue's possession of the letter, its purchase and whereabouts, through the Church, knowing it would end up with Simon, knowing it would end up with his thief of choice, KC. Iblis knew he could never call her up, ask for her help in stealing both the chart and the sultan's rod; besides having a moral center, she knew him and his dark ways, his affinity for death. It had been ten years since they last spoke.

Iblis was shocked at Venue's knee-jerk decision to have them killed for their affront. But when Venue pushed the buttons to send KC to Chiron Prison, when he paid off the warden to have her executed, Iblis had no fear for her. For he had educated her, shaped and formed her; he knew she was capable of escape. But to help tip things in her favor, he sent a picture of Simon in shackles to the Vatican along with the information regarding where he was being held and his date of execution. He found the business card of a Stephen Kelley in KC's pocket—another lawyer, he hated lawyers—and imagining she had it for a reason, included it in his little package of info.

He figured the cavalry wouldn't rush in for a thief, but a priest . . . no one would sit still for the execution of a man of the cloth.

KC was part of Iblis's overall plan in Istanbul, one that he couldn't fulfill without her help. He needed to ensure her escape not out of affection, but to ensure that she would supply the help he would need to pull off the two jobs in Istanbul. It was all part of his plan, a plan he didn't dare share with Venue.

Iblis drove along the seaside road among a plethora of cabs all racing for the airport in hopes of one more fare for the night. The limo had no chance of spotting him. As he watched the black car weave in and out of traffic, he imagined what KC was thinking.

Iblis knew KC: how she thought, how she felt, what moved her and scared her. And he used that knowledge to control her now. She would do his bidding out of fear; she would do it for her sister, just as she had taken to a life of crime to raise her. KC's motivation had never changed. Whether it was stealing a watch to buy Cindy school books and food, or an artifact to save her life, she was motivated by the bonds of love between sisters.

Iblis's mind refocused from its momentary sentimentality. He discarded his emotions as he had done so often, pulling his thoughts back to the task at hand. He watched the limo glide up the service road and slide through the gates of the private air terminal at Ataturk International Airport, slowing and disappearing into one of the private jet hangars. Iblis found a parking spot that afforded a perfect view of the doors, turned off the engine, and sat back.

Iblis had no doubt that KC, despite the danger her sister was in, despite the fact that her friend was bloodied and battered and in imminent danger of succumbing to his wounds, would consider stealing the chart. The chart had been her and Simon's initial quest, the reason for her breaking into Venue's office, for stealing the letter to learn of the chart's location. He knew that she would recognize its greater importance, that it would be a perfect bargaining chip.

He knew that beyond the fear, beyond the desperation that filled KC's heart, she wouldn't play the pawn, she wouldn't be so easily manipulated; she'd want to hold all the cards, and those cards included the chart.

Iblis found it an irresistible challenge to go head to head with his former student, to test her, to have a battle of wits. He was enthralled to see her again, his heart skipping whenever she was in his sights. But this was not a game and he had no intention of her ever truly getting the Piri Reis chart underneath Topkapi.

As much as Iblis cared for KC, as much as he actually loved her, if she betrayed him, prevented him from completing his task, he had no compunction about killing her, about tearing the lungs from her chest.

MICHAEL PULLED BACK the carpet in the center aisle of the Boeing jet, exposing a large rectangular floor panel, and made quick work of the screws. He lifted up the metal door to uncover a host of electronics, reached in, and hoisted out the fake electronic pallet to reveal a four-by-eight compartment. It was a tight fit, but it held those things that could never stand up to scrutiny. Michael climbed into the small hold and handed three large black duffel bags up through the opening into Busch's waiting hands.

Busch unzipped a bag with a gold tag, searched through reams of climbing gear, digging to the bottom, and pulled out a sheathed knife, compass, and two coils of rope. He opened the next bag to find several gun bags and boxes of ammunition.

"Jesus, Michael, it's a good thing you don't fly commercial."

Michael ignored his friend as he climbed out of the belly of the jet and opened the third and final bag: It was filled with electronics and gadgets, basic dive gear, and four blocks of clay wrapped in clear plastic. Michael went through each bag, inventorying everything in his mind.

Michael sat back and thought for a moment. He stood and went to a back closet in the plane, returning with four three-foot-long leather tubes. Each had a leather shoulder strap and appeared like a satchel that held architectural drawings. He opened them to reveal a steel tube with an airtight flip top.

"Is that your everyday stolen-artifact bag?" Busch quipped.

"Very funny. They're actually for transporting paintings; they're waterproof and you can vacuum-seal them."

"And you have them because . . ."

"Give me a break," Michael said as he tossed them into the first duffel. He zipped each bag up and reset the false electronic panel. He spun the screws into place and rolled the wall-to-wall carpet back, tapping it down with his foot.

"Point of no return," Busch said as he handed Michael the compass and knife.

"That was actually hours ago," Michael said as he slipped the compass and knife into his pocket. He threw the two coils of rope over one shoulder and a black duffel over the other and headed out the jet door.

Busch hoisted the remaining two black bags and carried them down the jet's stairs, throwing them in the open trunk of the limo next to Michael's bag. He closed the trunk and looked through the window at the back of KC's head. He finally turned back to Michael.

"In my opinion, your point of no return . . ."

"Yeah?"

". . . was six weeks ago when you kissed the girl."

CHAPTER 19

Iblis watched as the enormous blond driver emerged from the limo. He was all-around large: tall, thick, and muscular. There was no question he functioned as more than a driver as he walked around the car, opening the door for his passengers. Mikla Iki restaurant on Tavasi was one of the most exclusive restaurants in the city, known for its seafood and atmosphere; it was a place that required reservations weeks in advance. But that didn't seem to be a hurdle for KC. She and her male friend stepped from the limo. The man was already heading for the door when KC stopped. She turned and scanned the area. There was no doubt in Iblis's mind: She was looking for him. He stared at her from his vantage point in the cab down the road. Her blonde hair and tall stature turned the heads of pedestrians, who wondered if the striking woman was someone they should know.

Iblis had tailed the limo as it left Ataturk Airport and loosely followed them back into the city, which was in full swing for the night. He was in the process of checking out KC's two companions, but had so far only learned that her dinner partner was the son of the wealthy American attorney whose business card was in her pocket. Iblis hated lawyers, finding them no more than self-important, self-promoting, arrogant interpreters of the language of legalese. On the occasions when he had killed one, he had taken special pleasure in knowing that he was doing the world a service.

He wasn't sure about the brown-haired man, but he appeared to be an intimate of KC's—something that gave him pause, that gave him a feeling he had never known. Iblis felt a sudden tinge of jealousy and it began to grow.

And then the American took KC by the arm, admonishing her for who knows what, and hustled her into Mikla Iki. As they slipped from sight, Iblis felt his jealousy peak. A dark rage began to pour through him, as if KC's escort had personally attacked him.

Iblis committed the man's face to memory. He was more than angry at him for touching KC; he was suspicious of him and his intent. He didn't know who the man was or how close KC and he were, but Iblis would find out. In his field you had to know everyone and everything, with the greatest threat coming from where one least expects it.

A well-dressed attendant approached KC's large driver. He was no more than twenty-five, filled with piss and vinegar. No one was parking illegally in front of the restaurant on his watch. Iblis watched as the body language of the two stubborn men slowly escalated into a full-on argument. The blond driver towered over the slight Turk. Fingers pointed and their shouting carried over the din of the night. Finally the American stalked back to his car, reluctantly got in, and drove off with his middle finger pointing skyward.

Iblis sat a moment debating whether to follow the man but opted to remain in place for when KC exited. While KC was very good at what she did, she wasn't foolhardy enough to run off and try to steal either the chart or the rod unprepared, with less than eight hours' notice. She would plan it well, leaving nothing to chance just as he had taught her.

And her actions would be just as he planned, as if she were but a marionette on his strings. KC had no idea what was coming.

CHAPTER 20

Michael and KC lay prone, head to head atop the ten-foot granite wall surrounding the grounds of Topkapi Palace, both listening, both looking. The wall was like a border between two realities: one alive with people and vendors, diners and nightlife, the other a silent world of the past, tranquil, serene, and abandoned for the evening. They both took a slight roll and silently landed like a pairs team on the grass of the Courtyard of Janissaries. Michael scanned the grounds and noted that most of the guards were milling about the locked Imperial Gate entrance fifty yards away while two guards walked patrol.

The guards were oblivious, lost in conversation, never seeing Michael and KC race along, coming to a stop in the dark shadow of an ancient supply building.

Staying in the shadows, they worked their way past Hagia Eirene and the Imperial Mint, past the collection of old brick buildings and supply houses, constantly on alert, finally coming to a stop within a stand of cypress. They lay down, their dark clothes blending with their surroundings. KC had tucked her hair up into a dark stocking cap to hide her long blonde tresses. Michael carried the two coils of rope across his shoulders with a watertight satchel at his hip.

They had walked straight through Mikla Iki restaurant and out the back door to where Busch was waiting. The thousand-dollar tip to the maître d' helped ensure not only their privacy but their alibi. They hadn't seen Iblis but they were sure he or his men were watching the restaurant. They paid double for the private dining room along with generous tips for the entire staff for their ensured privacy. KC doubted Iblis would come into the restaurant, but if he did he would be none the wiser. Still, they couldn't "eat" forever without raising suspicion.

They figured they had two hours.

Ahead of them was the Gate of Salutation, large and imposing against the nighttime sky. Two guards stood within the arched entrance in front of the large dark door, talking in hushed tones.

Michael pulled the map from his back pocket and spread it on the grass in front of them. KC passed him a small pin light, its red lens diminishing any glow as he ran it over the map. They both silently scanned it, looking back and forth between the map and the guards. On the leftmost edge, the fortress wall abutted the archeological museum, heavily shadowed by foliage and the surrounding structures.

With two fingers, Michael pointed at KC, then at his eyes, and finally at the guards, indicating where to fix her gaze. Michael continually scoped the grounds for any sign of movement, and without a word they cautiously moved within the trees toward the far corner.

They sprinted along the open ground and slid to a stop at the inner wall that wrapped the palace proper. Made of squared stone and brick with a heavy mortar aggregate, it was a rock climber's challenge.

"I got this," KC said as she looked up the twenty-foot barrier.

Michael shook his head, dug his fingers into the mortar seams, and began his climb before KC could react. The wall was ancient, but it had been well maintained through the years. His hands and knuckles burned as he ascended the brick wall, his fingertips finding precarious purchase in the half-inch seams, which grew shallower and shallower as he climbed. The shadows played out along the wall in varying patterns, forcing Michael to change position to remain concealed. He made the top in a minute's time, removed a coil of rope from his shoulder, quickly affixing it to a scupper, and dropped its length to KC's outstretched hand. She scurried up hand over hand, and within ten seconds was sitting at his side.

From Simon's notes and his own earlier reconnaissance tour, Michael knew the high-tech security of Topkapi was reserved for the public locations, where the objects of value were stored, while the route they were taking and their destination held little appeal for anyone.

"Now, will you tell me where we're going?" KC whispered.

"It's nice up here," Michael said as he looked around. The palace grounds spread out before them, the moon casting a pale blue tinge on the Ottoman sanctuary. The palace was vast, a growth of structures of varying size drawing on the architectural heritage of both East and West: Middle Eastern arches, European towers, Asian roofs—a true reflection of Istanbul's varied cultural past. Michael finally turned back to KC and smiled as he pointed across the second courtyard to the third inner circle.

KC turned and squinted, her eyes finally falling on the host of orange cones that circled a dark hole next to the white marble Library of Ahmet within the third courtyard.

"Earlier today, I saw the construction cones around that

hole when we came out of the Treasury." Michael pulled out a modern electrical schematic and spread it on the rooftop. "Simon had this. It shows where they are excavating, where they are going to put in some new conduit. With all of the renovation and digging going on, they pierced some open space, which they need to shore up and cover over."

"Yeah, and . . . ?"

"And," Michael pulled out a second map that showed two of the eunuchs' passages. "Feel like taking a look underground?"

Michael folded up the papers and tucked them in his pocket. "Let's go for a walk." He stood, throwing the coil of rope over his shoulder, and headed off without waiting for a reply.

KC sat a moment watching Michael walk among the shadows of the rooftop before getting to her feet and jogging to his side. As they walked, it was like being in an alien world. Rooftops, no matter where they are found, are worlds seen by few, worlds whose views can be unparalleled and awe-inspiring, and Topkapi's was no exception. It afforded a perspective seen by only a handful of people through the centuries. The hoi polloi below raced about their day, unaware of the peaceful environment just above their heads.

From this point of view, the palace of Topkapi seemed like an organic growth, without any grand plan or design, or any symmetry to speak of. Sections grew off in all directions: up and out, down, right, left, east and west, all tied together by blue leaded roofs and domes, minaretlike towers and chimneys. Michael felt as if they had been walking for days, making their way across the low-pitched and flat roofs, constantly remaining back from the edges, out of sight of any guard patrolling the grounds. They walked past the Tower of

Justice, unamused at the irony, over the harem and around the Circumcision Pavilion, and finally over onto the roof of the exhibition of miniatures and manuscripts. Michael looked out on the open ground: In the middle of the construction site was a small, dark pit; like a black hole it seemed to suck in all the surrounding light.

They scanned the area, confirming that no one was around, and made their way to the edge of their roof, jumping down the ten-foot drop and rolling out into a crouch. They sprinted to the white library building, skidding along the ground till they arrived next to a series of orange cones and a backhoe.

Michael affixed the two ropes to the steel frame of the backhoe and without a thought, grabbed tight and jumped into the pit. He slid twenty feet down into utter darkness, pausing to look up to see a silhouette of KC sliding down the adjacent rope beside him. He hung in nothingness, his breath echoing off the cool walls around him.

Michael pulled a flashlight from his satchel, flipped it on, and the world exploded into view. They were in a shaft of stone, water trickling down its sides. Michael shone the light below and found it reflected back by a watery landing point.

"This is your great idea?" KC whispered, annoyance in her voice as she switched on her flashlight.

Michael didn't bother looking at her as he slid down and away from her complaints.

It was a twenty-foot drop; the end of his rope was coiled upon the water's surface like a snake waiting to strike. Michael halted his descent inches above the water and shone his light about what he now realized was a cavern. The air was cool, and lime leached out of the rounded, domelike ceiling into an organic tapestry of crystalline shafts that painted the roof above. Michael took his time absorbing it all, slowly spinning on his drop line, shining his light to and fro. The open room was oblong, stretching thirty feet wide by ninety feet long; the walls were made of ancient stone and brick that sparkled with moisture and amplified even the most silent of drips as they rained from above.

"It's a cistern," KC said.

"Yes and no." Michael lowered himself slowly into the water, finally hitting bottom at five feet, the surface lapping around his shoulders. The water was as clear as glass; Michael judged it to be a cool sixty-five degrees. "It's a lot more than a cistern."

Cisterns, large underground bodies of water, dated back centuries. They were fresh water supplies, man-made reservoirs for royalty and the upper class. There were hundreds hidden under Istanbul, lost to living memory but occasionally finding their way back into the city's consciousness.

KC lowered herself into the chilly water, gasping as it covered her body.

Michael pulled a compass from his bag, looked at it under the glow of his light, and headed north through the blackened cavern.

"What did you mean, yes and no?" KC threw the beam of her light along the walls, upon the ceiling, into the water, warily looking about as if something might emerge from the darkness.

Michael continued slogging, his flashlight leading the way, until something caught his eye. On the far wall was a remnant from pre-Islamic times. The symbol was carved directly into the stone, and while it had chipped and deteriorated, there was no question as to its Christian meaning.

"Before Topkapi, before this cistern, this used to be a monastery. It was in the notes that Simon had. Dating back to the times of Constantine. It was common practice to build atop older buildings and foundations, and even more common practice to use pieces of older structures to help build new ones."

Michael realized what the room had originally been. He saw crucifix after crucifix carved in the wall; underneath them were large recesses, dug out of the stone and crumpled earth. And within each hollowed-out space was a stone container, a stone coffin.

"It's a crypt," he said.

"Great, as if the place wasn't spooky enough already."

They looked around. Most of the coffins were intact; the ones that were broken had crumbled to piles in which bone was indistinguishable from marble casket.

"Glad I wasn't drinking this water," KC said.

Michael and KC kept moving, the chilled water affecting them both, slowing them down. They finally reached the far wall, an absolute dead end. Michael shone his light about but found no opening. KC peeled off to the left, examining the walls as she went, looking for an opening, a sign of a sealed-up room.

Michael examined the stone and brick wall, walking along its edges, and that's when he felt it. It was a subtle stirring, a current. Michael shone his light about, and without warning dove under the water and disappeared.

KC turned, suddenly alone, clutching her flashlight as if it would somehow protect her from the darkness. "Michael?"

But he did not surface.

"Michael?" she said in a loud whisper. "Dammit."

She waded through the water to where Michael had

disappeared, aiming the beam of her light under the water, looking for any sign of him. She felt the current washing about her body. Thirty seconds gone. She shone her light and spotted a four-foot dark pipe under the water. She waited. One minute gone.

What KC hadn't told Michael, what she never really shared with anyone, was her fear of the dark, a phobia she had had since the age of six, when she would lie alone in bed watching the shadows on her wall as the voice of her mother came from her bedroom. Her mother would scream and whisper, laugh and cry as if talking to a room full of guests, as if there were actually people in the room with her. And with her mother's breakdowns, the shadows seemed to dance, seemed to reach toward her to pull her into some other, frightening world. Her mother would often break down in tears or lash out in anger at the disembodied ghosts of her mind, sending terror through young KC's heart. KC's eyes would dart about the darkened room in anticipation of being snatched away by some unseen demon into a realm where the darkness consumed her.

As the years went on, KC had mastered her emotions, but the fear never really left her, and sometimes when she was in the dark, when that fear rose up, she thought she could hear her mother's voice again calling to her in whispers and screams, pulling her back to those terrible nights.

Now, as KC stood alone, clutching the flashlight in the dark cavern, her nerves began to fray. Where was Michael? Was he trapped, and if she went through the pipe would she become stuck also? Would they drown together? A minute and half. Her fear became anger. She was pissed.

"Dammit, Michael." And she dove under the cold water.

KC shone her light through a wide pipe, thankful that

Michael's flashlights were waterproof dive lights. She kicked against the mild current, using her free hand against the slimy tube to guide her. And before she knew it she was through, emerging into a smaller room, an anteroom of the cistern, its waters reaching her shoulders.

But there was no sign of Michael.

"Michael," KC whispered, as if she would somehow disturb the dead, as if someone would hear her. She directed her light about a three-foot-wide walkway that circled the room one foot above the water's surface. She grabbed the lip and pulled herself up and out of the water. Though the air was cool, it was far better than the water's chill, which was seeping into her bones. She shone her light about the walkway, finding it completely dry; Michael hadn't gotten out of the water. She had risen to her feet when suddenly Michael exploded up out of the water on the far side of the room, gasping for breath in deep, heavy sighs.

"What the hell are you doing?"

"What?" Michael looked at her, bewildered and confused. "There's another pipe, about forty feet long; it leads to another room. I was checking it out."

"Don't you ever do that again!" KC yelled.

Michael looked at her as he regained his composure. "You okay?"

KC glared at Michael, wanting to punch him.

"Were you worried about me?" Michael couldn't help breaking out in a smile.

"What do you think?"

"You look like you saw a ghost." Michael swam over to the ledge and hoisted himself up.

"Did you find anything?" KC asked, trying to change the subject.

"Far as I can tell, this ledge runs the circumference of the room." Michael pointed to the opposite wall. "There's an old doorway over there, with three rising stairs abutting it. That must be the sealed stairwell that led up into the harem. On the other side of this wall, where I just came from, is another antechamber. It looks like the cistern control room, with a high shaft." Michael paused. "The shaft leads right up into the Turkish baths in the harem that we saw this morning." Michael held up the quarter she had tossed in. "I got you a full refund."

Michael pointed to the wall on his left. "We know the way we came in through the cistern is behind that third wall . . ."

KC rose to her feet and walked to the fourth wall, running her hands along it.

"That's the only one with nothing behind it." Michael walked around and came up next to her. "Look at the walkway."

KC looked down, her eyes following the pathway around the room. "Yeah?"

"It's six inches narrower here," Michael pointed out as he crouched. He patted the wall. "This wall was built well after they constructed this walkway."

"Michael, that doesn't necessarily mean that the chapel is behind this wall."

"I know, but I think this symbol does," Michael said, pointing to some ancient symbols etched in a stone at the near corner of the wall. They were small and crude, and at first glance, looked like nothing more than a mason's notation of looping lines and letters.

Michael pulled out a photocopy of the letter that KC had stolen from Venue and held it up. Though wet and beginning to run, the symbol in the upper right-hand corner was a match.

"This is the symbol of Grand Vizier Sokollu Mehmet, and Simon has written beneath it, *The Sons of Abraham.* That's what the grand vizier believed. He was a man of understanding and appreciated different beliefs—three religions, Judaism, Christianity, and Islam, united by a common God, a common prophet, Abraham." Michael stepped back, walking out along the walkway to the far side of the cistern antechamber, taking in the wall, the room. His eyes focused on the structure before him. "I'm sure the chapel that he built is behind this solid wall."

"That's great." KC paused, looking at the stone and mortar and the impossible solidity of the barrier. "How the hell are we going to get through that wall?"

"Don't worry about it; we found what we came for." Michael checked his waterproof watch: It was after ten-thirty. "We have to get back to the restaurant to avoid raising any suspicion in your friend Iblis."

"Please don't call him that," KC said in all seriousness.

"Sorry." Michael nodded.

KC jumped into the water and made a beeline for the drainpipe. "You still didn't say how you're going to get through that wall."

Michael jumped into the water behind her and waded over to the pipe before glancing back at the stone and brick barrier. "I suppose I'll have to use something that goes boom."

"Great. That makes me feel so much better," KC said as she dove under the water.

CHAPTER 21

Michael and KC came through the back of the restaurant, slipped the maître d' another two hundred, and walked out the front door. They stood on the sidewalk in the dry clothes that Busch had kept in the car for them and watched as their friend drove around the corner and stopped the car right in front of them. Busch came around and, with a wink, opened the rear door for them to enter the limo they had just exited not two minutes earlier and one block away.

They had climbed out of the cistern and back onto the roof of the palace, working their way around to the front of the building. Still dripping, and with the coiled ropes on their shoulders, they slipped over the far western wall into the side street, where Busch picked them up.

"You know there are going to be hundreds of people here tomorrow night, and who knows how many guards, cops, and undercovers."

"Which is all the more reason to do it," Michael said. "People won't be expecting someone to be foolish enough to pull any kind of stunt tomorrow. And Iblis—it's the last thing he'll suspect, especially if he watches you go into Hagia Sophia."

KC nodded.

"And good old Paul here, he'll be keeping an eye on Iblis to make sure he doesn't do anything unexpected."

KC and Busch exchanged smiles through the rearview mirror.

"Speaking of which," Michael said, "where is our friend?"

"Five cars back," Busch said. "He watched you guys walk in and out of the restaurant and didn't move a bit."

Michael and KC turned and looked out the rear window but saw nothing but a sea of yellow taxis. "How you can see him is beyond me," KC said.

"He's got two guys with him now. I imagine they'll be watching the hotel for the night while he goes and gets some shut-eye." Busch paused. "So this thing is a go?"

"We've got some kinks to work out on my end." KC turned and smiled at Michael. "And Michael needs to find something that goes boom."

"I can't tell you how dangerous it is for him to handle anything flammable; even a match in his hands can prove world-ending." Busch laughed to himself as he pulled up to the hotel. "I think I'm going to hit the hotel bar. I'll see you bright and early."

"Good night, Paul. Thanks is such an inadequate word," KC said.

"From you? It's better than anything I could wish for."

KC and Michael stepped from the limo and headed into the hotel lobby.

"Well, that was the most unique date I have ever been on," Michael said.

KC smiled at Michael. "I don't know if I would call it a date."

"What would you call it?" Michael walked a little closer to her as they neared the elevator.

"Michael," KC said softly, suddenly at a loss for words.

Michael could see the regret forming in her eyes, the air between them growing suddenly uncomfortable.

"I don't think you and I—"

The elevator arrived and they stepped in.

As they stood alone in the elevator cab, the air was thick; what had been easy banter had fallen to an uncomfortable struggle for words. The doors had begun to close when a hand shot through and pulled them back open.

"Hold up," an elderly man with a French accent said. And suddenly a crowd of eight poured into the cab meant for six. Michael and KC were forced together, their bodies thrust up against each other.

"Sorry." Michael looked deep into KC's eyes.

She couldn't help the warmth that poured through her. Their lips were only inches apart as the crowd shook and jostled, trying to make room for the door to close. "Me too," KC whispered.

The elevator rose slowly. Michael and KC were in their own worlds, ignoring the laughing and chattering French crowd. The elevator came to a stop on the third floor and the French all poured off in a cacophony of merriment, leaving Michael and KC alone in silence.

The doors closed and opened again moments later, letting them out on the fourth floor.

Michael walked KC down to her door. He couldn't help looking at her blonde hair in the soft hallway lights, her body as it gently swayed beside him.

"Michael," KC said, and though she turned her head

toward Michael she averted her eyes. "I'm so sorry I have dragged you into this."

"You didn't drag me."

"I can't get the image of Cindy's tears out of my head, and Simon . . ." KC paused. "I lied to her about everything; I lied to you."

"It's okay."

"No, it's not, you thought you were with one person, someone upstanding, someone truthful . . . but that's not me. Our time together was based on lies."

"KC," Michael said, seeing her pain.

"I'm done lying, I'm done hiding."

"You lied for a reason."

"We can't lie to the ones we love. I see what that has done to Cindy. I need to tell you the truth."

Michael smiled warmly.

"I think some people aren't meant for love and I think some people are meant to be loved unconditionally." KC took a breath. "I can't replace your wife—"

"I'm not asking you to—"

"Let me finish. I don't know how to do this. You are such a good person, you deserve so much, and I have nothing to offer . . ."

"KC, this isn't the time to be thinking about these things. Let's focus on getting your sister and Simon back, then we'll figure this thing out together. No one knows how to play the relationship game, least of all me." Michael reached out and warmly ran his hand down KC's cheek. "Let's just put things aside for now. There's always tomorrow."

KC looked into his eyes, their faces inches apart, the moment hanging in the air.

"I'm sorry, Michael." KC stepped back as she slid the electronic key card in her door. "Good night."

THE DOOR CLICKED shut as KC walked into her suite. She headed straight upstairs, went directly into her over-sized bathroom, turned on the shower, and undressed. She stepped into the granite stall, allowing the hot water to beat down on her body, hoping that it would somehow restore her. After five minutes, with exhaustion filling her soul, she turned off the water, wrapped herself in an oversized towel, and emerged back into the marble bathroom.

A sudden fear ran through her; momentarily shaken, she grabbed her pants off the floor and dug into a front pocket, thinking it was gone. But her hand wrapped around it and pulled it out. She clutched the tiny object tightly in her palm and slid down the wall to sit on the floor as the steam from the shower slowly dissipated from the room.

She had done everything in her power for it not to be found by the guards when she was frisked in Amsterdam, when Iblis patted her down and found Michael's father's business card in her pocket. She'd been able to shift it around when she arrived at Chiron Prison with no one ever the wiser. Its resale value was nothing spectacular, but its sentimental value was priceless. It was the only gift some-one had ever given her out of love. She read the inscription, *There's always tomorrow*, and slipped the Tiffany locket around her neck. She closed her eyes and held it tightly, as if she was holding Michael's heart, and dozed off upon the towels on the bathroom floor.

MICHAEL STOOD ON the balcony of his hotel suite, look-ing out at nighttime Istanbul, across the Bosporus at Asia, his mind lost in KC's words. She had reawakened in him something he thought had died, something he thought he had buried with Mary. Somewhere, deep down within him, she had found his heart.

Despite her trepidation, despite her words, Michael could not let her go that easily. She was strong and smart, her emotions were being tested against seemingly insurmountable odds, and yet she pushed on with a smile. They were so much alike, not only in what they did, in their less-than-conventional skills, but in personality and character.

But throughout their harrowing day and its pressures there was an issue that gnawed at him, which they had yet to discuss: KC's safety. She spoke as if she knew what she was doing, and he had no doubt she did; Simon never would have used her otherwise. But Michael, more than anyone, knew there were always dangers. There were those unexpected turns that could rob you of your life before you even realized what was happening. He had had too many close calls, and what scared him now, what gave him pause, was wondering what would happen if KC faced one of those turns: Would she survive or would she be ripped from Michael's life?

Michael refocused. If they were to get the chart, if they were to save Cindy and Simon, Michael had to be completely vigilant. He had to put his thoughts for KC, his fears and emotions, aside and concentrate on the job at hand. That was how they would succeed, that was how they would survive.

Michael stepped off the balcony and climbed the stairs to his bedroom. He undressed, climbed into his bed, and pulled out a folder containing several documents. They were Simon's, from his satchel, but Michael had yet to read them. On first glance earlier in the day, he had opted to put them aside, and to save them for later. Certain words had caught his eye, and he thought it best that certain things not be so quickly shared. Simon had been evasive at best when Michael queried him about the chart and where it led, and Michael knew he was holding back for a reason. So, as Simon was his friend, and as Simon had been somewhat elusive about the facts, Michael thought it best to read the contents of this particular file on his own before he shared it with KC and Busch.

Michael flipped open the folder and looked at a drawing of a Turkish corsair, standing with one foot upon the bow rail of his ship, the wind blowing back his long dark brown hair, which was tangled with an overgrown beard. He was dressed in billowing dark maroon pants held up by a deep blue sash. A long dark robe wrapped his shoulders, riding the heavy sea breeze, while in his hand he clutched a long, curved scimitar.

Kemal Reis was a Turkish corsair who became an admiral of renown in the Ottoman Empire. His real name was Ahmed Kemaleddin from Gallipoli, and he sailed the seas for forty years, capturing and plundering ships in the Mediterranean, the Black Sea, and as far as the Indian Ocean and China Seas, accumulating tremendous wealth and power through his ventures.

Michael removed a paper clip from the picture to find a copy of a letter written in a foreign hand, attached to which was an English translation.

The attached entry was written in the ship's log by Bora Celil, the captain of the lead ship in Kemal Reis's fleet.

April 16, 1511, by the Julian calendar

While sailing the oceans of India we have come upon a Chinese junk, a massive ship, over seventy-five meters long, its sails loose and torn, flapping in the wind. The Chinese are not known for worldly voyages, so much excitement has roiled the ranks. Kemal Reis, myself, and a crew of thirty boarded the vessel to find the entire ship's crew dead, as if a horror had boarded the ship. The Chinese crew had torn out their own eyes, severed their own limbs, plunged daggers into their own hearts, their bloodied fists still gripping the hilts. As corsairs, we had witnessed death and brought it upon the innocent more times than there are stars in the sky, and it was as normal to us as breathing, but the sights before us stilled our hearts. This was not the doing of men.

Kemal and I ordered the crew to stand guard as we took three of our men and headed into the depths of the ship. We found the lanterns all lit, all of the food stores intact, but like the crew, the livestock was dead, having turned on each other. The usual stench of quarters was overpowered by the decaying Chinamen we found below, all dead under similar circumstances, all by their own hand. Kemal found the captain's quarters at the rear of the ship. The Chinese captain was a tall man, over four cubits; he lay upon the floor, his sword still in his death grip while his head lay on the far side of the room. His long black hair was matted in dried blood; his half-open eyes were glazed white, while his mouth hung open.

We didn't linger over the body but instead turned to the chart table. There were hundreds of charts, all stored neatly in shelves below the working surface. Kemal ordered us to tie up the charts as quickly as we could, as he became lost in a map that lay open upon the draft table. It was enormous, with exquisite detail; we had never seen a chart of such refinement and scope. But as we stood there, our men having left the room with the collection of charts, we thought we heard voices. We looked about but saw no one and wrote it off to the ramblings of our minds, brought on by the ghastly sights we had seen.

But then we heard a low humming, barely audible. We drew our scimitars from their scabbards, grabbed an oil lamp from the wall, and opened the door. We followed the low droning to the forward hold, where we found a locked room.

With a few blows of Hadrid's hammer, we removed the locks.

As Kemal slowly opened the door, he held the lantern high and was nearly blinded. The room was filled with gold; no section of the floor was visible under the piles of precious metal, scattered among which were precious jewels: diamonds, rubies, and sapphires, exquisite and larger than we ever thought possible. In the far corner were stacks of books and scrolls, ancient parchment, notated hides and skins, even etched stone in languages unfamiliar to us.

And in the middle of it all sat a man. He was bald, old beyond years, though he possessed a smooth, unlined face, as if he had never smiled or frowned, never experienced emotion. But for a single scar that ran down the man's right cheek, his skin was unmarred by time.

He sat cross-legged upon a large velvet pillow, his hands wrapped around a dark rod that lay upon his lap as he hummed slowly to himself. His skin was the color of dull tea, his body devoid of hair. He wasn't Chinese or Indian, he wasn't Turkish, European, African, or Middle Eastern. He appeared to possess traits of all men and none at all. The man was calm, the essence of peace. He slowly opened his eyes and looked upon us, studying our faces, our mode of dress. He didn't appear to be guarding the treasure; he possessed no weapon and showed no signs of aggression. We didn't know if we were looking upon a crew member, pirate, prisoner, or guardian. He was dressed simply in wool peasant clothes and wooden shoes. And as the man stood, we could see the rod in his hands. It was one and a half cubits long, made of a dark, unnatural wood. It was wrapped, coiled with two snakes along its length, their mouths opened, ready to strike from the top of the rod. Their eyes were of blood-red rubies that twinkled in the firelight; their fangs of silver glimmered, poised, ready to sink their teeth into one another.

Kemal asked the man who he was, but received a response in a dialect we had never heard before. The man started to speak slowly, deliberately, his language seeming to change with every phrase until we saw our first mate Hadrid's head snap to the right in recognition. Hadrid Lovlais had been part of our crew for five years, a large, dark, fierce warrior who came out of the jungles of India. He began to speak slowly, conversing with the man. It was polite, soft, contrary to Hadrid's character, and an approach we were seldom accustomed to at sea.

Hadrid finally turned to Kemal. And said three words . . .

"We are dead."

Hadrid explained that the man had traveled with the treasure for countless months, a treasure that had been stolen again and again since it was removed from a mountain tomb where it had lain hidden for centuries. The man called it the Devil's treasure, a treasure that was said to be stolen from hell itself and whose possession would bring only insanity and death.

The elderly man with tea-colored skin did not beg, he did not implore, he merely asked that Kemal and his crew return the treasure to its proper resting place.

Kemal was sixty years old; he had won countless battles,

plundered more treasure than could be spent in one hundred lifetimes. He had seen life and death, holding it in his hands daily, playing the role of a god since before he could remember. But through it all, he had been a spiritual man, a devout Muslim who had followed the five pillars, the five duties incumbent on all adherents of Islam. And as such, he believed in Allah, in Muhammad, he believed in angels, and, in particular, he believed in hell. He had encountered evil firsthand, he had seen the Devil's work, and what he saw on the ship around him was its true manifestation.

The spiritual man slowly extended his hand to Kemal, to the chart under his arm. Kemal passed it to him and watched as the man unfurled it, indicating a spot on the chart that the treasure must be returned to.

We loaded our ship, transferring the gold and jewels to the largest holds of our three lead ships. We have selected a crew of two hundred and charted a course through the Indian Ocean, up into the Bay of Bengal. From there we will sail upriver into terra incognita and travel across land with the spiritual man as our guide, up into the highest reaches of the earth, with the intent to return the treasure to the Devil himself.

Kemal has passed the array of Chinese charts on to his nephew Piri and appointed him to sail the fleet down around the African Cape of Storms, up to the Mediterranean and home to Istanbul.

Michael sat there, digesting the words of the Ottoman captain, understanding where Piri had received much of his information for the eastern section of his map, and while the tale of treasure and haunting would still the heart of many, Michael did not understand why Piri had chosen to tear up his chart because of a single corsair's fears.

But then Michael read the final translated note in the packet. It was brief, addressed to Piri with a notation saying it was delivered after a fourteen-month journey by the corsair Hadrid Lovlais, who died two days after conveying the package.

September 24, 1513
Piri,

I am sending you this serpent staff, which we have come to know as the Key of Forever Night, on behalf of your Uncle Kemal, who implores you to hide it away along with the charts that were taken from the Chinese ship and any reference to our destination. We offer no explanation of what we have found but know that the entire crew but myself, Hadrid, and three others, including Kemal, have all perished. And know this: Man is not ready to learn the truths we have found; it is not the place of men such as us to determine when and what knowledge the empire and the world is entitled to. Understand there are some things that are never meant to be learned, some things that are never meant to be found.

Salaam,
Bora Celil

Michael pondered Bora Celil's fatalist words; he suddenly understood why Piri had torn his chart in half after painstakingly creating it. The pieces of the mystery of what Iblis sought were beginning to fall into place.

Michael took the picture, along with the two letters, affixed the paper clip, tucked them back into the folder, and decided he would not be sharing them with KC. What he had read, what he had learned, would have no bearing on what lay before them; it would not affect how they carried out their thefts; in fact, it would prove nothing but a distraction. He thought it best to keep Bora Celil's words to himself and heed his warning:

There are some things that are never meant to be learned . . .

CHAPTER 22

The Boeing Business Jet rolled out of the hangar, its white skin glittering in the golden dawn. It taxied down the empty runway and was wheels-up, sailing west into the sky, by 6:15 A.M.

Busch stood inside the cavernous private hangar, watching as the jet became but a pinpoint in the sky. He rubbed his tired eyes and turned his gaze to the yellow Fiat that had followed them from the hotel. Iblis wasn't driving; Busch had not expected him to personally maintain surveillance twenty-four/seven. The driver was a dark-haired Turk, tall, with a pinched face. Leaning against the car, he, too, had his eye on the disappearing plane. Busch watched as the man finished his coffee, threw the empty cup on the ground, got back into his car, and left.

For the time being, KC would be Iblis's sole focus, allowing Michael and Busch to operate and prepare unencumbered for what lay ahead.

"Awful waste of jet fuel," Busch said, his voice echoing in the high-ceilinged, vacant space.

"They're only going to Greece; they'll be back tonight," Michael said.

"Still a waste of money."

"Not if it keeps Iblis away from me. As long as he thinks I've left the country he won't suspect what we are up to."

Michael stood before a long workbench in the back of the hangar. Ataturk Private Co. leased the buildings and crew out to the business and private jet set, offering everything from full jet maintenance by certified mechanics to stocking the fridges and bars of the luxury aircraft. Michael had paid off the crew for the day and had the vast space, with its plethora of tools and supplies, at his disposal.

He hoisted the three large black duffel bags onto the workbench that ran along the long rear wall. Unzipping each in succession, he began to methodically withdraw their contents: from the first bag, six coils of kernmantle climbing rope, two harnesses, and four carabiners; a small toolkit with a screwdriver, a Leatherman multitool, and a small crowbar; and finally, the four leather art tubes. He reached into the next bag and extracted four Sig Sauer pistols, a box of clips, four boxes of bullets, a Galil sniper rifle with laser scope, and two holsters. He laid them out next to two rubber-handled dive knives, four two-way radios, and the climbing gear.

"Are we stealing a chart or going to war?" Busch said as he walked up and pulled a bag over.

"Give me a break; I'm not sure what I need yet."

Busch pulled from the duffel a large plastic bag filled with small black boxes.

"Portable alarms," Michael said. "Like trip wires. They send a radio signal when the pin laser is broken."

"Don't let Jeannie get hold of these. She still thinks I get home at eleven."

Michael smiled as Busch pulled out four poker-chip-sized electronic chips. He read them closely, seeing the acronym GPS engraved in the side.

"Afraid you'll get lost?"

"Hey, they're good enough at finding my dogs; I tuck them in their collars when I run or go hiking."

"You haven't hiked in two years," Busch said in a dismissive tone.

"Aren't we cranky at six-thirty?" Michael said. "That's what you get for staying out till two."

"Thanks, Mom." Busch shook his head. "And yes, I did brush my teeth."

"Somebody's got to mind your ass when you're away from the wife." Michael smiled as he picked up a chip. "We should each have one in case we get lost. They feed to this." Michael held up a small dash-mount flat-screen receiver. "Works anywhere."

"Anywhere?"

"Anywhere on earth, at least."

"Remind me not to carry one."

"FYI, Big Brother is already watching. They put a much cheaper chip in cell phones now and triangulate off cell towers. It's pretty hard to get lost in the world these days."

"Thank you for the education, George Orwell."

From the last bag Michael pulled what looked to be a coiled roll of putty.

"Jesus," Busch said. "You had that in the plane?"

Michael didn't bother looking up as he removed and placed three squares of C-4 next to the coil.

"You could have blown us out of the sky."

"Don't be ridiculous," Michael said as he held up a bag of small electronic blasting caps. "Not without these sticking in their guts."

"You're going to wake the neighbors with that stuff."

"Only if I use it."

"I don't think KC will be all that happy if you blow yourself up."

"I'm not saying I'm *going* to use it. It's just for backup."

"Did you figure out how KC is going to lift the lid off that dead guy yet?"

"You mean the lid on Selim's tomb?" Michael looked at his friend and slid him a hand sketch of a Rube Goldberg–like contraption.

"Looks great." Busch glanced at the paper and turned to walk away. "I'm going to rustle up some breakfast, see what kind of fixings they got. Hopefully some traditional bacon and eggs. You don't suppose they have bagels, do you?"

Michael ignored Busch as he walked across the large hangar to the oversized kitchen and vanished inside.

Michael picked up his sketch and headed into the maintenance supply room. It was filled with everything one could imagine for plane and auto repair, from valves and oil to leather seats and instrument panels. Michael focused his attention on the hardware along the rear wall. He grabbed six long rubber hoses sheathed in cloth; they were heavy-duty and were used in the pneumatic control systems of jets. He took several pieces of copper pipe and four aluminum frame supports, grabbed a handful of brass fittings and a hand pump.

He carried it all back to the worktable and laid it out before him. He smoothed out the piece of paper with his sketch and studied it for a moment, thinking, planning. He pulled over the oxyacetylene torch, fired up the thirty-two-hundred-degree-Celsius flame, and set to work.

CHAPTER 23

Iblis sat in Honessa's, an outdoor café in the Spice Bazaar, sipping his morning coffee.

His man Jahara stood across from him, just having reported watching the Boeing Business Jet rocket into the early-morning sky carrying KC's male companion out of Istanbul. The plane was the Cadillac of private air travel; Iblis had, in fact, considered one for himself but passed. Why waste the money when Venue's jet was at his beck and call 365 days a year?

Iblis ignored Jahara as he watched the tourists pass by on the sidewalks, his eyes scanning the crowds, looking for someone. He finally dismissed his underling with a wave of his hand as his eyes fell on an elderly man.

He wore a wrinkled houndstooth suit, his thin gray hair slicked back over an overly large head, his shoulders slumped forward with the years weighing heavy upon them. The approaching man leaned with one hand on a knotted pine cane for balance and carried a black leather briefcase in the other.

Ray Jaspers was another expatriate, hailing from Chicago forty years earlier. His law firm, based in The Hague, had been on retainer to Venue for over twenty years now.

Despite his weathered, hobbled appearance, Jaspers was a king of information who dealt in corporate espionage, who knew what companies were vulnerable, who knew what CFOs were skimming the till and exactly where everyone's skeletons were buried. His sources were never questioned and never wrong. Where Iblis was Venue's lethal left hand, Jaspers was his right, keenly laying the gunsight upon the target.

Jaspers arrived at Iblis's table and sat without invitation or a word. He laid his case down, opened it, and withdrew a thick manila folder.

"Coffee?" Iblis offered.

"No, it will only make me need to piss in fifteen minutes," Jaspers said in a gruff, smoke-addled voice. He looked about the market as he withdrew his pocket square and dabbed his sweating brow. "Are you on schedule?"

Iblis nodded as he sipped his coffee. There was an undeniable tension between them.

"I hope so." Jaspers's words were accusing. "Venue will be here tomorrow. He's growing impatient."

"He's been impatient since he was conceived," Iblis said with annoyance, unable to mask his feelings for Venue. "There's nothing to worry about."

Jaspers slid the manila folder across the table.

"This didn't take you long." Iblis pulled the file out from under his hand.

"Nothing ever does. I think you'll find this very interesting," Jaspers said as the old man stood up.

"Leaving so soon?" Iblis said with a smile.

"No offense, but we have nothing to talk about," Jaspers said matter-of-factly, turning and walking away.

Iblis watched the old man shuffle down the sidewalk

until he was out of sight. He waved his hand at the waitress to fetch him more coffee, settled back in his seat, picked up the file, and began reading all about Michael St. Pierre.

BUSCH DROVE THE limo past the Imperial Gate, the main entrance to Topkapi Palace— though "crawling" would have been far more accurate. The streets were flooded with delivery trucks, catering trucks, news trucks, and almost every kind of truck Busch could imagine.

Hundreds of people scurried about like ants, pushing carts laden with supplies through the giant arch, unloading flowers and tables onto the sidewalk, focusing satellite dishes atop news vehicles. Everyone walked in double time, hustling about, shouting at those who stood in their way. It was as if the Super Bowl or the Olympics had come to town and they only had one hour to get ready.

Busch's eyes fell upon the guards and police who flanked the archway, heads turning diligently, looking about. Everyone who passed them wore an ID badge hung on a lanyard from his neck. A flatbed truck pulled up and the driver waved at the police, who in turn waved him through. There was no mistaking the cargo: four additional airport security scanners.

"You had to pick tonight, huh?" Busch said as they came to a dead halt.

"Everybody likes a challenge now and then," Michael said from the backseat, his nose pressed up against the smoked glass.

"So is KC a challenge?" Busch put the car in Park and turned around to face Michael.

Michael shot him a withering glance. "We back-burnered everything."

Busch sat there, the moment dragging on until he couldn't take the silence.

"Not to be nosy or anything, but which one of you decided that? You or her?"

"I did," Michael lied. "We've got more important things to focus on at the moment."

"That's good. Not that I don't like her, I like her a lot. Not sure I can trust her yet, but she's good people. I actually thought you guys were perfect for each other—beyond the whole bad career choice thing—you seemed to be in synch even when you were fighting. But I've been wrong before. Only you know if it's right or not."

Busch turned around, put the car in Drive, and continued ahead five whole feet before coming to another stop in motionless traffic. He put the car back in Park and turned to Michael.

"Don't take this the wrong way, but are you looking to fill the hole in your life that Mary left? Because it won't matter who you meet or who you love. They'll never be her and they'll never fill that chasm; that pain is with you forever. New love, when you find it, it will be different; you may not love her more, you may not love her less, but it'll just be different. So if you do care for her—"

"Thanks, Freud," Michael cut him off. "But I'm fine."

"So, you don't love her?"

"No." Michael continued looking out the window.

"Just checking . . ."

Busch pulled up to the Four Seasons and parked the limo in front; he grabbed a black duffel from the trunk along with a three-foot compact blue bag. As he closed the trunk, he caught sight of Iblis sitting across the street, his eyes fixed on the hotel.

Busch carried the bags into the lobby and took a last look, confirming Iblis's presence and counting one other person in the car with him.

He had dropped Michael off on the other side of the Sultanahmet district at a small no-questions-asked apartment where he would lie low until dark and the time arrived when everything would become frantic. With Michael ostensibly flying out of the country, they figured Busch was free to roam as KC's assistant, acting as a liaison to get supplies from Michael to her, perform as her chauffeur, and keep an eye on her safety. As he would not be venturing into Topkapi, he wouldn't create concern on Iblis's part, appearing as her driver.

Busch headed straight to the elevator, rode to the fourth floor, and went down the hall to find KC waiting for him. She was wearing an oversized T-shirt, her hair pulled back. Busch couldn't help staring. Even without an ounce of makeup she was stunningly beautiful.

They smiled at each other, headed into the room, and closed the door behind them.

KC picked up a blue gown by its hanger off a side chair and hung it in the closet.

"Nice," Busch said as he looked at the dress. "Somebody's getting fancy. "

"It was in the boutique downstairs. I usually buy these things with nowhere to wear them to, but tonight . . ."

"For Michael?"

"For the job," KC corrected him. "In case he needs my help."

"Of course," Busch said with a knowing smile. "Or in case a special occasion pops up."

"Well," KC said, changing the subject. "You're looking like a regular summertime Santa."

"Well . . ." Busch unzipped the black duffel. "I do come bearing gifts."

He pulled out the three-foot-long leather tube and handed it to KC, not needing to explain its purpose. He pulled out a handheld radio and an earpiece with a built-in microphone. "Channel one is the main for you two, I'll be on channel two."

KC took the radio and laid it on the table. "How is he?" KC asked.

"Michael?" Busch asked. "He's fine. How are you doing?"

"I'm fine," KC said. "Why?"

"Just checking. I heard you guys kind of cooled it."

"Yeah," KC said softly.

"Listen, I know he may have said some things, I know he wanted to slow things. But that doesn't mean—"

"He said that?" KC asked in surprise.

"I know it hurts when things hit a patch."

"He said *he* broke up with *me*?" KC was getting a little upset.

"He didn't?" Busch asked, realizing that his friend had lied, that the decision had been KC's.

"I can't deal with things that are trivial compared to getting my sister back." KC's words sounded more as if she was trying to convince herself.

"I can understand that," Busch agreed, and turned back to the duffel filled with supplies.

KC leaned down and took the bag from Busch, rummaging through the stuff herself. She pulled out two black boxes.

"He said to give you those portable sensor alarms; you can have them signal you through channel three if someone breaks the plane of the sensor."

"I know how they work."

KC continued looking through the bag, finding a Sig Sauer pistol, several clips, a rope, knife, small crowbar and two waterproof dive lights.

"Things are so complicated," KC said defensively out of nowhere. "I can hardly think straight. I've never been in a long-term relationship. He's been married; I could never live up to the memory of his wife."

"No, you couldn't," Busch said honestly. "But who said you have to?"

The conversation died again. Busch was unsure how much he should say. He hated being the intermediary in relationships; that was something for his wife, Jeannie, to do. She was the relationship expert.

KC pointed to the blue bag. "What's that?"

"Michael said, and I quote, 'If you're not strong enough to lift the lid of the sarcophagus, here's a little help.'" Busch pulled from his pocket a page of handwritten instructions and handed it to KC. "He said to practice using the dining room table, if that makes sense."

KC stuffed the directions in her pocket.

"What else did he say?" KC asked, sounding like a teenager.

Busch stood up straight, rising to his full six-four height, and looked down at her, running his hand back through his mop of dirty blond hair as he exhaled. "KC, you want my two cents? Don't let him get away. He cares about you very much and I know you care about him. You'll never do better, that I can promise. And you know, I don't think he'd ever find anyone better than you."

KC looked up at Busch, a sad smile growing on her face.

He wanted to hug her and tell her everything would be okay, that they'd save her sister, that they'd be reunited with Simon, that she and Michael would make it work, but he was unsure.

There was a knock on the door, saving Busch from the moment.

Both their eyes widened in confusion. No one else knew they were here.

Busch motioned KC to stay back as he approached the door. He withdrew his pistol, flicked off the safety, and held it at the ready. He inched up toward the door, hugging the wall.

In a quick motion he grabbed the knob and pulled the door open, his gun aimed at the man's head.

"Paranoid?" Michael said as he looked down the barrel.

"What the hell are you doing here? I could have killed you. If Iblis sees you . . ."

"Not a chance," Michael said as he stepped into the room. "I paid a delivery truck to back me right into the garage. I came straight up the service elevator, making sure every camera along the way was obscured."

"What are you doing here?" KC emerged from the far dining area of the apartment in her T-shirt.

"I think we have to run through everything, both jobs, to make sure we've got everything covered." Michael tried to keep his focus off her attire. "The more I think about it, the more it seems to me that our prep time is next to nothing, and we could be rushing into hell if we're not careful."

"My end's covered," KC said defensively.

"Really," Michael said as he looked at the unopened blue bag on the floor. "How do you even know how it works if you haven't tried it out?"

"Like I've had a chance," KC said. "Busch just got here."

Michael walked into the room. "Let's order some food and go over this."

"I said, my end's covered."

"Yes, you did, but we're still going to go through it," Michael said slowly. "Both your job and mine."

"I know I'm suggesting this a little late," Busch interrupted, "but maybe we should try to find Cindy and Simon. He's got to be holding them somewhere near."

"How?" KC turned on Busch.

"If we tried to follow him, he'd know," Michael said. "He's not stupid. They could be anywhere."

"Where does he live?" Busch asked.

"Give me a little credit," KC shot back. "You don't think I've already tried to find him? He's a goddamned ghost, always has been."

"Sorry," Busch said, his hands raised in surrender. KC and Michael were more alike than either wanted to admit.

"He's got my sister, for Christ's sake."

"I know," Busch said calmly as he sat in a suede club chair and put his feet on the ottoman, "and he's got Simon."

"Stay focused, guys," Michael said, his voice filled with optimism. "We need to be thinking on the palace and Hagia Sophia. Once we have what he wants, what he needs, he's not going to screw up his chance of getting his precious objects."

"And you're just going to turn these two things over to him?" Busch asked.

Michael remained silent as he looked at his friend.

"What does that mean?" KC asked, looking back and forth between the two. And then it dawned on her. "Don't even tell me you're screwing around on this. You can't keep these artifacts even if it's Simon's wish. It's not your call to make. This is my job, I call the shots. This is my only family."

"Relax. I'm not—"

"Don't tell me to relax. It's an old sea chart and a damn stick. I don't care what they're worth. They're not worth my sister's life. If we need to trade them to get her and Simon, then we trade."

"KC." Michael leaned forward. "Everything is—"

"Don't 'KC' me, I don't want to hear that 'everything is going to be all right' speech, I'm not a child. I know what we are up against and what we are about to do. Don't forget we are doing this to get *my* sister. And if we have to give them the chart, that's what we are going to do."

Michael was doing everything in his power not to launch right back at her.

"Who the hell are you to start to say what we are going to do and not do?" KC continued.

"What the hell do you think we are doing here?" Michael finally responded, his voice rising. "Why do you think I'm doing this? I don't give a shit about what we're stealing, I care about getting two people back safe. And that's what we're going to do, but we're not going to do a thing until I've gone over every single detail of both jobs."

"You know, I have a little experience at this," KC said defiantly. "I'm not the one who was convicted and sentenced."

"No." Michael could no longer control himself and lost

it. "You were the one caught and sent to prison to be executed. What a short, ungrateful memory. Remember, I am not the one who needed to be saved."

"You know what? I can do this myself."

"You couldn't steal a simple letter without getting sentenced to death."

"Oh, my God." Busch erupted out his chair. "The two of you go back to your corners."

KC and Michael fell silent, watching the bear of a man turn about.

"You." Busch pointed at KC. "We're all pissed and frustrated. Quit taking your anger out on the people who are here to help you, and keep it focused on Iblis—he's the cause of this, not Michael. Why is it that we can so easily lash out at the ones we're close to yet we keep our mouths shut at the people who really piss us off?" Busch shook his head, his anger escalating as he turned to Michael. "And you, Mr. 'We have to keep our heads clear and straight,' take some of your own damn advice for once. We've got a lot of shit to review, I've got a wife and family at home, and I plan on seeing them again, so we'd better not screw this thing up." Busch's face was red with rage. "And last but not least, I'm goddamn hungry and I want some food."

IT WAS FOUR o'clock. They had spent the last three hours running over every minute detail of both jobs. Michael knew KC was a thief, and he suspected she was good or Simon wouldn't have been involved with her, but Michael didn't know how good and questioned her relentlessly on every "what if" scenario, upsetting her no end. Fortunately, Busch stayed between them, ever the mediator.

The contents of Bora Celil's letter floated about in Michael's head, his words of warning to Piri Reis ringing in his ears. They weren't just warnings to Piri, they were warnings to all. Iblis wanted this rod for a reason, and Michael feared that the reason went way beyond its commercial value. KC would be the first person to hold it in five hundred years, and it was an object that had been hidden away for a reason, an object that had been feared even by the corsair Kemal Reis, one of the most feared men of the sea. Michael finally banished the matter from his head, as it was fogging his concentration; it was already hard enough to focus after his recent fight with KC.

Michael looked at KC, who was busying herself with the machine he had built for her. He could see the focus in her green eyes as she disassembled the contraption; he watched the gentle curves of her lithe frame, agile and strong as she packed up the blue bag.

"Iblis is going to watch KC," Michael said as he pulled Busch aside. "Paul, you have to follow him; don't let him out of your sight. I'm afraid as soon as she emerges from Hagia Sophia, he is going to grab the rod from her and probably try to grab her, too."

"Don't worry about her. She can take care of herself." Busch looked KC's way. "But I'll watch her back, just in case. What about you, though?"

"What do mean?"

"What do you mean, what do I mean? You're the one running into a palace filled with 750 of the world's movers and shakers. You're the one with the far tougher theft, if you ask me. And one other thing . . ."

"What?"

"What if we underestimate Iblis, what if he goes for the chart? What if you run into him, who's got your back?"

"Look, worry about KC for me. I'll take care of myself."

"That's what you always say, and then you know what happens? I practically have a heart attack trying to save your ass."

"Thanks for the concern," Michael said, slapping his friend on the arm.

Michael walked to the window, where KC now stood looking out at her destination, her mark, Hagia Sophia, the late-afternoon sun dancing along its enormous dome.

"I've got to go," Michael said softly.

KC turned and looked at him, a world of emotion passing between them.

Michael looked at KC. "You be careful," he said.

KC stared back into Michael's eyes. "You too."

"Guys." Busch snapped his fingers, breaking the moment as he held up his watch. "Time's a-wasting. The drama between the two of you is getting ridiculous. You both know what you're doing. I'll have Iblis in my sights the whole time. Let's get this done so we can leave this place for good. Capiche?"

THE VAULT DOOR silently swung open, the light of the room dancing on its brushed-silver surface reflecting back along the dark wood walls. Iblis walked into the room dressed in a classic Armani tuxedo.

Cindy stared at him from her vantage point on the leather couch, where she sat watching TV and sipping a Diet Coke as if she were in a living room instead of a walnut-paneled prison. Iblis walked across the room to the cot and checked the nearly empty IV bag. As he looked down on Simon, he was surprised to find him staring up through half-mast eyes, his head subtly moving side to side.

"Mmm, didn't expect to find you awake," Iblis said in his deep voice.

Simon didn't respond, his eyes intermittently drifting shut as he tried to focus.

Iblis changed the IV bag, tossing the nearly empty one into the wooden trash can. "Now, don't you slip into a coma and die on me, at least till I'm finished with you."

"He needs a doctor," Cindy insisted.

Iblis ignored her, turning and walking over to the mirror on the far wall. Looking at himself, he brushed the hair off his unlined, tan forehead and pulled the lapels of his black jacket, smoothing out the shoulders.

"Where are you going?" Cindy asked.

"I'm going to a party," Iblis said as he straightened his tie.

"God forbid we interfere with your social life," Cindy said. "How long are you going to hold us?"

Iblis turned. "If all goes to plan, you'll be out of here by three o'clock tomorrow."

"You're not going to kill us?" Cindy asked with mock courage.

"Not unless I change my mind, but who could hurt a cute face like yours?" Iblis smiled coldly, his eyes not showing a hint of humor. "Then again, if your sister double-crosses me . . ."

"What if Simon gets worse?"

Iblis looked at her and shrugged his shoulders. "Got to go. It's going to be a pretty spectacular night, lots of stuff going on, don't want to be late," he said, more to himself than to her, as he walked back to the giant vault door.

"Where's the party?" Cindy couldn't help asking.

"Nice place, a palace actually, called Topkapi. I've got a little rendezvous planned."

"Really, with whom? You and my sister going out for a night of crime?" Cindy said in a voice filled with disdain.

"Actually, I'm going to see her boyfriend, Michael St. Pierre."

CHAPTER 24

Michael ran up the hill, the envelope of night embracing him as he stayed within the shadow of the trees. A neoprene satchel of supplies was strapped over his right shoulder and bounced against his hip with every stride. He had never used the black scuba-dive bag on land, but figured it would help keep his tools dry in the cistern with its double-wide seals. Strapped about his waist were a flashlight and his knife, while an empty leather tube was strapped across his back, awaiting his hoped-for quarry. He had hiked up from the train tracks that sat above the road that wrapped the tip of the Golden Horn, which overlooked the Bosporus.

The forty-foot rear wall of Topkapi Palace loomed at the crest of the hill 150 feet above Michael, casting its giant shadow over him like a beastly challenge. Constructed five hundred years earlier, its position was the most strategic in Constantinople, overlooking and defending the sole waterway to the Black Sea while offering the perfect vantage point for monitoring Asia on the far shore and any enemies looking to attack. But since the fall of the Empire, since the end of the sultans, there were no more sentries looking for interlopers, no more threats, no more enemies looking to penetrate the great palace, only daytime tourists watching the passing ships.

"Couple hours, we'll be done," Michael said into the small microphone that was joined to the headset hanging on his ear. "We'll have your sister and Simon back by tomorrow. You okay?"

"I'm good. I must say I've never done anything like this before." KC's voice came clear as crystal through his earpiece. She sounded focused and upbeat.

"You told me you've been doing stuff like this for years," Michael joked.

"Not with a voice of reason in my head."

"Don't let me be your conscience." Michael continued hiking up the steep hill.

"That is the last person you need as a conscience," Busch's voice cut in.

"You sound a little winded there, Michael," KC said. "Kind of like when I beat you in basketball."

Busch laughed. "You never said she beat you in basketball."

"Whoa, she didn't." Michael arrived at the base of the forty-foot wall, coming out of the darkness. "Enough chatter for now."

"Hey, you're the one who started yapping," KC said.

"He gets a little sensitive when he loses," Busch added.

Michael flipped off his radio, looked up at the wall that loomed above him, and began to climb.

KC WALKED ALONG the cobblestone walkway of a huge garden with a camera strung about her neck; she carried the three-foot blue duffel on her shoulder and an oversized black Prada bag in her left hand. She was dressed in stylish tight black pants and a form-fitting dark top. Her blonde hair was brushed out and golden under the nighttime lights of the commons. Looking every bit the tourist, she stopped occasionally to take photos of the tremendous Hagia Sophia, which filled her line of sight. Lit for the night, its four minarets appeared to be standing guard around the ancient domed structure.

Honeymooners sat on a bench lost in the deep kiss of a new life together. KC couldn't help staring as she walked by, the thoughts of love and marriage alien to her, something she thought she would never experience. And while it had been fate's fault, while she had used the excuse of Cindy and caring for her to avoid falling into a relationship, she could blame only herself now. She had turned her back on Michael, told him she couldn't find it in her heart to carry their relationship on.

And as she thought on it, she knew it was fear, fear of commitment, fear of finding love and happiness that had compelled her to tell Michael she couldn't fill the shadow left by his wife. It was the reason she had exploded at him earlier; her anger was at herself, at her situation, not with him.

She snapped out of her pity party. She would figure this thing out with Michael, they weren't over; she'd figure out how to make it work, but first things first.

The security was minimal at best for the former mosque, former basilica, current museum. While it was a building of historical significance, it was not a common target of anyone beyond tourists, and all vigilance had been targeted at Topkapi.

Beyond the kissing newlyweds, the area around the walled perimeter of Hagia Sophia was vacant; it was as if all the world's eyes were focused across the street, watching the rich and powerful enter the big EU party. All eyes except for Iblis's, the ones she felt boring into the back of her head.

THROUGH HIS BINOCULARS, Busch watched Iblis, who in turn had his eye on KC as she walked through the park on the far side of Hagia Sophia. Iblis was one hundred yards away driving his yellow Fiat taxi. The service light on the roof was, as usual, conspicuously off. Busch had followed him from afar as soon as he spotted him in front of the hotel. KC had emerged at eight-forty-five, supplies in hand, looking more like a model than a tourist, and walked the short distance to the grand mosque museum. Iblis had started up his car and followed, unconcerned with whether she knew he was there . . . In fact, Busch realized, Iblis wanted KC to know he was watching. He was keeping the pressure on her and would know her every move.

Iblis drove around the perimeter of the former mosque and finally headed into the tremendous flow of traffic making its way to the festivities at Topkapi. The traffic was at a crawl, which made Busch's job all the easier. The majority of vehicles on Babihumayun Caddesi and Kabasakal Caddesi were limousines, so Busch could get lost among the crowd while not being so concerned that the little yellow sports car would zip into traffic and escape his watchful eye.

Busch had made a promise to Michael: He would protect KC at all costs, he would ensure that Iblis never got his hands on her, and if he even got close, Busch would gladly crush his little head in his bare hands without an ounce of guilt.

MICHAEL DASHED ALONG the rooftops, the sound of music, party chatter, and laughter growing upon his approach. The European Union party was in full swing, the bright lights of the festivities rising in a glow into the sky from the second courtyard of Topkapi, a party the likes of which hadn't been seen within the palace walls in over a century. With various museum doors alarmed and locked tight, the fear of a robbery was at a low, the rationale being, who would be foolish enough to rob a museum that had never been robbed on a night of high security? And while the suspicion was low, Michael reassured himself that the world wasn't even aware of what was hidden below the grand palace. Security was focused on the party on terra firma, on the dignitaries and their protection.

As he arrived at the roof's edge overlooking the third courtyard, which sat quiet and empty for the evening, he scanned the area, noting two guards who stood at attention within the Gates of Felicity, their backs to the third court-yard as they looked out at the revelers within the second courtyard.

Michael looked down upon the construction opening, surrounded by cones and barriers, the blackness of the hole seeming to seep out onto the ground. The area sat in heavy shadow, made all the darker by the lights of the party on the other side of the Gates of Felicity. Michael leaped down to the ground, quickly pulled a kernmantle rope from his neoprene bag, and tied it off to the axle of the adjacent backhoe. He took one of the work tarps and laid it over the rope, then placed some shovels and rakes over it to better disguise his line.

Michael checked the straps of the empty leather tube, pulling them tight on his back; he resealed his waterproof satchel, wrapped the line about his body in a juggler's knot, and slipped into darkness. Fifteen feet down, he passed through the mouth of the shaft and stopped his descent, hanging twenty-five feet above the water in the wide, open cavern. He switched on his flashlight, shining it about, looking at a structure that predated Topkapi, that had been built over fifteen hundred years earlier and yet still remained. Designed and constructed in an age lacking modern technology, it had stood the test of time and was more sound than many structures built by modern man, which could barely last twenty years.

"KC?" Michael said into his microphone.

"Yeah?" she whispered. Her voice was static-filled.

"How you making out?"

"All's good."

"I'm going to lose radio coverage," Michael said. "So . . ."

"Where are you?"

"Just dangling. You?"

"Watching the guards, timing their rounds, hiding in the shadows. Remind me again why you get the fun heist."

Michael looked around the cavern, at the dark water, as he spun on his line. "Next time you can have the cold water and explosives, I promise."

"Yeah, right. Be careful."

KC RAN ACROSS the courtyard to the east of Hagia Sophia, staying tight to the shadows. She had put on a black stocking cap, her blonde hair tucked up inside. She had slipped through the service gate on the side of the building, the lock taking her less than five seconds to pick. While Hagia Sophia was a museum, it was not a place of artifacts but rather a place of reverie. The structure itself and its inlaid mosaics and outer tombs were the attractions. Its security detail was minimal, as was fitting for a place where there was not much to steal. The guard and the caution were directed at deterring vandals and pranksters, resulting in a less than attentive staff who went about their shifts in boredom.

The world within the fifteen-foot walls of the holy structure was silent and asleep for the night, standing in sharp contrast to the bustling world outside, the sounds of cars and laughter seeping in to remind KC she was still in the modern world. The main sidewalk ran up the center of the courtyard from the side door of the museum, past the three tombs, ending at the large locked gate to the parking lot.

KC ducked into the shadow and sat with her back against the stone wall surrounding the ancient mosque, behind the trunk of a cypress tree. She looked at her watch; the guards had made two passes around the grounds at twenty-minute intervals. Both times their eyes were on each other, and they were lost in conversation. Their attention was lax, as the chance of a break-in at one of the three mausoleums was practically nonexistent.

Watching the movements of security for almost an hour had left KC too much time to think. She fought to keep her mind focused, to keep it from dwelling on Cindy and Simon and the danger they were in. But she fought the thoughts off, knowing that if she was distracted she would fail, and in so doing . . .

She banished her morbid thoughts and turned her attention to the entrance to Selim's tomb, which sat across the courtyard.

MICHAEL SURFACED IN the antechamber, the beam of his flashlight dancing on the surface. He briefly looked about the smaller cistern adjacent to the cavernous chamber he had rappelled into next door. The water seemed colder, feeling like small knives upon his body.

Michael hoisted himself up on the ledge of the eastern section and unzipped his satchel. He reached in and pulled out a handful of glow sticks, cracking them and tossing them about the walkway, lighting up the stone and brick cavern. In full light, it appeared like a lost grotto, the orange light shimmering off the cistern's clear waters, reflecting off the rounded ceiling. The acoustics amplified his breath and exaggerated the sound of the droplets of water that intermittently fell from the ceiling. It was easy to imagine the eunuchs and harem girls making their way around the walkway five hundred years earlier. Michael wondered if the echoes of their voices still clung to the stone walls.

He stood and ran his hands along the wall. They hadn't just sealed up the doorway; they had built an entirely new partition, made of stone and mortar. It was fifteen feet from walkway ledge to ceiling, and forty feet wide.

Reaching into his dive satchel, he pulled out the coils of detonation cord, a thin, malleable explosive of pentrite wrapped within a soft, pliable textile that appeared to be a long strand of nylon rope. Designed for demolition, its workability enabled it to be used with surgical precision, concentrating its blast to cut rock or steel girders. Michael took four five-foot-long strands and worked them into the mortar joints three feet off the ground, spread at five-foot intervals. He inserted a thin metal rod—which looked very much like a golf tee—into the center of each piece of cord. Each electronic blasting cap had a small radio receiver on its tip that dangled on two thin wires, awaiting the signal from a detonator.

By spreading the charges, Michael would be removing

only small sections of the wall so as to prevent the total collapse of the façade, which might not only render his mission over but end his life along with it.

Michael walked around the perimeter of the cistern, stepping over the glow sticks that littered the walkway, and jumped into the five-foot-deep water at the far side. In his right hand he held a waterproof radio detonator, much smaller and far more practical than the old-style TNT plungers that Yosemite Sam loved to wrap his hands around. Without a second thought, Michael flipped off the safety switch, thumbed down the green button, and dove under the water.

The four sections along the wall exploded simultaneously, throwing mortar and rock about the cistern, the four balls of flame curling upward and licking the curved stone ceiling. The muffled explosion was concentrated, its focused force blowing out four three-foot sections that were spaced along the length of the wall exactly as Michael had intended.

Michael surfaced and climbed out of the water. He walked slowly, working his way around the cistern, making sure the walkway wasn't compromised. Arriving at the wall, he inspected the first hole and found, as he had suspected, that there was a wall behind the wall. The façade had been constructed flush against the interior wall. He moved to the next hole, kicking the rock and debris into the water, and found the same. It was on the third section that he found what he was looking for. The three-foot hole did not reveal another stone wall but rather a dark opening. Michael pulled his flashlight from his waist, shone it into the dark recess, and smiled.

* * *

THE EUROPEAN UNION party was in full swing. Dignitaries, VIPs, and celebrities were arriving, exiting their limos and walking up the royal blue carpeted sidewalk through the Imperial Gate of Topkapi Palace to the party within. News trucks sat across the street as video cameras rolled and reporters commented on the night's festivities. The flashbulbs of the paparazzi lit up the faces and surrounding area in a constant strobe of pale blue light. Guards conspicuously flanked the gate, ten strong, with rifles clutched to their chests, sending the message that Turkey would guard the European Union with the same fervor with which it guarded itself. After years of opposition, discourse, and rhetoric, the country that spanned two continents, the society that had long embraced all faiths, had finally been embraced itself and welcomed into the union of twenty-seven European nations.

Busch sat behind the wheel of the parked limo; he could see both the Imperial Gate of Topkapi Palace alive with activity, a quarter mile away, and Hagia Sophia sitting directly across the street, serene and quiet for the night.

The yellow Fiat was lost in a sea of taxis two hundred feet ahead of him, quietly idling at the side of the road. Iblis sat in the driver's seat, his attention upon Hagia Sophia, no doubt rooting for his protégée's success. It had been twenty minutes and Busch's legs were already twitching. He had hated stakeouts when he was on the Byram Hills police force. Hours upon hours of tedium, waiting for someone to make a move, waiting for something to happen. But in this case, Busch was watching to make sure something didn't happen.

But then it did.

Iblis emerged from his small car and, realizing what

was happening, Busch's heart doubled its beat. Iblis wasn't going toward Hagia Sophia; with a hyperactive walk, he was heading left toward the Imperial Gates, dressed in a crisp black tuxedo, a tan briefcase in hand. This had been Iblis's plan all along: He was going into Topkapi; he was going for the chart.

Busch checked his gun and holstered it. He turned off the engine, grabbed his radio, and nonchalantly exited the limo. He walked across the street and up the sidewalk towards Topkapi. With a quick pace he halved the distance to Iblis, one hundred feet away and closing. Busch wasn't sure what he would do; he was running on instinct and hoping he would react appropriately. Iblis arrived at the gate and had begun walking up the blue carpet when a guard stepped from formation and stopped him.

And then suddenly, much to Busch's surprise, Iblis turned and looked straight at Busch, looking him right in the eye. The small man smiled and nodded, and finally, turning around, he pulled a card and flashed it at the guards. And like that the guard stepped aside and Iblis disappeared behind the walls of Topkapi Palace.

MICHAEL CRAWLED THROUGH the three-foot opening, shining his flashlight about the dark room. It was small, no more than twenty feet square. There were three rows of pews facing a crucifix that sat behind a small altar, and an open area covered in a large prayer rug. It had a star within a crescent moon woven into one corner, facing a wall where the rising sun of dawn glowed upon a city. A medium-sized tabernacle was set off to the side of a second altar, the Star of David carved into the small wooden cabinet door.

It was a private chapel in which friends of different

faiths could worship together praying to their respective gods. A room in which they could all join as òne, a room created to allow those who had been stolen from their homes, from their Christian and Jewish lands, to secretly worship the gods they had been forced to renounce. But in truth it was one God, three faiths, all tracing the route of their faiths back to Abraham, the common denominator of a common God.

Michael looked upon the altars, the symbols of faith, at the crescent moon and star, at the Holy Cross and the Star of David, pondering the wisdom of the man who had built this chapel and the insight of those who clandestinely swept worshippers through its doors. He wished that their understanding and tolerance might be heard more resoundingly.

Millions upon millions had been killed in the name of God, by people who believed that the almighty being was on their side. Michael wondered if God really was a Yankees fan or whether he preferred the Red Sox; whether he lined up with the communists or the capitalists. He wondered who God listened to when soldiers on both sides prayed for victory or whether he had grown tired of those who battled and killed in his name and turned a deaf ear to all. Michael shook himself out of his philosophical reverie. Whatever the case might be, the wisdom of the overseers of this room had led them to close it up, to hide it from the world, and to hide a greater secret somewhere within.

As he walked about the room, scanning the five-hundred-year-old religious artifacts, the intricately detailed wall painting of ancient Constantinople, the exquisitely tiled artwork upon the rear wall, he found no safe, no chamber. The ground was of solid rock, the walls of granite. It was a sanctuary carved from the earth. Each altar was of solid stone, the pews and chairs of cypress, the carpets of tightly woven wool, the organic materials standing true for half a millennium.

Michael stared at the rear wall, at the beauty of the mosaic tiles that covered a large section of the back of the chapel. There were three images, pictures rendered in stunning detail. The first was of lush gardens, centered on two large fruit trees, their green leaves seeming alive within the ceramic design. Around the trees, beyond the garden, were cities, thriving metropolises of the past. There were no cars, no trains, but there were three-masted ships sailing waters of incredible blue, the pyramids of Egypt off in the distance, the thriving world around Jerusalem, Mecca in all its glory, Rome when it had not yet crumbled.

It was a rendering combining various holy eras of the ancient world: images from five hundred years ago, from a millennium ago, from before the time of Christ, all depicted as a giant time-spanning world of peace joined by the seas, by the ancient ships that sailed her waters.

As Michael looked up at the tile masterpiece, the blue skies above the world faded into nighttime darkness. Star-filled skies gave way to what could only be described as heaven, tranquil, serene, the supreme promise of salvation. Angels mingled with men and women. Clouds floated among the masses, a peaceful gathering of the best of humanity, a depiction of all races, all creeds and colors. Priests and imams, rabbis and monks. Muslims, Christians, and Hindus; Buddhists, Jews and Celts, all gathered as if in supreme understanding of eternity. And it filled Michael with optimism. He didn't know why, but the fact that this artist's rendering, this mosaic from history's past, depicted what so many thought of as an ideal filled him with hope.

But it all washed away as Michael's eyes were drawn to the third and final piece of art. It sat below the rendering of man, beneath the cities and people. It seeped out of the darkened earth into an utter manifestation of hell, a world of singular evil, a land filled with people overcome by suffering, weeping, holding the dead. Dark creatures lurked in shadows, their yellow eyes peering from the darkness. A world of blazing heat and bone-cracking cold, of torment and anguish. Bodies broken, limbs torn away and cast about, cities aflame, rivers filled with corpses floating upon the blood of the dead. Giants holding swords dripping with crimson, severed heads attached to their belts.

Michael was overcome by nausea; he keeled over, his hands upon his knees, swallowing, trying to catch his breath. It was as if the depicted evil had suddenly invaded his mind and heart. What would drive an artist to create something of such darkness was something Michael couldn't—wouldn't—grasp. And the horror of it shocked him back to the moment.

It finally occurred to Michael where the chart was hidden, and it broke his heart. For what he had to do was surely an act against God, against one of man's truly great creations, against a depiction of realms that stirred humanity's base emotions, a work of art that truly captured man and his destiny. A work of staggering accomplishment that would never be seen by the modern world.

Michael removed a ten-inch chisel and hammer from his bag and walked to the tiled mosaic.

He laid the chisel upon the center of the wall and raised the hammer high. He closed his eyes, asked for forgiveness, and with all of his strength brought the hammer down upon the chisel and struck it hard.

The city of Jerusalem shattered, spiderweb cracks erupting up and out through the ancient worlds as if God himself were destroying mankind. The tiles fell to the floor in a glass-shattering crash. Again and again he smashed the masterpiece until its center had fallen away.

At first he thought it had been a useless gesture, a needless marring of the room, but then, as he brought his flashlight closer, he saw it. It was faint at first, an outline in black, blending with the earthen wall. It was pitch, the dark tarlike substance, waterproof and sticky, used for roofs and boats. As Michael ran his hand along the dry surface, he could hear the hollow behind the wall. He ran his chisel along the perimeter. It was a two-foot-by-two-foot section, the black organic substance forming a watertight seal. Michael made quick work of the pitch and revealed a wooden box. He pried it from its confines, removing it and placing it upon the floor. The box was made of cypress, coated in black tar, brass hinges at the rear. The lock was nothing more than ornamental, easily popping off as Michael pried at it with his chisel.

He slowly lifted the lid, his breath held tightly in his lungs. Filled with anticipation, he laid the lid back and picked up his light, shining it upon the contents. The box was dry; its waterproof seal had remained true, preserving the objects before him. Michael reached in and pulled out a handful of coins. They were of gold and silver, copper and tin. Stamped faces of sultans, of kings. There were Roman coins and Egyptian tender. Michael reached in again and withdrew a rolled-up chart—coiled and bound, made of tanned and supple animal skin. Michael cut the cord and slowly rolled the chart out, finally exhaling.

He looked at the chart. It was large and detailed, with notes and legends upon the perimeter.

And Michael's heart sank. This was not the second half of the Piri Reis map. This was not the map that would free KC's sister or save Simon. It was a chart—of that there was no doubt—but not the goal of his search. It depicted cities and routes. It was of Europe and the Middle East. It was a chart that led the world to the holiest lands of the three major religions. Mecca, Jerusalem, and Bethlehem; Medina, Mount Sinai, and Hebron. It was a chart that pointed man to the places where one could be closest to God, to Allah, Yahweh on earth.

Michael sat back, overwhelmed at his failure. He had pieced it together from Simon's notes and KC's research. He hated relying upon others, and his stubborn way of solitary action and responsibility had never failed him, but now, without the time to confirm information himself . . .

Michael refocused; he wasn't about to give up.

He looked up at the tile masterpiece above and without hesitation jammed his chisel into heaven. The tiles of angels and saints fell away. Where the star-filled realm once stood was now nothing more than rock face and a recess covered in pitch, where a second box rested.

Michael knelt over the second case, wasting no time in reverie, and smashed off the lock. He lifted the lid and gazed in. But this time it was worse. He stared at books and scrolls. He removed an ornate Bible, meticulously created before the age of printing presses. Its leather cover was adorned in rubies and sapphires, its Latin pages illustrated with painstaking detail. There was a Koran, exquisite in design, its Arabic wording elegant, and a giant scroll, a Torah, wrapped in cloth and sealed with golden end caps.

As Michael looked upon them, confusion skittered in his mind. He could not grasp the reason for hiding away these Holy Scriptures; while exquisite and surely of great value, they were far from unique. And the chart, upon first review, didn't appear to be earth-shattering in detail, didn't seem to reveal any great secret.

But then KC's words echoed in his mind. *Maps. Guides.* The holy books were the maps to heaven, the charts that, if explicitly followed, would lead one to one's final reward, to redemption, to everlasting life. They truly were maps. Just as the chart in the first box led to earthly destinations, these charts would lead to the celestial.

Michael suddenly understood the meaning of the artwork upon the walls, the reverential depiction of the worlds found through the use of the guideposts within.

And then it hit him. A sense of pain and dread such as he had never felt in his life. There was no doubt where the eastern half of the Piri Reis map was hidden.

Michael looked at the final depiction, the final pieces of tiled art that sat beneath heaven and earth. He longed for the images he had just destroyed, wishing for their holy depictions to wash away the nightmare that would be before him for months to come as he stared at the depiction of hell.

CHAPTER 25

K C watched as the two guards walked lazily by on their half-hour rounds, oblivious to her presence and intentions. She counted off a minute and emerged from the shadows of the Hagia Sophia wall, pulled two small black boxes from her bag, and laid them opposite each other across the main sidewalk. She pushed a small button on top and lined them up until the high-pitched beep sounded in her ear, confirming that the unimpeded laser beam was aligned. She hit the button again, resuming the silence, activating its invisible barrier.

She sprinted to the circular building containing the tomb of Selim II and placed another alarm pair twenty-five feet from the door. As she turned the box, the alarm sounded in her ear, this one higher-pitched and louder, more dire. It would provide her with only seconds' warning, but a short warning was far better than a sudden surprise.

As ancient as the structure before her was, the lock was as modern as they came. Though it was covered in a worn green patina, giving the impression of age-old lead, the inner workings of the Caprice wheel ball lock were mechanically advanced. Known as a pickless lock, advertised as unbreakable, it was all the rage, but as with any security software, nothing was impenetrable. KC slipped the flat mirrored key into the narrow cylinder; she held it in place as she pushed the rear button, which activated the polished sensors, which in turn fed back the laser release. Her key had cost her fifteen thousand euros in Germany and she wasn't very happy when she learned that Michael had bought this particular one for $3,500 for his security business back in New York.

The key turned easily and the lock slipped open with a thunking echo.

She quickly slipped through the door, closing it behind her, and reset the lock. She laid the blue duffel and her bag on the ground, turned, and stared at the elaborate room. Tiled and graced with beauty, it was an elaborate tribute to a man whose accomplishments paled next to those of his father and grandfather; they paled, too, next to those of his grand vizier, whose accomplishments he so often took credit for; they were nothing compared to those of the wife who was buried at his side, who rose in prominence as their son Murad III ascended to the vacated throne of his father. But he was a sultan, the ruler of the largest empire in the world. And this room was his tribute.

KC stood before the coffins, each covered in a green shroud. There were forty-four in all, and while the thought of the sultan's and his wives' remains didn't disturb her, the small child-sized coffins did. Children, brothers and sisters and sons, murdered to prevent their growing up to steal the throne. Murder in the name of stability of the empire, a practice more common in the Middle Ages and ancient times than anyone was willing to admit. Paranoia was common among kings and sultans, pharaohs and emperors, all living with a wary eye for those around them. For once you were at the top, there was nowhere to go but the grave.

There were no elections, no orderly presidential transitions of power; there was only succession through death.

But Selim II was felled not by sons or brothers, not by his viziers or admirals, nor by poison, sword, or dagger. It was by accident; his sultanship was felled by a fall. He succumbed to injuries sustained from an undignified drunken tumble in the royal baths in 1572.

It took four years to construct his tomb, a seemingly long time in an age when a king or sultan could marshal thousands to construct a palace in three years. The tomb was designed by the great architect Mimar Sinan, who designed over three hundred of the Ottoman Empire's greatest structures, including the Topkapi Harem, Selimiye Mosque in Edirne, and the Suleiman Mosque in Istanbul. Living to the age of ninety-nine and a close friend of the grand vizier, Mehmet Pasha, he was considered one of history's greatest architects and was often compared to Michelangelo.

The bodies and coffins were moved in under cover of darkness and the tomb was finally opened in 1577 for the viewing public.

KC slipped off the green coffin shroud to reveal an ornate sarcophagus made of stone and carved cypress. Its cover depicted Selim II dressed in a large turban and royal robes, standing upon a great mountain, his kingdom spread before him, his subjects prostrate in worship.

KC worked her way around the tomb, examining it, assessing it. It was truly fit for a king. Set upon granite block footings, it was the work of craftsmen who must have toiled months to create it. She looked about the room, wondering if such tribute, such craftsmanship, was afforded his wife and children, whether he even cared about those who surrounded him in the afterlife.

Growing curious, she removed the green coffin shroud from the tomb immediately to the left, the tomb of his first wife, Nur Bana, who died eight years after her husband. It was much simpler, made of carved cypress, its top adorned with the image of her sultan, an image of Topkapi and Hagia Sophia.

She was born Cecillia Venier Baffo, a young Venetian noble who was captured by the Ottomans. Her son Murad III succeeded his father, and as a result, she grew in power as the Valide Sultan, the king's mother. She ran the government with Grand Vizier Mehmet Pasha for eight years, only to die under mysterious circumstances. KC smiled as she thought how a woman had ruled a world in which women's rights were suppressed.

KC ran her hand over the lid, over the exquisite design afforded a wife who knew she was just one of many possessed by her husband. She noted the simple hinges affixing the lid to the coffin and wondered why back then, as now, coffins were built to be opened; it wasn't as if the residents would be leaving or anyone would be paying them an up-close visit.

KC laid the coffin shroud back over the woman's tomb and returned to the sarcophagus of Selim II. There were no hinges on this tomb, no simple switch to throw to open it. She wished that she could simply lift the lid, grab, and go.

The lid weighed at least fifteen hundred pounds. Made of solid stone, it would take a team of men with dexterous fingers and tools to open.

And she smiled; Michael truly was gifted at compromising security, at cracking the difficult barriers and entering impossible places. She had always turned away from crimes when the obstacles grew difficult, when the physical compromise exceeded her ingenuity and required lithe acrobatic entrances and exits. But Michael was the type who liked to perform the impossible.

KC reached into the blue duffel bag and pulled out the aluminum pieces, thankful for Michael's ingenuity.

She affixed the stabilizing frame to the rear of the coffin, sliding its thin foot under the coffin proper, raising its bracing up along the back and onto the top. She placed a thin wedge against the seam of the lid and gently tapped, the echoes seeming to sound like a jackhammer as the thin piece of steel slipped into the lid's seam. KC laid the framing rod against the wedge and affixed them together. Michael's design was simple, easily assembled, and even easier to disassemble. Made of reinforced aluminum members used for airplane wings and copper piping, the portable lift that Michael had crafted could probably hoist a truck, yet it fit into a small duffel bag. Its base was affixed to the ground by the sheer force of the weight of the coffin, while the lifting arm remained in place due to the overall pressure. It was as simple as a car jack.

She repeated the procedure on the three remaining sides. She pulled out and affixed the pneumatic tubes and attached the small air cylinder. Grasping the cylinder tightly, she pumped the arm, and after a moment of pressurization, the tomb's seal broke with a gasp, a sudden intake and exhalation of history. The lid began to rise, slowly at first, the ancient wood and stone creaking in protest. It gradually elevated by fractions of an inch, as KC's muscles grew tired.

KC continued pumping; the lid was five inches up now. Unable to resist the temptation, she flipped on her flashlight and peered inside.

And what she saw frightened her, terrified her, for it was far from what she and Michael had expected. She was suddenly afraid for her sister, for what she was looking at she was entirely unprepared for.

And then the alarm in her ear cried out. Someone had broken the plane of the sidewalk beam. Someone was coming.

KC flipped the release valve; the lid of the tomb fell back in place with a great hiss from the pneumatic valves. She grabbed the four stanchions and threw them into her bag, then draped and smoothed out the green coffin shroud upon the tomb.

The second ring sounded in her ear. The guards were on the walkway and they were coming.

KC spun about, looking everywhere, her eyes finally falling on the tomb of the sultan's wife. She folded back the green cloth cover. Without thought, she rammed the chisel into the hinge pin, thankful it was not of the heavy design of her husband's container, and flipped open the coffin.

She looked at the remains of Selim's wife: the sheer white veil draped across her skull, her long dark hair appearing freshly combed. The few remaining pieces of skin were like paper-thin leather, dried and flaking against her ivory bone. She was small, barely five-two, by KC's estimate.

The noise grew louder, the guards coming closer.

KC shoved the bony corpse aside, threw her two bags in, and quickly climbed into the coffin.

She gingerly held the green cloth as she lowered the lid, ensuring it fell back into place.

As the lid quietly fell shut, KC was enveloped in darkness and the musty smell of death. She fought the revulsion, trying to shield her mind from the horror next to her as her fear of the dark rose up out of her soul. But it was to no avail.

Her mind screamed in terror.

* * *

MICHAEL STARED INTO the depths of hell, at the suffering and anguish of its inhabitants. He closed off his mind and drove the chisel into the heart of the heinous work of art. He smashed it with a vengeance, as if stabbing the heart of the Devil, making quick work of the entire depiction. While with the two tile works above, Michael had left intact the sides and perimeters, depicting heaven and earth, now Michael left nothing of this underworld, annihilating the entire scene till not a single tile remained.

Michael reached into the exposed recess and withdrew a large box, three feet long by one foot wide. He hesitated as he looked at the wooden case, hoping he wasn't opening a Pandora's Box, hating that he was in this position. But he thought of KC and the pain she was feeling, the guilt that was overwhelming her over her sister and Simon.

Michael tore open the lid, shattering the hinges and lock, and reached in for what he knew was there. He laid the chart out on the ground. Its gazelle hide was surprisingly soft and supple, the torn edge leaving no doubt of its authenticity. The chart was rich in detail, depicting eastern Africa, the Indian and Pacific oceans, India, Australia, and the Far East.

And Michael's eyes were drawn to the mountain range, the Himalayas, drawn in precise detail, with a refined depiction of a five-peaked mountain in the uppermost section of India. Of all the landmarks, of all the notes, none were more detailed than the pathway up through the rivers of India, from the water's edge into the heart of the continent. While Michael couldn't read the Turkish notes, he imagined what they said. After what he had read of Kemal Reis's journeys, of this chart's secretion in this very wall, he had no doubt the notes on this chart were warnings.

Michael pulled his waterproof digital camera from his satchel and took multiple shots of the chart before sliding the camera back into its compartment. It was a backup, rudimentary at best, but he liked redundancy, preferring to call it covering one's ass.

He rolled up the chart, pulled out the leather tube, and unwound its top flap. He opened the internal hasp, slid the chart into the waterproof tube, and locked the airtight seal with a barely audible whoosh. He flipped down the leather flap, laced it tight, and threw the leather strap over his shoulder. He stowed his tools in the neoprene satchel, sealed it, and threw it crosswise over his other shoulder. Michael checked his watch and tried his radio, to no avail: The walls were just too thick. His nerves were on fire for KC's safety, hoping she was long done with Selim's tomb, hoping she was already waiting for him.

As he took one final look at the room, at the damage he had caused, he prayed it would not be in vain. As the images of the final tile depiction, of the world of suffering that was burned into his mind, filled his thoughts, he decided he would not tell anyone what he had seen, not KC, not Busch. He would not tell them of his suspicion about where the chart led or what it possibly meant. It was an unwanted knowledge, expertly imparted by Mehmet through the artwork in the chapel, a knowledge he would never pass on to others.

Michael would get Simon back, he would ensure Cindy's safe return to KC, but there was no question. He would never let this chart out of his possession.

KC LAY STILL, fighting the need to breathe, partly to conserve her air, partly to avoid filling her lungs with the air of death, fearful that it would somehow infect her. Though the woman had passed away five hundred years ago, the odor of decay still permeated the wooden casing. As KC moved her aside, she was amazed at the lack of mass; it was like shoving aside a small pile of sticks, her bones clattering and scratching.

And then the outer door crashed open, the sound rumbling through the coffin where KC was concealed. She listened closely, hearing the guards walk in, two voices, urgent, speaking of disturbances and security and wondering why they had to have the dead shift.

She left her flashlight off, fighting the image of the body she lay up against; she'd seen it only for a brief moment, but it would be with her for life. She fought her turning stomach, her revulsion at lying with the dead, as she heard the footsteps of the guards.

She interpreted the muffled conversation, hearing just snippets and snappets. The conversation seemed to drag on for hours, though the guards' round of the room lasted only minutes.

But as terrifying as where she lay, as what she was lying next to, as the possibility of being caught was, what she had seen in the tomb of Sultan Selim II chilled her heart far more.

And then the loud crash of the door and the lock falling into place reverberated. It was a moment before the alarms sounded in her ear, signaling the guards had crossed the first barrier, and then the second beep told her of their departure.

KC slowly lifted the lid, illuminating the body next to her: The head had detached from the body, the once graceful hair tangled about her. KC jumped out of the coffin in revulsion but was overcome with shame. She had disturbed the peaceful rest of the dead, of this innocent woman. KC thought of realigning her body but knew she was running out of time.

KC quickly set to work on the sultan's sarcophagus. It took her only a minute to remove the green cloth, to set up the support rods, and another minute to raise the lid—but this time she went far beyond the five inches; she pumped the lid up two feet.

She flipped on her light and shone it into darkness and what she'd found earlier.

There was no body; there was no sultan or rod. The coffin was beyond empty. It was bottomless. It was the entrance to another world. It was the entrance to the real tomb.

And now she understood why it had taken four years to construct: It was because of the tomb below. Hagia Sophia used to be a church, a grand basilica, and it was common practice to build churches over crypts. They all had them: the Vatican, St. Patrick's in New York, Notre Dame in Paris. When Hagia Sophia was built as a Christian basilica in the sixth century, it, too, had its crypt. But when the Christian church was converted into a mosque in 1453, there was no mention of what became of the crypts below. Now, as KC looked into Selim's tomb, it all became clear.

KC draped the green shroud over the raised tomb; she grabbed her two bags and the cylinder, lifted the green cloth, and slipped into the coffin. The stairs were stone, steep and narrow, carved out of rock over four hundred years earlier.

KC held tight to the cylinder, the air hose protruding back out to the lift arms, and opened the release valve a fraction. As she allowed the lid to slowly lower down upon her, it crept down with a hiss, enclosing her in the ancient world. Inches from an airtight seal, she closed the valve, stopping the lid's descent just above the air tubes. From out in the room nothing could be seen but the shroud-covered tomb, and unless you were an expert, the one-inch difference in height would be unnoticeable. But if the lid were to fall, crimping off the hose, KC would become a permanent occupant, residing with whatever horrors lay below.

KC headed down, her flashlight leading the way into the hidden world. And as she stepped down the final stair, she found herself in a necropolis. It was an old crypt; as grand as the former basilica was, this was its equal in design. Built at the height of the Byzantine Empire, it was arched and columned in marble with Ottoman additions and renovations. The walls were adorned with busts and mosaics depicting Christian saints, Muslim rulers, and the glory of paradise.

KC stood in a vestibule fifteen by fifteen, tight and confined, a world beneath the dead.

She shone her light and found a dark hallway, following it into a large, open room where, in the center, sat the true sarcophagus. Grand Vizier Mehmet Pasha was far more deceptive than anyone had realized. The room was festooned with treasures of the Ottoman Empire, sabers and Korans, tiled blue walls, spoils of war none of which Selim II had accumulated himself, for he never went to war or even strategized, leaving it all to his advisors yet taking all the credit.

There were chalices from Rome, jewels from Egypt, statues of pharaohs and kings. KC was shocked at the inscription upon the wall, etched in gold, the sheen still lustrous after centuries: It was written in Arabic, Turkish, and Latin, a warning to all the world. As she read, the grand vizier's words were clear: Whoever removed the contents of the tomb would suffer a subjugation in hell, a *fatwa* against the soul.

It explained why none of the artifacts had been removed, the warning tempering temptation, wiping the greed from the souls of those who built the tomb, from the souls of thieves that might have made it down here.

But KC would sacrifice her life, her soul, if she knew it would save her sister. She would gladly trade eternity for the life of the sister she had raised. She would do anything to ensure her safe return, and to ensure that her friend Simon would survive.

KC stood over the sarcophagus. It was ornate, made of gold, glimmering under her light. She felt as if she were Howard Carter, the first to see King Tut's tomb. She was looking upon a secret held for centuries. The detail was rendered by true artisans as if wielding a paintbrush upon canvas, working their intricate magic into a depiction of heaven.

She dug her fingers under the lid, its seal easily broken, its weight manageable as she lifted, but then she lowered it again.

KC looked around the room again, at the wealth, at the artifacts of lost history, her eyes finally falling upon the warning once more. Subjugation in hell. She thought on eternity, of what it would be like to be cast into the underworld, and whether such a place existed. She had been raised Catholic and held tight to her faith, in constant awareness of her breaking of countless Commandments. But as she had so often done, as Michael had so succinctly explained, she rationalized that sometimes we are forced to do the unthinkable, to break the laws of God and man to save those closest to us, despite the consequences. KC believed in destiny, she believed in heaven, and as she reflected on Iblis and Chiron Prison, she surely believed in hell and that it waited with open arms for those deserving it.

Curses be damned. KC lifted the lid of the coffin.

Sultan Selim II lay in repose. He had not fared as well as his wife. His face was sunken, caved in in sections. What little hair he possessed was gray-streaked brown, a rat's nest of tangles. His elaborate hat had fallen to the side, half of his skull remaining within it. He wore a cloak of white stitched with gold thread, a green sash wrapped around a nonexistent waist. His withered body was but a husk of shattered skeleton.

And clutched in his bony hands was the rod, grasped like a scepter, on his chest. The core of the rod, formed from dark wood, carried a maroon hue that shimmered under KC's light. And as described, two snakes rose along the shaft, intertwining on their rise, their heads flaring outward and their ruby eyes locked in a deadly stare-down, their silver viper teeth poised, ready to strike.

KC had never robbed the dead, had never thought of the necromantic nature of such a deed. In any other circumstance it would have repulsed her, but this was different. This meant saving lives, it meant saving her sister and Simon.

She reached into the coffin with both hands and wrapped them about the rod. She slowly lifted, the skeleton resisting as if he was fighting from the heights of heaven or the depths of hell. And it frightened her; she was fearful that, however improbable it sounded, the dead king would sit upright and kill her with his bony hands.

But then, with a cracking sound, the sultan relinquished

his prize. KC lifted the rod, examining it more closely. The snake heads were detailed right down to the scales of their skin. Their red eyes seemed to flicker with life as she stared.

And all at once she felt dizzy, overcome with nausea. She was surrounded by death, having to slip into hell to save the life of her sister. It was becoming too much; her mind was fogged into confusion as she stared at the corpse before her, as she thought of lying with Selim's dead wife, of staring into the eyes of this hideous serpent.

She fought to refocus, averted her eyes, and quickly stuffed the rod into the leather tube that Michael had given her, sealing it in the airtight cylinder within, vowing never to look at it again.

CHAPTER 26

B usch sat in the limo, under the long shadows of Hagia Sophia, the a/c on high as it fought back the heat of the Istanbul summer night. Across the street, the VIPs continued to pour in for the celebration: dignitaries, royalty, Istanbul's captains of industry, all heading up the blue carpet into Topkapi as if they were heading into the Academy Awards.

Busch continued to try to reach Michael on the radio to warn him of Iblis's entrance into Topkapi, but to no avail. It wrecked him that the small man had slipped away from him so easily. He longed to get his hands around the skinny neck of the man who had so ruthlessly kidnapped and beaten his friend, who had kidnapped KC's young, innocent sister.

The rear door of the limo flew open and a dirty, grimy KC slid onto the backseat. She laid the blue duffel and her large Prada bag of supplies on the floor, took off her hat, and shook out her long blonde hair.

"Well?" Busch said.

KC held up and waved the leather satchel, finally laying it on the backseat.

"Where's Michael?" KC grabbed a glass from the bar, filled it with ice, and poured herself some water. "I can't reach him on the radio."

"Not out of there yet."

"Where's Iblis?" KC crawled across the back of the limo, leaned over the front seat, looking through the windshield, scanning the cars outside. She took a large swig of water.

"I lost him," Busch said, unable to look at KC.

"What do you mean, you lost him?" KC's voice grew frantic.

"I lost him. He slipped into the VIP crowd and disappeared into Topkapi."

"Jesus, does Michael know?" KC scooted to the back of the limo, pulled out her radio, but heard nothing but static. "Iblis is going for the chart; he'll kill Michael to get it. How could you let Michael slip into such danger?"

"You don't think I'm dying here? I couldn't get into that party if I had an invitation. I've been trying to reach him for over a half hour now. Remember, he is my friend."

"I know," KC said. "I should have gone with him."

"Michael knows what he's doing; he can take care of himself. I know him."

"Yeah, and I know Iblis." KC spat out her teacher's name as if it were poison.

KC tore off her clothes without regard for Busch or modesty. She grabbed the bottle of water off the bar, poured it on a napkin, and ran it about her face and arms, wiping away the dust and death she had carried back from the coffins and tombs. She quickly applied her ruby-red lipstick and brushed on a subtle eyeshadow, thankful for a face that didn't require heavy makeup. She reached into her Prada bag and pulled out the long Oscar de la Renta gown she had bought in the hotel boutique, midnight blue and stunning. She slipped into it, the gown hugging her contours like a second skin. It was slit up both sides, revealing more leg than Busch thought was humanly possible. It was perfect, not just in a haute couture way, but functional, unrestricting to the legs, allowing her mobility for actions not typical in society functions.

"I knew you'd find an occasion to wear that dress," Busch said.

KC ignored Busch as she ran a brush through her blonde hair; she took off the Tiffany necklace Michael had given her, tucking it into a small jewelry bag, exchanging it for a diamond choker and diamond stud earrings. She affixed the jewels, slipped on a pair of three-inch Prada heels, picked up her purse, and opened it.

The purse was custom-made, its interior waterproof, filled with pockets that stored her polymer lockpicking tools, several glow sticks, money, a thin knife that looked like a nail file, and in one sealed compartment, a twelve-diamond necklace of silver with a blue sapphire pendant in the center. She had had it for over five years now, stolen from a German businessman who would proffer it to young girls, luring them with its promise of things to come, only to ship them off to the Southeast Asian sex-slave market. Upon stealing it along with his computer files from his Berlin penthouse, she had contacted the police and provided his information to the families of his victims. He was dead by morning.

She had held on to the necklace in case she ever needed its universal currency to bribe her way out of trouble. It revolted her every time she looked at it, and, she'd resolved not to sell it except in the most dire circumstances. She dropped in her lipstick, tucked her radio, cell phone, wallet, a miniflashlight, her long black shirt, and her pair of lightweight flats in and zipped the bag up. She grabbed the leather satchel containing the rod—her prize from the tomb—and tucked it under her arm.

"What the hell you bringing that for?"

"It's my ticket in," KC said as she opened the door.

"In?" Busch looked across the street to the celebrants entering Topkapi. "You can't go in there, especially with that," Busch said as he pointed to the narrow case.

"You don't think so? Watch me."

KC stepped from the car and slammed the door behind her.

Busch shook his head in anger. "Michael always picks the stubborn ones."

KC HAD TRANSFORMED herself from a grimy, dust-covered thief to a woman of model caliber. She carried herself like royalty, projecting an air of confidence and celebrity as she strode across the street and straight up to the blue carpet. Heads turned, a collective murmur hummed, trying to figure out who the statuesque blonde with the deep green eyes was.

KC walked right past the flashing cameras and paparazzi and straight up to the security detail as if this were her own party.

"Good evening, gentlemen."

Three guards manned the airport-sized metal detector. They were dressed in the tan outfits and black-brimmed hats of the local police. They wore unrelenting stares upon their faces and Glock pistols upon their hips.

"I don't have my invitation," KC said in apology as she opened and reached inside her purse.

"I'm sorry, miss, but—"

KC handed over a flipped-open billfold, presenting her

ID along with a picture badge. The lead guard took it and examined it closely. "The European Union . . . ?"

KC smiled, her friendly look disarming and practiced over many years of deceit. An expert in the use of her feminine charms, she glanced at the guard's badge. "Yasim," she said, addressing him by name, speaking in the familiar to relax his attention, "I'm presenting this on behalf of Ulle Regio of Switzerland, the president of the EU, repatriating this artifact as a token of welcome to Turkey from the European Union collective."

The two subordinates looked at their leader as he motioned KC to open the case.

KC flipped open the latch and lifted the cover, displaying the snake-head staff, its head with silver teeth and ruby eyes dazzling beneath the bright security lights.

KC continued to smile as she fought the sudden sickening feeling in her stomach; the rod that she had sworn not to look upon again stared back at her, filling her with dread, making her skin crawl. She hoped it was not an emotion felt by the guards. "The embarrassment for all if I do not present this will mean the end of my career." KC hoped the insinuation of lost jobs was carried in the subtext.

Yasim stared at KC, his look conveying no emotion. KC never broke eye contact or diminished her disarming smile. The moment dragged on until Yasim finally averted his eyes, looking back at KC's ID. He closed the billfold and handed it back, nodding KC through. "Please behave yourself. Neither of us wishes to experience a career-ending moment this evening."

"Thank you." KC smiled at the man as she closed the case. Yasim waved KC around the metal detector and she walked through the welcome archway into the Courtyard of Janissaries.

KC entered the reception and followed the crowd as they moved toward the Gate of Salutation. The walkway was lined in flaming torches, their orange glow painting the ancient buildings a golden hue, sending tendrils of black smoke dancing skyward.

As KC approached the second gate she broke off to the left and stepped beyond the lamps' illumination. She reached into her purse, feigning a makeup break, and scanned the area. The crowds were all heading through the arch of the Gate of Salutation and into the second courtyard where the main festivities were taking place.

KC watched as a team of guards made their rounds, scanning the crowd, looking for anything unusual, but KC knew much of it was for show, the guards relying on the diligence of their brethren at the entrance. The body of people here tonight were not the ones to be concerned with; they were not the rabble-rousing, unlawful bunch that gave pause to civil society. At least, KC thought, most of them weren't.

KC headed left into the shadows, taking the familiar route that she had ventured upon with Michael the night before. The shadows were deep and were made all the darker by the glowing torches along the walkway. She wandered along, her eyes flitting back and forth as she kept an eye on the movement into the party, on the guards who were half enamored of the celebrity of the moment, doing everything to avoid being seen. She finally arrived at the shadowed corner where the thirty-foot wall that wrapped around the actual Topkapi Palace abutted the archaeological museum. KC quickly slipped off the impractical heels, put them in her bag, and dug out her flat running shoes, putting them on.

She had no idea where Michael was, but Iblis was on the loose and not many knew him better than she did. She knew of his cunning, brilliant mind, she knew of his lethal approach to achieving success, and she knew he was somewhere within Topkapi, racing for a head-on collision with Michael. Two thieves, two different approaches, one avoiding harm to others at all costs and one harming any and all in pursuit of winning no matter the cost.

KC had been so consumed with worry for her sister, with fear for Simon, she had put aside her own wants and needs, but her heart came racing to the forefront as soon as she heard that Michael might be in danger. She couldn't let him come to harm; he had so selflessly saved her, and had never hesitated in helping her break the law to save her sister. This in spite of the danger and risk involved, where being caught meant the possibility not only of prison but also of death. And now the threat of death hung over three people. A friend, a sister, and . . . She realized she could no longer hide her feelings for Michael.

Risk be damned, KC thought, looping the strap of the leather case over her head and shoulder, and doing the same with her purse; she dug her fingers in and began to climb the wall.

MICHAEL EMERGED FROM the chapel, crawling through the three-foot hole, and shone his light about the cistern, the quiet and solitude made more apparent by the echoing of the drops of water slipping off the ceiling. So much of the world was hidden, so much of it just steps away from unaware society. And it wasn't just in Istanbul, it was the same in much of the world: Rome, Moscow, Shanghai, the American West. Much of it was mercifully lost to the modern world, for once breached, the unleashed secrets of the past would bring nothing but trouble.

As Michael looked back at the hole leading into the hidden chapel, he knew he had unearthed things meant to be hidden. There would be no disguising the breach, no hiding the recent destruction and theft. It pained him that he had opened history only to lay it to waste, but in life there were some things that carried greater weight.

Michael checked and rechecked the vacuum seal on the tube that contained the chart and jumped back into the five-foot-deep cistern. The chill of the water shocked him back to the moment. He held his light above his head and slogged back toward the first wall, the sound of his aquatic disturbance reverberating around him.

Arriving at his exit wall, he took a quick breath and slipped under the water, gliding through the five-foot tube to emerge in the main section of the cistern. As he broke the surface, his light exploding around the cavernous room, the air left his lungs in shock. He aimed the beam ahead and saw the rope, his means of departure, floating atop the water, cut from its perch above. He shone his light up to the hole in the ceiling where he had entered, a wasted search, for he knew he would find nothing there.

Without a moment's hesitation, Michael dove under and swam back through the tube. He surfaced once again in the antechamber, quickly shining the light on the wall thirty yards away, tucked his flashlight into his belt, and began swimming as fast as he could. Trudging through the water would prove too slow to allow him to escape. There was no doubt in his mind that he had securely tied the rope to the backhoe; when it came to safety he never made mistakes. It hadn't fallen by accident.

Without breaking stroke, Michael snatched the light from his belt and dove into the tunnel of the next wall.

The tube was longer, a slight current fighting his advance. Confined and dark, over forty feet, it seemed to never end, until he burst through to the surface. He never left himself with only a single means of egress, and he was determined to make it to the second exit. He fought back the thought of who had cut his cord and where he was, knowing that if fear entered his mind it would lessen his chances of success.

Michael emerged into another cistern anteroom. But this one was far different. It was tall and narrow, reaching upward twenty-five feet, where shafts of light pierced through a ceiling grate. It was a well, leading up into the heart of the Turkish baths of the harem. The well was part of the cistern that provided a constant supply of cold, fresh water back in the days of sultans and their multiple wives, only to be forgotten, as so much had been lost to memory.

There were three tubes at seven-foot vertical intervals up the side wall. Three feet in diameter, they protruded several inches from the main wall, spaced far enough to make the climb difficult, with leaps and precarious handholds, but difficult was always better than impossible.

Michael stared up at the grate in the ceiling, three by three; it was easily large enough to get through if he could detach it from its setting. Michael climbed up into the first tube, glad to be out of the water, and he fought against the involuntary shivers that struggled to bring his temperature back up to normal. The cold of the water had sapped his strength, cramped his muscles, and removed any sense of feeling from his fingers—and all combined to make his climb even more precarious.

Michael reached into his dive bag and withdrew a screwdriver and the small crowbar, affixing them to his belt next to his knife so that the tools would be easily accessible once he completed his climb and available for breaching the grate of the harem proper. Michael sealed his bag and stood precariously on the upper lip of the first pipe. He extended his arms upward, his fingers just shy of the next tube. He took a deep breath, focused, and leaped up, his fingertips just catching the lip of the second tube. His forearms burned as he hauled himself up, pulling up into the pipe, where he collapsed, leaning against the rounded wall of the tube.

Michael rose to his knees, rechecked the tube, resecured the bag at his waist, and leaned out of the pipe, casting his gaze from the pool below to the grate above that would lead him out of this pit.

And then, suddenly, he heard a sound, subtle at first, then growing, approaching with a roar like thunder. All at once, great gasps of air blew through the tube where he sat, a gale wind upon him, blowing his brown hair about his face. The pounding sound was coming from the tube, and not just from the one where he sat, twelve feet above the water, but from all three tubes. Hurricane winds whistled through the pipe, up through the cistern anteroom and out through the three-foot grate. Michael knew what was coming.

Without hesitation, he leaped out of the shaft, falling fast but not fast enough, as a torrent of water exploded out of each tube, knocking him in midair against the wall. He tumbled down head over heels into the pool below, three tremendous waterfalls pounding into his body. He was churned about like a rag doll, with no sense of up or down. He struggled to breathe against the splashing water and mist, his lungs burning as he coughed, expelling the water that had entered his throat.

The water level rose quickly, rising above the first tube,

turning the lowermost tube's escaping water into a death-like Jacuzzi, spitting Michael haplessly about.

Michael tried to swim down through the rapidly rising waters, only to be churned around like flotsam. The volume of water was tremendous, pounding him about in the midst of its cacophony of sound and unrelenting pressure.

The leather tube and his neoprene dive bag conspired to pull him in two, each object taking on a life of its own and trying to pull away from his body in opposite directions.

The water climbed rapidly up the walls, overtaking the second tube, carrying Michael's bobbing body upward toward the grate. He would reach his destination but not as he wanted; he would never be able to unscrew and open the grate as his body was tossed to and fro.

The water built up into slurry, bubbles churning, currents pulling his body up and down. He kicked for the surface only to be sucked down again, feeling assaulted by thousands of blows. He struggled to stay afloat but there was no doubt that, despite his efforts, he was drowning. His lungs were on fire, white spots moving around the periphery of his vision. He fought with every ounce of his being; he couldn't fail KC, he couldn't let her down.

And then out of nowhere, someone grabbed him, pulling him toward the surface. Michael's head violently rammed into something, but he paid it no mind as he gulped air, as he finally found the oxygen his straining lungs craved.

The water around him was a roiling froth as he slowly got his bearings. The water had slowed its rise a foot short of the ceiling. Michael realized his head had rammed the grate that, minutes earlier, had been twenty-five feet above him. He grabbed tight to the metal cross rods, holding on as he continued to be stirred about in the churning waters.

"You must be Michael," a voice said.

Michael looked up through the grate to see a man crouched down, looming over him, dressed in black tie with a white dress shirt, the sleeves rolled up. His hair was slicked back and carefully groomed. He was beyond thin; the veins on his forearms and neck were pulsing in unison. His tanned skin accentuated ghostly, pale blue eyes, creating an appearance two steps short of human. There was no question he was staring at Iblis.

"So, KC's dating a thief," Iblis said.

Michael glared up at the man, surprised at his American accent.

"You've got quite a resume, Mr. St. Pierre." The roar of the churning waters almost drowned out his words.

Michael struggled to breathe as the water splashed his face.

"I needed KC's assistance, but I never imagined she'd bring help. Y'all not only found the chart quicker than I expected, but saved me from getting my hands dirty."

Michael saw a small coil of rope on the floor beside a tan briefcase, and he could just make out a host of tools scattering the floor.

Iblis walked around the polished metal grate, circling Michael like a bird of prey.

"I knew she had resources in the Vatican, but . . . who knew she was sleeping with another thief? What, did she dangle a little bit of flesh to get you to do this? Get you to risk your life for a little roll in the hay, for a little taste of booty?"

Michael suddenly pulled himself up with his right hand and lunged with his left, in a vain effort to grab Iblis. But Iblis merely smiled and stepped back, laughing at Michael's anger, at his aggravation, at his arm protruding from the grate in the floor.

"Offended because I hit the nail on the head? Or protective of your bonny lass?" Iblis taunted, his voice filled with vitriol. "What do you know of her? She's just another tall blonde piece of ass to someone like you. I'm the one that plucked her off the street. If anyone gets to claim her, it's me. I made her, shaped her, built her. If anyone holds her heart in his hand, if anyone holds her life in the balance, it's me."

Despite his near drowning, despite the futility, Michael tore at the bars. "You touch her and I'll—"

"You'll what?" Iblis said as he stomped on Michael's fingers, crushing them into the metal grate.

Michael instinctively released his grip, to be pulled under the roiling waters, spun about the whirlpool like a rag doll, his mouth and nose filling as his lungs emptied of air. The two bags affixed to his body, though secured, whipped and smashed against him like errant shutters in a storm.

And with a sudden focus he thrust his hand above the surface to grab the metal grate, once again pulling himself up into the narrow pocket of air.

"Enjoy your swim?" Iblis leaned his face close to the bars, taunting Michael. "Have you ever had to discipline a child, to punish someone you care about? Maybe I should just take KC away from all of this, set her soul free."

Michael grabbed tight to the bars with both hands and pulled himself up into Iblis's face. "Don't you touch her. If she so much as has a broken nail, I'll find you—"

"What?" Iblis exploded, his voice echoing off the marble walls. He took a moment, regained his composure, and, finally, softened. "Did you think you could best me? I'd be very surprised if this was her idea."

Michael crushed the bars in a white-knuckled grip, his frustration overflowing as Iblis laid bare his plan.

"She knows me," Iblis said. "She knows the risk of betraying me, and knows full well what the price would be, what would happen to her sister if she didn't follow my instructions to the letter." Iblis paused. "You know what I think? I think it was your idea to try to steal the chart and trade it for Simon and Cindy. The two-bit idea of an arrogant, overconfident, second-rate thief."

Michael shook the bars in total rage, coughing uncontrollably as the water splashed up over his face.

Iblis took a moment, studying Michael, looking at the cauldron he was immersed in. "Have you ever had blood on your hands, Michael? Well, tonight, the ultimate price will be paid; someone must die for your ineptitude and lack of caution."

Michael pulled his face up flush with the bars as the water continued to whip his body about. His eyes filled with rage as he growled, "Without this chart, you have nothing."

Iblis leaned in close; Michael could smell his foul breath through the grate as their eyes locked.

And without warning, something clamped Michael's left arm. Michael was so enraged, so drawn into the staredown with Iblis, that he never saw the handcuff slam around his wrist, the other end affixed to the grate. Michael instinctively pulled against the restraint, kicking back and forth in the water, but it was useless.

"Relax," Iblis said in an oddly calm voice. "It'll keep you from sinking. Now, I'd like that tube on your back."

He turned away from the small man, as if that would keep the tube out of reach. Michael grabbed the strap of the case in his right hand and pulled it from his back, holding it under water as far from Iblis as he could in his restrained condition. He held tight to the grate with his left, cuffed hand, fighting to steady his body as the water continued to roil about him, tossing him to and fro.

Suddenly, Iblis thrust his arm into the water, trying to snatch the tube from Michael, who fought to hold the buoyant tube down and away from Iblis.

Iblis withdrew his arm from the water and smiled, long and with no sense of humor. "So you know, the police will be called, given a complete description of you. A breach of the palace will be reported, inferences will be made about robberies and potential harm to the guests upstairs. Even if you get out, there's nowhere to go. And I'll tell you, they are not going to be happy with what you've done, stealing such a significant artifact, part of their heritage, on the night all the world's eyes are focused on them."

Without warning, Iblis again stomped on Michael's hand, crushing his fingers. Michael automatically released his grip to once again be thrust about in the churning pool, fighting to keep the water from invading his lungs, his left wrist bloodied and throbbing from its awkward handcuff restraint. He willed himself to survive as exhaustion took over his body.

And then Iblis began unscrewing the grate from its perimeter anchor points. Michael once again grabbed the grate, gulping air, but he could do nothing but watch. His left bicep throbbed; it was past the point of failure at trying to hold his body steady and above the surface. He held the tube below him with his right hand, wishing he could somehow weigh it down, drop it into the depths, but it was more than buoyant, fighting to stay above the water as much as his lungs were, as if it were fighting to get away from Michael and into the hands of Iblis.

Iblis made quick work of the grate, removed the final screw, and pulled the small iron-barred barrier sideways, yanking Michael to the left. Michael could see the strain in Iblis, the grate far heavier than he expected. He moved the three-foot-by-three-foot iron square, angling it, but he had no intention of pulling Michael out.

Without a moment's hesitation, Iblis dropped the grate through the hole, inexorably dragging Michael by his handcuffed wrist downward to what would surely be his death—but before he sank away, Michael was once again pulled toward the surface, this time by his right hand, or rather the strap of the tube that he held tight to.

Michael broke the surface and, with sudden terror, realized Iblis held the other end of the tube. It was a tug of war, a challenge that if Michael was to lose, so would they all. Michael held tight to the tube's leather strap while his other arm was pulled nearly out of its socket by the heavy grate affixed to his wrist, which fought to drag him to a watery death. He was trapped between two hells.

Then Iblis withdrew a knife; he looked at Michael without a smile this time, without emotion in his dead eyes. Iblis's left arm was flexed, the muscles straining his tight shirt. He placed the blade against the leather strap and unceremoniously cut it through. The strap snapped and the tube shot upward into Iblis's hand.

And without fanfare, without a scream, Michael disappeared beneath the surface, the anchor about his wrist dragging him to a watery grave.

CHAPTER 27

KC raced along the rooftop of Topkapi Palace, the leather tube lashed tightly across her back, her bag clutched in her right hand. She ran above the harem, working her way to the third courtyard, staying low and tight to the shadows. She occasionally glanced at the vast crowd lost in celebration within the second courtyard, all drinking, all congratulating themselves on deeds surely accomplished by others but for which they took credit, all the while oblivious to the illicit happenings above and below.

KC flipped off her radio for fear that its squawk would alert the world to her presence. She stayed close to the chimneys and away from the edges, scanning the rooftop for guards, trip wires, anything out of the ordinary. She was cautious but didn't slow her run, her blue gown hiked up around her waist so as not to impede her stride.

She arrived and stood atop the Exhibition Building of Miniatures and Manuscripts and stared down at the backhoe in the third courtyard. The barrier-wrapped hole was a black spot among the dark nighttime grounds. The grounds were mercifully empty, devoid of guards but for the two who stood in the distance within the doorway of the Gates of Felicity. Their attention was on the party and keeping people at bay, and they were unaware of the occurrences behind their backs.

KC crossed herself, grabbed the edge, hung down, and jumped. She landed in a crouch within the low shrubs and a nest of garden hoses, a shock of pain vibrating up her body from the rapid ten-foot descent.

She scurried to the work zone and sat within the shadow of the backhoe among a host of shovels, rakes, and hoes. She pulled the radio from her purse, lowered the volume, and thumbed the switch. "Michael," she whispered. "Michael, are you there?"

But KC didn't wait for a response; her fear was already confirmed as she saw the rope upon the ground. It led up to where it was anchored on the backhoe's axle but ended before ever reaching the hole in a tattered, frayed mess.

Without thought, KC grabbed a long garden hose from the bushes, pulled out her flashlight, and shone it into the dark hole. It was as narrow as she remembered and she could see the reflection of the water as the spray of her light danced about the cistern. She removed her dress, her naked skin glowing in the rising moonlight, and stuffed it, along with the flashlight, into the bag. She slipped into the long black shirt and tied back her hair. She wrapped the hose twice about the frame of the backhoe's undercarriage, crudely tying it off.

She looked at the case containing the rod and hoped the leather satchel was as waterproof as Michael said it would be. Not that the wood and precious-metal object would be damaged by moisture, she just didn't want to get it wet or risk damaging it before she had her sister back. She thought of hiding it along with her purse but decided against the risk. Murphy was always lurking around the corner, ready to throw his law at the unprepared or foolish. She threw the satchel crosswise over her shoulder and across her chest and did the same with her purse, the two straps looking like a fashionable bandolier.

KC looped the hose around her body, gripped it tightly, leaned back, and began her descent into darkness. She slid the forty feet down into inky blackness, her determination holding her phobia at bay, and hit the cold water, sending an icy chill through her body.

And she felt it: The water was no longer still as on her first visit; it was like entering rapids, the water churning about her, a raging river of unknown origin far different from the placid water of twenty-four hours earlier. And the noise: Where she had felt a peace before in this silent uninvaded world, now the cistern echoed with a modulating roar.

KC held tight to the hose, steadying herself in the darkness, removed her flashlight from her bag, and flipped it on. She looked about the cistern, shining her light back and forth. The water was flowing like a mountain river in spring swollen with snowmelt and the temperature wasn't much warmer. It flowed past her toward the southern wall, the waves ricocheting back. The water was rising. KC was sure the water had been at chest height before; now it neared her shoulder.

Her eyes finally fell on the source. Water raged from the far wall, sending whirlpools and eddies in all directions. The center of the wall looked like a boiling cauldron percolating with swells and breakers.

And something floated against KC, startling her; it slithered about, dancing upon the water. It was Michael's rope, hung up on a ledge, skittering upon the surface of the flowing water. Though it was frayed and wet, there was no mistaking the knife cuts.

She looked at the distant wall, the one the cistern flowed to, debating which way to go. The strength of the current there diminished to an almost safe serenity. She knew solutions were never in the easy direction; she turned and headed for the cauldron.

She walked against the current, her feet fighting for purchase on the slippery bottom. She balanced and gripped the stone and brick wall as she approached the torrent, hoping to God that Michael was okay, that he was still alive. She banished that fear, and all of her nerves, as Michael had told her: Remain focused on the task at hand; don't let emotion cloud judgment.

Reaching the far wall, KC inched her way toward the froth and bubbles of the water's point of ingress. The current was strong. As she remembered, the tube was wide and short, no more than five feet in length with a three-foot diameter. She pulled two glow sticks from her bag and cracked and shook them out, watching as their green glow lit the wall and surrounding area. She laid them on the wall edge, flipped off her flashlight, and stuffed it into her purse.

Without thought she went under and straight at the pipe, grabbing the rim as the water buffeted her body. She thrust her legs into the ground and pulled with every ounce of energy into the thunderous flow. Inch by inch she moved into the pipe against the raging water, and then suddenly she was thrust backward, caught in the current, launched out of the tube like a tumbling rag doll. She surfaced with rage in her eyes and charged back at the pipe as if in challenge. She checked the satchel and purse on her back, ensuring the straps were holding, inhaled, and dove under. She once again grabbed the rim of the pipe and pulled herself into the current, her arms burning in protest as she tried to gain purchase with her feet against the slippery pipe, but once again she was violently spat out, the force of the water's flow propelling her backward. She surfaced, spitting water from her nose and mouth. Without anything to hold on to, without a surface on which to get a secure foothold, she wouldn't make it through. She tossed her frustration away; it would get her nowhere and would serve only to delay her from finding Michael.

She pulled out her flashlight, flipped it on, and looked up the wall for a way to breach it, for any other way through, but found nothing. She thought if she could get a rope to the other side she could pull herself through, but there was no way without tools, nor was there anything to anchor the rope with, even if she managed to penetrate the wall of water.

And then it hit her. KC turned and raced back toward the dangling hose. It took her no time, as the current helped to carry her along with every step.

She restowed her flashlight in her purse, grabbed the gray rubber hose tightly in hand, and began to climb. She was thankful for the coarse rubber surface, which aided her wet hands and feet in her ascent as she shimmied up. She breached the surface, back into the grounds of Topkapi, cautiously looked around, and climbed out. She spotted the pile of garden tools by the truck, grabbed a rake and a hoe, and slid back down into the cistern.

She quickly made her way back to the hole, the two long tools helping her walk against the current. Both tools were five feet in length, with thick wooden handles. The rake formed a T on the end and the hoe was a perfect hook. Both were ideal for sticking through the pipe and grabbing the lip on the other side.

KC went under and thrust the two tools through the water, the current resisting her efforts as they slid up the base of the pipe. She turned each until she felt them grip the lip on the other end, and without bothering to take another breath, began pulling herself through. The torrent shook her body, whipping her blonde hair back, roaring in her ears. She could feel the tube and her purse fluttering on her back, trying to rip free.

Within seconds she was through, and she quickly moved to the side, surfacing, holding tight to the garden tools. She filled her lungs in thanks as her ears filled with the crashing sound of a waterfall. The room glowed with a dim orange light from Michael's fading glow sticks.

The anteroom of the cistern was a world of watery chaos. Where on the other side of the wall she had faced a strong current, what she saw now was nothing short of a tsunami coming from the wall on the other side of the room. Water exploded upward as it flowed in under the surface, rocketing up and out ten feet like a geyser. The pressure was nothing short of a violent aquatic war.

KC looked around the smaller anteroom, the water already up to her chin. There was no doubt that if the flow didn't stop, the entire room would be under water by morning.

And then she saw the hole in the side wall. She fought against the waves, made her way to it, and climbed up to the ledge. The three-foot hole was blackened from an explosive breach. She pulled out her flashlight, shone it in to see the altar, and felt the calm of the room as she glanced about at the various religious symbols of peace and hope. Then her eyes fell upon the shattered wall. A pile of colored tiles lay upon the ground. Above them were three holes of varying heights. Whatever had been hidden away was gone. She prayed that it was Michael who had achieved success in here and not Iblis.

"Michael," she called in the chapel, hoping he would answer and they could leave. But there was no response.

"Michael," she called louder.

But again there was no answer. He wasn't in the chapel, he wasn't in the large water-filled anteroom or the main section of the cistern. As she looked out at the water geyser launching out of the pipe beneath the surface, she knew she could never get through there. Even if she could get close, the force of the water would crush her.

She looked again into the chapel . . . and a sense of dread filled her soul. As she turned back and looked at the mayhem of exploding water, she had no doubt where Michael was.

It all came racing in: her fear, her anger, and her rage. At Iblis for doing this to her, at her mother for killing herself, at her father for abandoning them as children, at the world for being so cruel. Without the map, Simon and her sister would surely die, and now because of her, because of who and what she was, she feared the worst for Michael. He was down here for her, selflessly risking his life only to have it . . .

Over the sound of the roaring water, the thundering cascade in front of her, she finally screamed louder than she had ever screamed, a rage-filled cry of frustration, of love lost, of pain and anguish. "Michael!"

IBLIS WALKED OUT of Topkapi, his cell phone pressed to his ear as he reported suspicious activity at the palace to the local police. He headed straight to his car and, as he drove off, he checked his rearview mirror. The tall blond American who had followed him around earlier in the evening still sat in his limo, oblivious to what had just slipped through his fingers. Iblis drove up the street and around to the rear of Hagia Sophia and parked.

He opened the tube and poured the chart out onto the seat. He stared at the tanned gazelle skin, amazed at the intricacies, at the level of detail: the deep reds and browns, the finely sketched mountains and oceans. Pictures of animals upon the lands, ships upon the waters. Islands and atolls, coral reefs and rocky shorelines, all depicted with a stunning level of complexity from a time before theodolites, GPS, satellites, and cameras, two hundred years before John Harrison established accurate longitudinal measurement.

Like the first half of the Piri Reis map, the one depicting the Antarctic landmass, under a mile's worth of ice, that had not been mapped until the late 1950s, this chart held secrets, too—far greater secrets.

The handwriting was intricate, from an educated hand, descriptive and concise. And as Iblis read the Turkish words written five hundred years earlier, it all made sense. Iblis understood what the chart pointed to and why the grand vizier, Sokollu Mehmet, chose to hide it away from the world. This was not just a sea chart, it was truly a land map, a depiction of the world drawn from many sources, pointing to objects and places that were of great controversy in his time, concise directions to things that were not meant for the common man to know, secrets that were meant only for sultans, kings, and gods. Iblis realized why Philippe Venue wished to possess it and all that it led to. It wasn't just some treasure, some prize to be won. It was a place of legend, a mystery sought by rulers, kings, and despots for millennia.

The chart that Iblis held in his hand led to a world lost in the hazelike tendrils of forgotten myth.

MICHAEL HIT BOTTOM, the grate, handcuffed to his wrist, leading the way, dragging him to a watery death. And as soon as he touched down, his body was caught in a current, a riptide that violently snagged his body, pulling him feet-first toward the pipe at the base of the wall. But he stopped short of going through, his wrist still locked to the grate, to a virtual anchor. His body was tossed to and fro, vibrating up and down with the flow of the water, the violent surge flowing around him, seeking to escape under enormous pressure. His neoprene dive bag of tools pounded against his hip like a bag of stones. Michael struggled to see, but his vision was met with nothing but foam and bubbles whipping by him out of the well.

It had only been five seconds, but his lungs were already burning. Between the struggle above and the struggle below, Michael knew he had less than thirty seconds before his air ran out, before he involuntarily gasped and flooded his lungs with death.

Michael reached for his belt, thankfully finding the screwdriver, and clutched it tightly in his right hand. He pulled it from its holster and reached up toward the handcuffs. He closed his visionless eyes and tried to imagine the dexterous maneuver he had performed so many times in daylight without the encumbrances of water and pressure, of sightlessness and currents. Michael's chest was on fire, his wrist bloodied and numb; desperation was taking over as he struggled to keep his hand calm and accurate.

He quickly guided the thin blade up his arm to his wrist and jammed the screwdriver in the edge of the cuff's arm slot, only to miss, the screwdriver's blade digging into his palm. Michael focused, ignoring the raging current, ignoring the pain in his hand, within his lungs. He focused his mind and thought of nothing but the lock. He tried again, slowly, like threading a needle, and this time the slim blade slid in, pressing the catch away from the teeth, releasing his wrist.

And with the grate no longer attached, with his body free of the anchor, Michael was violently sucked into the tube with the ever-escaping raging waters.

He was banged against the walls of the forty-foot-long pipe, his head and body careening off the sides before he was finally squirted out into the pool of the cistern's anteroom. Michael broke the surface, his mouth wide as he gulped the misty air. He gasped as the adrenaline shakes took over, quavering his hands, chilling him, as the blood slowly returned to his skin.

Michael floated on his back, his eyes closed, regaining composure, his mind clearing, though the pain throughout his body fought to distract him. Iblis had gotten the better of him. Michael hated himself for thinking he was in competition with the guy, that it was a race to get to the chart, when all the while Iblis had been waiting for Michael to do the heavy lifting, and then simply snatched it from Michael's hands.

He didn't know what he would tell KC, but he had time. With the access to the harem flooded, his ropes cut away, he would have to find another way out. At least she was safe, he hoped; he imagined she was already out of harm's way in the safety of Busch's protection.

Michael finally opened his eyes, looking around, surprised that his glow sticks still carried light. As much as he wanted to get out, he was glad to see the room; it meant that he was still alive.

And then he heard a sound, echoing off the walls, slogging toward him. Michael sprang to his feet in the neck-deep water and came face to face with KC.

Both were soaked; exhaustion filled their faces.

"You okay?" KC whispered, her voice beyond tired.

"Yeah." Michael nodded.

They stared uncomfortably at each other as a host of emotions ran through their eyes. Both beaten and fatigued, neither reached for the other, the lack of physical contact magnifying the uncomfortable air. The silent moment dragging on until Michael finally snapped back.

"What the hell are you doing down here?" Michael tried to contain his confusion. "You're supposed to be with Busch."

"I came to help you," KC said.

"I don't need help." His words were as much a challenge as a rebuttal.

"Really?" KC said in disbelief, lost for words as she looked at Michael's battered and soaked body.

"I was doing just fine before you got here."

"Yeah," she said facetiously.

"Did you get the rod?" Michael asked.

KC turned and removed the tube strapped to her back, holding it out as a prize. "Did you find the map?" KC fired back.

"Yeah . . ." Michael began to say, but didn't continue.

"In there?" KC pointed at the broken wall leading to the chapel.

Michael nodded.

"Well . . ." she looked at Michael's body, seeing no evidence of the chart.

"Well . . ." Michael said defensively as he unconsciously ran his hand over the neoprene bag at his hip.

KC's eyes grew stern. "Iblis?"

"Don't worry."

"Don't worry?" KC turned her back on Michael and looked at the lost world around them, the water rushing in from the pipe, stirring up a frenzy. "How the hell are we going to get my sister back now that he knows we tried to steal the chart?"

"Relax—"

"Don't tell me to relax," KC said, her back still turned.

"Iblis may have the chart, but what he really needs"— Michael pointed at KC's leather tube as he lowered his voice to a calming tone—"is in your hand. He won't risk your not turning it over. Cindy and Simon are fine as long as you hold on to that."

KC stood there without acknowledging Michael, looking at the leather tube in her hand that held her sister's and Simon's fate.

"First things first," Michael continued, trying to keep them on track. "We've got to get topside."

KC turned back toward Michael. "I've got that covered."

"Oh, really?" Michael tried to temper his skepticism with a smile.

"Really," KC said, as if that were obvious. "I'll have us out of here in no time."

Michael grinned as they resumed the silent stare that they had greeted each other with.

"Of course," Michael finally said as he turned away in disbelief and headed to the far wall and the exit pipe. Without another word, and half ignoring KC, he floated on his back, the current carrying him toward the five-foot tube that was now acting as a drain.

KC restrapped the leather tube to her back and followed, trying to contain her anger.

As Michael approached the pipe, he took a deep breath and went under, quickly getting sucked through the tube feet-first, his hands held out, deflecting him from hitting the sides. He was spat out, ejected into the main cistern. The world was pitch black; no glow sticks left glowing in here. Michael reached into his bag and pulled out his flashlight, its beam exploding off the walls as he flicked it on. He turned around, shining the light in the direction of the wall to see KC come rocketing out like a log from a flume, rubbing the water and her blonde hair from her face as she surfaced. Michael couldn't help smiling, thinking of her love of extreme sports, wondering if this qualified.

She stood and pulled out her flashlight, flipping it on, and saw his smile.

"What?" KC spat out. There was no question his smile pissed her off.

"Nothing," Michael said in amusement. He and KC began sloshing through the shoulder-deep water in the cistern, both shivering in the chilled waters.

"You know, before we walk out the front gate," Michael said without stopping or even turning to KC, "we need to actually get out of here."

There was no response from KC as they continued.

Michael finally stopped and turned around, facing her.

"What?" KC said, exhausted by the verbal sparring.

Michael's body language asked the question.

Without a word KC shone her light up and down along the hose that ran from the water and disappeared into the ceiling.

"Okay, well, halfway home." Michael nodded in surrender and smiled.

BUSCH SAT IN the limo, apprehensive. The last of the VIP partygoers had long since moved inside, the paparazzi departed to get a drink and regroup so they would be energized and lying in wait for the inevitable drunken stumble of the society ne'er-do-wells.

The world had seemed to calm a bit, a hush falling over the ancient section of the city as the buzz and revelry of the party disappeared behind the walls of Topkapi, when suddenly a host of police cars came careening in, skidding to a stop at the entrance. Eight cars disgorged a team of thirty cops, guns drawn, moving in various directions but with total purpose. Teams of four ran east and west along the perimeter as four teams ran into the palace grounds.

Busch's heart pounded in his chest. He knew they could be there for only one reason.

MICHAEL AROSE OUT of the hole, climbing hand over hand up the rubber hose. He crested the lip and rolled onto his back, catching his breath. He cast his eyes up and behind him to see KC crouched in the shadow of the backhoe, quietly staring at him.

"Don't tell me that wiped you out . . ." KC whispered, her words half-serious.

"Don't start." Michael hopped to his feet and looked about the darkened courtyard. The party noise—music sounding a lot like U2 competing with the idle chatter and laughter—washed over the Gates of Felicity, which acted as a partition between the second and third courtyards. This was one of the true inner sanctums of the sultan and his family back during the height of the Ottoman Empire, a sanctuary seen only by the sultan's family and most trusted associates. To their left were the Treasury and the Costume Museum, with the white marble Library of Ahmet III in front of them. The two guards still stood within the Gates of Felicity, their backs to the third courtyard, unaware of the thieves seventy yards behind them.

As Michael and KC scanned the grounds, listening, feeling the air, they found there were no other guards or cops, but they both knew that wouldn't last.

"So," KC whispered as she headed toward the northeast marble wall where a large black iron door sat at the end of a walkway. She looked over her shoulder at Michael. "Time's ticking."

"Where're you going?" Michael pointed at the wall behind them. "We go over the wall out the back."

"We go through the harem," KC retorted.

"We'll get lost in the harem."

"We'll get caught going over the wall. Even if we get over and make it to the streets, look at us. If some cop sees us, we're done."

Michael looked down and couldn't argue: The two of them were a waterlogged mess. "And I suppose there is a change of clothes inside the harem?"

KC tilted her head and smiled.

With sudden agreement, Michael walked past KC along the cobblestone path toward the iron door.

Without missing a step, KC reached into her bag, withdrew a leather billfold, and opened it up.

"Nice," Michael said as he looked over her shoulder at a set of thin angled black tools, each no longer than a pencil. "Custom?"

KC nodded. Her lockpicking tools were twelve years old and, ironically, had been a gift from Iblis—not that she would acknowledge that fact. They arrived at the large black door; Michael bent and already had a pick in the door lock. "I make mine myself."

KC shook her head as she put the billfold back in her purse.

Michael briefly stopped, unsealed his black dive bag, reached in, pulled out two rectangular slabs the size of a pocketknife, and passed them to KC. Without a word, and as if they had practiced, she leaned her ear to the door and ran the two magnets along the top of the jamb, stopping as she heard a slight click and releasing the first magnet with a pop as it adhered to the metal frame. She continued tracing the door, running the second magnet down the side of the jamb until she heard the second sensor of the alarm react. She released the magnet to the jamb, its attractive properties holding back the alarm contact on the other side. It was one of the simplest of feats: a fifty-cent magnet overriding a thousand-dollar contact switch.

Michael turned back to the door and, with a dexterous hand, pushed the small internal pins of the cylinder's mechanics back, releasing the lock, and opened the door.

The two slipped into a darkened hallway. To their right were the apartments and the Courtyard of Favorites, those who held the sultan's interest above all, some of whom bore sons and would go on to become his wives.

As Michael and KC headed deeper into the harem of the palace, they found themselves in a virtual Ottoman labyrinth; countless hallways, hundreds of rooms. None of the arched halls looked familiar from their tour the previous day.

They passed the Imperial Hall, the maroon, blue, and gold banded space where the sultan sat upon his throne and watched all forms of entertainment, be it readers of verse, European actors, Far Eastern magicians, Eastern minstrels, Indian snake charmers, or African magistrates with lions, zebras, and other exotic animals.

Michael and KC raced past stairs, along blue-tiled hallways, past columned arches of white and maroon marble, none of which had been on the tour schedule. They picked up speed as they ran through the columned Courtyard of the Black Eunuchs and finally arrived at an open hallway whose small windows looked out upon the palace grounds and the evening's party.

They both looked out at the large reception.

"We can't go out there looking like this," Michael said, alluding to their wet condition.

KC scooted around the corner and pulled her blue dress from her bag. Mercifully, it had stayed dry in the watertight seal of her bag, but the wrinkles were another matter. She smoothed them out as best she could and slipped it on. She brushed out her long blonde hair, tied it back, and slipped on her Prada heels. In a matter of moments she transformed herself from tomboy back to model. She hoped the wrinkles were not as obvious in the nighttime lighting and that the crowd was on their third drink, with fading vision.

Michael couldn't help his heart skipping a beat as he saw her.

KC handed Michael her purse and the leather tube containing the sultan's rod.

"Where are you going?"

"To get you a suit."

KC slid through the harem door and stepped into the

shadows of the Divan, the overhang and large columns serving to blot out the party lights, masking her entrance from the restricted door. She walked out from under the arch, carrying herself with confidence, and mingled with the crowd. The party was huge: 750 strong. A large dais and greeting area was set in front of the Gates of Felicity just as it was five hundred years ago when the sultan would sit upon his throne greeting the masses. A bandstand was set off to the side by the kitchens, while a large tent covered over one hundred tables, all bedecked in white linens and fresh blue irises. Large royal blue bags sat on each table, filled with party favors and donated marketing gifts. KC casually walked to the tent and picked up one; she didn't know what the canvas bag contained, but thought its contents might come in handy.

She turned and stared at the crowd: the power elite, easily spotted by their barely out-of-teenhood arm charms; the Armani-suited businessmen of all nationalities working the crowds, seeking deals, financing, or companionship while the politicians pressed flesh and wore never-diminishing smiles. It actually made her skin crawl as she looked around, wondering if anyone remembered what this party was about, wondering if anyone actually understood what a milestone it was for a predominantly Islamic country to be joining the European Union, an organization of predominantly Christian countries. It was truly a bridge between two worlds.

She looked toward the main gate and saw two policemen talking with the guards. As she scanned the grounds, she spotted more guards and cops paired up, milling about.

And then KC could feel the eyes upon her: not the guards, not the cops. He stood among a group of middle-aged men, all with drinks in hand, leering like panthers in the bush waiting to pounce.

KC slowly turned and caught the man's eye. He was perfect, five-eleven, broad-shouldered, impeccably dressed in a dark Zegna suit. The Hermès tie matched perfectly with his European Union blue pocket square. She judged his shoe size at around an eleven. She couldn't be sure, but hoped they weren't too small. She glanced at his face and smiled before demurely averting her eyes. It was her favorite baited trap, one that worked easily on men: Show even the slightest bit of interest and they think that you want to take them right there on the spot, never imagining any other intention.

The man disengaged from his friends and headed her way, grabbing two flutes of champagne from a passing waiter. His hair was black as night, his brown eyes hidden under heavy, dark lids. He looked more terrorist than businessman in his elegantly expensive attire, but she knew better than most that the clothes people wrap themselves in can't hide one's true heart for long.

The man smiled on approach and handed her the glass.

"Good evening."

KC smiled in response.

"Jean Frank Gittere," he introduced himself as he chinked their glasses.

"Katherine," KC said, shielding her eyes.

"Are you here alone?"

KC nodded.

"What a coincidence."

KC couldn't help glancing at the wedding band on his finger.

"Have you eaten?" Jean Frank asked.

"Too much, I'm afraid. I'll need to run extra far tomorrow." KC softly ran her hand over her head, her movements slow, seductive.

Jean Frank smiled, entranced. He finally looked toward the band that was just starting another set. People rose from their chairs, converging on the dance floor. "May I ask you to dance?"

"Thank you." KC smiled. "But no. I'm a terrible dancer, I don't want you to get the wrong impression of me. Perhaps a walk?"

Jean Frank smiled in triumph as he pointed out his elbow. KC took it and they headed toward the Divan.

"Why are you here this evening?" KC asked.

"My company works closely with all of the member states; we're a large contributor to this evening's festivities."

"What do you do?" KC feigned interest. They continued, slowly walking arm in arm under the overhang of the Divan, the shadows concealing his eyes as he glanced at KC's low-cut dress. They finally stopped right in front of the entrance to the harem.

"Import-export."

"Goods or people?" KC joked. She stopped and turned to him, looking up into his eyes, extending an invitation.

"Wine, actually," he stuttered briefly, lost in her eyes. "Only the finest."

"I love wine," KC said softly, causing him to lean in to hear her.

"And you?" he whispered back. "What brings you here?"

"I'm here for my sister," KC said in all honesty.

Jean Frank never got the chance to ask about her sister, as Michael grabbed him from behind, his forearm wrapping around his throat, cutting off the air and the blood flow to his brain. Michael dragged him through the open door into the harem, kicking and clawing, reaching back toward Michael to no avail. He was unconscious in less than ten seconds.

Michael dragged him toward a window and made sure the coast was clear.

"You love wine?" Michael said as KC closed the door.

"Give me a break, I caught him, didn't I?"

"You looked like you were enjoying yourself," Michael said, half in jest, half out of jealousy.

"Maybe I was." KC leaned down and unlaced the man's shoes.

Michael stripped Jean Frank of his clothes and quickly put them on. He dressed the unconscious man in his wet clothes and used his belt and KC's wet shirt to truss him up.

"He'll have some explaining to do to his wife." KC turned to Michael, seeing him looking out onto the party.

"There are a lot of cops," Michael said to himself. "What's in the bag of tricks?"

KC dumped out the blue canvas party favor bag finding magazines, perfume, posters.

"I meant your other bag," Michael said, pointing at KC's purse on the ground.

"Besides makeup? A knife, cell phone, flashlight—not much in the help department. You?"

Michael opened his neoprene dive bag. "Detonation cord, several electronic blasting caps, transmitter, flashlight, my cell phone and radio, hammer and chisel, lost my crowbar and screwdriver in the cauldron of hell, but I still have my knife." Michael looked out at the party.

"With Iblis tipping off the police, everyone's radar is going to be up. We're going to need some major distraction to get out of here."

"Hey." Michael could see the stress in KC's eyes. "We're going to get Cindy and Simon back."

"But Iblis has the chart. What if he forgoes this?" KC held up the tube containing the rod.

"He won't."

"How do you know?"

Michael thought on the letter from Bora Celil, Kemal Reis's trusted captain, of his words of warning and mystery not only about where the chart led but about the rod itself. There was no question they were linked. Venue needed both the chart and the rod to achieve whatever his goal might be. There was no question: Iblis would not leave Istanbul without the rod KC held in her hands.

"I just know," Michael finally said. "And don't worry about the chart, I'll get it back." Michael pointed to the leather tube containing the rod. "You don't let go of that, okay?"

"How are you going to get the chart back?"

"You just have to trust me," Michael said.

"I'm sorry," KC finally said, her face relaxing as she considered his words. "I'm sorry I got you into all this."

"You kidding? What else would I be doing on a Saturday night?"

KC smiled, glad that Michael had a sense of humor in the face of danger.

"Not to put too much pressure on you, but whatever we do, don't let that rod out of your sight."

Michael pulled a strand of detonation cord and cut it into five foot-long pieces. He inserted an electronic blasting cap in each and tucked them into the blue bag.

"Michael, people will get hurt."

"KC," Michael tilted his head. "I'm not going to blow anyone up. Have a little faith."

Michael checked the knife that was strapped to his ankle, assuring himself of its presence. He straightened his tie and checked the pockets, finding a wallet. He pulled it out and tossed it on the man's unconscious form. Michael pulled out the small detonation transmitter from his bag, checked the kill and safety switches, and slipped it into his front pocket.

He opened his neoprene bag and took out his cell phone and the radio, tucking them into his pocket. He grabbed the spare blasting caps, hammer, and chisel, laying them on the floor next to the unconscious Jean Frank, and strung the black dive satchel over the man's shoulder.

KC picked up the blue canvas bag and put the leather tube containing the rod inside; though it protruded, it wouldn't attract the attention it would if it were to ride against her backless dress. She held the blue bag open to Michael, who picked up the magazines and posters and laid them atop their illicit party favors, the bag looking pretty typical for someone who was leaving a function. KC threw her purse over her shoulder, turned, and smiled.

Michael opened the harem door, allowing the music to flow in. He turned back to KC and held out his hand. "Would you like to dance?"

Busch sat in the limo, waiting. He always felt as if he was waiting. Waiting for Michael, waiting for his wife, Jeannie, waiting for his kids. And usually he didn't mind the wait. But since he couldn't get the Yankees–Red Sox game on the radio—he couldn't find any sports radio here in Istanbul, for that matter—his waiting became interminable. Michael went into Topkapi, Iblis went in, KC went in, and he had no idea what was going on. And now the police had poured into the party, no doubt in search of his friends.

His cell phone rang and he quickly answered. "It's about time."

"Good to hear your voice, too," Michael said.

"Do you mind telling me what you're doing?"

"We're dancing."

"Dancing?" Busch yelled. "You've got to be kidding me."

"Listen, we're coming out in a few minutes along with seven hundred of our closest friends. Pop open the trunk so we can spot you."

"Shit, you're not going to cause a problem, are you?"

"You know me better than that. But look," Michael said, "if you see some cops on our tail, just ignore us, and get the hell out."

"That makes me feel so good," Busch said. "Need I remind you that I was once chasing people like you as opposed to running with people like you?"

"Paul . . . ?"

"I'm not leaving you," Busch said defiantly.

"And you're not joining us in jail, either."

CHAPTER 28

The evening was winding down; the band, with loosened ties and unbuttoned shirts, was in its third set. The early birds were beginning their good-byes with kisses and feigned laughter. The night had gone off without incident. And while the police had come in with reports of a possible robbery, the suspicions were not confirmed. The Treasury had been checked, the exhibition of miniatures and manuscripts inspected. Everything of value was accounted for. The police had begun to suspect that the call had come from a disgruntled employee looking to disrupt one of Turkey's finest moments. Well, that didn't happen; the night was a true success.

The guards had begun to relax; while posts were still manned, food and nonalcoholic drink was being passed around. All shared in the celebration of a new era, an era that had begun on an evening of secure merriment.

Michael and KC danced under an enormous blue tent. It housed the ten-piece band that played upon a riser, a sea of tables for dining, and a long wooden dance floor that was filled with the nostalgic, inebriated, and horny, each with a different goal for the evening's outcome.

Michael led KC toward the central tent pole, which

climbed thirty feet up, supporting the center of the canvas like a circus tent. Four inches in diameter, it looked like a small white tree, ringed in small potted tulips and wildflowers.

Michael reached into the blue bag that hung from KC's shoulder and palmed a small piece of detonation cord. He crouched, feigning tying his shoe, and as KC stood cover, he quickly looped the cord about the base of the pole where, behind the potted plants, it was obstructed from common view.

Michael stood, kissed KC, took her by the hand, and led her toward the bar, looking every bit like a married couple.

The bar was under a second tent set off to the side. More than half the bottles were empty, hardly any ice remained, and but for a single elderly gentleman, no one was there but the bartender. KC bellied up and ordered herself a Diet Coke, engaging both men in conversation as Michael stepped to the side toward a white tent pole along the perimeter. He held the blue gift bag and placed it on the ground, masking his quickly placed explosive.

Michael returned to the bar, smiled at the elderly man, and took KC by the arm. They walked about the festivities, their heads turning, looking, getting the layout of the party grounds memorized. Working their way around the open, grassy courtyard, they placed the small explosive charges in strategic locations. No one paid Michael any mind as he tucked the three remaining pieces of detonation cord in unobtrusive, out-of-the-way spots. KC was the perfect distraction, all eyes drawn to her beauty as they ignored her escort, who seemed to busy himself with his shoes and bags.

While KC was the perfect distraction, she was also impossible to miss. Yasim, the head guard whom she had confronted when she forced her way into the party, caught her eye. KC tried to avert her glance but it was too late.

The officer approached them, carrying a can of soda and a piece of cake. He wore a disarming smile, much different from his stern appearance when she had arrived. "Hello again."

"Hello," KC said, taking hold of Michael's hand as she hoisted the blue bag onto her shoulder.

"Your presentation went smoothly, I trust?"

"Very well." KC nodded and smiled.

"I'm glad." Yasim took a bite of cake as one of his guards arrived at his side. Yasim nodded to KC. "Enjoy your evening."

But as he turned to leave, his eyes caught the tube protruding from KC's blue bag. He stopped and turned back. "They did not wish to keep its container?"

"No." KC smiled her usual disarming smile. "It was just used to transport it."

Yasim's cordial demeanor dissolved. "Do you mind opening it?"

KC tilted her head to the side in question.

"I'm sorry, but we received a report of a robbery, yet we have found nothing stolen. I'm sure you understand." Yasim turned his eyes to Michael. "I don't recall you coming in."

Michael laughed as he looked around at the enormous crowd. "You remember 750 people?"

Yasim remained silent as he placed his cake and soda on an adjacent table.

"I arrived at eight-thirty," Michael said defensively. "Michael Paulson, guest of Tram Industries."

"Of course." Yasim nodded. "You won't mind me seeing your ID, then, Mr. Paulson." He turned back to KC and pointed at the tube. "May I?"

Yasim removed his radio from his belt.

Two police in the distance took note of Yasim's body language as he picked up his radio and began to wander over, their pace growing swifter the closer they got.

Michael feigned exasperation as he glanced at KC. She looked at him with a soft smile, no sense of danger or fear behind her eyes as she crouched to the blue bag and wrapped her hand about the leather tube.

The two policemen arrived, their hands on their holstered pistols. They spoke in a quick burst of Turkish to Yasim, who responded while pointing at Michael.

"Sir," the lead policeman said, "he really needs to see your identification."

"Of course." Michael smiled as he tucked his hand in his pocket and wrapped his fingers around the detonation transmitter.

And time seemed to slow.

KC slowly rose from her crouched position, the tube containing the rod in her hand. Her cleavage pulled the focus of the two policemen. Yasim was speaking into his radio; Michael couldn't deny he was a man with a well-tuned intuition. The crowd noise fell away; Michael could no longer hear the band's rendition of "We are Family." His peripheral vision took in his surroundings: who was to his left, his right, where the openings were, where the other milling guards and police meandered.

From within his pocket, Michael thumbed back the safety on the transmitter. He looked at KC, who had risen to her full height. And as if on cue, they smiled at each other.

Real time caught up and Michael hit the switch.

* * *

THE FIVE CHARGES exploded simultaneously, tearing apart the night. The three central tent poles disintegrated, the enormous blue tent collapsing upon the band, the dining tables, and the dance floor of inebriated VIPs, billowing out heaps of air as it buckled.

The tent above the bar fell on the bartender. The ice sculpture exploded in a shower of snow and mist.

Mayhem infected the crowd of 750, all reacting as one and charging for the gates. Shouts and screams filled the air as confusion reigned. There was no longer a stratification of the attendees; be they royalty, celebrity, elected official, or waiter, they were all united by the most basic of instincts as they fled to safety.

The guards at the gate were well trained. At the sight of the charging crowd they pulled back the tables and chairs, the security scanners and barriers, leaving the single exit unencumbered. Their shouts for calm were unheeded by those fearing death.

All charged, pushed, and shoved as the masses squeezed out the Gate of Salutation and raced across the wide-open Courtyard of Janissaries toward the Imperial Gate and out to freedom. Some fell, some were trampled only to be picked up by a heroic stranger or guard who had presence of mind in a crisis.

Yasim, his partner, and the two police jumped at the explosion, instinctively ducking and covering their heads, their attention drawn to the collapsing tents and screams. Confusion ruled the moment as clouds of smoke curled up into the night sky. But as Yasim looked about, he saw no bodies, he saw no death; this attack was not an attack at all, it was a deception, an extreme distraction to draw everyone's focus away from reality.

And when Yasim finally got his bearings, he realized the deception had worked perfectly. Michael and KC were gone.

AT THE MOMENT of the explosion, Michael and KC were already in a full-out sprint at the lead of the mass. And as the crowd's shocked reaction abated, the throng grew into a full-on stampede behind them.

KC and Michael raced through the Gate of Salutation, a sea of people around and behind them, and headed across the open ground toward the Imperial Gate, their longed-for exit to freedom. But they both saw them at the same time, a phalanx of guards and police at least twenty-five strong who had raced in at the sound of the explosion. Their startled looks at the wave of people heading for them quickly shifted to an attitude of command.

Guards and police were on their radios, nodding, and then suddenly looking, scanning the crowd. Several began shouting to one another and abruptly pointed at KC, who was impossible to miss at five-foot-ten, with long blonde hair, in a blue gown.

Seeing the guards focus upon them, Michael cut right, heading for the far wall.

"I hate these things," KC said as she kicked off her heels and broke into a barefoot dash along the wide-open lawn.

Michael grabbed the leather tube from KC's clutched fist, threw it over his back . . . and they doubled their speed.

The police and guards tried to fight their way through the charging mass of panicked partygoers. Some were knocked aside, some couldn't get a foot forward, but five managed to pierce the crowd and ran after the two thieves.

Michael and KC made the far wall, leaping upon it and scaling the fifteen-foot façade like animals fleeing a flood.

They flipped over the parapet, landing on the flat, graveled roof of the Archaeology Museum.

"Well, that was smart," KC mocked Michael as she dug her flats out of her bag and put them on.

And as they looked back down on the Courtyard of Janissaries, they saw the five guards charging their way, guns drawn, anger filling their faces.

And without warning, the bullets erupted.

Busch stood next to the limo, his trunk open, his emergency flashers glowing as a beacon to Michael and KC. Busch had heard the explosion, and though it startled him, it held no surprise. When it came to Michael, at some point there were bound to be explosions. Though Michael preached disdain for guns and firearms, he was not prejudiced against bombs. Michael had a habit of blowing things up. He would never intentionally put someone in harm's way, but if he could use an explosive charge to accomplish his goal he never seemed to hesitate.

Busch watched as the swarms of elegantly dressed people poured out of the Imperial Gate, flooding the streets and sidewalks. Car horns blared at the human gridlock as the panicked voices screamed and cried in relief at their survival.

Busch scanned the multitude of partygoers but saw no sign of Michael or KC. He picked up his radio and clicked the Talk button but got no response. He pulled out his cell and quickly dialed Michael, but there was no answer.

For three minutes he watched the crowd pour from the entrance, but Busch knew Michael wasn't coming out. It wasn't instinct that told him, it wasn't a voice inside his head, it was experience. Michael never did anything the easy way.

The traffic was backing up fast; cars filled the streets with nowhere to go, and the scene was dissolving into utter chaos that would take hours to disperse.

Busch slammed down the trunk lid, hopped into the driver's seat, turned the key, hung a quick U-turn, much to the consternation of the other drivers, and headed east. He wasn't sure where he was going, but when Michael called in a panic—there was no doubt that he would—Busch needed to be ready, he needed to be able to get to him as quickly as possible.

MICHAEL AND KC raced across the two-hundred-foot-long rooftop of the Archaeology Museum, hell bent for leather. Michael was amazed at her speed; she kept up with him stride for stride as if floating above the surface.

The gunfire continued, bullets skipping along the gravel, ricocheting off the bulkheads and parapets. Three of their pursuers had made it onto the roof and were chasing them.

"They're shooting at us!" KC yelled.

"Really?" Michael yelled back sarcastically.

"Why would cops be shooting at us? They don't even know if we did anything."

"They're not cops. They're the guards hired to protect the palace, and they failed. They think we not only stole something but blew up their heritage. We may even be terrorists in their eyes. They're pissed."

"Is there anyone *not* after us?" KC said through staccato breaths.

They both saw it at the same time, up ahead, the end of their proverbial road. The roof ended.

"It's ten feet; you can jump ten feet, right?" Michael asked.

"How do you know it's ten feet?"

"Can you make the jump or not?"

KC ran harder.

As they arrived at the parapet, neither slowed; both, in fact, picked up speed. Without breaking stride, they hit the parapet and leaped out into the nighttime air. They sailed across the ten-foot alley, neither looking down as they flew across the gap and landed upon the tarmac and gravel roof of the Kreshien Heritage Building. They shoulder-rolled and came up in a run, ignoring the small sharp pebbles embedded in their backs.

Their pursuers were ten seconds behind when they stopped at the edge and had to restart their jump, losing precious time.

In seconds, Michael and KC were halfway across the rooftop of the Kreshien Building. "Next one's eight feet, can you make it?"

"Just shut up," KC said.

They hit the next parapet and flew across the eight-foot gap, this time both landing on their feet. The small flower shop building was actually half a story lower than the Kreshien. They cut across the small store's rooftop and stopped at the edge, looking down onto an awning. Michael slipped over the side, rolled down the awning, and jumped the eight feet to the concrete sidewalk. KC landed beside him two seconds later. The gunshots stopped; there was no sound of anyone running along the rooftops, no sound of anyone chasing them.

They were in a residential neighborhood of cobblestone streets and small, stuccoed houses. Built up over the last three years, it had become a haven for the young Turkish professionals who longed to recapture some heritage living in the Sultanahmet district as in the days of the great Ottoman Empire.

"We need a car," Michael said as they raced up the sidewalk. The street was lined with them, both sides. BMWs, Fiats, Audis—but Michael ignored them all, keeping his pace until he spotted his mark: an '88 Buick, the blue car's exterior clean, the wheels new.

Michael smashed the driver's-side window; the alarm screamed in protest at him as he reached in, lifted the lock, and opened the door. KC jumped in the passenger side, closing the door behind her. The interior space offered no solace, the blaring alarm only acting as a beacon to their pursuers, who would be upon them any minute. Her hand began nervously tapping the armrest, her head spinning about.

And then she saw them, the five guards, a block away, their eyes drawn toward the car alarm. Michael tossed KC the leather tube with the rod, momentarily distracting her from her nerves.

Michael dug under the dashboard with his left hand while his right grabbed the knife from the sheath strapped to his ankle. In a fluid motion, his hands came together, a fistful of wires in one hand, the razor-sharp blade in the other. In a second-nature move, Michael quickly found and spliced the ignition wires. The car roared to life and the alarm suddenly stopped.

The guards were only fifty yards away, their guns once again drawn as they shouted Turkish commands.

Ignoring them, Michael slammed the door, threw the car into gear, and dove out into traffic. The wheels spun as they fought to grip the roadway. Cars bobbed and weaved around him as they lay on their horns.

"You couldn't pick out a newer car?" KC said as she looked over her shoulder out the back window. Their pursuers were hauling out radios, shouting God knows what commands into them.

"Most cars after '95 have ignition kill switches attached to their alarms; they're dead before you even go near the wires."

Three cop cars came squealing around the corner, fishtailing out, the large engines of the French-made Peugeots muscling the cars forward. Michael punched the accelerator, downshifting the automatic transmission of the Buick, and drove as fast as he could.

"Do you have any idea where you're going?" KC yelled. The police were closing in, and fear filled her eyes. She had never been on the run like this; capture meant her sister's death, Simon's death. She gripped the satchel tighter.

Michael said nothing as he pulled out his cell phone, blindly opening it and hitting the speed dial. He flipped the speakerphone button on the Motorola, and the cell shouted out for a half ring before Busch answered. "What the hell—"

"No time. Three cops on my tail. Heading up . . ." Michael paused as he floored the car and whizzed past a street sign. "I'm on Atmeydani, the main drag in front of the Blue Mosque. You gotta talk me out of here."

There was silence on the other end. "Paul?" Michael shouted.

"Two seconds, I'm waiting on the GPS."

"We don't have two seconds—"

"Make a right on Ozbekler, then a quick right on Katip Sinin."

Michael spun the wheel, barely making the turn.

"How far back?" Busch yelled over the phone.

"Less than a block," KC said, grabbing the phone from Michael.

"What are you driving?"

"Blue Buick, blowing every light and stop sign; we're pretty hard to miss."

"After Katip, go two blocks and hang a hard left onto Piyerloti, then a quick right onto Pertev. The street's about as narrow as they come. Whatever you do, don't slow down."

KC looked back; the lead car was closing. "Turn right—"

But Michael was already turning, the wheels spinning, fighting to hold the road as they left streaks of rubber upon the pavement.

"Paul, you want to tell me what you're doing?" Michael shouted.

"Buying you time. I've got no solution but I can help you get a bigger head start on whoever is trying to crawl up your ass."

Michael spun the wheel left onto Piyerloti and quickly right onto Pertev. It was barely wider than the car, the walls whipping by, the air whooshing through the broken driver's-side window. And the cop cars never broke formation. They were like a linear herd of horses, never straying from their path.

Michael accelerated through the intersection; he caught a glimpse of a black car flying up perpendicular to them, nearly plowing into him.

And then there was sudden screech. KC turned back to see the dark limo pull across the intersection, blocking the narrow street. The cop cars locked up their brakes, wheels smoking and crying as they all came to a sudden stop.

Michael rammed the accelerator as he bolted out onto the main thoroughfare.

As KC looked back, she could see Busch and the cops erupt out of their cars, arms flying in anger, body language screaming.

Michael drove for eight more blocks before he spotted a group of teens, their swagger and looks not conveying innocence. Michael slammed on the brakes.

"What the hell are you doing?" KC shouted.

"Let's go." Michael jumped from the car, not waiting for an answer.

"Hey," Michael shouted. The five teens turned, their piss-and-vinegar attitudes looking for a fight. The lead punk walked toward Michael. Michael held his hand out toward the car in offering. "Have fun."

The teens looked at each other, confused, spinning about as if this was some sort of trap. But before anyone could protest, they hopped into the running car and took off.

Michael charged up the road, nearing a full-on run.

"What the hell did you do that for?" KC asked as she fell in stride beside him, the leather tube banging against her back.

Multiple sirens screamed out in the night; the three cop cars, their flashing lights lighting up the rough neighborhood, flew after the '88 Buick. The sirens seemed to be coming from all directions now. In front, behind . . . others were joining the chase.

KC's mind was on overdrive. Paranoia was slipping in, which scared her, for she knew that once that flowed in her veins she was through: Her mind would fill with supposition, worst-case scenarios that would destroy her focus on getting the job done, on getting out of wherever here was.

Michael never let up. He kept running, looking to his side at KC as if they were out for a jog.

KC ran like she'd never run before. It was not the speed, it was the fear. While she'd always maintained supreme focus, her thefts did not involve lives hanging in the balance. The consequences were always hers and hers alone. But now, she realized, if she fell, if she was caught, it would literally be the death of her sister and Simon. Both lives depended on her and Michael eluding their pursuers.

Michael came to a sudden stop in front of a nondescript white building that sat midway down a cobblestone street. The section of the city was old, but since it had never been upgraded, no one thought of it as historic. The first floor was a run-down butcher shop that sat behind a large-paned glass window with paper signs, Turkish words decreeing hours and specials.

Michael opened a mottled white door set off to the side, ushered KC in, and closed it behind them. Michael led the charge up three flights of narrow stairs, arriving at the top floor to find a long hallway, both ends exposed and wide open to the elements. Michael raced down the hall to the last door on the left, tried the handle, and it opened right up. He held the door open for KC and followed her in, closing and locking the door behind them.

They stood in a dark room, their hearts thundering, the adrenaline still surging through their veins as the scream of the sirens faded to silence. Their eyes slowly adjusted, the city lights filtered through the narrow slatted windows. The room was starkly white: the walls and floors, the furniture and sheets, as if all color had been sucked out of the world. The room lacked any sign of personality, no photos, no pictures on the bare walls. The space was not much larger than a hotel room. The sitting and sleeping areas were one. There was a small kitchenette with a pass-through and an even smaller bathroom. A large balcony sat off the bedroom, facing the Grand Bazaar, offering sweeping views of old Istanbul.

KC raced to the window, which was covered in large wooden shutters; she cracked the slats and looked outside.

"It's okay," Michael said.

KC could not stop panting, her heavy breaths coming not from exertion but fear. "No, they'll find us."

"We're safe," Michael said.

"How do you know?" KC was beginning to shiver, the adrenaline shakes making her voice quiver.

"It's a safe house."

KC turned to him in shock.

". . . safe room, really—I set it up."

"How could you know?" KC said in surprise.

"I get chased a lot. Had a feeling I wouldn't be breaking that habit. I'm full of surprises."

"You're sure?" KC looked through the slats down onto the vacant streets.

Michael nodded.

"You're *sure*?" KC's fear wouldn't abate.

Michael placed his hand on her shoulder, turning her around. "I promise."

"What if someone . . . what if the police check?"

Michael shook his head. "I promise."

And in that moment, with the echo of the words "promise" and "safe," KC felt something grow in her chest. Michael cared for her, was taking care of her, something no one had done since she was a child.

There was never a boyfriend buying flowers or opening doors, no husband leaving presents under the tree at Christmas. No one protecting her, assuring her that life would go on. And the regret poured in, for a life missed, for a life sacrificed for a sister who could die in spite of everything she had done to protect her. KC had no children, no one to share her life with, no one who had loved her for her. She had thought it impossible, inconceivable, as a result of her unconventional career. There was no way to explain what she did for a living to any man, to any suitor, if she was to hope for an honest, permanent relationship. Hers was to be a life denied all such comforts, a sacrifice made out of love, at the highest of prices. But now, a feeling filled her body, overwhelming her, a warmth, an outpouring that was beyond her control. And it all came flooding up.

Michael took KC in his arms, gently pressing her head into his shoulder, rubbing her back as her tears poured forth. All of her anger, all of her sorrow and shame, the frustration and anxiety, was released as she broke down.

She had not cried since the death of her mother. She had been strong from that day forward, had shown that strength for her sister, had assumed that tears were a sign of weakness, shed by too many women on too many mundane occasions. She vowed she would never be that way. She learned to bottle up her feelings, to contain the agony in her heart: When she and her sister were desperate for food, when she feared being caught, when she spent sleepless nights thinking of her sister being taken away, she locked it all in her soul. She feared prison, she feared loss of control. She feared being alone. But it never showed; she met life and the problems it threw at her head-on, with a smile and the answer that she was fine and happy to be breathing.

But now as Michael held her, she could contain it no more. It was too much; her world was crashing down around her.

Despite it all, the peril and jeopardy, the shame and anxiety, all the danger, anger, and harsh words she had thrust upon him, Michael was there. He didn't run, he didn't condemn her. She looked up and became lost in his eyes; she leaned in and he kissed her, softly, with passion. And it was like a key opening her heart, opening her soul to emotions she had buried long ago. She kissed him back, long and hard, and he responded in kind. They held tight to each other, Michael's hand stroking her face, running through her blonde hair, down her back.

And the heat rose: She clawed at Michael, tearing his shirt open. They fell to the floor in the throes of passion, her agony replaced with lust. It was primal, a lust from the soul, pure and innocent, filled with love and compassion, promises and commitments. It was physical, both reaching for release, coaxing it from each other as if in a dance. And in it, their fears washed away, troubles and obstacles disappearing as they were consumed by the moment, as their clothes scattered the floor. They banished all thought of sisters and friends, of assassins and police, all their troubles obliterated by their feelings for each other. Both reached for completion, lost in the tangle of flesh, their entwined hearts carrying them to a place neither had been before. When they had made love for the first and only time five weeks earlier, it was different. It was respectful, filled with love and tenderness. This was beyond that. They urged each other to new heights, as if the heat of the moment would burn all their troubles away and meld them into one.

It was warm and tender, moist and alive, their lips running about each other's body, earnest and uncontrollable.

They finally collapsed, both achieving the physical and emotional release they had denied themselves for too long.

They were as one, finding in each other completion, finding a love that few would ever know.

And after it all, they fell asleep, arms and legs wrapped about each other, their breathing and hearts in perfect synch.

CHAPTER 29

KC drifted upward from her dreams. She couldn't remember them but they were calm, filled with smiles and peace, filled with Michael. She tried to fall back into them, resuming where she left off, but the world began to intrude upon her. She heard the Islamic call to prayer, cried out in singsong voices from the minarets that dotted the Istanbul skyline, and the light of dawn poured in through the slatted windows across her eyelids. KC slowly opened her eyes, acclimating to her surroundings, to the safe room. She looked beside her but Michael was not in the bed; she glanced at the closed bathroom door and smiled.

It was the most restful sleep she had had in months—not that being awake and in peril didn't exhaust her and contribute to her sedation. She had awoken with a new-found confidence; there was no doubt in her mind that they would get Cindy and Simon back. Michael was right; in the rod they held the most important piece of Iblis's puzzle. He wouldn't harm them as long as she held his prize.

KC slowly arose from the bed and walked to the window. Pulling the shutter aside, she glanced down on the streets already in the midst of the early-morning rush, pedestrians walking quickly to their mosques, vendors setting up shop: Istanbul was waking up.

She stepped to the bathroom door and rested her bed-head blonde hair against the jamb. "Good morning," she whispered to the door, smiling as she rubbed the sleep from her eyes.

She crouched and picked up her panties and bra. She couldn't remember the last time she had slept naked, the last time she had felt so free. She had sat on the bed and begun to dress, when she realized there had been no response from the bathroom. There was no sound of water, no shaving or showering. She walked to the bathroom door again. "Michael?" she said louder.

But there was no response. She knocked, quickly, a sense of urgency pervading the three raps. But again, nothing. She tried the handle and, to her surprise, the door opened right up. The bathroom was dry as a bone, unused and unoccupied.

KC spun about and raced for the bed, the fear already upon her as she lifted the dust ruffle. The leather tube with the rod was gone.

CHAPTER 30

Cindy sat on the couch, soda in hand, the TV tuned to FNN. She hadn't slept a wink, her thoughts bouncing between anger and fear all night. She'd showered at 5:00 A.M. Though she'd been wearing the same clothes now for two days, she tried her best to keep up appearances.

Simon lay on the cot; she was unsure if he was unconscious or sleeping: He had mumbled and stirred through the night but had yet to open his eyes. She got up and leaned over him. His wound had grown darker, continuing to swell, and she feared if he didn't get medical attention soon, he might die before her eyes. She looked at the IV bag; it was on a slow drip and whatever it was did not seem to be serving any purpose beyond keeping him hydrated. She spun the bag around, expecting to see a 100 percent saline solution, but was surprised to find something far different.

While the drip was keeping Simon hydrated it contained the sedative Sedine benzodiazepine. Iblis wasn't taking any chance of Simon becoming fully awake. As she looked down upon Simon she wondered how much of his condition was a result of the blow and how much was caused by the medication pouring into his veins.

Cindy heard a subtle spinning sound like a top coming from the vault door. Iblis was coming.

She looked back at Simon; he was in terrible shape but if he were at least awake maybe he could figure a way out of here. Cindy heard the gears of the safe spin toward release.

She quickly grabbed Simon's left arm and lifted the bandage concealing the IV needle. She plucked the thin metal tube out and bent it, impeding the IV flow to a bare minimum.

The whooshing sound at the door continued. Cindy knew she had only seconds.

She lay the bent needle flush against Simon's skin and reaffixed the bandage tight around his arm.

And the large vault door clicked and swung open. Iblis stalked into the room still wearing the black tuxedo pants and shirt but no longer the jacket or tie.

Seeing Cindy standing at Simon's side, he laid the long leather tube he carried on the small card table, walked to Simon's unconscious form, and leaned over him. He briefly looked up through his blue, haunted eyes at Cindy, assessing her as much as Simon.

"He needs to get to a hospital," Cindy said, her eyes alive with fear of being caught.

Iblis checked the half-empty IV bag, flicking the tube with his finger. Ignoring her, he walked to the far wall. He moved aside a picture of a lion taking down a gazelle to reveal a wall safe.

"So cliché." Cindy shook her head. The relief of not being caught emboldened her.

"I'm sure you already found this while I was gone," Iblis finally spoke.

"Not afraid I'm going to break it open?"

"This thing is four inches thick; it can withstand a direct blast, fire, and most definitely you. Besides, even if you got it open, you're not getting out." Iblis pointed to the large vault door. "I'm sure you noticed, there is no handle on the inside."

Iblis spun the dial back and forth until the wall safe opened. "Did you know your sister's boyfriend was a thief?"

"There's a surprise." Cindy dismissed the information. She stared at Iblis as if looking at a stranger. "All those years, I thought you were a friend, I thought you were one of the few people I could trust."

"I never lied to you." Iblis's voice was deep and matter-of-fact. "I never brought you to harm. I treated you and KC like a surrogate family."

"Please, stay away from my heartstrings."

"Honestly, Cindy? I never thought you had any," Iblis shot back with a smile.

"How was I to know when I answered the door that the person standing there, someone I trusted for so many years, would kidnap me, would be so violent?" Cindy cast her eyes on Simon's unconscious form before glaring with accusatory eyes at Iblis. ". . . would turn out to be a criminal just like my sister?"

"And what she does shames you?"

"More than you could know," Cindy said with pure disgust.

"You know, you're despicable. You walk around with this holier-than-thou attitude, passing judgment, yet you forget what she sacrificed for you. So you could get your sheepskin, tell the world you graduated from Oxford. Is her name on that diploma? It should be. Everything in your young life came from her."

"She lied to me my entire life. She's a common thief."

"Careful what you say," Iblis said slowly.

Seeing Iblis's dead eyes boring into her, Cindy fell silent.

"Your sister is anything but common." Iblis paused. "She'd risk her life for you. Would you do the same for her, would you risk your life for your sister?"

"You defend her, yet you're prepared to kill her if she doesn't do what you say," Cindy said in challenge. "You're screwed up."

Iblis walked to the small fridge and pulled out a Coke, cracking it and downing half before answering.

"Do you know what fear is?" Iblis placed the satchel on the table and walked toward Cindy. Cindy froze in the thought that she had gone too far as Iblis leaned close to her ear. "You have no idea what fear is."

"No idea what fear is?" The anger washed over Cindy. "You threaten us with death and then say something like that?"

"Do you fear death?" Iblis said, sounding like a preacher.

Cindy was floored by the question, her hands shaking, her palms instantly sweaty, at a loss for words. This man before her had been a friend to them in their youth, providing money, guidance, a shoulder to cry on, and yet all the while he had lived his life in the shadows, dealing in the underworld, a world of crime. And now she was nothing more than a living, breathing incentive to get her sister to do his bidding by holding a proverbial knife to her and Simon's throats.

"Fear is our instinctual motivator, it is what keeps us alive, is our most basic of instincts that ensures our survival. It is what makes us resourceful in times of crisis, it is what makes us think of solutions we could never imagine when we are safe and secure.

"Fear in the hands of someone skilled can be used to achieve goals, to attain success, money, fame. When you know what scares someone you can get them to do almost anything you want. Some people work harder as they fear being fired, most live their lives in fear of death, which provides a motivation to believe in the Almighty.

"For centuries, for millennia, fear is what was used to rule. The benevolent ruler, the benevolent king was one of fairy tale. Kings were feared, sultans were feared.

"Why is it that when fear overwhelms us we begin to pray? Pray for divine intervention, pray for a solution, pray for delivery from what scares us, be it monsters, death, and even sometimes ourselves?

"But fear can also bring out the best in people. Do you know what scares your sister? It's not death, not the boogeyman. It's anything that threatens *your* continued survival. It is what has always pushed her forward. She was terrified of losing you, not being able to support you. That pushed her to do things most people would never consider, things that the high-minded, moral society frowns upon. And yet she never complained about it. Yet you, for two days, live in fear while condemning her for the sacrifices she made for you.

"I hope you're scared; I hope you're terrified." Iblis finally paused, moving closer to her once again. "I hope you know that I hold your life in the palm of my hand."

"You think I'm afraid of death?" Cindy tried to be bold.

"There are things and there are places worse than death." Iblis's cold eyes bore into her. "Far worse than death."

"Death is the end of all things," Cindy said in protest, as if in debate. "There is no afterlife. We simply cease to exist."

"That's what you believe?" Iblis smiled.

"Can you prove otherwise?" Cindy asked.

"They educated the God right out of you, didn't they?" Iblis shook his head.

Cindy was suddenly angry, offended by Iblis's comment. "For people like you and KC, I would think that would be a good thing. No final judgment for your deeds."

"Need I remind you, your lack of faith is just as grave a sin?"

Cindy rolled her eyes. "I'm not getting into a theological debate with a psychotic."

"Really?" Iblis said.

"Trust me, you'd lose."

Iblis smirked under arched eyebrows. "You're more concerned with being right than learning the truth."

"You can't prove the existence of God, the Devil, or an afterlife."

"Have you ever taken anything on faith?"

"I only believe in what is real, what I can touch, what science can prove."

Iblis nodded. "What science can prove?"

Cindy stood there obstinate and angry.

"You play in the financial world, corporate raiding. Cashing in on the misfortunes of others; every time you make money someone else loses it."

"That is completely legal," Cindy defended herself.

"But is it moral?" Iblis paused, letting his point sink in. "Don't you, of all people, talk to me about morality."

"The company you are going to work for, they're probably paying you a fortune."

"I'm paid what I'm worth," she shot back.

"Do you believe that? What if you were to find out you were just a pawn in a much bigger game? Isn't that what most worker bees in a corporation are, pawns grinding out their everyday existence in order to make the hive bigger, the company stronger, the boss richer? Doesn't that bother you? You with your Oxford degree?"

"My time will come," Cindy said.

"Are you sure?"

Cindy stood there, unable to hide a hint of rising doubt.

"Since you were ten, you've been after the big payday; you always said thirty million by thirty, three hundred million . . ."

"By forty," Cindy reluctantly said.

"Wealth comes to risk takers, Cindy, not worker bees, not people who play it safe, and you're playing it safe, Miss Polly Purebread. You believe in the promises of your chairman, you have faith in him, faith in the almighty dollar, yet your success is not a given. They'll probably screw you with worthless options and a twenty-five-dollar retirement watch."

"They'll take care of me; I trust them."

"And yet not your sister," Iblis said as if proving a point. "So let me get this straight. You can have faith in a boss you've never met, you've handed over your future to him for the promise of a dollar, yet you refuse to even explore the existence of forces greater than man, of God, for the promise of eternal life."

Cindy stared into Iblis's eyes; she had little doubt of his fragile sanity, as he spoke of God yet wouldn't hesitate to kill them if it meant getting his heart's desire.

"We're born, we live, we die. That's it, nothing before, nothing after. No God, no magic or mystery, no heaven and hell. There is nothing you could do or say to convince me otherwise."

"What if I showed you something?" Iblis unlaced the

top of the leather tube, then unlatched the interior hasp. He removed the chart, reverently rolling it out on the table.

Cindy stared at the elaborate chart, never having seen anything like it in all her years. She looked up into the cold, lifeless eyes of her captor, curious about what he was showing her and why.

"What if I told you a secret," Iblis continued, "that would change the way you think about everything?"

CHAPTER 31

KC came down the three flights of stairs and cracked open the large white metal fire door. She peered out into the Istanbul morning; the heat of the day was already on the rise, the humidity straining each breath. The cobblestone street was vacant but for a few shopkeepers going about their routines to prep for the coming day.

She remained in the doorway, her heart racing, her feet ready to run, not sure if she was being watched by the cops, stalked by Iblis, or hunted by some unknown. And Michael—her mind was in a jumble over his betrayal. She had trusted him, made love to him. She didn't question their passion, but that didn't negate the fact that he was gone, along with the rod that she had stolen. She hoped he wasn't trying something foolish. If Iblis was to find Michael still alive, she had no doubt the assassin wouldn't fail the second time. She had less than five hours to find him and get the rod to Iblis, otherwise her sister and Simon and who knew who else would be dead.

And then the limo rounded the corner, moving slowly, heading her way. KC ducked back in the vestibule, leaving the door cracked open to watch its approach. The black car was out of place in this run-down section, incongruous among its surroundings. It wasn't here by accident.

The car was creeping, searching, approaching as if it was ready to pounce. And as it finally rolled to a stop, the window came down.

KC released the building door, allowing it to fall shut with an echoing thud, and retreated into the recesses of the stairs, ready to run up.

"Good morning," the voice called from outside.

And KC's fear slipped from her mind. She opened the door to see Michael standing beside the limo, holding the car door open with his left hand, a brown paper bag in the other.

"You hungry?" Michael asked.

KC walked outside, glancing left to right, unable to contain her paranoia, and jumped into the back of the limo. Michael slid in behind her, closing the door, sealing them into the first safety KC had felt since waking up. The smell of fresh bread and coffee filled the car; the air-conditioning was on high, already fighting back the early-morning heat.

Michael smiled at her as he opened the bag and pulled out two flaky borek pastries and a bottle of water.

"Where the hell were you?" KC exploded, all her rage and frustration pouring out. "I've been calling. Can't you answer your phone?"

Michael silently looked at her, his face awash in confusion. He slowly raised the brown bag. "Breakfast?"

"And you couldn't leave me a note?"

Michael glanced to Busch, who manned the wheel. KC followed his eyes and verbally launched into Michael's large friend. "And what's up with you? You don't answer your phone, either?"

But Busch said nothing, turning his attention to the road as he put the car in gear and drove off.

"Where's the rod? What the hell did you do with it?"

Michael held up his hands as if warding off a stampede. "Relax—"

"Relax, my ass. You had no right taking it."

Michael held her eye as he lowered the breakfast bag and picked up the leather satchel from the floor, passing it to her. KC ripped it from Michael's hands and fell silent, looking out the darkened window in a huff, like a child who had gotten her way but still wasn't happy.

Michael handed her a borek and the bottled water; she snatched it from his hands, ignoring him and the gesture, and turned her attention back to the city as it whizzed by in the rush hour.

Busch drove into the morning traffic, the car jumping and jerking, starting and stopping as they made their way across the ancient city. He had finally gotten the hang of driving in Istanbul, realizing it was an every-man-for-himself traffic blitzkrieg that could only be managed through aggressive selfishness, a game of ultimate chicken, with those who hesitated left in a snail-like crawl across town.

They all sat silently, each lost in thought, as they made their way past the Blue Mosque, its worshippers flooding out into the street upon the conclusion of morning prayers, past the Grand Bazaar and out onto Ataturk Bulvari. They drove across the Ataturk Bridge and into the modern world of the Asian side of the city.

It was all cosmopolitan, fresh and new, standing in stark contrast to the ancient masterpieces and district behind them.

"Do you mind telling me where we are going?" KC looked at Michael.

"Not particularly," Michael was lost in his notebook computer that sat upon his lap.

KC ignored his flip response and scooted along the bench seat up to Busch.

"Will you tell me?" KC asked.

Busch was focused on a GPS display, following it as he drove. Two red blips intermittently shone: one in the center of the screen, the other in the upper right-hand corner. "What is that?"

"Did you eat breakfast?" Busch asked in hopes of changing the subject.

"What is that?" KC asked, getting annoyed. "Will someone please tell me where we are going?"

Busch glanced up at the rearview mirror, his eyes meeting Michael's, and noting his acceding glance, Busch briefly turned an eye to KC. "We're going to get your sister and Simon."

THE PRIVATE ENCLAVE sat on five acres of manicured lawns behind ten-foot stone walls. The three-story Mediterranean-style house overlooked the water and sang of wealth beyond compare.

An imposing wrought-iron gate served to warn of the security that sat behind the large walls. Two guards flanked the entrance while three cameras sat rather conspicuously atop tall white metal poles.

"Where the hell are we?" KC asked.

Busch removed the GPS monitor from the dash, the two red lights flashing side by side in the center of the screen. "We're chasing the leather satchel with the chart."

He turned to KC and held up a small chip, the size of a piece of chewing gum, placing it in her hand. "It's waterproof. The battery is good for forty-eight hours."

KC looked at him, confused.

"You flip that little switch on the side to activate it." Busch's enormous finger dwarfed the pinhead-sized button on the side of the chip.

KC flipped the switch and a third red dot appeared in the center of the GPS. She smiled. "Son of a bitch."

"You're not the first person to call him that. My feelings exactly." Busch grinned.

KC's brows furrowed as she looked closely at the digital GPS display. "If one is in that house, one is in my hand, where's the third?"

Michael held up the leather tube containing the rod. "I had put one in here yesterday just in case. I borrowed it from you this morning to change the battery."

"Why didn't you tell me?"

"I didn't want to wake you," Michael said sheepishly.

"I mean, that these had tracking devices in them."

"Sorry, bad habit." Michael cast his eyes down. "I have a tendency to keep things to myself. I've never worked with a partner before."

"If we can't trust each other . . ." KC let it hang, looking Michael in the eye. She didn't need to finish the statement. "You put these in the tubes . . ." KC said, more to herself than to anyone.

"I figured Iblis would try to steal the chart from us at some point," Michael said as he crawled along the seat to the front of the car. "I was actually hoping he would."

"How could you know?"

"It was more of a precaution, but a fortunate one."

KC looked up the street at the mansion. "The chart's in there?"

Michael nodded. "And I'm pretty sure that's where your sister and Simon are."

"How can we be sure?"

"We can't, but I've got a way to find out."

KC SAT ATOP the Kiritz Hotel, binoculars in hand, her eyes trained on the courtyard of the Blue Mosque. It was twelve-fifty, ten minutes before the Islamic midday *dhuhr* prayer, ten minutes before the time of the designated hand-off of the sultan's rod to Iblis.

The Blue Mosque couldn't be more public; the mass of tourists would swell with the arrival of the observant Muslims. One of the greatest tourist attractions in Istanbul, it had been completed in 1609 and was named for the exquisite blue tiles that lined the walls of its vast interior. It was surrounded by six towering minarets: four fluted, narrow towers, each with three balconies, sat at the corners of the mosque, while two stood in the forecourt. The thin, pencil-like structures reaching nearly two hundred feet into the midday sky were the trademark of Istanbul as the Eiffel Tower was of Paris and the Statue of Liberty was of New York. The main structure was formed by a succession of cascading semidomes enveloping the enormous central dome that climbed into and reflected the midday sky.

This was where the palace of Grand Vizier Sokollu Mehmet Pasha once stood. Purchased and destroyed by Sultan Ahmed I to make way for his grand creation, its foundation, vaults, and undercrofts still remained beneath the historic place of worship. As KC looked upon the beautiful structure, thinking of its buried history, its rich foundation, she knew that it was here that their journey had started so many years ago. It was beneath this house of Allah that Sokollu Mehmet Pasha's letter to his brother had originated. It was within his former palace that he had devised his scheme to hide away the dark half of the Piri Reis map and the accompanying rod of the sultan.

KC's eyes focused back on the present, her hands involuntarily clutching the binoculars, her blood beginning to boil, because of the image that filled her field glasses. He stood in the inner courtyard of the Blue Mosque, dressed in a white linen shirt and matching pants, looking every bit the local. He removed his sunglasses and stared across the two-hundred-yard span straight at her, right through the twin lenses into her soul.

A smile slowly creased his innocent face as he stood among the swelling congregants and tourists who passed him, all oblivious to the evil that stood not twenty yards from the holy house. He continued to stare at KC as if in challenge, as if he knew her every move. And he finally bowed: It was subtle, an Asian-style greeting, a sign of respect before battle.

KC stepped from his line of sight, picked up her phone, and dialed.

Michael answered on the first ring. "We're a go?"

"Yeah," KC whispered as if Iblis were standing right next to her.

"Be careful," Michael said with genuine concern in his voice.

"You too," KC said. "Please don't let anything happen to my sister."

"I'll protect her as if she were you."

BUSCH KNEELED ON the backseat of the limo, watching. The barrel of the Galil sniper rifle rested on the sill of the smoked rear window. It was Michael's, gifted to him by Simon. Michael never had the nerve or need to use it but kept it with his bag of tricks in case the need ever arose.

Busch rested the wooden stock against his shoulder, wrapped his finger about the trigger, and clutched the rifle as if it were his wife and they were ready to dance the paso doble. He rested his eye in the scope's socket cup, the black rubber sealing out all light but for that which poured through the telescopic lens. He moved the weapon about, back and forth, getting used to the feel, scanning the streets of the upscale neighborhood. His vision came to rest on the large wrought-iron gates of Iblis's home. Unlike many of the gates of the rich, these were not ornamental—no fancy design, no family crest on the heavy bars, just thick double-welded iron in all its forbiddingness. Busch looked up at the three staggered video cameras, perched on tall white poles, their range of vision covering the sidewalk and gate, leaving nowhere to hide. He touched his finger against the trigger of the Galil; the laser scope responded, painting a sharp red dot on the white pole, center square to the scope's crosshairs, and he smiled.

Busch was an excellent shot, sniper-trained for the police force, but fortunately had never had to bring the training to bear. He laughed to himself that since his retirement, Michael had caused him to draw on more of his police training than he had used in his twenty years of service.

Busch finally swept the scope back to see Michael walking up the sidewalk adjacent to the ten-foot stuccoed walls that wrapped Iblis's home. He was dressed in a tan summerweight shirt and khaki pants, a large leather bag strapped to his shoulder, which bounced against his hip with his every step. Busch moved the rifle back and forth between Michael, the iron gates, and the video cameras, truing up his site, training his eye, awakening the muscle memory that had lain dormant for so many years.

As Michael drew to within twenty-five feet of the gates,

he raised his hand to his head, briefly running his fingers through his wavy brown hair, signaling Busch.

Busch twisted and craned his neck, inhaled, and, in that moment, pulled the trigger. He hit his target on the first try and held his finger against the trigger, refusing to release, as would so often be the practice.

But there was no shot, no report of the gun shattering his ears. The darkened window he aimed out of was unmarred by the shot, as there were no bullets in the gun.

It was not a mistake; he had hit his target as planned. The laser beam on the scope shone its pinpoint through the smoked rear window, 150 yards up the road, and hit the lens of the security camera dead on. He held his finger down, the invisible beam's red dot carrying across the street and up the road unhindered, hitting its target true.

The infrared cameras were designed for both daylight and low-light viewing, providing a quality image both day and night. Therefore, the camera's lens was highly susceptible to corruption via overexposure. The electronic video lens was overwhelmed by the rifle's laser pointer and would provide Michael a narrow path for entry into the grounds.

MICHAEL WALKED ALONG the upscale residential street. The gated mansions were scattered so as to provide the best possible views of the Bosporus and the European side of Istanbul. The area was quiet and deserted in the middle of the day. There hadn't been a car in five minutes; not even the barking of a dog broke the stillness. Michael cinched the leather bag on his shoulder, checked the Sig Sauer pistol that rested under his shirt in the small of his back, quickly looked up and down the street, ensuring its continued vacancy, and scaled the white stucco and brick wall. He hurtled the coping stones and landed in a crouch roll within the blinded sight line of the camera.

The grounds were lush with heavy green shrubbery and bright flowers, all expertly landscaped. The house was a whitewashed Mediterranean with a barrel-tiled roof and two stories of at least five thousand square feet per floor, no doubt purchased with the fruits of Iblis's illicit deeds.

Confirming the coast was clear, Michael dashed along the wall to a stone guardhouse that sat just inside the gates. It was small and unnoticeable, as it sat under the shade of a sycamore tree. A golf cart was parked at its side. Michael cautiously slowed and ducked under the rear window of the guardhouse; he worked his way around the small building and ran headlong into the guard.

He stood six-three, his blue blazer working overtime to contain an overdeveloped physique. But before he could react, Michael hit him square in the throat, crushing his windpipe. The man's hands instinctively went for his neck as he doubled over, his air supply nearly cut off. Michael drove two uppercuts into the man's face, sending him careening back into the guardhouse, where he collapsed on the hardwood floor. Michael drew a roll of duct tape from the bag at his hip and made quick work of securing the unconscious guard.

As Michael stepped into the guard's hut, he was greeted by a host of twenty security monitors, their blue lights providing a spectral effect in the cramped quarters. There were four lockers along the back wall; three pairs of street shoes sat on the floor in front of them. There would be at least two other guards to contend with somewhere on the grounds in addition to his friend on the floor.

The upper left monitor was awash in white light, overwhelmed by the laser scope; Busch's aim was spot-on perfect. The other images were of both the interior and the exterior: a Romanesque pool and cabana, the gardens, the rear wall that faced the Bosporus, various living rooms and bedrooms. Each monitor was appropriately labeled, indicating its location and compass point direction.

It was the lowermost bank that caught Michael's eye. His heart ran cold as he saw Simon lying motionless, an IV running to his arm, his head wrapped in bloody gauze.

Cindy's image filled the next monitor. Michael couldn't make out her face completely but her auburn hair left no doubt it was she. She sat in a large leather chair watching TV, sipping a bottle of water, fortunately appearing no worse for wear. They were both being held in a room labeled *Lower Lounge*.

Michael pulled out his cell phone and quickly dialed.

"They're here," Michael said as soon as KC answered. "Be careful, and whatever you do, keep your head, stick to the plan."

Without another word, Michael hung up and dialed Busch. "Let's go."

The whitewashed monitor instantly refocused on an image of the wall, painting a clear picture of the sidewalk and gardens that it bisected. Within moments, Michael saw Busch jogging up toward the gate. For a six-four, 225-pound man, Busch still moved like a teenager.

Michael pushed a red circular plunger on the security console; there was a heavy click and the large iron gates parted. Busch ran through and into the gatehouse.

Busch pulled out his Sig Sauer, drew back the slide, popped out and reinserted the cartridge, and finally flipped up the safety.

"We've got at least two," Michael said as he grabbed a walkie-talkie off the desk and tucked the earpiece in his ear.

"Did you all of a sudden get a gift for language?"

Michael threw him a glance.

"It's not like you're going to be understanding a single word they say."

Michael's look shut him down.

"Do you have any idea where we are going?"

"No," Michael said as he shook his head.

"Okay, well, let's go, then."

They stepped out of the guardhouse and both caught sight of the golf cart. Without a word they hopped in and drove up the drive toward the house. The grounds within the high walls appeared to be around five acres, every inch of it expertly maintained. Michael drove as they headed along the front of the house and down the drive toward a six-car detached garage that sat in the back. There were three cars there: a Mercedes limousine, an Aston Martin Vantage Roadster, and a Maserati GranSport Spyder.

A man rolled out on a mechanic's creeper from underneath the Spyder and turned a curious eye toward the two strangers in the approaching cart. The slight man, not more than 140 pounds, gradually got to his feet as the golf cart rolled to a stop. He suddenly realized he was moving too slowly and reached for the gun at his side. Busch jumped from the passenger side, instantly overwhelming the small man with his size. He ripped the gun from his hand and forced him facedown in the driveway. Michael quickly duct-taped the man, wrapping him like a Christmas present. Busch grabbed the struggling man by the waist of his pants, carried him into the garage, and stuffed him into a storage locker.

Without a word they both got back into the cart and drove around the back of the house. The view from the rear was spectacular: passing ships and yachts, sailboats with billowing white sails, the blue waters that divided continents and connected the Black Sea with the Sea of Marmara and the rest of the world. Michael had never known that Istanbul held such beauty, such spectacular views, such utter importance to ancient world economies. Looking across the Bosporus Strait from Asia, Michael was reminded that having fixed notions about cities as urban worlds of concrete and glass was like saying New York was a one-note town.

"You would think he would have more guards," Busch said.

"You would think—"

And the gunshot ricocheted off the front of the golf cart. Michael and Busch dove from the moving vehicle and belly-crawled to the side of the house. Michael pointed up toward the front corner of the house.

Busch rose to his knees. "Take a shot every fifteen seconds."

"What—" Michael began to answer, but Busch was already gone, heading around the back of the house.

Another shot rang out. Michael responded, shooting up in the general direction the gunfire had come from, but he saw nothing to aim at. He hated being pinned down and hoped Busch knew what he was doing, but quickly admonished himself for doubting his friend. They had experienced more life-threatening situations than any man should. Busch had always been there for him. He might verbally abuse him for it, but Busch never hesitated when it came to protecting Michael. Michael fired off two shots at the unseen sniper, wondering where Busch was.

Michael prayed that Cindy and Simon were okay. Despite seeing them on the monitor, Michael couldn't help feeling a sense of dread that he was walking into a trap that could kill them all.

Two shots rang out and then a fusillade erupted, thirty seconds of a barrage of gunfire before the world fell silent again.

Michael lay there in anticipation. Fear began to creep up his spine. Until . . .

"We don't need duct tape for this one," Busch said as he finally emerged from the far corner of the house and jogged down to Michael. "Now what, genius?"

They walked back to the front of the house, tried the door, and found it open. "That's not good," Michael said.

"He's got guards, security, and a big-ass wall, why lock it?" Busch said.

Michael didn't voice his fear of being set up to his friend and stepped into the house.

Michael and Busch walked across a marble foyer into a large, modern great room. Twenty-foot windows overlooked an aquamarine pool, trimmed in blue tile that looked as if it had been taken out of the Blue Mosque, its vanishing edge seeming to fall off into the Bosporus, which sat less than half a mile away. A poolhouse sat off to the side, its white pergola supported by pallid marble columns.

The midday sun filled the great room. The furniture was cold and modern: brushed-steel tables, acrylic chairs, a black armless sofa. The room had no personality: no family pictures, no heirlooms, no character to speak of. It was something out of a catalogue, impersonal and lacking comfort. It might have been Iblis's house but it certainly wasn't a home.

"Hey," Busch said.

Michael turned to see Busch holding up the leather tube, its outer skin water-stained. Busch quickly unlaced it and opened the inner seal. His head snapped up to look at Michael.

"That would be too easy," Michael said. "He either stuck it in a safe or has it with him."

Michael wasted no time and quickly found a wide set of stairs leading to the lower level. Heading down, they both clutched their guns at the ready, expecting the unexpected.

They walked about the lower level, cautiously opening doors. There was a home theater; a glassed-in gym filled with free weights, a treadmill, and a stationary bike; a fully stocked wine cellar; a vacant bedroom. They met in a large game room, a gentleman's playroom—pool table, card table, a large mahogany bar, a flat-screen TV mounted on the far wall in front of a large sofa.

But as they stood there looking about, they both came to the same conclusion.

"You sure you saw them on the monitor?" Busch asked.

"Positive. The monitor label said lower level."

"Well," Busch said, "they're not down here."

Michael looked around, feeling the walls, pounding the floors. All solid.

"They're somewhere else," Busch said. "Why would Iblis put a label pointing to where the people he kidnapped were being held?"

"Mmm." Michael shook his head. "They're here."

"This level matches the footprint above. There's no place for a hidden room."

"Iblis is a thief," Michael countered. "He's also human. He has his trophies, his keepsakes. He's a prideful son of a bitch. There is no way he lives in this sterile environment."

"Maybe he lives in the poolhouse," Busch half-joked.

Michael walked over to the bar and slipped behind it. The floor-to-ceiling bar was crafted of a dark African mahogany, trimmed in brass. Ornamental brass lights sat on either side of the large decorative piece, their bulbs dimmed, glowing warmly. The ice maker was full, the bar fully stocked with every liquor imaginable, from ginger wine to rum, absinthe to tequila, vodka, whiskey, Frangelico and Grand Marnier, to twice-distilled anise-flavored Turkish raki.

Michael examined it all carefully. The back wall was lined with segmented cabinets and liquor caddies made of the dark African wood. He ran his fingers along the seams, felt under the bar lip, opened the lower drawers and doors. He peered behind the bar. Though it abutted the rear wall, he could still see what he was looking for.

"I don't think he lives in the poolhouse, but maybe . . ." Michael pulled back the brass ornamental light on the right side of the bar. "Maybe he lives under it."

The left side of the bar separated from it, swinging out on whisper hinges to reveal a large metal door.

It was a seven-by-three-foot vault door with no discernible handle, lock, keyhole, or flywheel. Michael examined the door, running his hands up and down the steel frame, tracing the hair-thin door seam. He laid his ear against it, listening, thinking.

Manufactured by Matrix, it was one of the American firm's best sellers, three inches thick with four protruding dead bolts on each side of the door that anchored into a steel frame and a Magna-Lock sill plate. It was one of the finest security devices in use. There was no key, no traditional combination flywheel. It was accessed via an electronic keypad that could be located away from the safe, an additional precaution against thieves in the night.

Michael turned and looked back at the room, his mind spinning, his eyes darting about.

"What are we looking for?" Busch asked.

"A keypad. It's probably hidden behind a panel or behind some artwork."

Michael and Busch opened every drawer, looked behind the bar, checked behind the cheap framed movie posters from *Casablanca, North by Northwest,* and *Spartacus* that adorned the walls.

Busch gripped the edge of the wall-mounted plasma TV and tilted it on its hinge. It only angled a few inches, designed to accommodate anyone sitting at the bar, but it was enough for him to see the wall behind it. "I hate that," Busch mumbled to himself.

"What?" Michael said as he crouched behind the bar, moving aside a dozen crystal glasses.

"They buy them for show. What a waste."

Michael stood up, tilting his head in question.

"Would you spend thirty thousand on a seventy-eight-inch plasma and not bother hooking it up?"

Michael stood there a moment semiannoyed at the distraction before crouching back down and moving the glasses. But then it hit him. He popped back up, his eyes searching the room. "Shit. He hid it in plain sight."

"What?"

Michael grabbed the remote off the bar and examined it. It looked every bit like a TV remote, down to the manufacturer's label: It had colored buttons for on and off, video feeds, DVR features, but most important, it had a numbered keypad.

"He accesses via remote?"

"Makes sense. You can leave it in plain sight, carry it around with you if you want. No one's the wiser."

"And if you're like everyone else . . . you lose it every single night." Busch looked over Michael's shoulder. "How big's the combination?"

"Nine digits."

"Nine digits? That's over a million combinations," Busch said.

"Three hundred and eighty million, actually," Michael said as he opened up the back of the remote. He pulled a set of miniscrewdrivers from his leather satchel and removed the cover face.

He looked around the room, his eyes quickly falling on a small maroon sensor above the bar. He climbed atop the mahogany cabinets and removed the cover face of the infrared receiver. He dug the maroon-colored box out of the wall, leaving it to hang on its three wires.

He hopped down, looking at the room as if for the first time. The couches, the bar, the table. His eyes finally stopped at the black audio/video cabinet that sat below the plasma TV. He walked over, looked behind the unit, and found a bundle of wires exiting the wall before disappearing into the back of the black case.

"Now what?" Busch asked. "Can't you break the code? It's only 380 million possibilities . . . smart-ass."

Michael ignored his friend. "You never put the control computer for an electronic vault inside the safe. If it fails you are locked out in the worst of ways with no access to reset the system."

Michael opened up the video cabinet and found the illu-minated video system: DVD player, DVR, VCR, tuner, and on its own shelf behind a smoked-glass panel, a computer and flat-panel display. The screen read *Central Station*. Michael removed the clear panel and looked closer at the computer. "You don't use a twenty-thousand-dollar computer for iTunes."

"What do you use it for?"

Michael pulled out the black computer tower and removed the back. "It controls your vault."

He pulled out a flashlight, examined the inner workings of the computer, and popped out a small nickel cadmium battery. "All computers have a small battery that provides power to certain memory functions even when the system is down." He examined the motherboard and popped out a black chip, holding it up for Busch to see. "MRAM is a non-volatile memory chip that doesn't need power to maintain its data. It's where the security memory for this particular system and the vault door is stored, so in the event of a power failure, hard-drive crash, or corruption of the system, you can still access your vault. But if we take it out, along with the battery backup for the BIOS . . ."

Michael turned off the computer, waited thirty seconds, and fired it back up.

The screen glowed green and the display read: *System initialization. Reset system. Reset password.* Michael quickly typed and the system restarted. Now granted full access, he worked the computer for thirty seconds and, with a flourish, hit Enter.

A large whoosh followed by a heavy click sounded within the mechanics of the safe door.

The three-inch-thick door pivoted out to reveal a darkened hallway. And as the door moved to its extreme open position, lights flicked on in succession, moving down the hall, to reveal another world, a refined world of elegance and style, of trophies and secrets.

Michael and Busch stepped into the hall and found it lined with dark mahogany walls and recessed shelves. Thick blue and green Persian rugs covered rich hardwood floors. Paintings, lit under pin spots, mingled with sculptures and antique books upon the shelves. As they moved down the hall, Michael recognized the first piece of art: Pablo Picasso's *Nature Morte à la Charlotte*. It had been stolen from a restoration studio in Paris in 2004, no clues left behind, no witnesses or leads, never to be seen again. Michael shook his head as he walked on, but suddenly stopped and stared at an exquisitely detailed painting on a wooden pallet of the Virgin Mary holding Baby Jesus. The deep colors, the pride-filled eyes were rendered in lifelike, heartrending detail. Stolen in 2003 from the Duke of Buccleuch, Da Vinci's *Madonna of the Yarnwinder* was worth over $100 million.

"Nice," Busch said, not comprehending what he looked at.

Michael said nothing as he came to a heavy mahogany door and opened it. The room was softly lit; a single chair sat in the center. What Michael looked at was beyond comprehension. Upon the walls were three Rembrandts, a Johannes Vermeer, an Edouard Manet, and five works by Degas. Michael stood staring in wonderment at the haul from a theft in Boston over fifteen years ago, one of the most renowned unsolved thefts of modern times. This room alone was worth over $400 million.

"Hey," Busch called, looking at his watch.

Michael closed the door and they walked down the hall.

Iblis was a thief beyond compare. There had to be over a billion dollars' worth of works of art down here, none of which he had chosen to liquidate, looking at them as trophies, badges of honor, successes that he could never share. Iblis was not vainglorious: He appeared to be self-satisfied, with no need for congratulations or back-slapping compliments for a job well done.

The hallway passed a small open lounge, a couch and two chairs focused on a single piece of art lit with three hidden pin spots in the ceiling. The seventeenth-century painting hung on the far wall of the room, the centerpiece of Iblis's illicit collection. There was no question he considered it his greatest achievement.

As Michael's eyes fell upon *Concerto de Oberion*, an oil masterpiece painted by Govier, his professional admiration for Iblis quickly dissolved.

Four people had died in that theft from the Franze Museum in Berlin: two grad students, each with a bullet through the temple, a twenty-year-old secretary with her throat slit—but it was the curator's death that chilled the art world. Hans Grunewald—the name had appeared on the news for weeks—had had his ears sliced from his head, the skin of his face filleted off, lye poured in his eyes, all while he was alive; tortured to give over the museum's security codes. He had lingered for ten days, but had no recollection of the thief who had not only robbed the museum but robbed Grunewald of his senses and eventually his life.

Michael's stomach twisted as he thought of Iblis displaying the Govier for the first time, how he applauded in a self-congratulatory fashion every time he sat before this work of art obtained through the death of four innocents.

Michael turned away in disgust, and what his eyes fell upon next nearly tore the heart from his chest. He looked upon a mahogany bookcase on the side wall next to the Govier; it was filled with books and mementos, keepsakes and photos. And it was the photos that disturbed him, far more than the Govier, far more than anything he could have imagined. Each of the pictures sat in a silver Tiffany frame, displayed in reverence, displayed with love, all of one individual. The pictures were through the years, teenhood, early twenties, the most recent appearing just days old, taken surreptitiously here in Istanbul within the grounds of Topkapi Palace, the subject entirely unaware. And each photo was meticulously presented with affection, exhibited with love, as if the subject was the greatest piece in all of Iblis's collection. There was no question of Iblis's feelings for his subject, no question that he stared upon her nightly, entranced by her green eyes, her long blonde hair. There was no question in Michael's mind that Iblis loved KC.

Without another thought, Michael stepped from the lounge and continued to the end of the hall to find Busch staring at him.

"You see a ghost back there?" Busch asked.

"Let's pray to God Cindy and Simon are down here so we can get out of hell."

"I'm pretty sure I found them," Busch said as he stepped aside to reveal another vault door, this one with a traditional flywheel in its center. Its brushed-steel exterior was made all the more stark by the surrounding warm dark wood walls and Persian carpets. There were no computers on this one, no reliance on modern electronics. The door was a Sands-Meanne, an old-fashioned mechanical door that dated to the 1920s.

Michael pounded on the steel as hard as he could.

He waited a moment before pounding again. "Cindy, can you hear me?"

Michael and Busch waited, the moment hanging in the air.

"Michael." Cindy's voice was barely audible through the thick metal door.

"Is Simon with you?"

"He's in bad shape, Michael, you have to hurry."

CHAPTER 32

KC walked across the grand courtyard of the Blue Mosque, the grass recently cut, the hedges thick and lush. Her heart pounded in her chest; she could practically hear her own pulse. Except for the night he'd caught her and Simon in Amsterdam, she hadn't seen Iblis in ten years. He hadn't said a word during their brief encounter in the Netherlands but there would be words now. Her mind was a mixture of fear and anger at the man who formed her, who molded her into what she needed to be at the time. She wondered if he knew it was like starting an addict with free heroin. He had hooked her, and in so doing, made her what she was today.

Iblis had been like her family, like an older brother, and at times he was even like a father. She had found herself actually fantasizing about him as her father on more than one occasion when she was young. He was the only one to care about her and Cindy, the only one who came to their rescue, in a Dickensian kind of way.

But as time wore on and she started to learn about his true methods, about his penchant for blood, disregard for life, and disdain for anyone who did not serve his purpose, she began to regret her paternal fantasies, horrified that she had looked up to a man who killed without remorse.

And despite the illusion that he cared for her, despite the history they shared, he was holding Cindy and Simon for ransom. Simon was a man who knew the risk, who had faced danger and death many times throughout his life, risks he brought upon himself. But Cindy . . . she was innocent. Not only in her lack of knowledge about Iblis's and KC's less-than-legal careers, but in the traditional sense of the word. She had no horse in this race; she couldn't affect her salvation or demise. She was but a pawn in a game between KC and Iblis.

The crowd around the Blue Mosque was thick with tourists who respectfully made way for convening worshippers arriving with the calls from the minarets for their midday *dhuhr* prayers. KC had lost sight of Iblis when she re-entered the Kiritz Hotel and made her way down to the street, but knew she would find him. This was the one meeting in life he would never miss.

She took her time exiting the building, walking up the street and through the mosque's courtyard. Though she had seen Iblis from the rooftop and he had seen her, she was in no rush to arrive at his side. She would do everything she could to give Michael and Busch as much time as possible to pull Cindy and Simon out of Iblis's house. She walked with purpose, not too slow, not tipping her hand that she was stalling, but she would draw out her arrival as much as she could. She held tight to the leather tube that was strung over her shoulder. It was all part of Michael's plan, but as is the case with mice and men, even the best laid plans have a tendency to take unexpected detours. She prayed to God that Michael was already successful and away.

"Taking in the sights?"

KC turned and came face to face with Iblis. She looked down at the man. His flawless skin hadn't aged in the ten years since they had parted ways; the eyes she had thought of as caring in her youth frightened her now in their blue opaqueness. Dressed in his white linen shirt, with his black hair and tan skin, he looked every bit the local, but she knew the man was anything but what he appeared.

"I half expected to see you with a gun in your hand." Iblis smiled.

"How dare you kidnap my sister," KC tore into Iblis; she couldn't help herself.

"Correct me if I'm wrong, but I didn't think you'd help me if I asked you nicely," Iblis said. "It's good to see you too, by the way."

"Is Simon alive?" KC tried to rein herself back.

"When last I saw him," Iblis said.

"You're pathetic."

"And you've matured." Iblis looked KC up and down. "Grown into a real woman. I guess that makes you even more deadly."

KC tried to keep the conversation on track but failed. "You sent me to die in prison."

"No, I didn't. That wasn't my idea," Iblis protested.

"And yet you let it happen."

Iblis pulled a business card from his pocket and handed it to KC. "Look familiar?"

KC looked at Stephen Kelley's business card, the one Michael had given her in case Cindy ever needed to talk to someone about starting her own mergers and acquisitions firm.

"I had no idea why you would have the business card of

a Boston attorney, but I sent his info along with the execution and prison details to Rome. I figured the Vatican would intervene diplomatically. Didn't think they'd have much sympathy for a thief like you, but one of their own, a priest, being executed has a tendency to create sympathy, to force people to action."

"That makes no sense."

"Oh, it makes perfect sense; I needed your help to get the Piri Reis chart and the sultan's staff. You couldn't very well help me if you were dead, now could you?"

"You think you saved me? You're as delusional as ever."

"Be that as it may, I'm glad to see you standing here, looking very much alive. Whether the Vatican helped you or not, KC, I had my doubts that anyone could ever hold you for long."

KC stood there refusing to believe that Iblis had done anything to save her, but it was the only explanation. Someone had tipped off the Vatican, and only a handful of people had known of their incarceration and scheduled demise.

"May I see the rod?" Iblis pointed at the leather satchel hanging from her shoulder.

"What guarantee do I have that you won't kill Cindy and Simon?"

"I gave you my word."

"Which is worth less than nothing."

"Despite your feelings toward me, KC, you are the one thing I found good in this world." Iblis paused, looking at the throng of people passing them by. And for the briefest of moments, something arose in his eyes. "I see part of myself in you."

"I'm nothing like you," KC said with revulsion. "You're a murderer."

"You're more like me than you know." Iblis nodded. "Tell me you wouldn't kill me right now if it meant saving your sister."

"I'd gladly take your life to save hers, but I would never kill someone for personal gain." KC paused and looked at him with disgust. "You take pleasure in it."

"I deny that. I feel nothing when I kill; I've never felt remorse, regret. And you know why? Because I've never felt. I don't say that to arouse pity, I say that because my heart just can't feel except when it comes to you."

KC stood there in shock, her fear rising at his words.

"I don't live behind illusions. In fact, I'm more honest with you than you are with yourself. You're a thief, KC, living outside the law. The degree to which you live outside the law is irrelevant. You're a thief, don't forget that as you sit in judgment of me. You sure took to my mentoring when you needed it."

"That's before I knew what you really were."

"And what's that, what am I?"

"You're darkness. You're without a conscience or soul."

"Why don't you come work for me?" Iblis smiled, ignoring her condemning words. "Or with me? We were so good together."

"What do you want with this?" KC disregarded his offer as she thrust out the tube.

"It's not for me."

"Bullshit."

"You know who it's for?"

"Since when do you need to work for someone?"

"There are times in life when we all answer to someone, KC."

The moment hung in air as the crowds passed them by without interest.

"Give me the rod and you can take your sister and your friend Simon, if he's still alive."

"If he's still alive . . . you son of a bitch." KC did everything to restrain herself from hitting him.

"I'm living up to my end of the deal even though you betrayed me by sending Michael—yes, I know his name and all about him—after the chart."

"You've got the chart and you killed him in the process," KC exploded.

Iblis tilted his head. "You used to be the best liar I knew, KC."

KC said nothing as the rage poured from her eyes.

"Surely you knew that I wasn't about to let someone else get hold of the chart. He was a good thief, from what I saw." Iblis paused, looking deep into KC's eyes, and softly asked, "Was he your lover?"

KC's eyes burned with rage as Iblis's emotions were laid out before her. As dark and as dangerous as she knew him to be, she had never thought, never fathomed a jealous side, a side that could prove far more irrational, far more dangerous.

"How dare you ask—"

Iblis held up his hand, stopping her in midsentence. What little shred of emotion he showed dissolved from his face and he pointed at the leather tube hanging from her shoulder. "Now, can I have the rod?"

"What the hell is it?" KC held up the tube. "How are this and the chart connected?"

"Your priest friend never told you?"

KC shook her head.

"Then it's best you don't know."

"Now you're trying to protect me? Don't bullshit me."

"I'll stop bullshitting you when you stop lying to me."

"What?"

"Where is Michael?" Iblis's voice grew stern.

"You killed him—"

"Come on," Iblis cut her off. "You used to be the best of liars; you could convince a cop of your innocence with a smoking gun in your hand. Is this what happens when you fall in love? Your skills begin to weaken with your knees?"

KC stared at Iblis as anger began to grow in him.

"I warned you not to attempt anything foolish."

"What do you mean?"

"He's trying to save Cindy and Simon, isn't he?"

KC stepped back, unable to answer.

"You never listen; you always have to do things your own way. It's a shame, really."

"What the hell are you talking about?"

"Michael may be smart enough to make it into my house and to where they are being held, though I doubt he will be smart enough to get them out."

A sudden realization poured through KC.

"The room your sister and Simon are in is secure beyond compare, filled with its share of precautionary countermeasures."

"Countermeasures?"

"Think booby traps. Your *good* friend, Michael, by thinking you're stalling me here while he breaks into my house, is going to have some blood on his hands. If he tries to open the room she is in . . ." Iblis paused. ". . . Cindy will die."

CHAPTER 33

Cindy stood at the vault door listening to the banging and jostling of metal on metal. A feeling of relief washed over her as she looked back at Simon.

Her mind was a jumble of confusion with all that had happened in the last few days; KC's escape from prison, the fact that she had hidden another side of herself, that she was a criminal. And then to be kidnapped by a family friend. She felt like a child again, control of her life in everyone's hands but her own.

But what stirred in her mind now made all other thoughts pale. Despite the rage she felt toward Iblis, she had listened to his tale of the chart. Where it came from, where it led, and the secrets it would reveal. Iblis had laid bare all of the fallacies in her life: the truth about KC, about the father she never knew and why her mother wanted them to witness his burial, about himself and how he had taught KC all she knew about dealing in the underworld. Iblis had revealed just how many secrets there were in the world.

She looked at Simon as he lay unconscious, wondering how much he knew and what his part in all of this was. She had spoken with him only briefly, but while he at first appeared cold and detached, she realized that was only his focus. She had warmed to him in their brief conversations in the limo and at the hotel, seeing his caring manner.

"Simon," Cindy said as she walked to his side and leaned over him. But there was no response. She checked his pulse; it was weak but it was there. She hoped that removing the IV from his arm had been wise; while it kept him unnecessarily sedated, it was providing him the hydration that was so important. He stirred, looking up at her through half-mast eyes as she spoke. "I don't know if you can hear me, but your friends are here."

"It's about time." Simon nodded and closed his eyes, falling back to sleep.

"We're going to be okay," Cindy whispered, in reassurance more to herself than Simon.

MICHAEL KNELT ON the thick Persian rug, his bag of tools open on the floor beside him. He had removed the numbered flywheel from the central cylinder of the vault door, laying it on the floor behind him. He attached a small dial—it looked just like a miniature flywheel—to the spindle that protruded from the door. There were four half-inch holes surrounding the spindle, used for grasping the door during installation, a feature that went out of style in the 1930s. He was glad to be able to avoid the tedious task of drilling as he had been forced to do on certain prior occasions.

He inserted a thin gooseneck device into the upper left hole and placed a sight cup against his eye. The narrow fiber-optic viewer was self-lit, bringing the inner workings of the vault door to life. Michael maneuvered the scope, looking about the innards until he caught sight of five interlocking gears. With each turn of the wheel, the first gear would turn until the first designated number was precisely arrived at, at which point a narrow metal post that lay in wait would fall into a thin notch on the first wheel, locking it to the second wheel. The flywheel's direction would then be reversed, carrying that pin and wheel until the second combo number was arrived at, whereat the second post would fall into the third wheel. This process would continue for all five numbers in the combination, at which point, with all five pins in place and all five gears lined up, the lever could be turned and the door opened.

"How long is this going to take?" Busch asked. But Michael's focus kept him from answering.

Michael began by spinning the miniflywheel three times to the right, his eyes focused via the scope and his ears tuned to the moment of the gentle click. He had opened similar vault doors both in his legitimate security business and in the course of his more illicit affairs. He was thankful they were not on a clock lock as banks were, restricting the times that the combination would work to specific hours and minutes.

Like a laparoscopic surgeon, Michael watched through his scope closely until the first pin fell into place. He slowly spun the wheel back until the second pin clicked in, and so on through to the fifth and final pin.

Michael eyed Busch; a mutual smile began to crease their faces.

Michael stood, his right hand holding tight to the flywheel, keeping the pins in place while his left hand grasped the handle. And with a gentle nudge, the steel bar handle began to turn.

But Michael suddenly froze. A high-pitched beep began to rhythmically pulse. It came from the other side of the door, from within the room.

"Cindy?"

"Michael, what's that noise, that beeping?"

Busch turned to Michael but said nothing as he saw Michael's intensity rise.

"Listen to me, Cindy. Quickly look around, follow your ears, I need you to locate the source of that sound."

"Iblis would blow this all up?" Busch asked as he turned and looked back down the hall toward all of the artwork.

"No," Michael said. "The blast will be contained to the vault room, but it will be more than enough to kill Cindy and Simon."

KC STARED AT Iblis. She and Michael had walked right into a trap.

"Getting past my guards I'm sure proved easy. Finding my private sanctuary where I store my art would prove far more challenging, but if he's as good as you think he is, he'll make it through the security, which will lead him to the last obstacle before reaching your sister. He'll be feeling confident as a result of his success and fall for the simplest of traps.

"The bomb is made of Semtex, encased in a score of razor blades and nails. They'll not only be incinerated but shredded into hundreds of pieces. And it will all be your fault. If you'd trusted me, I would have let her go, I'd even have let Simon go if . . . you hadn't betrayed me."

KC quickly withdrew her cell phone.

"Don't bother," Iblis said. "There's no signal down there. Now give me the rod."

KC's heart thundered in her chest; her sister was dead by her hand, an innocent victim. KC took a step back, her mind in a fog as the guilt overwhelmed her.

"KC, don't force me to do the one thing I would regret," Iblis said in all seriousness. "I'm not leaving here without the rod."

As KC stared at Iblis, at the man who had taught her everything she knew, bile rose in her throat, utter hatred began to consume her, and it took everything she had to stay her hand. She decided right then that he deserved pain and suffering, he deserved to be punished.

But suddenly, with a lightning hand, Iblis snatched the tube from KC's grasp. He flipped up the leather top and then the interior metal seal; he peered into the case to see the twin-headed snake with ruby eyes. He closed it back up and looked at KC.

KC stood there at a loss for words as Iblis held her eyes. For a moment she was beyond vulnerable, she was in too much shock to have reacted if he tried to kill her. But without a word, without raising his hand, Iblis turned and walked away across the courtyard, down the shrub-lined path.

KC wrapped her head in a scarf, took a seat on the bench, pulled out her cell phone, and dialed. It rang on and on, each ring like the toll of a death bell. She hung up and redialed, but again there was no answer. KC tucked the phone back in her pocket and did all she could possibly do in that moment: She wept.

The tears poured forth at her sister's death; she had failed her. And to compound the situation, Cindy had died hating her, their last words spoken in anger. She had hoped that they would reunite, that she would be able to explain that the unfortunate path her life had taken was taken out of necessity, out of love. But the tears of reunion would never come, only the tears of grief and anguish that covered her face now.

She finally looked up to see Iblis approaching the exit of

the grounds of the Blue Mosque. He never looked back, he never suspected.

The police swarmed in from all directions, thirty strong. Iblis had nowhere to run as he was violently tackled to the ground, his hands cuffed before he could even struggle.

THE WINGBACK LEATHER chair in the corner of the room was pulled aside. Upon the floor sat a foot-square black box, its lid flipped back. The sound of the beeping cut through the room and Cindy's ears like a hot blade. The sound corresponded to a red LED timer that was counting down. Cindy had never seen one before but she knew exactly what she was looking at as the panic flooded in.

"Michael, it's a bomb!" Cindy screamed. "And it's ticking down from ninety."

Michael looked through the scope into the vault door, moving the fiber-optic gooseneck around before finally finding the cause of the current threat. It was a simple mechanical switch attached to the handle, its wires running out of the door and into the wall. Michael was beyond angry at himself for not checking first. He could have easily removed it, but his impatience had caused him not to be mindful of such traps. He had played right into Iblis's hands.

Michael quickly cleared his mind. "Cindy, I need you to focus. Describe it to me."

"I'm terrible with this kind of stuff, I can't even set my alarm clock." Cindy's voice, on the brink of hysteria, was barely audible through the door.

"Listen to my voice, focus, or you'll die."

"Hey, she's scared enough—" Busch began.

"Better scared than dead," Michael said without turning around. "Cindy . . . ?"

"It's black, the timer is on top, red numbers ticking down, my God, seventy seconds."

"Do you see any wires?" Michael looked at his watch and hit the stopwatch function, synchronizing to the seventy-second countdown.

There was total silence. Until . . . "Four wires coming out of the wall into the box. There are a bunch of wires inside the box, two metal spikes are protruding from the inside case, there are wires coming out of the timer—Jesus, Michael. I can't do this!"

"Cindy, what color are the wires?" Michael knew it was a foolish question; there never was a blue wire to cut, or a red one, for that matter. There was no standard wiring for bombs. No anarchist handbook for wiring explosives.

"White, black, red, green, striped. It's less than fifty seconds, Michael, help me."

"Open the door, Michael," Busch said as his hand grabbed the handle.

"No," Michael shouted, pushing his large friend back. "It'll blow; didn't you hear what she said? Four wires from the wall. Iblis has not only a timer switch but a trigger switch on the door."

"She's going to die," Busch said.

"Cindy?" Michael looked at his watch: Twenty seconds left. "I need you to reach into the box—"

"Michael," Cindy's voice was calm, her panic evaporated. "Please tell KC I'm sorry—"

"Reach into the box, you can do this," Michael said calmly. "You can tell her yourself."

But there was no response. Michael glanced at his watch again. Ten seconds . . . Five seconds . . . "Cindy!!!!"

Michael crushed his eyes closed, braced himself against the thick vault door . . . two . . . one . . .

Michael's watch ticked to zero, the numbers going negative past five seconds, ten, a half-minute gone by, but there was nothing, not a sound, not an explosion, not a voice.

"Cindy . . . ?" Michael said as he turned a questioning eye to Busch.

Suddenly the door creaked. Michael stood up and away from the door as it slowly swung open. Michael and Busch stood there, their hearts in their mouths, waiting until finally the room was revealed.

Cindy sat against the wall, her knees pulled tight to her chest, her head buried in her arms. Her body was racked with uncontrollable sobs.

"Took you long enough."

Michael turned to the familiar voice.

Simon sat on the floor propped against a leather chair, his head wrapped in a large blood-encrusted bandage. He was pale, his eyes barely open. Michael finally looked at his right hand to see a red timer and a host of dangling wires wrapped about his splayed fingers, the unexploded bomb on the floor next to him.

CHAPTER 34

Busch laid Simon across the back of the limo. He had carried him up from the basement, and even though he prided himself on his strength and fitness, he felt as if his heart was going to explode from carrying his two-hundred-pound friend.

Busch backed out of the limo to see Michael closing his cell phone. "KC will meet us at the hospital."

"She's okay?" Busch asked.

"Yeah, relieved." Michael nodded as he looked at Cindy, who stood in the shade of a large cypress tree. "You really should talk to her."

"Is my hotel on the way to the hospital?" Cindy asked, ignoring Michael's suggestion.

"Don't you want to see your sister?" Busch asked as he walked around the car and opened the trunk.

"No," Cindy said. "Not particularly."

"You said to tell her you were sorry . . . ?" Michael said.

"That's when I thought I was going to die."

"That's cold," Michael said, much to Cindy's surprise. "She just went through hell to get you, she risked her life to save you."

"Yeah, and she is also the reason I'm here, the reason

Iblis used me to make her steal. None of this would have happened if she wasn't a thief."

"You know what, you're right," Michael said. "But you know what else wouldn't have happened? Your life. Your schooling, your career. You would have been stuck in foster care and out on your own at eighteen. Why don't you think about that? Why don't you think about what she gave up for you, instead of being so goddamn self-centered?"

Cindy looked at Michael, unsure how to respond. And then it hit her. "You love my sister."

Michael said nothing as he stared at her.

"The way you defend her; I can see it in your eyes," Cindy said with a smile.

And Michael was suddenly disarmed.

"What are you going to do about all that artwork down there," Cindy said as she pointed at the house, completely changing the subject.

"When we're clear, we'll call it in to the police," Busch said as he walked over from the limo. "Can you imagine the press that this is going to get? Some of that art has been missing for decades."

"I thought you were a thief," Cindy said to Michael. "None of that stuff interests you? You'd have millions."

"Billions, actually," Busch said.

Michael smiled. "I'm not that kind of thief."

"What about the chart? Isn't that why I was just put through hell?" Cindy asked.

"We don't have time to look for it. I've got digital pictures of it. Let's go," Michael insisted as he began to climb in the back of the limo. "We need to get Simon to the hospital."

"Michael, she's right. That's the one thing you can't leave in that house," Busch said. "Simon wanted it for a reason."

"Look who's getting all hot and bothered." Michael smiled. "I thought you didn't give a shit about this stuff, that it was a bunch of bullshit."

"It is bullshit. I don't think it should be in anyone else's hands, though. It would make a nice present for Simon when he wakes up."

"You're so thoughtful," Michael joked. "But I have no idea where it is."

"I do," Cindy spoke up.

"You don't even know what it looks like," Busch said, dismissing her.

"A big map, on some kind of animal skin? This big," Cindy said as she held her arms apart. "There's only one problem."

"Yeah, what's that?" Busch said.

"It's in a wall safe."

Michael and Busch looked at each other and smiled.

"Take him to the hospital," Michael said to Busch, pointing into the limo at Simon. Michael grabbed his leather bag of tools off the car seat and began walking back toward the house. He turned to Cindy. "Why don't you come with me?"

Cindy looked back at Busch, unsure what to do.

"This won't take long, then I'll drop you at your hotel," Michael said.

Cindy headed toward Michael.

"How are you going to get back?" Busch asked as he opened the driver's side door.

"I always wanted to drive an Aston Martin Vantage."

CHAPTER 35

Iblis sat on the cold metal bench of the police van. His hands and feet were manacled, the chains jingling with every pothole they hit on their way out of the Sultanahmet district on their way to the police station. Four policemen, dressed in dark uniforms, sat with him, their eyes filled with hate.

A large dark-haired man arose from the passenger's seat. He had a slight paunch but his harsh face diminished any sense that the man was soft, that he couldn't crush someone's spine in his bare, callused hands. He patted the driver on the shoulder and walked back among his men and the prisoner.

Kudret Levant was a fifteen-year veteran, a senior detective. He had been awoken twelve hours earlier by an enraged Ahmet Baghatur, the chief of police, who had just had half his ass removed by Prime Minister Erdem. Levant had twenty-four hours to find the terrorists responsible for the fiasco at Topkapi Palace if he had any interest in keeping his job.

Levant smiled to himself as he stared down at the short, skinny man; he had accomplished his mandate in less than twelve. And it wasn't terrorists or extremists; in fact, there appeared to be no political agenda to the night's chaos. It was simply about money, that universal motivator.

The anonymous call came into the police station giving the name and description of the perpetrator and his location. It was one of hundreds of tips, but it was a tip provided without incentive or demand for recompense, giving a description of what the man would be carrying and of the motive behind the night's events. He had sent his men at the prescribed hour, all bursting as they lay in wait watching the man who perfectly fit the description carry the long tube out of the grounds of the Blue Mosque. Their gruff supervisor had ordered them to hold their position until their mark was back on the public street; they could ill afford an incident at another of their most revered tourist attractions.

Levant stood in the back of the van, holding the leather tube that matched the description given by the woman. He glared at the thief.

"You caused great embarrassment to us," Levant said harshly, his voice deep and scratchy from years of smoking.

The baby-faced thief remained silent as he stared back with icy, emotionless eyes.

"On the world stage, no less," Levant continued. "Sometimes I hate the laws that bind us, as I'm sure someone of your profession does. They restrict us from carrying out those impulses, those feelings where we just want to mete out justice on the spot. Where we just want to reach across the van and snap the skinny neck of the guilty."

Levant turned his attention back to the satchel, opened the top of the tube, and peered inside. The eyes of his men were upon him as he reached into the long leather tube and withdrew the long bubble-wrapped object. Two of the officers let out slow whistles of admiration as their eyes fell upon the jeweled heads that were exposed above the wrapping. They all stared at the two snakes, the serpents poised to strike each other. Levant looked at the bubble wrap and slowly unwrapped it. And as the shaft of the rod was exposed, he looked at his men, who all shook their heads in confusion. He turned and held the rod before Iblis.

The shaft was a simple piece of wood, pine, brand-new. Levant flicked his index finger against the head of one of the snakes; he grasped one of the mouths and its left silver fang snapped off in his finger.

"Is this a joke? This is a piece of crap," Levant said.

Iblis sat there, not a trace of emotion in his eyes as he looked upon the false rod.

Detective Levant looked back into the tube, tilted his head in curiosity, and turned it upside down. The object trickled out like water into his hands. He held it up for all to see, the diamonds glinting in the sun that poured through the truck's rear window. The bejeweled necklace was exquisite, diamonds joined along a string of silver with a blue sapphire pendant in the center.

A slight change washed over Iblis's face.

"You jeopardized Turkey's reputation for this?"

"I want to call my lawyer," Iblis said quietly, with no hint of emotion.

"You can call ten lawyers; there is no one who will save you from your fate."

As Iblis sat there, resuming his silence, none of the police could see his cuffed hands behind his back. The blood was already beginning to drip, pooling on the wooden bench as he gouged the flesh of his left forearm with his fingernail, digging in, tearing the skin away.

Iblis finally turned his head, his eyes widening as if he'd suddenly woken up; he looked at Levant, and smiled.

* * *

KC BURST THROUGH the door of the Occidental Suite at the Four Seasons Istanbul.

Michael sat at the dining room table, the two leather satchels of their stolen goods before him. Upon the table was a host of documents, an open bottle of Jack Daniel's, and two cell phones.

"Where is she?" KC said, her breath coming in fits as she hurried into the room.

"She's in the shower," Michael said as he sorted through his paperwork.

"*How* is she?" KC's face squinched up, concerned with the answer.

"She's fine. Pissed"—Michael looked at her—"but fine."

"Pissed?" KC stopped in her tracks. "Does she know what *we* went through?"

Michael sat quietly, bracing himself, letting her vent.

"This is the way it has always been. She doesn't even take my phone calls." KC pointed to Cindy's cell phone on the table. "Did she see my number come up? And ignore me?"

"Well . . ." Michael didn't want to answer her question.

"Did she?"

"She looked at her phone, saw it was you. Decided to go take a shower."

"Doesn't she realize I have sacrificed my life for her?" KC began pacing, thinking, finally turning back to Michael. "And she has the nerve to ignore me?"

"KC," Michael said, his voice gentle, quiet. He finally stood and walked over to her as she stopped her aimless meandering. "She needs to work these things out in her head. She was kidnapped; she never faced her own mortality before. She's never dealt with anything like this. That's a rough thing. I remember my dad, my adoptive father, said just because you love your kids, that doesn't mean you like them every day, but you never, ever stop loving them. It doesn't make one a bad parent, a bad child, a bad sister. It's one of life's things; life is never steady, it's up and down all the time. We can't just love someone when things are good, when life is rosy; if we truly love someone we love them even more on their bad days, their worst of days."

"It hurts, Michael," KC said softly.

"It's the people we love the most who can hurt us the deepest. You have to remember, the ones we love, we take their trust in our hands and we try not to crush it as we protect them."

"You're defending her?" KC asked with a tinge of appreciation.

"I'm defending two people who love each other. You're sisters, the only family either one of you has. I know you guys will work it out."

KC relaxed and exhaled as she looked into Michael's eyes; his calming voice, his sense of balance infected her. A smile creased her lips as she understood what Michael was saying.

"Do you mind?" KC picked up Michael's glass of whiskey. "I kind of need it." KC's mood lightened as she looked at the two satchels on the dining room table.

"I can't imagine what's going through Iblis's head right now," KC said as she picked up and opened the leather tube, looking in at the twin snake heads, their red eyes and silver teeth glinting under the lights of the chandelier. "How the hell did you come up with a false head?"

"I made it early this morning while you were sleeping. I took a mold of the head. It's pretty crude."

"It was good enough to fool him. Where did you make it?" KC closed the container and laid it back on the table.

"In the mechanic's shop at the hangar."

"You didn't sleep at all last night, did you?" KC said, shaking her head. "I would have gone with you."

"You needed the rest."

"And you didn't?"

"But your necklace, that was a pretty pricey thing to frame him with."

"Trust me," KC said. "It couldn't have been put to better use."

"Wait until they check out his house, the art world is going to have a field day."

"What did he have, anything good?"

Michael paused, emphasizing the moment. "Da Vinci's *Madonna of the Yarnwinder*."

"What?" KC said in genuine surprise.

"Picasso's *Nature Morte à la Charlotte*," Michael continued.

"Holy shit, he was good."

"He did the Gardner Museum in Boston."

"You saw the Rembrandts?"

"And the Vermeer, the Manet, and the five Degas."

KC couldn't help laughing at the enormity of what Iblis had done.

"KC?" Michael said solemnly.

"Yeah?" She was shaking her head, lost in thought.

"His favorite painting, the one on most prominent display, was *Concerto de Oberion*."

KC's smile of wonderment dissolved.

"He killed those people in Berlin," Michael said, his voice filled with contempt. "He tortured the curator."

KC and Michael fell into silence, pondering the depravity of Iblis and the life he led, the moment dragging on as if in respect for those who had died six years earlier in the Franze Museum.

"Can I see the chart?" KC downed the rest of Michael's glass of whiskey, looking to change the subject.

Michael smiled as he picked up and opened the second tube. He removed the gazelle skin and rolled it out on the dining room table before KC. They both stood under the chandelier, quietly looking at the detail.

"It's so intricate . . ." KC whispered as if in the presence of something holy.

And it truly was. It depicted eastern Africa across the Indian Ocean to the South China Sea. It illustrated in great detail Australia, Indonesia, the minute specificity of Micronesia all the way up to Japan. Many of the grand rivers of Asia from the Ganges and the Padma to the Yangtze, the Yellow and the Zhu Jiang rivers were meticulously drawn, with cities and towns highlighted along their banks.

Her eyes caught sight of a giant serpent, a dragon, on the uppermost regions of the map. "Please don't tell me that's what this leads to."

"No," Michael said with a laugh. "That's terra incognita, unknown lands. Some cartographers liked to label unexplored regions on their maps with fancy depictions of mythical beasts."

KC smiled and sat atop the table as she resumed studying the chart. Her eyes were eventually drawn to the Himalayas, and to one particular peak. It was surrounded by a great deal of Turkish writing that sat next to pictures of gold and silver, jewels, books, and grain.

"So that is what everyone is so interested in," KC said softly as she traced her finger along a highlighted path from the Bay of Bengal up the Padma River and the Jamuna River and then trekking over land through to Darjeeling, India, and finally into the peaks of the Himalayas. "What do you think is there?"

"Don't know and I don't want to know," Michael said.

"Not the least bit curious?" KC joked.

"If it scares Simon then it scares me." Michael rolled up the chart and inserted it in the tube. "I need to bring these to him."

"I'm going with you. I just need to speak to Cindy first." KC smelled her armpit and arched her brow in question. "And maybe a real quick shower?"

"I think that would be for the benefit of all," Michael joked. "Besides, we don't want you infecting anyone at the hospital. Maybe I'll grab a shower, too. Simon's not awake yet anyway." Michael looked at his watch. "Half hour?"

"Thanks." KC sat on the table.

Michael gathered up his papers and cell phone and picked up the satchel with the real rod.

KC smiled and picked up the tube with the chart. "Do you mind if I look at the chart again?"

"Of course not," Michael said as he slung the satchel with the rod on his shoulder. "Do me a favor, though, don't let it out of your sight."

KC hopped off the table and walked over to Michael; she paused a moment as she became lost in his eyes. She reached up and ran her hand through his hair and pulled him into a kiss. It was deep and sensual, and time seemed to slow. All of their effort, risk, and worry was behind them as they became lost in the moment. They held tight to each other, the minutes dragging on, running their hands over each other, their contact conveying their rising emotions.

"I don't suppose . . ." Michael began.

"Later." KC tilted her head toward the upstairs bedroom where Cindy was.

"Great, I love taking cold showers," Michael said as he turned and walked out the door.

CINDY OPENED THE bathroom door, her body wrapped in a large white towel; she ran a brush through her wet auburn hair as she walked into the bedroom.

"Are you all right?"

Cindy jumped in surprise as she saw KC sitting on the bed.

The two sisters locked eyes, looking upon each other as if they were strangers. Cindy turned back to the mirror and continued working on her hair as if KC weren't even there.

"I'm sorry," KC said softly.

Cindy turned to her closet and drew out a tan Chanel dress wrapped in dry-cleaner plastic, hanging it on the door.

"I never meant any of this to happen." KC bowed her head.

Cindy continued to ignore KC as she unwrapped the dress, balling up the plastic and throwing it in the garbage.

"I thought I was going to die," Cindy said, her voice trembling just above a whisper. She spun around, tears of anger filling her eyes, the hairbrush vibrating in her shaking hands. "I was scared to death, but it's not the kidnapping, KC. You know what hurts the most? It's that the one person I trusted deceived me about everything. If you had been honest with me, this wouldn't have happened. And for God's sake"—Cindy shook with disgust—"you're a criminal. You are what Mom fought so hard for us not to be: You're a criminal just like our father was."

Cindy fell silent; she turned back to the mirror, grasping the dresser as she tried to calm herself.

KC looked about the room, uncomfortable in the moment, searching for something to say, when she realized what was missing. "Where are your bags?"

"I sent them ahead. I've got an evening flight to London. I never want to see this place again." Cindy removed the dress from the hanger and draped it over her head, pulling it down, smoothing it out over her body. "I'm probably going to lose my job."

"You won't," KC said in her big-sister way.

"Like they'll understand?"

"You were kidnapped," KC said as if pointing out the obvious.

"Do you ever stop and think? I can't tell them I was kidnapped, do you know how pathetic that sounds? That's worse than 'The dog ate my homework.' Did you ever call the cops, fill out a missing persons police report? No, you didn't. You were probably afraid you'd be arrested. You see, there's no evidence I was kidnapped. And how do I tell them I was set free?" Cindy threw open her hands in mock appreciation. "'My sister and her boyfriend went and stole an ancient sea chart and then broke me out of some lunatic's vault.' No . . . I can't imagine that going over well with the HR department."

KC sat there listening, the truth sinking in.

"If my bosses were to find out that my sister is a thief, what do you think that would do to my chances of retaining my job? Now I'm going to have to be like you and come up with some lie. Any advice?" Cindy asked coldly.

"Integrity, KC, they value integrity. They asked in my interview who was the person I most admired, who I looked up to, who influenced my life the most, and you know what the answer was?" Cindy shook her head in disappointment. "The answer to every question was you."

Cindy picked up her brush and ran it through one last time before fixing her hair with a large black hair clip.

"I don't know what to say," KC whispered in defeat.

"What do you even know about work, real work?" Cindy paused. "Legal work?"

KC could slowly feel their roles reversing: She had always been the one in charge, calling the shots, pontificating about right and wrong, telling her sister what to do, holding up a standard for her to aspire to. But now, as Cindy stood over her, her words like daggers upon her heart, KC felt like the child, felt as if she was the one who didn't live up to expectations, who brought shame on their name.

"Look at the bright side: Dad would be proud." Cindy turned and stepped back into the bathroom.

KC remained on the bed, her heart pounding more than it had in the past several days, more than when she feared she would be caught in Hagia Sophia, more than when she and Michael were running for their lives. While then she had been afraid for her life, had faced the fear of losing everything she held dear, it was nothing compared to her feelings now.

She was more afraid of Cindy's choosing to walk out of her life, to leave her. Cindy was all she had. A cell phone rang, startling KC out of her self-pity. Cindy emerged from the bathroom, walked out of the bedroom, and headed downstairs. KC could hear her answer, speaking softly. Left alone with her thoughts, KC felt suddenly alone. Cindy had already packed up physically and emotionally.

"That's great," Cindy said as she briskly walked back

into the bedroom. "I thought I would be going back to London to fight to keep my new job; now I have to fight to get it back. Thank you for destroying not only my trust but my career." Cindy grabbed her purse, a leather Longchamp bag, and walked back to the door, finally turning back and glaring at KC.

"Stay out of my life," Cindy said with measured anger. And she left.

KC's guilt was overwhelming: She had destroyed her sister's life, her career, her trust and hope. Everything that she prayed Cindy would never face in life had happened, and it was all because of her.

KC heard the hotel door slam and walked out of the bedroom onto the landing that overlooked the great room. She looked down at the leather satchel that sat upon the dining room table. Without even being revealed to the world, it had already begun to destroy lives.

KC descended the stairs, her eyes intent on the bottle of Jack Daniel's that Michael had left behind. She poured herself a drink and looked out the enormous windows at the minarets of Hagia Sophia tickling the sky. She thought of how peaceful and carefree one must feel standing upon the uppermost balcony, high above the city, away from life's troubles.

She picked up the leather tube and unlaced the top; she flipped up the hasp of the internal metal tube and turned it upside down. She'd take one more glance at the object that had laid such trouble upon her shoulders, at the artifact that was so filled with secrets and had struck such fear into Simon.

But nothing poured out, nothing came forth. The tube was empty; the chart was gone.

KC's cell rang. She plucked it from her pocket, her thoughts filled with mind-numbing confusion as she tried to figure out what had just happened. Her eyes ran over the room and back to the tube.

Her phone rang again. She looked with hope at the number, but it wasn't Cindy calling. It wasn't Michael. In fact, she didn't recognize the number. She thought of letting it go to voice mail but in all her sudden confusion she flipped it open and answered.

"Hello," she said, though her mind wasn't focused on the caller.

"Hello, KC."

KC's heart suddenly went cold. The room felt as if it were rapidly closing in, constricting her lungs. Her eyes darted about nervously as the voice filled her ears. All thoughts of the missing chart vanished.

"Do you remember what I said would happen if you betrayed me?" Iblis whispered.

CINDY WALKED THROUGH the lobby of the Four Seasons Istanbul and straight out onto the street.

"Good afternoon, ma'am." The doorman nodded. "May I get you a cab?"

Cindy ignored the man as if he didn't exist while she looked up and down the Istanbul street. She spied the limo driver holding the sign that said "Ryan," leaning against his black Mercedes just south of the hotel. With her Longchamp bag slung on her shoulder and purse in hand, she made a beeline for the car, looking every bit the society woman in her Chanel dress and Prada pumps.

"Enjoy your evening," the doorman said.

Cindy never even bothered to acknowledge the man's

existence as she approached the driver, who held the door open. He was tall and wiry, an obvious local. She avoided eye contact and remained silent as he greeted her.

She slid into the darkened limo, the door slamming shut behind her. Three large men sat silently in the opposing seat, guns conspicuous on their laps, as the clunk of the locks echoed about the air-conditioned car.

IBLIS STOOD WITH a cell phone pressed to his ear. Blood ran down his arm, momentarily pooling at his elbow before dripping onto the metal floor of the police van. Each drop added to the mayhem that surrounded him.

The four guards lay in a puddle of mingled blood at his feet, all randomly twitching in various throes of death as their bodies came to terms with their souls' abrupt departure.

In Iblis's other hand he held a thin, four-inch metal blade. He held it like a champion clutching his hockey stick, holding it with pride after scoring the winning goal. But Iblis didn't score goals.

With blinding speed, he had eviscerated the four policemen, quick strokes along the neck, each guard falling in turn as the crimson flood shot from their veins like water through a broken pipe, splattering the walls, the ceiling, and each other.

The thin, sharp blade had rested in an equally thin plastic sheath. A year earlier, Iblis had used his hunting knife to slice open his forearm and insert the medical plastic that he had formed into a thin knife holder under his skin. He stitched his arm up and felt as if he had wrapped himself in a security blanket as he buried his secret. The knife was tungsten, with a hair's-breadth edge that glinted in the light of day. It was impossibly narrow and was the perfect tool for the removal of handcuffs and the picking of locked doors, and it was outstanding for rending flesh from the bone.

He had placed it under his skin in the event of emergency and had endured explaining at every security checkpoint the "metal rod" that held his ulna together, displaying the "surgical" scar that ran up his forearm as incontrovertible proof.

He had dug it out of his flesh, using his nail to burrow under the skin, digging down to the lower dermis. The pain was like nothing he had ever felt; ripping into his own skin without the benefit of anesthesia or sight proved difficult, but he actually looked upon it as an achievement. Taking pleasure in the sensation of agony it brought him, he had finally felt the tip of the plastic sheath and pulled upon it, further tearing his skin in a ragged line. He had hoped no one in the van would hear the shredding of flesh as he extracted the bloodied sheath with a wet pop. Holding the tool he had hidden away like treasure one year earlier, he smiled at his Boy Scout–like preparation and set to work.

He had made quick work of the handcuffs, using his freed hands to carry out the execution of his unsuspecting captors. The driver had died instantly as the thin metal blade was jammed into the base of his skull, scrambling his brains. The van never moved when the light turned green.

Iblis turned to the sixth man, the boss, Detective Kudret Levant, who had taunted him so, who had chided him on his apparent guilt, not realizing for even a moment that Iblis had been set up. Iblis might have been guilty of many crimes, but the one they had arrested him for was a ruse concocted by his prodigy, KC.

Iblis was far from guilty, and he resented Levant's accusing eyes, so he did the only thing he thought appropriate: He dug them out. Levant was trussed with his own handcuffs as his breath wheezed through the thin hole in his neck, an air slit courtesy of Iblis. Levant's nose and mouth were stuffed and sealed with rubber surgical gloves from a med kit, barring air from passing through them. Levant would slowly die as the blood around the slit in his neck congealed, slowly scabbing over, slowly suffocating him.

The van remained in the middle of the street, ignoring the green light, its own red and blue flashing lights discouraging anyone from blowing horns or approaching the police vehicle.

Iblis clutched Levant's cell phone tightly in his right hand, not a hint of nerves or exertion showing in his voice despite the executions he'd just carried out.

"KC," he said slowly, "you're going to listen very carefully to what I have to say."

CHAPTER 36

Michael emerged from the bathroom, the shower having done a world of good, bringing life back into his aching bones. He felt rejuvenated, and he realized it wasn't just from the shower.

His heart had warmed. He felt a tingling in his stomach as he thought about KC, a feeling he hadn't known since Mary died. And oddly, he felt no betrayal of the memory of his deceased wife. He had loved her with all his heart and she had loved him unconditionally in return. Michael knew she would be happy for him; she had insisted that he find love again, not only before her passing from cancer but in the letters she had left behind. They pleaded to his heart to reach out and find someone to complete him, to make him whole again. Michael clutched the gold wedding band he wore about his neck. He would always wear it in memorial to Mary; he would never stop loving her.

He thought himself lucky; love is the rarest of gifts, one that is seldom found even once in a lifetime. Most relationships start off as physical attraction or commonality of interests, both of which had occurred between him and KC, but true love goes far deeper than that. It is an unexplainable connection of the heart, one that endures triumph and tragedy, pain and suffering, obstacles and loss. It is something that is either present or missing—there is no "almost," "in between," "most of the time." It is the unexplainable reason that some marriages entered into after one-week courtships can last a lifetime. Its absence is why "perfect" marriages fall apart. It can't be quantified or explained by science, religion, or philosophy. It can't be advised on by friends or marriage counselors who can't take their own advice. There are no rules, no how-to books, no guaranteed methods of success.

It is not defined by vows or rings or promises of tomorrow. It is simply a miracle of God, that too few are blessed to experience. And, Michael knew now, he had been twice blessed.

Michael's cell phone broke him out of his thoughts.

"Hey," he said as he quickly flipped open his phone.

"You guys all right?" Busch asked.

"We're good. How's Simon?"

"He'll be fine. His body is in shock and he's got about one hundred stitches in his noggin, but I venture to guess he's seen worse."

"Is he awake?"

"Yeah, once they pumped him full of fluids. He's going to have to stick around here a few days while the swelling goes down."

"He could use the rest." Michael paused. "KC and I are on our way to relieve you."

"Do me a favor?"

"Name it," Michael said.

"Three cheeseburgers, fries, and a Coke?"

"Of course." Michael laughed. "See you in a half hour."

Michael closed his phone, threw on his clothes, and

headed downstairs. He walked onto the balcony and looked out at the Bosporus and the Sea of Marmara. He tried to slow his mind, taking in the passing ships, the view of the grand city, memorizing it so that someday when someone asked about Istanbul, he could describe it beyond its underworld and back alleys.

Michael pulled out his phone again and dialed KC. The phone rang and rang but there was no answer. He still didn't understand why women took such long showers. He didn't bother leaving a message, closed his phone, and tucked it back into his pocket.

He took one last look at the boats upon the water that divided Europe and Asia and headed back into his room, glad that he was looking at the world from the much-preferred perspective of a relaxed mind. He picked up the house phone, dialed room service, and asked for three cheeseburgers and fries for Busch, telling the concierge that he needed them as quickly as possible and that he'd pick them up from the kitchen.

He grabbed his room key and wallet from the coffee table, flipped off the lights, and walked behind the bar, where he had stashed the leather tube containing the rod.

There had been times in Michael's life when he had felt utter surprise, but it was only on the rarest of occasions. Michael had always been a lover of chess, of strategic games in which one had to think of all possibilities, of all potentials and scenarios. He had learned to anticipate people's actions, learned to forecast the outcomes of events as mundane as a business deal or a football game, or as complex as stealing a painting or rescuing his friend Simon from prison.

But as Michael looked down behind the bar, his heart sank. He had thought the possibility existed but had closed his mind to it. Busch had asked him how well he knew KC, but he had shut him down. Michael's heart never lied to him, his instincts were always spot-on.

Michael closed his eyes, breathing deep, trying to still his mind and heart, which were already in a full-on race. For in the spot where he had placed the leather tube, behind the crystal and bottles of wine, there was nothing.

The sultan's rod that KC had risked life and limb for was gone.

CHAPTER 37

The hospital room was antiseptic white, the smell of bleach filling the air. Ataturk Hospital was an old building—some joked it predated the historic mosques—but its doctors were some of the best in not only Istanbul but all of Europe.

Simon lay in bed, an IV mainlining him fluids as a half-eaten sandwich sat on a meal tray by the window. His head was fully bandaged but his color was back, his face looking healthy, his slate-blue eyes full of life.

Busch sat in a cheap yellow chair that barely accommodated his large frame, his legs extended, resting on the bed.

They were both in midlaugh when Michael stepped through the door, walked in, and stood over Simon. He clutched a briefcase, his knuckles white from his overly tight grip. For a moment he looked back and forth between his two friends, before his eyes settled on Simon. "You okay?"

"Yeah," Simon said in his Italian accent. "I'm good. Thanks. That's twice in a week. Either you're real good or I'm really stupid."

"I think it's a combination of both," Busch interjected. "But keep in mind that the common denominator in saving both of you is always"—Busch patted his chest with both hands—"moi."

Simon and Michael both looked at Busch with dismissive eyes before Michael continued. "Well . . . I'm just glad you're okay."

"If there's anything I can do . . ." Simon offered.

"Well, since you mention it." Michael stepped back, lost in thought, until he refocused and could no longer restrain himself. "What the hell is going on?"

"What do you mean?" Simon asked, genuinely confused.

"KC's gone."

"What?" Busch sat up.

"The chart and the rod?" Simon quickly asked.

Michael tilted his head. "She double-crossed me."

Simon sat up in his bed, thinking. "Do you really think that?"

"She picked the lock to my hotel suite and snatched the leather tube while I was in the shower. And the map—well, I checked her room and it's gone, too."

"You didn't answer my question."

"I don't know what to think." Michael shook his head. He was truly perplexed. He had been so filled with anger when he found that the rod was gone, he couldn't think straight. He raced down to KC's room to find her and the Piri Reis chart missing, sending him into an even deeper tailspin of confusion. But if she had double-crossed him, if she had stolen the two artifacts . . . the alternative was far worse.

Simon picked up the phone at the side of his bed and dialed nine. "Can you connect me to the Istanbul police?"

Michael and Busch remained silent, both realizing what Simon was doing.

"I'm calling about an arrest made earlier today outside the Blue Mosque." Simon paused, listening. "No, sir. No, I don't. I wasn't aware." Simon paused, listening intently, his face growing stern. "Of course, if I do you'll be the first to know." Simon hung up the phone as the person on the other end continued to grill him, ending the questioning midsentence.

He looked at Michael; he didn't need to say a word.

"Do you think he kidnapped her?" Michael asked.

"No, not KC, she's pretty hard to get the jump on. No." Simon took a deep breath. "Iblis would want to control her. He must have her sister again."

"Again? How can this happen again?"

"It's not what you think," Simon said ominously. "I think Cindy is working with Iblis; he seduced her."

"What?" Busch said with disgust.

"Not in the sexual sense, but in every other way." Simon paused. "They spoke, he showed her the map, told her all about it. I was barely awake, hiding behind closed eyelids, listening to everything he had to say. KC didn't betray you, but her sister did. She betrayed everyone."

KC SAT UPON a large bed in the back cabin of a luxurious private jet.

She had walked out of the Four Seasons Istanbul with the two leather tubes, one empty, the other containing the rod that she had taken from Michael's hotel suite. She headed toward the open door of the waiting limo but paused before getting in. She glared eye to eye with the driver who stood beside the car, the visible pistol in his waistband causing her no fear. As the moment dragged on, a black Mercedes limo on the far side of the street rolled down its window to reveal Cindy sitting between two large men, Iblis's men. KC needed no further prodding and entered the car.

The driver headed straight to Ataturk Airport, not a word spoken on the twenty-five-minute drive. They pulled up to the rear private terminal where a Royal Falcon business jet was parked, its engines idling, their exhaust shimmering the light around the wings.

The limo driver silently opened the door and motioned for KC to board. She headed up the gangway two steps at a time and into the luxury business jet. A blonde stewardess with a German accent directed her to the back of the plane. She entered a private bedroom filled with brushed-pine walls and a queen-sized bed, and before she could even turn around, the door was slammed shut.

It had been over half an hour, and no one had yet spoken to her. She gripped the two leather tubes tightly in her hand, wondering where they had taken her sister this time, and thinking about how foolish they all had been to allow Cindy to be taken once again.

With a jolt, the jet began to taxi. The engines revved to a full-on scream and the jet took off like a bullet down the runway, jumping into the sky at an extreme angle. KC held tight to the bed, the centrifugal force forcing her into the mattress. She looked out the small portside window to see Istanbul vanishing into nothing more than twin peninsulas on vast bodies of water.

She thought of Michael and the anger and confusion he must be feeling at her sudden disappearance, having stolen that which they had fought so hard to keep away from Iblis. But it was her sister, it was her welfare that once again controlled KC's life, as it always had. And as the jet continued to climb into the blue sky she realized she was leaving behind what she truly loved, her only chance at a real life. She knew there would be no coming back from wherever she was going, for there was little chance she would survive.

The door opened and Iblis stepped in. He looked at KC and smiled. His clothes were covered in dried blood, splatter marks dotted his face, his forearms looked as if they were covered in maroon paint. But his hands . . . His hands were surprisingly clean, contrasting with the rest of his macabre appearance. In his right hand he carried a small leather briefcase as if he were arriving for a business meeting.

"Where's my sister?" KC exploded.

"She's fine, KC. Relax," Iblis said as he laid the case on the night table.

"Where is she?" KC demanded.

"She's up front."

"Let me see her," KC said, her tone rendering an ultimatum.

And instantly, Cindy was standing in the doorway. She appeared out of nowhere, no worse for wear. Not a word was spoken, not a hint of emotion flowed between the two sisters as the seconds ticked by. All at once Iblis grasped the handle and closed the door, ending the uncomfortable moment.

Iblis stepped to KC and, without a word, took the tubes from her. His eyes flickered between her and the two cases. "Teacher always gets his way."

He removed the lid of the first tube, reached in, and pulled out the rod. He handled it gently, studying the snake heads, ensuring the silver teeth were real. He marveled at the jewel-encrusted skin of its body before sliding it back into the tube. He looked down the tube and back up at KC with disappointed eyes. "What, no diamond necklace?"

KC turned away, looking out the window as the world grew smaller and smaller.

"Oops," Iblis said in mock surprise as he removed the top of the second tube. "Something seems to be missing."

KC looked up at him but remained silent.

"Where is it?" Iblis said matter-of-factly. "Come now, KC, let's not play games when we are about to be traveling at thirty thousand feet."

"I don't have it."

Iblis nodded, slowly at first, then picking up in speed with understanding. "Let me guess, someone took it from you?"

"I said I don't have it," KC repeated defiantly through gritted teeth.

"Which is why sometimes it's best to have a backup, someone who can handle things in your absence." Iblis opened the briefcase that sat on the nightstand and pulled the Asian Piri Reis map out of his bag, holding it out in admiration.

KC's eyes began to burn with anger. She had suspected, she had known; no one else had been in the hotel room at the time the map went missing. But she had convinced herself otherwise, ignoring the obvious, all the while hoping that there was some explanation.

"I don't think I would have convinced her so easily if you hadn't disappointed her so much, if you hadn't lied to her. Your sister has proven more reliable and trusting this week than you."

The shock washed over KC's face.

"Not a good feeling, huh? It's always the ones we love

who hurt us the most. Funny how real betrayal can only come from those we trust."

"What did you do to her?"

"To Cindy? Nothing. I didn't need to dangle the death of a loved one before her eyes; her principles are far less rigid than yours. Once she learned where the chart led, once I told her I worked for a very rich man, she was happy to help."

"Happy?"

"Well, thirty million by age thirty, that was her motto. She wasn't going to get there with the job she had, whether she lost it or not. I told her, showed her where I was keeping the map, just in case you or Michael actually succeeded in taking me out. She could show you or Michael where it was so you could steal it and she could then surreptitiously swipe it from you and deliver it and have that thirty million far sooner than she had ever hoped.

"But I think what really motivated her was the little secret I revealed. About the man I work for, the man whose office you tried to burgle. Turns out, that was all the real motivation she needed. When she learned of his success and wealth, well, your little sister, those are the things she holds most dear.

"In her young life, she never met him, though she spent her life wondering about him. But all you ever told her was that he was a criminal, that he was evil, repeating what your mother had told you, what she emphasized when his coffin was laid in the ground. But truth be told, the only thing in that box was his name, his past, and the charred body that he left behind when he escaped. All of which was buried away forever, disappearing under six feet of earth."

KC sat there, the whine of the jet engine ringing in her

ears as her world spun out of control. Her bearings were lost; her mind could hardly hold a coherent thought.

"My father is alive?" KC finally asked.

"Of course he is," Iblis said with a smile. "Who do you think sent me all those years ago to train you?"

CHAPTER 38

Michael withdrew two large documents from his briefcase, unfolded them to reveal two exact photo replicas of the map, and laid them on Simon's bed. The first one was unmarked, the second annotated with English translations.

"Who did this?" Simon asked as he looked between the two charts.

"I took digital pictures of the map when I first found it, just in case."

"Always thinking," Simon said.

"I emailed them to my father in Boston; his law firm has access to translators. I'm sure he paid through the nose to get this turned around so quickly."

Simon studied the map, his eyes intent, his fingers running about the picture as if he could feel the topography.

Busch burst into the hospital room; he held the GPS tracker in his left hand. "A private jet left Ataturk a half hour ago; it's somewhere over eastern Turkey. Both tubes are on board. And get this." Busch paused. "The plane is registered to a Philippe Venue."

Michael turned to Simon. "Venue? The one who had you thrown in prison?"

Simon nodded.

"KC's on that plane, isn't she?" Busch asked.

"I would imagine with Iblis and Cindy."

"Do you know where they're going?" Michael asked.

Simon pointed to the center of the map and nodded. "Kanchenjunga. A mountain in the Himalayas, the third-highest peak in the world after Everest and K2. For many years it was thought to be the world's tailest mountain."

"What, did it get demoted?" Busch asked, half joking.

"It's partly in Nepal, mostly in India, not far from Darjeeling. Do you know what the name Kanchenjunga means?" Simon asked rhetorically, his eyes fixed on the middle of the map. "'The Five Treasures of Snow.' Pretty apropos."

Simon continued analyzing the annotated chart, reading the English translations, looking more closely at the marked route up from the Bay of Bengal through Bangladesh into India, his eyes growing wide with wonderment. He was lost in the map, as if Michael and Busch weren't even there.

"I'm sure you're finding this real interesting," Busch said, seeing Simon's concentration on the chart. "But I'm done being patient and you're done being a patient. In Michael's words, "What the hell is going on?"

Simon looked up, his mind snapping back to the here and now. He took a moment, adding to the anticipation. "There are places in this world around which fables have grown, worlds of peace whose legends have been placed upon mantels and been held up as the ideals of the ultimate utopian existence. Places like Shambhala, Shangri-La, the Garden of Eden, Ney-Pemathang, Aryavarsha, Hsi Tien, Land of Living Fire. The Hindus called it Meru, their

Olympus, said to be situated in the center of the earth. They say it was guarded by serpents who would kill those who tried to gain access to the realm of secret knowledge. They considered it the land of bliss. Some Hebrews spoke of a land called Luz, while the Cioces held tight to the legend of Stauricha.

"These worlds were thought to contain the mysteries of gods, the serenity of paradise. They were peaceful sanctuaries where the weather is perfect, society is kind and gentle, food is abundant, gold and jewels exist beyond the imagination, and, greatest of all, life is eternal. But as these places exist in legend, so do their counterparts, lands of darkness, lands of evil.

"The Greeks call it Tartarus, a place even worse than Hades; the Hebrews, Gehenna or Sheol; for Islam it is Jahannam; in China and Japan it is referred to as Di Yu; the Buddhists and Hindus call it Naraka. The Maya called it Xibalba, while the Sumerians called it the Great Below— many names, but all representative of the underworld, all representative of what Christians call hell.

"This chart, drawn by Piri Reis"—Simon waved his hand over the picture—"was informed by much older maps, maps from forgotten history. And what it leads to, the place that Piri's uncle Kemal Reis so feared being found, is a world that many have sought before. I don't know if it is Shambhala, Shangri-La, or Aryavarsha, but it is there, unrevealed to the world for a reason. Piri Reis's notes speak of his uncle's sailing up the rivers of Bangladesh, into India, then trekking by foot to return a vast treasure to a world of treasures, a repository for the words of gods. The English translation of Piri's notes says, 'No holier place, no place filled with greater darkness. A world of gods and demons, suffering and joy, love and misery. An existence protected and in balance and never to be disturbed.'"

"A mountain place filled with treasure?" Busch cut in, his voice filled with cynicism. "Hell, they call it the Mountain of Five Treasures. Seems obvious. And Shambhala, Shangri-La De Da is there? This has escaped everyone's notice, all the explorers, all the money-grubbing self-promoters, even the esteemed archaeologists? That makes no sense."

"Kanchenjunga makes perfect sense. One of the first persons to try to scale it was an Englishman by the name of Aleister Crowley, a man enamored of the occult. Some thought he was the author of the satanic bible, but that is pure fable. He was a member of Golden Dawn and was enraptured with myths and the mystical. No one was quite sure why he chose that mountain, but his guides spoke of his searching for signs of unknown civilizations along the way. Four people died during the trek and they never made it to the peak. As Crowley's life unfolded and the world learned more of Aleister Crowley, many concluded he was looking for Shambhala.

"During the thirties, Heinrich Himmler and Rudolf Hess led German expeditions in search of Shambhala, scouring the mountains of Tibet, Nepal, and India in hopes of finding the wealth and knowledge that would bring about the rule of the Third Reich."

"You can't possibly think a place like that exists," Busch said.

"The translation of the map is very clear," Simon said. "It may not be Shambhala as man has imagined in his books and fairy tales, but there is *something* there."

"All right," Michael said, cutting short Simon's dire

speech. "So even if this place exists, if it is filled with gold, or jewels, or repositories of knowledge, then why the rod? What does it do? Its value may be high, but its worth would be dwarfed if what you describe actually exists—unless it has some purpose."

"How can you buy into this?" Busch said to Michael before turning to Simon. "No offense."

"Do you doubt it out of skepticism or do you doubt it out of fear?" Simon shook his head in annoyance. "All myths can trace back to some truth, no matter how minute. How is it that so many cultures have the same myths, the same uniting themes?" Simon paused. "Is it because they have some basis in fact? Gods and demons, the great flood, heaven and hell, angels and beasts, earthly paradise, life after death. Every culture possesses similar tales about these things. Gives you pause, if you have half a brain to think about it—"

"The rod!" Michael interjected, defusing the argument before it twisted into a maelstrom. He shot a glance at Busch, who rolled his eyes and took a seat.

Simon calmed himself and turned back to Michael. "Each culture contains what is known as an axis mundi, a link between two realms such as heaven and earth. Sometimes it would be a mountain, such as Mount Sinai, where God spoke to Moses and gave him the Ten Commandments, or the Mount of Olives, where the Bible speaks of Jesus rising to Heaven, or a man-made thing such as a pagoda, church steeple, obelisk, or minaret. The American Indian has the totem pole, Egyptians have the pyramids, the Norse had the tree Yggdrasil. All places or things that would act as a conduit between man on earth and his god above.

"An axis mundi is sometimes considered the center of

being, the navel of Mother Earth, thought to be where the four points of the compass meet. And at that point there is rumored to be vast knowledge and wealth beyond imagination.

"KC told you about the rod of Asclepius and the Caduceus. Their central staffs are considered axis mundi, while the serpents are the guardians of the knowledge that passes through that link between heaven and earth.

"The sultan's rod is such an object, said to open a passage to heaven . . . or hell, but only if it is at the appropriate location. That location is where Piri Reis's chart is pointing. Whatever the name may be, wherever the chart points to is where the rod came from.

"I believe this place, this Shambhala, lies atop a keep, a temple where Kemal Reis and his men hid away the treasure. I believe it is a place of darkness and that the rod is needed to open its entrance. I believe what is at the end of this chart is a manifestation of heaven and hell on earth, and the sultan's rod is the axis mundi that links them, that opens them up."

Busch rolled his eyes, shaking his head, growing fidgety in his chair.

"Look, I'm not telling you what is at the end of this map," Simon said, seeing Busch's skepticism. "Be it boogeyman or monk, Devil or God, it is all speculation. But something is there beyond the gold and treasures that Kemal Reis returned." Simon held up the large photo of the map and underscored the English translation. "It says here that all but five of his men died up there, and only one survived to deliver the rod, letters, and the original chart to Piri. And what is very important to understand is that both Piri and Kemal were men of the sea, men who charted reefs and rocks to be avoided at all cost, to protect all who sailed so they might live to see a new dawn. This chart here"—Simon stabbed his finger at the picture—"depicted not a destination, but a place to be avoided at all costs.

"Kemal was warning his nephew, imploring him to hide the rod away and avoid Kanchenjunga. He was warning of the danger of opening this hidden world in the mountains to protect not only his nephew but everyone from what lay within.

"Make no mistake, Kemal Reis was a corsair, a pirate, an admiral, a man who instilled fear, who didn't cower in the face of danger. If Shambhala is heaven on earth then what lies beneath is nothing short of hell on earth, and if it were to be opened . . ."

Simon's words hung in the air as the hospital room grew silent. Echoes of nurses' voices and moving gurneys reverberated in the outer halls as Michael's and Busch's minds drifted about, absorbing Simon's story.

"Michael," Simon said, a tinge of foreboding in his voice, "Venue is a violent man, on the brink of insanity. He has three obsessions: wealth, power, and knowledge of the mysteries of the beyond. He's a fallen priest excommunicated from the Church not only for murder but for seeking out the devil, for seeking out alternative gods, for dabbling in mysticism. He went on to amass a fortune applying the lessons of his criminal past to the business world; he achieved tremendous power, rendering himself untouchable by the corrupt politicians and world's police, whom he expertly manipulated via money and blackmail.

"But his fortunes have turned; his empire has all but crumbled around him. The Church has found him and is looking to expose him, to hold him accountable for the murders of the seven priests who had him excommunicated from the Church. Where Venue was once invincible, shielded by his money, that protection has evaporated.

"So he has redoubled his efforts to find the location contained in Piri Reis's chart. Where it was once an avocation for Venue, a secondary quest intended to resolve the unanswered questions of his younger seminary years, it has now become his only hope for saving his world.

"If he reaches this so-called Shambhala, I fear he will find not only fortune but a darkness that he will use against those who cast him out: his sworn enemy, the Church."

Michael and Busch remained silent as Simon's tale soaked in. Michael understood Simon's fears and concerns, he understood his wanting to protect the Church, but Michael was not truly convinced of the threat. What his mind was focused on, what really caused the fear to build in him, was the thought of KC's fate as she was being dragged around the world.

"Michael, there is something you need to know about Venue. While I was being held by Iblis, during a lucid moment, I overheard him tell Cindy a secret that made the truth of the map pale by comparison in her eyes." Simon paused. "Venue is KC and Cindy's father."

Michael felt his insides contract, his world turned upside-down as his mind overflowed with confusion. He could feel Busch's "I told you so" eyes looking his way.

"And she knows this?" Michael finally said in anger.

Simon shook his head. "No, she has no idea. I had no idea. But it makes sense when you look at all the pieces. Iblis is the factor that ties it all together. He was not only KC's teacher, sent by her father when she was young, but also their protector, who would silence anyone who posed a threat to the girls."

"She never knew?" Busch asked as the seriousness of the revelation sank in.

"I imagine she is about to find out. Think what this will do to her. Remember, Venue already sent her to her death, knowing she is his daughter. I can't imagine what she will do when she learns the truth, that he is the man her mother taught her to hate, the man she thought she saw buried when she was a child."

"Simon, where are they flying to?" Michael asked, his voice urgent, thick with fury.

"Darjeeling, India. Then they'll grab either a helicopter or an off-road vehicle to travel the twenty-five miles to the mountain."

Michael looked at Busch. He didn't need to say a word.

"Shit," Busch said. "I'll call ahead, get the plane ready. Just stick another pin in my world map."

"I'm going with you," Simon said from his hospital bed, though he knew it wasn't possible with his condition.

"I wish you could," Michael said.

"Yeah," Busch added. "Then at least I'd have someone to drink with."

"Michael," Simon said. "Under no circumstance is the world below Shambhala to be opened. I fear it contains madness, evil of the darkest nature. In the hands of someone like Venue or Iblis . . ."

Simon didn't need to finish; Michael fully understood his warning.

CHAPTER 39

Michael and Busch were in the front of the limo two miles from Ataturk Airport. They had come straight from the hospital, bypassing the hotel, as they had nothing of real value there. Michael's gear was either in the trunk of the car or stowed away on the jet. Busch had already made the call; the jet would be prepped and ready for departure in less than an hour.

Busch was driving as Michael placed the GPS monitor into a cradle on the car's dash. The screen depicted a wide map stretching from eastern Turkey to India with two small red dots floating over the Caspian Sea.

"Michael, there is no question that there are two signals on that plane heading to India. But if they have the original chart and the rod, what is it that you had me lock away in the safe on your father's jet?"

"It's—"

Michael's cell phone rang. He looked down, saw it was KC, and flipped it open. "Thank God." Michael exhaled in relief. "Where are you?"

"God has nothing to do with this." The man's voice was deep and rich, a slight English accent polishing his words. "I understand you love my daughter."

Michael's senses ignited as he listened to Philippe Venue.

"If for some reason I do not get to my destination, if I do not achieve my goal, I will kill her. It's my prerogative as her father. So don't bother coming after her or me. Don't you be listening to that fool of a priest. If you try to stop me, I'll have Iblis here flay the skin from her bones. And it is such nice skin."

And the phone went dead.

BUSCH SPED INTO the hangar. The jetway door was already open, the Boeing Business Jet waiting for its passengers, its engines idling. Michael and Busch grabbed the bags from the trunk and ran up the gangway, closing the door behind them.

Michael headed straight for the safe under the bar. He spun the wheel and opened it to find the object of his interest. He pulled out the leather tube, untied the top, flipped open the interior metal hasp, and opened it.

Michael pulled out the sultan's rod, examining it, ensuring that it had not somehow magically disappeared. Authenticating it, he quickly slipped it back into its case and placed it back in the safe.

"Does KC know she has a fake one?" Busch said.

"She has no idea."

"That's some trust you've got going there between the two of you."

"You know me, I'm a bit of a control freak when it comes to these things. I was afraid for her when it was in her possession."

"Well, now that it's not, I think she is in far more danger. When they get where they're going they are going to figure it out. As soon as they try to use it—"

"Enough. I realize what I've done."

But Michael was not about to reveal that his deception was motivated by what he felt when he handled the rod. It was an overwhelming effect; it went beyond nausea, dizziness, and illness. It was as if it infected him with despair, robbing him of hope. It was an effect that he would protect KC from at all costs.

Michael had initially intended to make one replica, one doppelganger to fool Iblis, but after feeling the effect, he changed his plans.

He had left the comfort of KC's arms, leaving her sleeping in the safe house nearly eighteen hours earlier. It was just after midnight when he arrived in the private hangar at Ataturk Airport and headed straight for the workbench. The night guard was happy to vacate with one hundred euros in his pocket and a case of raki in the trunk of his car. Michael explained that he needed use of the lathe and press to repair some climbing equipment, but Michael didn't need to worry, the guard had no interest in the rich American's pastimes. He was already planning his night of drunken merriment with his three brothers.

Stephen Kelley's jet had sat behind Michael, filling three-quarters of the cavernous space. It had arrived back in the early evening, having taken its deceptive jaunt around the Mediterranean, with its pilot hunkered down in a nearby hotel awaiting instructions on when they would be leaving.

Four boxes of acrylic molding compound sat on the workbench in the rear of the hangar. Busch had picked it up earlier in the day from an art supply house and delivered it to the hangar along with some wood, quick-set resin, and various other supplies on Michael's shopping list.

Michael constructed the mold box out of plywood; it was simply a three-foot-by-two-foot-by-one-foot-deep hinged case, its seams joined with compound binding glue to provide an air- and water-tight seal.

Michael mixed the acrylic molding compound and poured it into the box, filling it halfway.

He opened the leather tube and pulled out the bejeweled rod. He laid it upon the table and photographed it from every angle, turning it about as he worked, paying particular attention to the dual snake heads.

Suddenly, Michael began to feel nauseated, dizzy. He felt no reason to continue, and pessimism infused his heart, a feeling that he was doomed to fail. It was a feeling such as he had never known, as if everyone he loved was about to die, leaving him alone for all eternity, and there was nothing he could do to stop it.

With great effort, despite his dark emotions, he placed the rod in the box mold and closed the top. Almost instantly the feeling diminished. He momentarily feared the rod emitted some type of radiation, but, if so, both he and KC would have felt it ever since they'd obtained the rod, as the leather and metal tube it was held in was incapable of containing any deadly emissions.

He didn't know what caused the feeling, but there was no doubt it came from the ancient artifact. He refused to speculate on the cause—he didn't need his mind running away from him—and remained focused on his creation. Nonetheless, he decided he would keep the odd effect of being in direct contact with the rod to himself and would create two replicas before dawn.

After five minutes, Michael opened the box. He brushed a coating of baby oil over the hardened half mold so that he could easily separate the cast when it had hardened. He mixed up a new batch of mold compound, poured it over the exposed rod, and closed the box.

Michael's adopted father, Alec St. Pierre, the man who had raised him, was an expert craftsman, a man who tinkered with and created everything from grandfather clocks and cars to furniture and electronics. Michael had learned many skills from him and had developed a great love of creating things from scratch. It was artistry, a skill that had proven more than helpful in his illicit past. Though Alec St. Pierre had passed away, Michael still cherished the memory of the father who raised him, a feeling that wasn't diminished by his relationship with his birth father, Stephen Kelley, the man who owned the jet in the hangar, the man who told him tales of his heritage, of his birth mother, and what she had been like before she died in childbirth. Michael considered himself more than lucky: He had lost the father who raised him, but cherished his memory, while being privileged to become friends with the father with whom he shared blood.

Michael flipped back the top of the wooden box, exposing a black hunk of rubber. He gingerly separated the mold into its two halves to reveal a perfect mold of the rod. Michael took out the original and tucked it back in its case, not wanting to experience the unpleasantness of its presence.

He removed the two sections of the hard rubberlike mold, and on the lowermost end by the tails of the entwined snakes, he used his knife and carved out a slit into which he placed a small copper pipe. He then took a drill and, with a one-sixty-fourth-size drill bit, punched ten holes along the length of the rod's outline.

Michael laid the two halves perfectly against each other and duct-taped them together. He carved a notch in his wooden box and dropped the mold inside, allowing the copper pipe to protrude from the box. He grabbed a tube of resin and injected it into the copper pipe, emptying the entire contents into the mold, then followed suit with five more tubes until the gel overflowed the top.

Michael placed the case aside, grabbed his camera, and climbed up into the jet. He headed to the small conference table, downloaded his picture file into his computer, and printed out the photos of the rod, studying them with a careful eye. He went to the bar, crouched, and spun open the safe, pulling out a black velvet pouch, tucking it into his pocket. Closing the safe, he headed back to the workbench.

Michael opened the case, unbound the rubber mold, and pulled out the resin replica. It was deep brown, a perfect match but for its overall color. Michael twirled it about, slapping it against the palm of his hand, and smiled: The quick-drying resin was as sturdy as metal.

Michael reaffixed the two halves of the mold together. He squirted more resin compound into the head section of the mold and turned back to his workbench. He set about grinding the sharp edges and imperfections off the replica. With his hand grinder, Michael ground down the raised areas that corresponded to the jewels on the original staff. He made quick work of the eyes, honing them down to concave sockets, and filed off the poised fangs.

With a delicate hand, Michael painted the bodies of the snakes in a rough reflection of the original serpents that intertwined up the shaft, distinguishing and highlighting them from the rod they wrapped around. He wasn't concerned about creating an exact replica so much as an authentic artifact that would suspend suspicion for the briefest of moments.

From the velvet pouch Michael extracted two ornate necklaces, each a gathering of a host of precious gems. Spoils from a theft many years in the past, they were finally being put to good use. Michael snipped the necklaces apart and epoxied the gems into the recesses he had created along the length of the rod. He inlaid four small rubies into the eye sockets and nodded at the likeness he had created. He reached into the pouch and withdrew two silver forks. He carefully cut the tines from the fork body and placed the first one in a vise. With a metal grinder, Michael honed the tine into a sharp fang, following suit with each tine until he had four perfect fangs. He rubbed them with a mixture of black paint and chalk, approximating silver tarnish, making them appear aged. He drilled four holes and epoxied the teeth into the snake mouths. He held up the rod and smiled. His creation could have fooled Sultan Selim II himself, but Michael had an even greater advantage: No one knew exactly what the rod looked like except for him and KC. It had never been on display in a museum, it had never been rendered in exact detail. It was an object of myth, so the duplicate wrought by Michael St. Pierre could fool the world.

Michael opened the mold and withdrew the second head, which was a virtual duplicate of the serpent head before him. He repeated the process of grinding and painting, creating a replica head of jeweled eyes and silver teeth. He anchored the head to a wooden rod, wrapped it in bubble wrap, and inserted it into the leather tube.

Upon reuniting with KC in the morning, Michael had passed off the perfect duplicate as the genuine article, and once he was sure that their plan had worked, without the need to surrender the original rod, he had Busch place the original in the jet's safe. Michael showed KC the wooden rod with the false head, which she would use to deceive Iblis. He was confident that Iblis would only peer into the container, not risk taking it out in a public place like the courtyard of the Blue Mosque. His ruse worked—he had fooled Iblis, he had fooled KC—but now as he stood inside the jet back in the hangar eighteen hours later, he condemned himself for his cleverness, for his deception might very well end up costing KC her life.

"Paul." Michael turned to his friend. "I don't care about this treasure, this place of peace or whatever horror may lie beneath it. All I care about is getting KC. When Iblis and Venue find out the rod she carries is a fake . . . " Michael paused, unable to voice his fears. "Mary died of cancer, there was nothing I could do to prevent it, I know that. But KC . . . I'm not going to have another woman I love die when I have the power to save her."

CHAPTER 40

KC lay upon the bed in the stateroom at the back of the Royal Falcon jet. They had been in the air for almost eight hours, heading east over the rocky, arid plains of Turkey. KC had occasionally looked out the window to see the stars and to note that their course had not deviated. They were heading into the heart of Asia, and KC knew where; she didn't know its name or its precise location, but she had seen it clearly marked on the chart.

It had been Iblis's goal—she stopped and corrected herself. It had been Venue's goal. Simon had implored them, with dire warnings, not to let the map fall into Venue's possession, and now . . . She felt as if she had laid it right in his hands.

She wondered if Simon knew who Venue truly was, but within seconds, she banished the thought. She felt in her heart he was too good a friend to hide such a devastating secret from her.

She had first learned of Venue before she and Simon raided his office to steal the ancient letter. She knew of his ruthless dealings, of his destruction of even his weakest competitor, and that he was suspected the world over of criminal underworld ties, but she never suspected that he was her father.

He had expertly buried his criminal past in St. Thomas Cemetery in Shrewsbury, England. Finbar Ryan had truly died all those years ago; she had witnessed his interment standing at her mother's side. Her father was wiped from the face of the earth, only to be reborn as Philippe Venue, trading in his holster for a briefcase.

And upon her mother's death, in a psychotically paternal action, Venue had sent Iblis to be their guardian, her teacher. She did not know Venue's motive, or why he had never attempted to contact them or send money. She was thankful that he had never reached out.

But the fact that he had set her on her life's path, that he had sent Iblis to turn her into a criminal by using her love for her sister to motivate her, twisted her heart. Her mother had explained that their father was a man capable only of taking, filled with depraved indifference. She understood full well why her mother hated the man, why she had taken them to his funeral so they could all bear witness to his demise.

But her fury at Venue—she would never think of him as her father—and her anger at Iblis were minute when compared to the pain and disappointment she felt toward her sister. She had raised her, sacrificed all for her, supported her, cared for her. Cindy had cried on her shoulder countless times over life, the absence of parents, school, and boys, never knowing that KC had no one to cry to. KC had listened to her sister's stories of heartbreak, never revealing that she wondered what it felt like to fall in love in order to have your heart broken.

And as Cindy grew up she became driven by success, by money, forever boasting of how she would one day care for KC when she made her millions. She became lost in the materialism of youth, in the craving to have it all, and it had finally consumed her, clouded her understanding of what was truly important in life and making her easy for Iblis to lure into a world of hollow promises, illusory wealth, and Philippe Venue.

As KC sifted through all the confusion and deception, she was filled with mind-numbing rage. At Iblis for all that he had put her through, at Cindy for her betrayal, but most of all at the puppet master, the man who had manipulated them, the man her mother raised her to hate: her father.

The fact that he was alive, that she had broken into his office to steal the grand vizier's letter . . . All at once she understood why the first painting she ever stole and sold, *The Suffering* by Goetia, hung on his wall. It was a prize, displayed with pride, as a coach displays pictures of his gold-medal protégés.

And then a final fact floated to the surface, the worst of all. Venue was the one who had sent her to her death in Chiron Prison, knowing full well that she was his flesh and blood. Was there any more heinous act than condemning your own child to death?

So many thoughts spilled about her mind. She had lived her life under false pretenses and suddenly felt like an utter fool. She sorted through the years, her sacrifices and self-denial, her longing for normalcy, for someone to reach out and pull her out of her life, embracing her, loving her, and making everything right with the world.

And her thoughts fell to Michael. She had gotten so close to a real relationship, one that had filled her heart and soul with joy. There was something shared, and it did not matter if they were angry, frightened, or tired, it was a constant and undeniable bonding of their hearts. In all the places, in all the situations to find love, she had never imagined it would occur under such circumstances. And with a man who made her feel every bit a woman, who made her feel confident and unashamed of her past and her career. He did not look for her to change in any way. He loved her in the most simple and most complicated of ways. He had soothed her when she was nervous, calmed her when she was frightened, and consumed her with his lust. She yearned for him now; she needed to feel the calming effects of his embrace, needed to be told everything would be okay.

For those brief moments of love, for indulging herself, however briefly, for this one instance of selfishness, she was being punished, dragged off to the ends of the earth by the two most despicable men she had ever known: one who had fathered her and one who had trained her. And the one person she thought she could count on, whom she had raised and was closest to, her own sister, had betrayed her and fallen in league with them.

KC walked about the small suite, rummaged through the fridge, and found some Italian sausage and cheese. She opened a bottle of wine. She wasn't going to play the martyr and not eat; she wanted to have all her energy when she tore into Cindy. She laid the food on a small desk and sat. She reached inside her shirt and withdrew the engraved necklace that Michael had given her, removing it from her neck, laying it on the table, reading the words of hope: *There's always tomorrow*. And for the first time since she had met Michael, she doubted that promise, not only doubting his words of wisdom, but doubting she would ever see him again. She dug through the drawers of the small desk, finding a notepad and pen.

And as her heart finally broke, she poured her wine and began to write.

Dearest Michael,
I'm sorry . . .

CHAPTER 41

KC watched the sun rise out the jet's port window, its dawn light painting the lush green forests below an orange early-morning hue. To the north she could see the peaks of the Himalayas and knew they were somewhere over India. No one had knocked, no one had entered the room since their departure. She knew both Cindy and Iblis were on the other side of the door and understood why they had left her alone. They both knew the wrath she would unload on them the moment their eyes met.

The jet began its descent and touched down twenty minutes later on a small private airstrip precariously perched upon a sharply rising hill bordered with ravines on either side. The surrounding area was awash in dense foliage and rolling hills of green. And in the distance, not more than forty miles north, she could see a mountain, larger than anything she had ever seen, its peaks blanketed in snow, outlined by a crystal-blue sky.

The jet taxied before rolling to a stop on the far side of the runway. KC could hear movement within the cabin and the mechanical wind-down of the jet as the main door was released with a hiss. She sat waiting for the door to her cabin to open, but no one came. She peered out the port-side window to see Iblis and Cindy descending the gangway stairs followed by seven of Iblis's men.

The hustle and bustle died off, the plane falling silent. KC waited at least a half hour before the door was opened by one of Iblis's men. He wasn't armed, nor did he say a word as he turned to exit. She followed him out of the plane into the chilly morning air; the surrounding temperature couldn't have been more than fifty on this summer day, confirming that they were at least several thousand feet above sea level.

They were in the midst of undulating hills covered in thick blankets of varying shades of green, thick grasses, rolling shrubs, and enormous trees. But for the makeshift airport, there was no sign of modern civilization. No towns, roads, no planes overhead. It was a timeless world that was imbued with a sense of peace.

KC followed the man, arriving at a wooden and tin hut that was covered in a spongy green moss. A stovepipe protruded from the slanted roof, light gray smoke floating out before evaporating into the cool morning.

The guard remained silent as he opened the door. KC peered into the shack to find an old woman kneeling at a cooking fire; she wore a deep red vest over a loose-fitting orange dress, with large Timberland boots. Her dark hair was pulled back, revealing a deeply tanned face that was painted with a smile that creased the skin about her eyes. The smell of food filled the air as she worked several pots and pans of eggs, stew, and meat. She nodded in welcome and dished out the meal on tin plates, filling dented mugs with coffee, pulling seasonings and utensils from a shelf.

As KC's eyes adjusted, she saw a large rough-hewn table on the opposite side of the room. It was covered with the Asian Piri Reis chart, the center of attention of the three who stood before it. They all turned as KC stepped in, their eyes falling upon her. She was struck by a fit of anger like nothing she had ever felt. Her sister stood with Iblis, her enemy. Both looked upon KC with expressionless eyes, and both remained silent, subservient to the man who stood between them.

KC's eyes fixed on the older man. She had merely glimpsed him in passing that night at his office. He was tall, at least six foot two inches, and what little hair he possessed had long gone to gray. He was dressed like someone out of an old Abercrombie and Kent safari brochure: tan khaki pants, a leather and fleece vest worn over a thick lumberjack shirt, all brand-new. There was no question that this was a man who thought his money could buy his way up a mountain.

As he took a step closer, KC became nauseated, for she truly saw the resemblance. She had his eyes, the same high cheekbones. He stood ramrod straight, his shoulders held back and confident. The man possessed an aura that filled the room; his presence commanded Cindy and Iblis, but KC ignored it, seeing it simply as arrogance.

"You're taller than I expected," Venue said as he stepped uncomfortably close, eyeing her as if assessing an object for purchase.

KC stared up into eyes that were much like hers.

"Far prettier than your sister," he said, not in compliment but merely as a point of fact. "Are you ready for a little family journey?"

"I'm not going anywhere with you," KC said through gritted teeth.

Venue stared at her, his eyes filling with anger; he was not accustomed to noncompliance. He slowly raised his arms, reached out, and gave KC a tight, unreciprocated hug. He tilted his head, coming cheek to cheek with her, his hot breath falling upon her ear. "Oh, my dear, you most certainly are."

Venue released KC and stepped back to the table. The three turned their attention back to the map.

KC stood in total shock at the man's conceit; she did everything she could to quell her emotions. "You sent me to die," she said defiantly.

"Yes, I did," Venue said without looking up from the map. "Now, why don't you come join your sister and me and see where we are going?"

KC ignored the invitation and the man's overconfidence and looked at Iblis. She saw something in him that she had never seen before. KC had known the man for years, had borne witness to his disregard for life, to his cavalier attitude in the face of danger. He could kill a man thirty times over, yet now she saw the one emotion she had never expected of the man: fear. Venue truly terrified him as he stood in his presence. Cindy, on the other hand, couldn't have been less afraid. She was enamored of Venue, a sense of pride drifting into her eyes as she looked at him. Seeing her naive admiration, Venue warmly rubbed her back, coaxing a smile, further ingratiating himself, further drawing her under his spell.

KC turned in disgust and spied the two leather tubes tilted against the wall of the ramshackle hut. She reached over and picked up the first, opening the top. It was empty, its contents being scrutinized on the wooden table by Venue. She picked up the second and began to open the lid. She thought twice about it, remembering the effect the rod had had on her when she first gained possession of it.

"I must give credit where credit is due," Venue said as he looked at the tube in KC's hand. "Iblis trained you well, but you exceeded my expectations. When I sent him to watch over you, to teach you the ways of the street, I thought your life of crime would be short-lived. Who knew it would become a lifelong career? You—" Venue cast a quick glance toward Cindy. "Sorry, my dear. You, KC, are truly my daughter."

KC ignored Venue, his words of praise falling on deaf ears. She was looking into the tube at the entwined snakes, at their silver teeth, their ruby eyes, and thought of the twin serpents as Iblis and Venue. She pulled it out halfway, looking at the blood-red ruby eyes of the opposing snakes, at their flexed jaws poised to strike each other, wondering what would possess someone to create such a vile piece.

"Do you realize what you hold in your hand?" Venue didn't wait for an answer. "That stunning object you stole is the key to a world few have ever laid eyes upon. It is the answer I have sought for thirty years."

Only the slightest of grins appeared on KC's lips as she fought to hide her smile, but that didn't mean she wasn't laughing on the inside. The rod had no effect on her: no sense of vertigo, no swirling images, no nausea. The rod was not encumbered with the disorienting effect she had felt when she first removed it from the sultan's tomb. And she knew why. Michael was far more resourceful than she had imagined, possessing a great deal of forethought. She realized the sultan's rod in her hand was, in fact, a fake.

KC's internal laughter warmed her soul, for as she looked at Iblis and Cindy, as she looked at Venue standing over his chart, patting himself on his prideful back, she knew that they might make it up the mountain, the chart might lead them to the place Venue had sought, but without the real rod, he would never get in.

THE BOEING BUSINESS Jet roared out of Istanbul and across Asia. Michael and Busch had hurriedly packed up, gathering their gear and weapons, stuffing them in the three large duffel bags and tucking them in the storage wells in the belly of the jet.

"Do you have any idea where we are going or what we are getting ourselves into?" Busch asked.

"Not exactly to the first question, but yes, I know what we are getting into."

"People don't climb the Himalayas in August unless they have a death wish," Busch said as Michael glared at him. "I'm just saying . . ."

"We're not going to the top. In fact, where we're going we won't need oxygen or many supplies."

"I thought you said you don't know where we're going."

"Not exactly. We'll follow the chart, but more important, we'll follow them. Michael pointed at the GPS screen in Busch's hand. "I did the heavy lifting for Iblis, now he can pay me back by showing me the way."

Busch looked at the GPS readout. The two red dots were merged, appearing as one. The tube containing the chart and tube containing the false rod were on the move again, traveling north out of Darjeeling, India.

CHAPTER 42

The four giant blades cut into the air, beating up a gale-force wind that swept the tarmac free of leaves, clippings, and debris like some enormous leaf blower. The HAL Dhruv helicopter slowly lifted off, its forty-three-foot-long rotors thundering over the lower valley.

The seventeen passengers sat in silence as the bulky tan copter, manufactured in Bangalore, India, pierced the midmorning sky. They were packed in and cramped, lined up as if for military deployment, sitting on two long rows of leather benches that rested against the metal sides of the spartan helicopter. Besides Venue, Iblis, KC, and Cindy, there were eleven formidable guards, Iblis's men. They were a mix of nationalities, a mix of criminal and military backgrounds, hailing from divergent parts of the world though united through their ability to speak English. In addition to being tough and skilled in the art of death, each possessed a quality that couldn't be taught: Each was completely loyal to Iblis as their leader, friend, and, most often, beneficent employer. They all had worked to varying degrees for the small man over the years, always on call, for everything from breaking into museums and private homes to driving and kidnapping sisters on a moment's notice. Dressed in heavy wool pants and dark sweaters, each wore a sidearm, had a radio piece in his ear, and avoided eye contact with the other passengers.

Two dark-skinned mountain guides sat between the guards on the hard-backed leather bench, dwarfed by the massive men who towered over them. Both came from a small village just north of Darjeeling, each bearing a heritage that was an amalgam of local peoples: Sikkimese, Nepalese, Tibetan, and Indian.

They were both aboard despite the protests of their wives and children. Their colleagues in the mountaineering business implored them to listen to reason, to not join the insane party that required their services to scale Kanchenjunga at this, one of the most dangerous times of year.

But to Sonam Jigme, the allure of the compensation, the fact that he was being paid three years' wages for one trip, caused any fear he had to evaporate. He was young and strong, his body thick and larger than those of most of the people of his village. If anyone was going to survive the impossible, he would. And if he did, his wife would have the home she had always wanted, his three daughters would have their education, and he would have the pride of knowing he had provided a far better existence for them than he could ever have dreamed.

Kunchen Tsering had always been the wisest of guides, the most knowledgeable about Kanchenjunga's five peaks. He had defeated the mountain eighteen times, more than anyone else on the planet. He was modest and soft-spoken, his hearty appearance belying his fifty-four years. He had been raised in the shadow of the Five Treasures of Snow and knew every approach to its five summits. When the tall, older European had made inquiries in the village,

Kunchen's name was on everyone's lips. He was expert at knowing the varied terrain, at reading the winds for changes in the weather, at delivering climbers to the heights of the world and returning them home safely.

But Kunchen was a man who couldn't be bought; his was an uncomplicated existence, and he took his joy from the simple pleasures of family and communing with the great Himalayas that provided for him. He had learned the nuances of climbing from his father's father, a man who survived avalanches and sudden storms that had taken the lives of countless men. Kunchen's grandfather had attempted to summit Kanchenjunga's highest peak for the first time in 1905 with a party led by an Englishman named Crowley. Four died on their unsuccessful journey and Crowley never returned for a second try. Kunchen's grandfather spoke of Crowley's quest, regaling Kunchen and his friends as they sat around the campfires of their youth. He spoke of Crowley's unsuccessful search for hidden temples and mythic villages secreted somewhere in the reaches of the great holy mountain. He told the story so often that Kunchen would have to pinch himself to avoid nodding off and to keep his eyes from glazing over the way most children's do as they listen to the twentieth telling of an elder's tales.

When the tall European upped his offer to five years' pay, Kunchen asked what so intrigued a man that he would pay such a wage to enable him to face certain death. Venue told him a story, one that Kunchen had not heard for decades, not since the roaring campfires of his childhood. Not since his grandfather had spoken of Aleister Crowley and his great quest.

In the end it wasn't the money, it wasn't the pleas of a desperate man that lured Kunchen. It was a chart, a highlighted chart depicting a route no one had ever taken, not only because of its treacherous route but because it ended at an impenetrable pass whose 130-degree rock face was forever covered in ice. Kunchen explained that the summit could never be reached via this route. But it was Venue's simple words that finally convinced him. "My destination is not the summit, it is something far greater," Venue had said.

They were the exact words that began Kunchen's grandfather's story; they were the exact words Crowley had uttered to his grandfather over one hundred years ago.

THE HAL DHRUV touched down on a wide-open stretch of snow-dotted land on the south side of Kanchenjunga. The mountain rose above an abandoned midmountain camp like a stairway to heaven, white-capped and majestic.

Iblis's men threw open the sliding doors on both sides of the helicopter, disembarking as if on a military mission. The roar of the helicopter's engine cut down to idle as the blades began slowing. The eleven guards unloaded ten crates of gear from the rear of the helicopter, quickly carrying it off to the side.

Cindy and Venue jumped out the port side, hand in hand, as if going on vacation. KC chose the starboard side, anything to stay away from the two.

The ground was hard-packed soil and rock, intermittently covered in snow. The temperature hovered around thirty-eight degrees Fahrenheit, the summer high for this part of the world.

Iblis's team quickly broke open the large crates and withdrew a table, unfolding it before Venue. They removed prepacked rucksacks and backpacks, tents and laptop computers.

Kunchen walked around the open rocky fields of grass and snow, occasionally pausing, smelling, appearing to taste the air. He spread his arms wide, spinning about as if in ritual. He looked up and read the blue sky, looking at the great sharp peak that loomed above them at twenty-eight thousand feet, studying the wisps of snow that curled off the jagged edges of the summit, looking like an Ansel Adams photograph.

KC turned from Kunchen's ecoanalysis and cast her eyes on the Piri Reis chart that had been rolled out on the table. Appended to the map were yellow Post-its written in English that Iblis had translated from Turkish during the plane ride. Sonam held down their fluttering edges, sheltering them from the slight breeze as he read. He turned his eye to the mountainous depiction of Kanchenjunga on the animal hide, tracing his callused forefinger along the red path. Venue, Cindy, and Iblis stood with bated breath awaiting his assessment, but he remained silent, his eyes falling closed at intervals of deep thought.

Abruptly he opened his eyes and turned to Venue with a broad smile filled with misshapen teeth. "Five hours," Sonam said as he pointed west toward a snowy mountain pass.

Venue looked at his watch and shook his head. "Three years' salary for five hours' work."

"Wait for destination before you start crying for discount," Sonam said in broken English.

"Not to worry," Venue said. "I have no intention of renegotiation."

Iblis turned to his men. "Secure the crates and suit up; we leave in ten minutes."

KC looked back at Kunchen, who was walking toward

Venue. The older guide walked slowly, his hardened eyes filled with warning.

"We cannot go," Kunchen said.

Venue said nothing as he watched the man approach.

"Why," Iblis barked.

"Storm's coming."

"Storm?" He looked up at the blue sky.

Venue turned and looked down to Sonam, his raised brow asking for a confirmation.

Sonam looked up at the wisps of curling snow as they wafted off the mountain peaks, and nodded in agreement. "Big storm."

"How big?"

"Down here, nothing to worry about. Throw up tents, make coffee, tells jokes, and in thirty-six hours we go."

"Thirty-six hours?" Iblis shot back.

"How long until it gets here?" Venue asked.

Sonam and Kunchen looked at each other.

"Six hours," Kunchen said. He was obviously the senior, the man of greater experience, and on the third-largest mountain in the world, experience always took precedence.

"We could make it to our destination if we leave now," Iblis said to Venue.

"Understand," Sonam interjected. "If we wrong, if we get slowed, if there's rockslide in our way, you could be added to body count of Kanchenjunga."

"Where I come from, weathermen are wrong all the time," Iblis said.

"That's because they learned their science from books." Sonam laughed. "We learned ours from God."

"I don't mean any disrespect," Kunchen said to Venue, bowing his head. "But where *I* come from, I'm never wrong."

Venue stood there thinking. He looked at the eleven guards now wearing backpacks. "Five hours, you said," he asked of Sonam.

"If all is right in the world. But I, too, can already taste the storm in the air."

Venue turned to Iblis. "Secure the base camp, keep everything crated. If the weather turns bad we'll turn back and make camp here. Let's take what we can carry, whatever doesn't slow us down."

A silent buzz overtook the camp as Iblis's men quickly got to work. Venue rolled up the map and tucked it into his backpack. Iblis grabbed the satchel containing the rod, throwing it over his shoulder. Cindy stood there like a fish out of water in her ill-fitting hiking clothes, looking like some sort of academic. Her hiking boots were poorly tied, her vest wide open, her hat rested in her pocket so as to avoid a matted head of hair. She was entirely naive about what she was facing, as though her intelligence had dimmed as she had fallen under the spell of her father.

KC shook her head in disgust as she picked up her pack, settling it on her back. She snatched the empty leather tube for the chart off the table as two of the guards broke it down. She watched as they stored the table inside the largest crate, along with the other bags of supplies, and began to close it.

"Wait," KC said, running over. She opened the top of the tube and slipped her letter to Michael inside. She closed it and passed it to the guard. "Only bringing what we need."

The guard said nothing as he tucked the leather case into the larger crate and sealed it, pulling down the hasps, securing it tightly.

KC looked around; there was nowhere to go, nowhere to

run. She hated herself for falling into this situation, for ever having listened to Iblis, for trusting her sister.

When she turned around she saw Venue, Cindy, and Iblis already hiking along the snow and rock toward the mountain pass one mile in the distance. The guards were heading up behind them in pairs. She had never thought she would die so young, but the possibility presented itself more strongly now than it had when she had been trapped in a jail cell, sentenced to die. KC turned to the two mountain guides who stood silently staring at her.

"This is a really bad idea," KC said as she put on a black wool hat, tucking her blonde hair up inside. She took off her pack and checked it, pulled out a bottle of water, and affixed it in a net pouch on the side. She looked at her watch, noting the time, put on her sunglasses, and looked at the summit of Kanchenjunga.

"You've climbed before?" Sonam asked.

"Nothing like this."

"At least you respect the mountain."

"It's going to get bad, isn't it?"

Kunchen nodded as he looked at Venue and his team heading off.

"Don't worry," Sonam said with a crooked-toothed smile. "You seem scared—more than any of this group—which is good. Maybe, out of us all, you'll survive."

CHAPTER 43

Banyo Chodan gripped the stick guiding his helicopter across the green foliage for the second time in four hours. The former Indian military pilot loved his job shepherding rich Europeans and Americans who picked mountains out of catalogues to add to their travel-experience collection. Mountain climbing had once been reserved for the hardiest, most adventurous of men: The great peaks had first been scaled only in the fifties, and climbs had been infrequent at best for the following decades. A sport reserved for intelligent, athletic risk-takers, it led to death and tragedy more often than any other. But now, with the vast amount of new money floating around, people thought they could buy their way up a mountain, could buy medals and badges of courage just like shopping for a new pair of shoes. Banyo did not mind that the jet-setters chose Kanchenjunga over Aspen, Tahiti, or Africa, he just had to be sure not to get too friendly, as the survival rate was not as high as Aspen and the death of his clients had a tendency to bring him down.

Banyo had arrived back at the airstrip to find the Boeing Business Jet taxiing toward him. It was larger than Venue's jet, which sat in the distance. With the cost of fuel these days, larger meant greater resources, more funds, which was confirmed by the brown-haired American and his large blond friend as they slipped the five thousand dollars into his hand.

Banyo explained everything he could remember about the European party and their foolishness at traveling in the off-season. He described the eleven large men and their militarylike countenances, the two guides, who were the best the area had to offer, the European Venue, his short, dark aide, and his young daughter. And finally, the beauty of the tall blonde with the look of defiance in her eyes, the second daughter, the one with a will of her own.

It took all Banyo's will not to break out in his usual belly laugh when they said they needed to go to the same place. Two thirty-million-dollar jets in a single day was no coincidence.

Banyo had called his two cousins Achyuta and Max, offering them as sherpas for a fee of five thousand dollars, and hit the two men for two thousand more for clothes, boots, and climbing gear. The American kept peeling off the bills, without protest, until Banyo finally overflowed with guilt.

All told, Banyo ended up with twenty thousand dollars to take this second party out to the mountain and be on call to snatch them back. It was definitely time to take another vacation with his wife in the Seychelles Islands in the Indian Ocean.

Banyo showed them to the back of the hut to change and pointed out the back door to a large natural steam bath that bubbled and fogged the cool air.

"Hot springs; you'll like them," Banyo had offered. "Not a bad idea in preparation for where you're going."

"No, thank you," Busch said uncomfortably.

"They are everywhere around the Himalayas, but here,

they are medicinal, no sulfur odor." Banyo sniffed the air. "See?"

"We really need to get going, if you don't mind," Michael had said.

And so they were flying out over the green, rolling mountainside, heading straight for the peaks of Kanchenjunga, the thrumming blades announcing to the mountain that more victims were en route.

BUSCH AND MICHAEL sat in the back of the helicopter, both wearing large yellow earphones equipped with microphones to communicate with each other over the engine noise. Achyuta and Max sat across from them, studying the large blowup picture of the untranslated map that Michael had given them. Neither of the young men who hailed from Sikkim was older than twenty-five, and their mahogany-brown skin seemed yet unfamiliar with facial hair. Both were reed-thin, which couldn't be disguised by their mountain wear. There was a joy and a sense of mischief in their eyes as they looked at the chart, pointing and whispering in their native Nepali language, the excitement on their faces unmistakable. They were heading into terra incognita, unknown territory, much as their fathers and grandfathers had before them.

But their adventure would be short-lived. Michael had already decided that once they were within an hour of their destination, he would send the two brothers back down the mountain; he had no desire to wipe the innocence from their eyes.

"Kind of makes me miss Istanbul," Busch said, seeing his breath coalesce in soft clouds before their eyes.

"Bet you're thinking of that nice hot spring and its nice

hot water right about now," Banyo's voice came over the headset.

"Yeah," Busch said in reluctant agreement as he pulled his backpack up onto his lap. He reached in, withdrew his GPS tracker, and turned it on. He magnified the image and found that the two red dots had separated, one stationary, the other moving northwest. He held it out to Michael. "It looks like they split up."

Michael rose from the wooden bench and, with his hand against the copter's ceiling to steady himself, walked to the front of the aircraft.

"How far up the mountain can you take us?" Michael said, thankful for the headset, which enabled him to avoid shouting.

"Not far." Banyo shook his head. He pointed at the mountain that loomed large in the windshield, its peaks silhouetted by dark, ominous clouds. "There's a storm coming in. You may want to reconsider and sit back for a day. I won't charge you again."

Michael shook his head. "Take us as far as you can."

The chopper rode low over the green hills, which gave way to rocky scrub. This part of the world appeared deserted, fresh, and unblemished by man, as if God was keeping secrets.

Busch made his way up to Michael and held out his GPS to Banyo, pointing at the stationary dot. "Can you take us there?"

Banyo nodded. And within five minutes they were touching down in exactly the same place he had dropped off the first team. There was not a soul in sight as they all disembarked, working together to pull off the backpacks and supplies.

Their equipment was de minimis; climbing, in the sense of using crampons, ropes, and spikes, was not what they would be doing. They didn't need oxygen, as they would be well below the eighteen-thousand-foot barrier for breathing, though fatigue would be a major factor. Michael couldn't imagine the foolish desperation that drove Venue and Iblis. Once they hit ten thousand feet they would be feeling it. And the climb to their estimated fourteen-thousand-foot destination would result in nothing short of sheer exhaustion. The terrain would be rocky and snow-covered at the higher altitudes, dangerous even to the sure-footed, but at least the gradient wouldn't exceed twenty degrees.

Achyuta and Max walked about the abandoned camp, the reproduction of the chart held before them. They looked at the looming mountain, pointing and speaking in hushed tones.

"You call me on the two way-radio when you're ready to come back," Banyo said as he stood by the open door of his helicopter. "And don't be stupid; it's always the ones with too much pride who die up there."

Michael nodded and shook Banyo's extended hand. "Thanks."

Banyo jumped in and started up the HAL Dhruv, pulling her into the sky; Michael watched it disappear south and turned around.

Busch stood among ten large wooden crates, each secured with large hasps and locks. He tapped his finger on one of them and then on his GPS display.

"Do you think they left something behind?"

Michael walked over, withdrew a small climbing ax

from his pack, and hammered off the lock. He flipped open the clasps and threw back the large top of the crate. He dug through the tents and duffel bags, pushing back a collapsible table, and found the leather tube.

He pulled it out and unsealed it. He briefly looked at Busch before withdrawing a folded piece of paper. Two pages. He unfolded it and began reading:

Dearest Michael,

I'm sorry to be leaving you this letter. I know it was something your wife did on so many occasions and that it was something special between you, but it is the only way I can contact you now.

I am not eloquent, my education has come through life, not books, but there is one thing I am certain of and thankful for. I finally know what it means to be loved, to have someone care for me without question; I know what it is like to allow my soul to be held in your warm hand. I know what it is like to become lost in an embrace, to feel the utter calm and security of love. To say that you opened my heart would be an understatement.

I love you, Michael, simply and purely. You have been the first thought in my mind when I wake and the final thought as I fall asleep. In the short time we have been together, I have found a lifetime of love. You live in my dreams and in my heart. I'm sorry for my words of anger and doubt, I'm sorry for rejecting you at my doorway when I should have invited you in. Please know the passion I felt when we made love filled my soul—they were the most complete, the most perfect moments in my life.

If you are reading this letter it means I'm on my way up

the mountain. I ask, no, I implore you not to follow me. We are heading for certain death and I could not bear the thought of your dying as a result of me.

I love you forever and for always,
Katherine Colleen

PS: I ask that you take this. It was the first gift of love I ever received and it was from you. I have worn it these past weeks, clutching it tightly for strength when I thought I couldn't go on. I ask now that you keep it and think of me and when you hold it in your hand know that I will always be with you.

Michael picked up the leather tube. He tilted it over his hand . . . and the silver Tiffany necklace spilled into his palm.

CHAPTER 44

Three hours into their trek, the sun well past its noonday high, Venue's party crossed the thirteen-thousand-foot mark. They had hiked through the mountain pass and up along a wide-open field of snow, winding their way along rocky terrain into a thirty-foot-wide trail bordered on either side with sheer granite, which gave the impression of being at the bottom of a chimney. The winds picked up, whipping about, making the thirty-degree air feel like it was fifteen. They had all thrown on their Arc'teryx jackets and Turtle Fur scarves, while their breathing sounded like straining locomotives.

Venue's movements were no longer spry, his cheeks red and moist with sweat, his age showing. But his words remained optimistic as he led and urged the team onward.

Cindy had fallen behind. No one waited as she continually slipped on the hard-packed snow. Unaccustomed to the rigors of outdoor life, she looked as if she had run two marathons without training.

KC had said nothing to her sister since they'd arrived in India, her anger helping to keep her climb aggressive. But seeing her sister's exhausted condition, she turned and walked back the fifty yards to where she was struggling.

"Are you all right?" KC asked.

"Fine," Cindy said defiantly.

"Good," KC shot back, what little sympathy she had drifting away. "'Cause if you weren't, make no mistake, he'd leave you behind. And when the storm comes . . . well."

Cindy looked up at the cloudless blue sky and shook her head. "Those primitive fools and their 'feel-it-in-the-bones' forecasts, they have no idea what they are talking about."

"Don't be a child. This isn't a balance sheet, Cindy. This isn't some financial model that you control with mathematical certainty. In case you don't realize it, you are way out of your element here and you would do well to lose the arrogance and pick up the pace. No one's carrying you up this mountain."

"You think I still need your safety net, KC. I haven't needed you in years. I've achieved so much more than you could ever hope for, all of it without your help. My life is my own; I do what I choose."

"And you choose to go up this mountain with that man?" KC pointed at Venue leading the pack that was pulling away from them.

"Yeah." Cindy began walking. "I do."

"He only wanted the chart; that is the only reason Iblis revealed who he is to you. He doesn't give a shit about you."

"Are you upset because I want to work with him, or because he likes me?"

"My God, Cindy, do you hear yourself? If he cared, why didn't he contact us all these years? He always knew where we were, who we were. This man is everything we fought not to be. He is a criminal."

"Oddly enough"—Cindy looked right at KC—"you seem to emulate him pretty well."

KC tried to ignore the dig, though she was growing frustrated with her naïveté.

"You know where we're going?" KC asked rhetorically, walking at her side. "You know how many people have died up here?"

"I thought you were all about taking risks, Miss *Extreme Sport*, Miss *I Love the Outdoors*."

"Yeah, I love risk, I love the feel of adrenaline. I've chosen to ride dangerous lines but I've never chosen suicide."

"Suicide?" Cindy looked at the team of men that were now one hundred yards ahead, rounding a mountain bend. "I think we're pretty well-protected."

"Protected from what?" KC blasted. "The weather? No one can stop that from coming. And if we make it to our destination, I have a feeling what's waiting for us will laugh at our protection."

"What the hell is that supposed to mean?" Cindy abruptly stopped.

KC smiled in irony. "Why do you think Simon, Michael, and I fought so hard to keep this map out of their hands? We couldn't give a shit about some gold or jewels. There's more to life than money, Cindy. There's something else up there."

"Do you hear yourself?" Cindy laughed despite her exhaustion. "Now who's the child?"

The flurries began, soft and airy, drifting about, caught in the updrafts. And suddenly the blue sky above was gone, replaced with thick, dark, foreboding clouds, casting the world into premature twilight.

A clap of thunder rumbled, echoing about the rock face, and the flurries became snow, falling steadily, cutting visibility by half.

"He's marching us to our death, whether you choose to believe it or not."

"I don't think our father—"

"Father? You're calling him Daddy now? I'm surprised you waited this long," KC mocked her. "It's amazing how close you've become."

"Go to hell."

"Funny." KC laughed as she began walking double-time up the hill, leaving her sister behind. "I think that's exactly where we're going."

CHAPTER 45

The air tasted of metal—aluminum, to be exact. The thinning atmosphere at fourteen thousand feet was dryer than any desert Busch had ever been in. He and Michael were enveloped in a blizzard of blinding proportions, their legs on fire from their four-hour trek while their bodies grew frigid from the dropping temperature and windchill.

They were both dressed in full mountain gear: down Gore-Tex jackets, gloves, face masks, yellow-tinted goggles, not a stitch of skin exposed to the suddenly harsh elements. The snow swirled about them, the silence intermittently broken by howling gusts and the sound of pouring sand as the snow was whipped against the rock face.

They had lashed themselves together with a hundred-foot strand of kernmantle rope. With visibility down to nothing, it was possible to lose each other while standing only a few feet apart. The roar of the wind drowned out and absorbed any noise that Michael and Busch made, forcing them to press lips to ears to communicate.

They had both pulled out their axes, using them to steady themselves against the wind and to better grip the icy surfaces.

"What would possess someone to do this on purpose?" Busch shouted into Michael's ear.

Michael shook his head, not knowing what to say. He had sent Achyuta and Max back down the mountain over an hour ago. With Busch possessing the GPS, the two young brothers were there only in the event of a failure of electronics, but for once, things seemed to keep working. While initially resistant, hoping to continue their first adventure, they both relented as the winds kicked up over fifty miles per hour.

Busch leaned against the rock face, and pulled out the GPS, shielding it with his body, and took a quick glance: The red dot was only a mile away, and it hadn't moved in over two hours. They both hoped that KC had made their destination, as the alternative would be nothing short of being buried forever in this abysmal weather. Michael banished the thought from his mind; he wasn't about to lose her.

Michael couldn't imagine what it was like at the peak of the mountain, twenty-eight thousand feet at the top of the world. They were at fourteen thousand feet, both in good shape, and yet they were heaving like pack mules as they struggled up the mountain.

They hiked up another wide-open field through deep powder, their legs burning with fatigue at every awkward step. With the low visibility, they might as well have been in a crater. All sense of direction was lost, forcing them to look at a compass to keep their bearings or risk being lost, traveling in circles in the snowy mass around them.

They came upon a wide-open mouth, a separation in the rock face that looked like a four-lane highway; it was well marked on the chart and in the direction of the red signal on the GPS tracker. They stepped through the mouth to find an icy path covered in fresh snow. It was like a mini-glacier, one of many frozen tributaries that channeled any water that melted off the mountain. Michael was more than surprised, as much of the ice seemed fresh and clear, as if it had been constantly added to, like a slow icemaker that made clear freezer ice.

They hiked up the walled path, which narrowed to a thirty-foot-wide crevasse that bisected the mountain granite. They fought against the wind, their feet slipping on the ever-icy ground, digging their axes in, forcing themselves onward. It took them almost an hour to go one mile, their bodies pushed beyond exhaustion.

They arrived at a dead end, a sheer rock wall that climbed into oblivion. The wind and snow was an icy hurricane around them. Busch looked at the GPS and feared it was broken; the red dot was on the other side of the wall. They looked about, feeling for an opening, a cave, a narrow passage that would allow them through, but there was nothing there.

Michael hoped they hadn't been on a wild-goose chase, following ancient maps, drawn before the times of precision instruments. He hoped that Venue had not somehow found the GPS tracker in the leather tube and led them astray.

But the fact that KC, Venue, and their party were nowhere to be found led Michael to believe they had missed something: a door, a passage, an opening. Somewhere along the way there was a breach that would allow them through to whatever sat on the other side of the granite wall.

Michael thought of erecting one of their tents for a brief respite but opted to seek a more solid shelter to allow them to rest and regain their strength. He and Busch began to backtrack, searching, hoping to find something they had missed.

One hundred and fifty yards back they found an overhang, a snowdrift over eight feet high obstructing it. A large natural window had formed in the snowy barrier, as if a warm wind had conspired to act like a beacon cutting through the icy wall. Michael and Busch dug fast, wiping the snow away to find a large boulder behind which was a small cave.

They scrambled in, kicking the snow from their boots, shaking it from their wool-covered heads. They pulled the Turtle Fur masks away from their mouths and collapsed to the rocky ground, gulping air as if they had just surfaced from a tankless deep-sea dive. They were surrounded by darkness but for the soft white glow of the snow that covered the entrance.

It was two minutes before Busch finally spoke. "People do this for fun? They climb these things for sport? What the hell happens at twenty-five thousand feet? This is stupider than golf."

"Easy there, peaches," Michael said.

"No, no easy. I'm going to wring this fucker's neck for dragging KC up here."

They both lay against the wall catching their breath, resting their legs. Busch pulled out the GPS, but they had no signal in the cave.

Michael reached into his bag and pulled out a water bottle and a flashlight. He opened the bottle and sucked it dry, the altitude having done the same to his body. He flipped on the light to find that they were in a surprisingly dry cavern. It wasn't large, no more than four feet high, but it left them plenty of room to move about. The back of the cave ran deep, its path lost in darkness.

Michael felt the walls. "They're warm."

Busch removed his gloves and ran his cold fingers against the rock. "Banyo said the Himalayas were dotted with hot springs and vents."

Michael felt the ground, removed his hat, and smiled.

Busch laughed. "I'll tell you this. If there's a hot spring in here, I'm in."

Michael shone his light deeper into the cave.

"What do you see?" Busch asked.

Michael pointed the flashlight into the tunnel: a scramble of boot tracks marred the ground.

"I'll be damned." Busch shook his head as he dug into his pack. He pulled out two pistols, unzipped his jacket, and tucked them into shoulder holsters.

Michael followed suit, holstering two Sig Sauers and strapping a knife to his inner left calf, and headed deeper into the cavern.

"Banyo said they've got eleven toughs, Iblis's guys—we can pretty much count on their knowing how to fight—plus Iblis, and that fucker would chew your face off if he had the chance."

As Michael and Busch moved through the earthen passage, the air began to warm. A gentle breeze began flowing. They kept walking through darkness and finally saw it up ahead: a faint light.

The tunnel narrowed before Michael finally emerged from the rocky passage.

He stood on a ledge and looked down.

Of everything Michael had ever seen in life, of everywhere he had ever been, of every place he had ever read about, nothing came close to the image before his eyes.

He stood there a moment, absorbing what he saw, his

mind fighting the irrationality of it all, but his heart over-ruled his mind and he smiled.

"What are you doing?" Busch said as he climbed out behind Michael. He was checking his gun, unaware of what Michael was looking at, but then finally he looked past Michael and out at the world before them, marveling at the sight, at the impossibility of what he saw. He actually did a double take as he whispered, "Oh, my God."

CHAPTER 46

Michael looked down onto a wide-open courtyard, nearly four acres in size. The grounds were green and lush, standing in sharp contrast to the bitter, frostbitten world at the other end of the tunnel behind him. Snow fell gently, drifting down, melting as it hit the warm ground. It was a world like nothing Michael had ever seen before. A rushing river bisected the grounds, the wash of water echoing softly in the enclosed valley. A warm fog rose and roiled above the flowing waterway, drifting off and condensing on the green riverbanks. It was forded by a natural land bridge and disappeared under the far wall. The grounds were entirely encased in rock face, as if a world sat at the bottom of a well. Michael looked up to see the swirling snows, their flakes carried aloft by the rising air currents.

Two small natural pools bubbled by the near wall, steam rising from their clear waters.

Michael ran his hand through the grass, over the rocks, along the granite wall; it was warm, radiating heat.

"This is incredible," Busch said. "But . . . it's impossible."

"It's geothermal, like the baths that Banyo showed us. Water runs along molten rock deep in the earth, turning to steam, and makes its way up through fissures in the granite, keeping the place warm," Michael said. "The warmth of the rock is heating the ground, keeping the lower air stratum at a moderate temperature."

A small flock of yellow birds flitted about, wings spread wide, riding the updrafts, then suddenly falling back before the icy chill of the mountain air froze them out.

A single impossibly large temple stood at the far side. It sat upon a small hill and seemed to grow out of the rock face. It was constructed of dark polished logs; its roof was slanted, sheathed in heavy tile. A wide covered porch wrapped the structure, while deep red filigreed wood accented the underpinning of the roof and adorned the corners, windows, and columns of the large building. A long flight of stairs led the way to an enormous carved door, its color darker than night. The building appeared of Oriental design, but was different, unique, out of an impossibly old fairy tale.

Colorful begonias, orchids, and marigolds scattered the rocky, well-tended gardens that sat on either side of the stairs. Rhododendrons grew up against the rock face, thick with green waxy leaves; juniper trees, their branches heavy and old, were interspersed about the grounds, several desperately trying to climb the sheer walls.

Every rock, every plant was in pure harmony, as if its positioning came from a divine architect, all perfectly manicured with the precision of a bonsai gardener.

"Hey," Busch said, snapping his fingers. "It's real pretty and all, but . . ."

"I know," Michael said, pulling back from his reverie.

"Do you think they know we're here?"

"Not thinking they're big on cameras or electricity up here. But there's only one way in and we've a good hundred yards of open space to walk across to get to the front door."

"Do you think they're in there?"

"They're in there and they either rounded up whoever lives up here or killed them already."

"You know," Busch said, "if this place is here, all that gold, all those jewels . . ."

"Yeah, and something else, and that's what scares me."

"Tell me you have a plan," Busch said with pleading eyes.

MICHAEL WALKED ALONG a natural stone pathway, his hands visibly open at his side, his Sig Sauer tucked in the small of his back, a black knapsack strung over his shoulder, concealing the glint of the pistol's handle. Busch lay prone in the mouth of the cave, the Galil sniper rifle tucked against his shoulder. This time the chamber was full.

Michael passed the steam baths, feeling the heat that emanated from them. He took a closer look at the trees and gardens, all recently pruned back, all thick and perfect. He had been filled with more than doubt when Simon had told him what lay up upon Kanchenjunga; he was literally walking in the midst of a legend, a world spoken of in hushed tones and myths.

Michael felt a slight cool rain as he walked, noting that the snowfall had slowed and what made it to the open area turned to drizzle before it hit the ground.

He made his way to the long flight of stairs leading to the temple's entrance. They were twenty feet wide with short risers and three-foot-deep treads that gave him the impression he was slowly floating upward as he climbed. They were bordered on either side by thick timber rails whose surface had been worn glassy smooth from centuries of use.

Michael's eyes constantly darted about, looking left to right for any sign of life. The stairs were free of footprints, as was the landing he now stood upon. The porch was wide and deep, the heavy polished timbers that supported the roof above contributing to the feeling he was standing in a nave about to approach the inner sanctum of the holy altar.

The double door before him was more than fifteen feet high and equally wide, made of a deeply stained burl wood that gave the impression of hundreds of eyes looking out on the world. The handles were formed of iron O-rings and rope.

Michael held his breath as he grasped the iron ring. He knew he would be leaving the protection of Busch's rifle within seconds and that he could be opening the gateway to his death.

He tugged gently on the door and it swung open without resistance.

CHAPTER 47

K C stood in a stone room, the recessed shelves filled with hundreds of small butter candles that cast an orange hue about the thirty-foot-square space. Venue and Cindy stood next to her, lost in a whispered conversation.

Sitting in a lotus position against the back wall were forty monks. Monks who were far from what KC had expected. They all wore robes, some white, some maroon, some blue, some saffron. But there was no single design, no universal theme.

Their hairstyles varied; not all were bald as one would expect in an Asian monastery. Though some shaved their heads, some wore their hair long, others in a modern style more akin to that of Wall Street suits. And it wasn't just the hairstyles that expressed individuality, it was the nationalities. The majority were Asian—Japanese, Indian, Tibetan, Chinese, Vietnamese—but there were also Africans, Caucasians, Middle Easterners, and Hispanics: a representative body of world culture.

And odder still were the adornments about their necks and waists. There was no unifying symbol. KC could plainly see the expressions of the world's beliefs: crucifixes of Catholicism, crosses of Christianity, Hebrew Stars of David,

Islamic Star and Crescent moons. There were Buddhist prayer beads and wheels of Dharma, a Hindu Omkar and several symbols KC didn't recognize.

The monks had been working about the temple and its grounds when KC arrived with Venue and his team, emerging from the cave into what she could only describe as paradise. Some monks had been tending gardens, some were kneeling in the sanctuary, others were meditating in small anterooms. None of them offered resistance as Iblis's men approached them with guns drawn; there was no surprise in their faces upon seeing the violent team, there was no fear in their eyes as they were shuffled inside, gathered up and forced into this room.

Throughout the ordeal, no one said a word except for a single monk they encountered in the sanctuary. He appeared to be Tibetan, of medium height, with dark bristle-short hair. He wore a green robe of silk, its sleeves and collar trimmed in gold. But for a single scar that ran down the man's right cheek, his skin was unwrinkled and pure. He stood at the altar, his fingertips touching in peaceful prayer.

He looked up as Venue and his men came through the large doors; his eyes smiled as he tilted his head. He stared at Venue for the longest of moments. An anticipation hung in the air until the monk spoke. The man of peace merely said, "You are making the gravest of mistakes."

And Iblis shot him, a single bullet that pierced the Tibetan's right eye, carrying half of the man's essence onto the back wall of the dais.

KC remained motionless at the violence, but the shock on Cindy's face could not be missed. She had never borne witness to Iblis's inhumanity. But for her kidnapping, she had lived a sheltered life, existing in her own little bubble, unaware of the cruelty that can exist in some people's hearts.

Though KC's face didn't register shock at the man's death, her mind did. It was not shock at the needless murder, or at the coldness that Iblis once again displayed, it was shock at what the monk had said. She corrected herself: not specifically what he had said, but how he had said it. The man seemed to know why they were there without hearing a word or demand from Venue or Iblis, as if he knew they were coming. But most shockingly to KC's mind, he had addressed them in perfect English.

KC looked across the stone room at each of the monks, who sat quietly, each of them calm, praying as if they were not being held hostage, as if they were oblivious of the barrels of guns that remained aimed at them.

Iblis appeared in the doorway, his sudden presence pulling KC back to the moment. He exchanged a knowing glance with Venue. "We found it."

"Let's go, girls," Venue said without looking their way.

They all followed Iblis out of the room and down a long stone corridor carved from the granite, lit by intermittent torches that reminded them they were no longer in the modern world. The corridor jigged and jagged left and right, deeper into the mountainside, until they emerged in a large vestibule, the torches burning strong and bright, fighting back the shadows creeping in from all directions. The circular room was over nine hundred square feet with walls of polished stone. The floor and ceiling contained an intricate design like nothing KC had ever seen before; inlaid with gold, it appeared abstract, yet with a deeper spiritual purpose she could not grasp. Seven corridors led off in every direction like spokes from a central wheel.

Iblis pointed to one of the corridors that led to a circular flight of stairs that dove into darkness. They all descended, enveloped in the virtual night. The journey took no more than a minute, but they kept their hands on the wall for guidance. They came out into a small vestibule where four of Iblis's men stood before a recessed door, with guns held at the ready. They finally parted upon seeing their boss, to reveal a large black doorway.

It was something out of a nightmare, made of thick ebony, carved with the effigies of hideous creatures, demons, and beasts, their mouths agape in rage and fear. Dozens of lost souls crawled along the surface: men, women, and children screaming for a redemption that would never come. Cindy recoiled at the sight, at the eyes of the children, alive with uncomprehending fear. She stepped back as if the door would somehow reach out and pull her into the same fate.

KC, though shocked, remained steadfast. She stared at the center of the door, at a hollowed-out recess. It was long and narrow, an absence looking to be filled, as if someone had carved out its heart and extracted it with an expert hand. And as she stared at the door adorned in terror, she finally understood the purpose of the rod, where it came from, where it belonged.

Venue stepped forward, the group separating around him, and held out his hand. Iblis placed the leather satchel in it and took several steps back as if in ceremony. Venue opened the lid of the tube, reached in, and extracted the dark two-foot rod, its bejeweled body, its ruby eyes alive in the reflection of the torch flame.

Venue stepped to the door, holding the rod as he would a newborn child. Without hesitation, he reached up and placed it into the door's recess, a perfect fit. Two black clips snapped over the rod, affixing it in place.

He stepped back, inspecting his work. The door was complete; the two dark serpents, their mouths ready to strike, were home. The jewels appeared to throb in the fire-light, pulsing like a heart come back to life. All breaths held, waiting, wondering. A collective hush fell over the room in anticipation of the unknown.

And then a subtle noise began, deep and guttural, as if the earth were speaking. The guards' eyes widened; they grasped their guns tighter. Cindy moved closer to the guards, as if they would protect her. Then, with a deafening crack, the rod snapped in two along its core. It slipped its bonds and fell to the floor, its opaque resin core exposed, its modern fabrication revealed to all.

Seeing the counterfeit rod, Iblis's eyes turned dark, his body shaking in anger as he turned to KC, his face a mask of primal rage. "What have you done?"

But before he could continue, Venue stepped in, his large frame dwarfing Iblis, stopping his verbal assault. He looked at KC, holding her eyes. He looked down at the broken rod and, much to Iblis's surprise, laughed beneath his breath.

"What did you do with the original?" Iblis shouted, try-ing to get past Venue.

"Let's take a walk," Venue said to KC and Cindy. He turned to Iblis. "Go look through the other rooms; this door is my concern. I will take care of it."

KC and Cindy silently followed Venue out of the room, back up the dark circular stairs. They walked back through the stone torchlit halls, past the room where the monks sat in silent prayer. They came to and scaled a flight of wide wooden stairs, heading to the second floor of the temple, and came out into a large foyer. The pine-log walls were decorated with religious iconography: mandalas and Madonnas, Abraham and Shiva, Muhammad and Shangdi.

Venue continued to a hall lined with doors; he opened the first, holding it open for his daughters.

The small room was the private quarters of one of the monks. A futon mattress was in the corner; large pillows were propped against the wall. There was a simple pine desk and chair. Venue picked up a journal from the desk's small shelf and leafed through it, finding the vertical Chinese language indecipherable.

The room, like all the interior spaces, was lit by small candles. Several joss sticks glowed red, their earthy smoke curling upward. Venue took a seat in the desk chair, leaned back, and inhaled the sweet smell of pine resin, herbs, and spices that fought to calm the room.

Cindy took a seat on one of the large pillows as KC remained standing.

"Could you imagine if your mother could see this?" Venue said as he looked between KC and Cindy. "Me and my two girls sitting in a temple that is over four thousand years old. She'd die all over again."

KC's eye bore fire into Venue, who only smiled at her stare.

"How dare you. You have nothing to do with us. You left our mother on her own."

"Prison has that effect."

"And you faked your death."

"Everyone has to die sometime." Venue let his silent threat hang in the air. "So this guy, Michael, he really cares about you."

"Don't you dare bring him up."

"Most guys can't be trusted. I guess most women, too, huh, KC? Sometimes things aren't what they seem; sometimes we think we know what's going on."

KC didn't respond.

"People can be so surprising, so unpredictable," Venue said as he stared at KC.

"What are you talking about and what the hell just happened down there?" Cindy blurted out. "What's behind that door?"

Venue looked between them. "Perhaps KC could answer that?"

KC stood in silence, staring at Venue, an unspoken argument going on between them. Cindy was a nonentity; the conversation and chess match was only between KC and Venue. "I have no idea," she said, not wanting to imagine the truth.

Venue relented with a smile. "It's got to make you think. This place predates Islam, Christianity, Judaism, it's older than Gautama Buddha and the gods of Hinduism. Makes you wonder who built it, who were they worshipping, who do they worship now? What are they protecting?"

"If they were protecting something, don't you think those monks would have tried to resist?" Cindy said.

"Maybe what they are guarding doesn't need protection," KC said, her eyes still on Venue. She paused, bringing home her point. "Or maybe they aren't protecting it from the world; maybe they are protecting the world from it."

Cindy nervously laughed. "Always such a drama queen."

Venue stared at KC as if not hearing Cindy. It was as if she wasn't in the room.

"Do they look old to you?" Venue asked KC as he shifted in his seat.

"Who?" Cindy asked, trying to enter their conversation.

KC remained silent. She knew Venue was making a point with his question; he wasn't looking for a validation of his observation. She had seen the same thing. While none of the monks were young, none of them were hobbled by age, or bent and broken by life. It was not that their hair wasn't gray, or their skin wasn't wrinkled. The wisdom in their faces came from experience, from many years lived, but each of them possessed young eyes, filled with life and optimism, eyes undiminished by hopelessness.

"There are things about this place . . ."

"What kind of things?" Cindy said, growing frustrated.

Iblis came quickly into the room. "We found the other rooms."

"Good," Venue said calmly as he continued to sit with no sense of urgency.

Iblis looked at him, confused. "Don't you want to see them? It's incredible."

"Not yet." Venue remained seated. "We're waiting for someone to arrive."

"Who?" Iblis asked.

Venue continued looking at KC, holding her eyes, and smiled. "Michael St. Pierre."

CHAPTER 48

M ichael stepped into the temple. It was cavernous and dark. Great columns bordered the central pathway, which led to a large altar. Large rounded cages hung from the twenty-foot ceiling on heavy chains, each with a glowing fire that provided a dim, constant light. Along the wall, hundreds of candles shone, their small flames refracting off their brass holders. The smell of incense drifted about in the smoky air, which rose and vented out of the cathedral's ceiling.

As Michael walked up the nave, he expected to see a large Buddha as a central figure, but nothing was at the temple's focal point. There was no crucifix or holy cross, no tabernacle or obscure deity. There was nothing but several purple and deep-red pillows stacked upon the floor.

The sanctuary was large, over one hundred feet deep and equally wide. There were no pews or chairs, though there were individual prayer rugs, fifty of them, in intricate designs, made of wool, filling the floor on either side of the aisle.

Michael walked to the edge of the raised platform and looked at the altar. He did not step up, out of respect: There was no doubt this was a house of worship, the dais reserved for those anointed or deemed worthy.

And then Michael saw the blood: It was fresh and new, staining the back wall of the dais and the ash-colored altar floor.

There had to be occupants, monks, but they did not concern Michael; it was Iblis and his guards who were a threat, who kept Michael on edge. Michael drew the Sig Sauer from the small of his back, flicking off the safety. He tightened his knapsack and moved off toward a hallway to the left. He hugged the corner, listening, but the temple was silent.

The stone hallway branched off; without thought, Michael took the left tunnel and continued through.

Michael arrived at a circular vestibule. Torches sat in wall sconces, their orange glow reflecting off an elaborate gold-inlaid mandala floor, its infinite concentric designs capturing the mysteries of the heavens. As Michael looked up he saw a perfect mirror image of the floor's design; its intricacy was beyond complex, a metaphysical representation of the cosmos. The walls were of polished stone while seven more corridors branched off from the central room like spokes from a wheel. Michael listened, holding his breath, halting all movement, but heard nothing.

He took a tentative step into the first darkened hallway, drew his flashlight, and turned it on; its beam became lost down a long corridor that jogged left and right. He walked for at least one hundred yards before arriving at a thick wooden door. He grasped the iron handle and pulled it open, and was greeted by a large circular room, the rounded ceiling over fifteen feet high, rows upon rows of shelves along its walls.

As Michael shone his light in, the room exploded in sunlight, beams of yellow erupted and reflected, seeming to grow upon themselves. Gold, shimmering in its purest form, sat upon the shelves that lined the walls. There were goblets and plates, shields and daggers, jewelry and religious ornaments, unformed blocks and malleable sheets. It was an unlocked storage vault whose value Michael couldn't fathom. If this was what Venue was after, it would make him wealthier than even he could imagine, but Michael feared this was not his primary goal. He was after something even greater.

Michael closed the door and headed back to the mandala vestibule, taking the next corridor, again traveling along hundreds of feet to find a far different sight.

The door was large and thick, tremendous iron hinges supported its weight, and to Michael's great surprise there was an enormous crosshatch lock. It was a four-bar design that rested upon the door's exterior, protruding into the stone door frame, the crossbars joined by an intricate steel gear in its center with a hole for a large key.

But as Michael admired the simple design, he wondered why it had not been fortified to any greater extent, for the door hung wide open, the steel lock shattered by gunfire.

If a room containing over a billion dollars in gold did not merit a lock, what was the value of the contents of the room before him?

Michaels's question was answered as he took a step in. Far larger than any of the other rooms, this was the true treasure of the monastery. This was the room of knowledge, the room of history. And as Michael stepped in and walked about, he understood it contained information far older and far more revealing than anything man had ever experienced. Upon endless shelves sat scrolls and parchments, vellum and books, even stone tablets, all meticulously arranged and labeled in five languages: Latin, Aramaic, English, an

Oriental language, and the largest markings, the oldest markings, which sat above the other four, from a language Michael had never seen before. The labels displayed language through the ages, from the protolanguage before him, through its evolution, reflecting the world's ever-changing dominant cultures.

There were simple hardwood tables and benches, and mirrors were strategically placed to reflect the torchlight, which was contained within vented stone pockets, at a distance from the flammable materials.

Michael walked about, examining the shelf tags, finding sections on Christianity, Judaism, Hinduism, Buddhism, and religions he had never heard of. Sections on prayer and meditation, divine intervention, evidence and proof of the afterlife. There were writings in the hand of Moses, Gautama Buddha, and Jesus Christ, lost gospels, and the philosophical treatise of Mein Na.

If the Ten Commandments were held as sacred, hidden away in the Ark of the Covenant, then this room, within this temple, within one of the world's largest mountains, was a repository of knowledge thousands of times larger, more monumental, and all the more sacred. The world had read no direct writings of Jesus but rather the written interpretations and observations of his disciples and chroniclers many years later. The teachings of Buddha were, again, penned by his followers and not by himself directly. The Ten Commandments were the only known direct writings of God. But now, with this room, the sacredness of it, the true divinity of its contents . . . It was as if Michael had stepped into the libraries of heaven.

The information was vast and all-encompassing, touching on all forms of faith, on all beliefs and interpretations of the afterlife. And there were not just writings on God and Allah, on paradise and the search for enlightenment. There were parchments and scrolls on the devils of the world's religions: Azazel, Lucifer, Abaddon, Belial, Satan, Angra Mainyu, Asmodai, Beelzebub, and the Islamic name that KC's teacher had usurped, Iblis. There were books on Shaitan, Baphomet, Mastema, Chutriel, Mephistopheles, the anti-Christ. They sounded like titles from a bad horror movie, but Michael knew these were nothing of the sort. Loki, the Norse god of mischief; Angat, a Madagascan devil; Arawn, the Welsh god of the underworld; Chernobog, the Slavic devil Black God; Mara, the demon who tempted Gautama Buddha; the Babylonian god Nergal, who reigned over the dead; Ördög, the Hungarian entity of legend; Pazuzu, the half-man, half-beast demon of the Assyro-Babylonians; Vritra, the adversary in Vedic religion; the Celtic demon Pwcca; Samnu, a devil to Central Asiatics; Supay, the Inca god of the underworld; T'An Mo, the Chinese counterpart to the devil; Sedit, a Native American devil. Their histories and biographies were present in unfathomable depth.

Michael finally arrived at the end of the collection, where empty shelves sat in wait of new topics, new introspective writings on the mysteries of the cosmos above and below. He turned to leave but suddenly stopped and turned back, all at once understanding why the door to this repository of heavenly knowledge had been blown off its hinges.

Michael's heart grew cold as he walked to the empty shelves. The conspicuously empty section was not awaiting new writings; the shelves were already labeled. There were hundreds of tags, yet their corresponding texts were gone. The empty section was vast, at least ten feet of vacant shelves six feet high, a collection of works gathered through time, since the beginning of man, a segment that could only be summarized as evil in all of its forms. "Demons" and "Darkness," the tags read, "Witchcraft" and "Malevolence," "Fallen Angels" and "Risen Beasts." There were prayers and incantations to the Devil and the unholy creatures of the deep. Labels that read "The Words of Lucifer," "The Gospel of Satan," "The Maps of Hell," "Summoning Pazuzu," "Possession," "The Rape of the Soul."

Michael had had his doubts about what Simon had said was below the temple, but as he looked at the empty shelves before him, as he read the titles of the books, scrolls, and parchments that were missing, a numbing fear consumed him. Venue was here not just for the gold; he was here for the power and secrets. He was here to unleash hell.

Michael stepped back and spun about, suddenly on edge. He wasn't sure why, but a fear rose in him, a fear he hadn't felt since childhood, unexplained and irrational; he white-knuckled his pistol as his eyes darted about. He had to find KC and get her out of here. He had to get her clear before he came back and stopped Venue and Iblis from what they were planning.

Michael headed back out through the stone tunnel, taking each of the hall spokes from the mandala room in search of KC. He found a room of silver; a room filled with jewels, precious and semiprecious stones; and a room filled with grains and food stores, understanding that "the Mountain of Five Treasures" was truly a literal interpretation.

Standing back in the circular hub, he was left with only two more passages. Michael felt like the Minotaur, forever trapped in a winding maze. One door led to a set of stairs that went down, while the other headed up.

Michael tilted his head, listening for any sound, any hint of where KC might be. Hearing nothing, he quietly ascended, his eyes scanning, his nerves on fire, gripping his pistol tight. He came out on a landing, where a door-lined hall drifted downward, but he found the stairs continued to rise. He proceeded to the third and uppermost floor to find a candlelit room wrapped in windows that afforded views in all directions. The storm had momentarily abated; the setting sun lit the outside valley in a glorious golden haze that filtered through the warped glass, filling the room with rainbow prisms and shafts of light.

The intermittent wall space was adorned with art that celebrated life, that celebrated religion. All religions: Christianity, Judaism, Islam, Zoroastrianism, Hinduism, Buddhism. Michael walked about, looking at the depictions; stories in varied languages hung below the art, telling tales Michael couldn't imagine. There were drawings of monks lying prostrate in the open sanctuary on the first floor. Pictures of magical sunrises and mystical sunsets. A drawing of a bearded man with long hair, his light skin in sharp contrast to that of the brown-skinned monks he sat with in this very room. An aura surrounded him, a subtle glow, as he spoke with open, outstretched hands.

An Indian prince, in long, colorful but tattered robes, stood in conversation in the gardens, walking with men of varied lineage while birds and animals fluttered and walked around him.

A tall man with long, flowing white hair and beard stood upon a mountain, clutching a long staff.

"Hello, Michael," a soft voice called out.

Michael turned around.

The man was of average height, his dark hair bristle-short. He wore a green loose-fitting robe of silk that hung to the ground, its sleeves and collar trimmed in gold. His skin was the color of weak tea, his face an amalgam of Asian cultures, while his shoeless feet were wide and thick with calluses. His eyes spoke of wisdom arrived at through an incredibly old age, yet his face was not harshly wrinkled; but for a single scar that ran down the man's right cheek, his skin was unmarred by time.

Michael couldn't help feeling as if the world had slowed, causing a time drag that was tranquil and filled the air with a quiet peace.

Michael looked at the man, he looked at the sketches and paintings, he looked out at the open valley and finally back at the monk.

"What is this place?" Michael said in a hushed tone.

"A place of prayer, a place of worship and study. A world in balance."

"I see that," Michael said with respect. "I don't doubt you know what I mean, though, in fact, I probably didn't even need to ask the question, did I?"

The man smiled. "Then you already know the answer."

"Shambhala?"

"Man has come up with names and ideals, some close, others that couldn't be further from the truth . . ." The man smiled. "This place has no name and yet it has many names."

"I don't understand."

"Does it matter that you understand? Do you question why you believe in God? Has anyone ever offered you undeniable proof of his existence?"

Michael's silence answered the question.

"And yet you are certain."

"Even more so now that I've seen this place." Michael paused, lost in thought. "You ask if I believe in God. But the God I refer to, the God of my religion . . ." Michael had trouble finishing his thought.

"Man insists on ascribing names to everything. Every religion seeks to make God its own, to make its God the greatest."

"Who's right, then?"

The monk smiled. "Everyone's right."

Michael smiled back as if they were in a mind game of philosophical challenge. He finally pointed to the depictions on the wall. "These pictures," Michael said. "They're beautiful. Who are they?"

"Again you ask questions to which you already know the answer."

"Yes, but this one." Michael pointed to the bearded man with white skin. "How can this be?"

"There are eighteen years of his life that are unaccounted for." The man smiled.

"But he was here?"

"He traveled many places. Someone looking to share wisdom, to learn of the world, travels often and travels far."

Michael stared at the picture, and finally turned his attention to the man in the tattered robes. "And this man—"

"Michael," the man cut him off. "Not all is peaceful here, not all is what it seems."

"How old is this place?"

"It was built before memory, built to hide a crack in the earth."

"It feels so . . ." Michael searched for the word, ". . . calm."

"As you feel the peace of heaven, so too does the torment of hell lie beneath our feet. And someone has arrived here to awaken it. To let it loose on the world. To steal the secrets hidden away here for millennia."

"Where is everyone?" Michael walked to the window looking out on the grounds, which at first he had thought of as peaceful but which now he could only think of as ominous.

"The people who live here have been taken hostage; one is dead."

"And the people responsible . . . ?"

"They're all waiting for you."

"What?" Michael asked, tightening the grip on his pistol. "Where?"

"You must not let them take anything from here."

"I've been in your rooms downstairs; they have full access to the gold, the treasury . . ."

"Those things do not concern me—"

"I've been in your library; they blew open the door. There is a shelf, its labels indicate things I could never have imagined." Michael paused. "The shelves are empty, Venue has already—"

The monk held up his hand. "They have nothing of true value. Those items, those scrolls, parchments, and books, were removed almost five hundred years ago. They have been stored away, in a room they will never get into."

The man looked at Michael, his eyes gentle but strong, fatherly in conveying an unquestionable sense of warning.

"Nothing must be taken from beyond the lowermost door of this sanctuary. They will unleash a darkness, a disease that will corrupt the mind as it creeps over the land. Venue seeks not only riches but the knowledge of God, the power of darkness."

Michael felt the weight of the knapsack on his back suddenly grow; a sense of guilt began to fill him. He turned away from the monk and looked once again at the pictures upon the walls, out the windows on the impossible world below. His mind was a jumble; he feared for KC. His only thought had been to save her, to rescue her from her father, from this place, but now the monk's words weighed heavily upon his heart. It was as if the man could read his mind, read his intentions; it was as if he knew exactly what Michael carried in his knapsack.

"They come now."

"Who?" Michael looked toward the door and raised his pistol.

"You must remember, Michael, stay in the light and do not listen to the voices, for they will lie to you, they will offer you your heart's desire; they know what you want, what you love."

Michael cast a glance toward the man, but he was gone, shafts of sunlight piercing the window where he had stood.

"Michael?"

Michael turned back to find KC standing alone in the doorway, the flames of the candles glinting off her moist eyes. They stared at each other, relief washing over Michael.

"What are you doing here?" KC said in anger.

Michael continued looking at her, shocked at the rude reception. "Are you all right?"

As Michael approached her, the shadows in the hall behind her came alive, and four guards emerged from the outer hall as Iblis, Venue, and Cindy came up behind KC.

CHAPTER 49

Busch lay upon the warm ground of the tunnel, clutching the sniper rifle in his hand. He occasionally moved it about, lining up the crosshairs on flowers and branches, truing up his line of sight. His body had finally shaken off the last remnants of cold, allowing his mind to gain complete focus.

He hoped Michael's plan was sound. It was rushed and was predicated on too many factors out of their control. But it was all they had. And KC was all that filled Michael's mind.

There was a lack of rationality when it came to love. It compelled men to do the most foolish of things, the most dangerous of things, sacrificing sanity in favor of those who held their heart. It had caused King Edward VIII of England to abdicate the throne for his mistress, it had caused Menelaus to send the Spartans to lay waste to Troy after Paris stole his wife, Helen, and it had caused Michael to break into an ancient palace to steal a map that shouldn't exist.

But what Michael was doing, while for love, was more than rational. He was saving her from a father who was undeserving of being called human; a father who would send his own daughter to prison to be executed, acting as her judge and jury, a father who would drag his daughter up a mountain for his own selfish gain, using his daughter as a shield. He was the antithesis of love, of a parent, standing in sharp contrast to everything a father should be.

Busch would die for his two children, he would sacrifice everything for their well-being, and he couldn't fathom what possessed a soulless man like Venue.

Between Iblis and Venue, Busch wasn't sure who was actually worse, but as he lay in the mouth of the cave, the butt of the Galil rifle hugged up close against his cheek, he hoped one of them would emerge from the door so he could make the world a little safer.

CHAPTER 50

"What are you doing here?" KC repeated to Michael, her voice desperate, pain-filled, as she stood in the hallway.

Michael looked at her, relieved to see she was alive.

"Hello, Michael." Venue stepped forward, interrupting their moment. "I understand you are quite the thief, quite the deceiver."

Pain rose in KC's face.

"Let her go," Michael demanded.

"How do you know she doesn't want to be here, that she didn't come of her own accord?"

"Give me a break," Michael said as he turned to KC. "He called me, said you would die if I interfered, if I stood in his way."

"You're not a very good listener," Venue cut in.

Michael opened his knapsack and pulled out the leather tube. "KC, it's not that I didn't trust you, I just didn't trust anyone else."

"It's amazing what one will do for love, huh, Michael? I didn't even need to ask you to bring it." Venue's eyes locked on the tube. "How do I know it's the real one?"

"I don't play with people's lives the way you do."

"Oh, aren't we the hero," Venue said in a dismissive tone. "Let me see it."

"When you let KC and her sister leave and I know they're safe."

"What?" Cindy spun about in confusion. "I'm—"

"Fuck this," Iblis said. He violently grabbed KC by the neck, pulling her back so fast that she had no time to react. Iblis twisted her body over, tilting her blonde head against his chest so she couldn't hold her balance, his blade resting against her carotid artery.

Michael held KC's eye as she struggled against Iblis. There was no fear in her, just anger. But Michael saw Iblis's eyes, his cold, dead eyes that clearly said that he wouldn't hesitate to slice KC's neck, despite how he felt about her, in order to get what they wanted.

Michael opened the tube and withdrew the true rod. He fought to remain focused as the object dizzied his mind.

"What the hell is that?" Iblis shouted, nodding his chin at the rod.

Michael held it up for Venue and all to see; the precious jewels sparkled in the firelight. But no one's eyes were focused on the jewels wrapped about the snake . . .

Intertwined with them like a third serpent was a tan piece of thin cord that ran tip to tip. Enveloping the two snake heads, the malleable explosive cord terminated in a small silver rod with two protruding wires that ran to a small box.

"I think you all know what this is. One of a kind, I would imagine. Held in the grasp of a dead sultan for the last five hundred years. Of course it does have my little design enhancement. Primacord packs a hell of a punch, 'scuse the double entendre. The silver thing, right here"—Michael said as he fingered the blasting cap at the head of the snakes that was attached to a small keypad—"that's my detonator. Now, before you think of killing KC or shooting me on the spot and ripping this out of my dead hands, you should know that if you try to release the box from the Primacord, it will go off. Only I know the code to disarm it. Once KC and Cindy are gone, you can have the rod."

"I'm not leaving; I'm not going anywhere with you." Cindy looked about for affirmation but everyone ignored her. "I'm staying," Cindy shouted at Michael, as if he was crazy, and took a step closer to Venue.

"Fine." Michael shook his head, not surprised. "Just KC, then."

"How do we know it's not another fake?" Iblis said, still holding the blade against KC's neck.

"Here." Michael handed the sultan's rod to Venue. "How's it make you feel?"

Venue rolled it about in his hands, turning it over and over as if just handed the key to his dreams. And then his eyes grew wide in wonder; you could see the effect on him in his face, in his overall appearance as his footing became unsteady.

"Trust me, it's real." Michael handed him the leather tube.

"I'm not letting the two of you walk out," Venue said in a commanding voice, trying to regain position. He was momentarily distracted as he placed the rod back in the tube and its effect faded, his balance returning. "You give me no reason to trust you, Michael."

"This is a trade, my life for hers."

"No," KC shouted, her struggle against Iblis returning with a vengeance.

"I'm the only one who can disarm this thing. And I'm certainly not going to do it while she's here."

"If I don't let her go . . . ?" Venue tilted his bald head.

"Then we all go boom."

"You'd kill the woman you love?" Venue smirked.

"You're going to kill her anyway and you're her father. I figured she and I at least get to go out together."

"Bullshit," Iblis said.

"Don't test me," Michael said to Iblis, his eyes alive with rage.

"I'm not leaving here without you, Michael," KC said, trying to break Iblis's iron grip around her. "Blow it up now. There's a door; you can't let them open that door."

Iblis pressed the knife against KC's throat, stilling her desperate struggle.

The seconds ticked on in silence.

Venue looked at Michael, holding his eyes, each assessing the other's mettle.

Venue finally looked at Iblis and nodded. Iblis released KC. She stood back up and turned 180 degrees, staring down at him. She didn't say a word as the rage poured out of her eyes onto the smaller man.

"You can't do this," she said as she turned to Michael.

"Yeah." Michael nodded. "I can. Please go, Busch is waiting."

"Michael," KC said defiantly. "I'm staying."

Michael stared at her. "It's time for you to go."

"No," KC said as if his words were an impossible request.

"Go!" Michael shouted, turning away from her.

"I'm not leaving you." KC fought to hold back her tears, but they began despite her efforts.

She turned her tear-filled eyes to Cindy, who merely stared at her, without pity or remorse, and said nothing as she took her father's hand.

Michael looked at Iblis. "When she is back in the cave with my friend, completely unharmed, then you'll get your prize." He then turned to Venue. "I don't care if you have to tie her up, you get her out of this place."

Venue nodded to Iblis, who instantly looked at the guard on his right. He was six-three, lumberjack-size; his obedient eyes instantly focused on his boss.

"Escort her back to the mouth of the cave. Don't hurt her, and call me when you get there," Iblis said.

"Your man will drop her off and start back while I still have a visual on her," Michael said.

"Suit yourself." Venue turned to the guard and nodded.

The large guard grabbed KC with a viselike grip about her left arm, leading her toward the stairs.

KC ripped away from the guard. "Get your hands off me."

But he wasn't in the mood for listening. He pinned her arm behind her back and lifted her in the air, heading down the stairs. Everyone followed as KC's screams reverberated throughout the temple. They emerged into the sanctuary and headed for the door.

KC kicked and screamed with all her might as the guard carried her out of the temple. "No, Michael, please . . ."

The door slammed shut. Two guards lifted a long, barrel-shaped piece of wood and laid it in the iron door sleeves, securing it tightly.

Michael stepped to the side of the door and watched through the small slotted window as KC continued fighting the man the entire 150-yard walk. A smile creased his lips as he saw her haul off and hit the man square in the nose.

Iblis stepped up and stood beside Michael as he looked out the window at his man rubbing his jaw.

"Get away from me," Michael said without turning to Iblis.

"Relax, I'm not going to try to drown you again."

Twilight was upon the mountain; long, heavy shadows fell across the valley. Nighttime would come much more quickly with the sheer rock walls surrounding the temple.

"Were you really going to slice her neck?" Michael asked, his eyes still fixed on KC as she approached the cave.

There was a long pause as Iblis's focus also remained out the window on KC. "Were you really going to blow her up?"

Michael and Iblis stood side by side as they watched KC reluctantly climb the incline and disappear into the mouth of the cave. The guard turned and began walking back.

CHAPTER 51

K C walked into the cave and found Busch lying prone, clutching a sniper rifle. She turned and watched as the guard slowly walked back toward the temple. Night had arrived quickly in the mountains of Kanchenjunga, but as KC looked down on the mysterious valley, as she stared at the temple that held who knew what secrets, she felt as if she were in another world far away from the mountain.

"You okay?" Busch asked, his eye pressed tight to the gun sight. A small fire glowed behind him.

"No, I'm not okay." KC's face was tired and tear-streaked. The walk from the temple had been the longest she had ever taken. She was walking away from the man she loved. He had come to save her; no one had ever come to save her in her life. It was something a woman dreamed of, a handsome man whose only thought was for her safety swooping in and snatching her from harm. But this was no fairy tale; there was no happy ending. Michael had traded his life for hers, and she thought it a far from equal bargain, the worst of trades.

Her father, her sister, her teacher, each selfish in his or her own way, had turned their backs on her. And Venue . . . her father, the paterfamilias, who like the Roman head of a household bore the power of *vitae necisque potestas*—the power of life and death over his children—had no trouble electing death. A man so obsessed with himself, he would do anything to save his crumbling empire, anything to bring havoc to the masses, who had no compunction about letting people die to achieve his ends, up to and including his flesh and blood.

KC never meant to fall for Michael; she never meant to involve him, yet she had. Whether unconsciously or knowingly she had condemned him by her actions; if anyone was to die, it should be her. This was not his price to pay. She had chosen her life, committing crimes, ignoring the laws of the civilized world. This was her karma, and, especially in this part of the world, *she* should fulfill her karma, not Michael.

There was no doubt that they would kill him; Iblis had said if he ever had the chance again, he wouldn't make the same mistake twice.

And the tears returned. She turned her back to Busch, not wishing him to see her weakness. She closed her eyes and held tight to the memory of Michael. They had had such a short time, much of it under pressure and confrontational, but throughout it all she could always see his heart. He had put her first in so many ways and helped her in the most dangerous of situations without question. Until six weeks ago, KC had lived a life denied, always wanting, always hoping to find someone who would complete her. She had gotten her wish only to see it destroyed.

"How's Michael?" Busch asked.

KC couldn't speak, afraid the voicing of his impending death would cripple her.

Phut!! The crack of the rifle echoed in the cave with a deadly sound, tearing at KC's eardrums, causing her to jump out of her skin.

"What did you do?" she snapped.

Busch looked up at her. "What? What do you think I did?" Busch held up the rifle.

"I don't understand." KC looked out toward the temple and saw the guard lying dead on the path. "You just killed that guy."

"Yeah . . . ?" Busch said, perplexed at her pointing out the obvious.

Busch finally saw KC's grieving face, stood up, and walked over to her. He looked down at her, smiling gently, and wiped the tears from her cheeks with his giant thumb.

"You don't think we're leaving him there, do you?"

"What do you mean?"

"KC, how much of the interior of that temple did you see?"

"A . . . fair amount," KC said slowly in confusion.

"And do you know where they've taken Michael?"

KC nodded.

"KC, Michael knew you wouldn't come out willingly. He was counting on you to learn the lay of the land so we could go in and pluck his ass out. Half the reason he sent you out was so you could come tell me where we have to go once we get back inside.

"I know he loves you and all, and don't get me wrong, he would give his life for you. But sure as shit, he's not going to be giving it today."

CHAPTER 52

Two guards flanked Michael as they walked along the stone hallway, heading deeper into the temple, finally emerging into the mandala room with its offshoot corridors. They turned and took the one route Michael had not ventured along, the route with the descending stairs. Michael was sure they were within the mountain as they traveled down the long circular flight of steps.

As they stepped off the final stair, Michael saw the door. It was more shocking than he had imagined. He wondered what would possess someone to carve such a thing, and how one could hold on to one's sanity as one completed the task.

Venue handed Michael the tube. "If you would be so kind."

Michael took it and flipped back the lid, but suddenly paused. The door filled him with a fear such as he had never known. He closed the tube back up.

"Now, Michael." Venue stepped into Michael's space, uncomfortably close, and whispered in his ear. "No time for second thoughts."

Michael turned his head until the two men came eye to eye, inches apart.

"Would you like KC's sister's death on your conscience?"

"You'd kill the daughter who actually likes you?" Michael said in shock.

"And I will make sure KC knows you let it happen."

Michael stood there. "I don't believe you."

"That's too bad." Venue looked at Iblis, the unspoken command issued.

Iblis pulled out his knife, walked over, and grabbed Cindy.

"Hey, get off me," she exploded, trying to pull away.

But Iblis said nothing as he violently dragged her over to a small wooden table.

"Make him stop." Cindy looked at her father in desperation, in disbelief, her face pale, her thin arms no match for Iblis's strength. "What are you doing?" Her cries were like those of a child.

Cindy looked at Michael, her eyes pleading. Michael could see the utter fear in her face; he watched as the hope left her eyes. And as he looked at Cindy, no matter how disloyal she was to KC, no matter how cruelly she had treated her, Michael could never live with her death. "Enough, stop."

Iblis ignored Michael, taking Cindy by the arm and yanking her hand down on the table. He pinned it, palm down, and looked her in the eye.

"I said, enough," Michael shouted.

Without hesitation, Iblis brought the blade down, severing Cindy's right pinkie.

The scream was like nothing Michael had ever heard before, bloodcurdling, like that of a wounded animal.

"Disarm it now," Venue shouted, in a violent voice that erased any notion of the man's humanity. "Or you will watch as Iblis dismembers her slowly, and that finger will be the biggest of all the pieces."

Michael tried to catch his breath. Cindy's desperate eyes begged him to help.

And his hesitation cost her. Iblis severed her ring finger with one blow. Cindy's head fell back in a faint, her fingers pouring blood like small hoses in a garden.

"Stop!" Michael yelled, unable to bear the torture.

He ripped off the top and pulled out the rod. He punched in a small sequence on the tiny numbered keypad and quickly removed the Primacord from the snakes' bodies. He stuffed it into the tube along with the detonator and handed the rod to Venue.

Michael looked at Cindy upon the floor; she was slowly regaining consciousness, moaning, clutching her mutilated hand.

"If you want her to live," Venue said, "you're going to open that door. I'm sure you can do it, a thief like you. You're going to open that door and then you're walking through it."

CHAPTER 53

M ichael placed the rod into the recess at the center of the black door and affixed the clasps; it was a perfect fit, seamlessly blending with the structure. It was an extension, a continuation of the horrific designs upon the barrier. He had never seen such renderings, so lifelike, as if they had leaped upon the door and been frozen in place. The mythic beasts with bared fangs and claws tormented the people who populated the lower reaches of the door, the men unable to protect their women and children from the hell around them.

Michael fought off the nausea, unsure if it came from the rod or the sight of the children's desperate eyes that reflected nothing but terror.

And then a noise rose. It was deep, rumbling the floor, the very walls; it was as if the entire mountain were shaking, in an earthquake triggered by his actions. Michael could feel it in his stomach. It was frightening, as if all the dead, buried throughout the earth, were speaking, angered at being awoken.

Suddenly, Michael thought he saw movement upon the door. It was shimmering, subtle, hazy. He was sure his eyes were playing tricks on him. The snakes that wrapped the rod began to writhe, to move of their own accord as if alive, burrowing into the carved structure, becoming one with it.

A great gasp leaped forth from the door's seams, a death rattle, but in reverse: a breath of life. Whatever lay behind the door was taking in the air it had been denied since before memory.

Iblis stepped to the door, reached out, grasped the rod, and tugged. The door easily gave way, gliding open. A blast of hot air poured forth. The guard shone his light into the inky blackness, revealing a flight of stone stairs. They were not stairs in the normal sense, evenly spaced, expertly carved. These were haphazard, a natural descent that had been augmented by man.

"Let us know what you find," Iblis said.

Michael stared at the little man, wanting to snap him in two.

"If you're scared, I'll send Cindy down," Venue taunted.

Michael looked at Cindy, her body racked with sobs as she clung to her mangled hand, wrapped in a bloody piece of her shirt. He saw her disillusionment, her hopelessness as she lay upon the floor wondering how long she had to live.

"Here." Iblis took a torch from the wall and handed it to Michael. "It will add to the mood."

"Don't you want the pleasure of seeing it first, you skinny shit?" Michael whispered.

"Canary in a coal mine," Iblis responded.

Michael heard the cocking of guns from the two guards who stood behind him.

"Silviu and Gianni will be right behind you, making sure you don't try to be too clever as you head down into the depths."

Michael glared at Iblis, ripped the torch from his hand, and stepped through the doorway.

CHAPTER 54

Busch and KC raced down the green rolling hill, across the verdant garden, past trees and steaming pools. The sniper rifle was strapped against Busch's back, and each carried a pistol. Their eyes remained fixed on the enormous temple.

They hit the stairs, taking three at a time, and came to the large black door only to find it locked tight. Without a word, KC darted along the front porch and leaped back on the ground adjacent to the farthest corner of the structure. She spun about, looking upward. Like a gymnast she leaped upon the porch rail, jumped, and caught the overhang, pulling herself up, and like that she was on the porch roof just below the temple's windows.

Busch followed suit, climbing up on the rail, thankful for his six-foot-four frame, as he merely needed to reach up to catch the lip; he knew he wouldn't have a prayer if he had to jump as high as KC had. He hauled his large body up, thankful that he worked out enough not to embarrass himself.

They ran across the porch roof to the first window and nudged it open. Its warped, bubbled glass hung on ancient hinges, creaking as it swung wide. It was a tight squeeze for KC and nearly impossible for Busch; his shoulders and hips were torn up as he forced his body through the small opening.

They landed in a small bedroom, a single cot on the floor, a desk against the far wall. The room smelled of incense and peace, reminding Busch of his childhood, when he would enter church and the chaos of the outside world seemed to disappear.

"Ten guards?" Busch asked.

"Yeah, not counting the one you took out already. They're well armed," KC said as she led the way out into the long second-floor hallway. She crept down the stairs, her gun held high and ready. Hitting the landing, they found no one there; all had retreated into the heart of the temple.

As they cut through the sanctuary Busch couldn't help staring about at the simple columns, the muted earthen colors upon the walls, the cagelike urns of fire suspended from the ceiling, their flames painting the world in a serenity such as he had never known. He was amazed at the simplicity and spirituality of the place, though there were no icons, no statues, crosses, or idols of worship; he had never been in a place where he felt greater peace and tranquility. He was suddenly filled with rage at Venue and Iblis for disturbing such a place, committing such blasphemous acts within the confines of this house of worship.

Busch and KC continued through the holy place and raced into a wide corridor that abutted a two-way juncture.

"This is where we split up," KC said as she came to a halt.

"There is absolutely no way I am letting you out of my sight," Busch whispered.

"That way," KC pointed, ignoring Busch's protest,

"leads toward a series of simple rooms; they're holding the monks down there. There are two guards. It loops around on the far side. We'll meet up there."

"KC, this is a bad idea," Busch said as he gently took hold of her arm for emphasis.

"I'll be fine," KC said as she held up the pistol. "I do know how to use it."

"I have no doubt, but that's not what worries me. It's your buddy, Iblis. I don't care how many bullets you have, I don't think he can be stopped."

"If there is one person in this building right now that I can handle it's him." KC tilted her head up and pecked a quick kiss on Busch's cheek. "Thanks for caring."

And she took off down the hall.

CHAPTER 55

Down Michael went, the two guards, Silviu and Gianni, a step behind, descending upon uneven rocks; the ceiling fell and rose above him. Michael could feel the heat rising, and he understood that he was near an earthen vent, the steam heating the walls around them. Deeper into the earth they traveled, his hand running along the rail-less wall. Five minutes they walked, the grade of descent waxing and waning until they finally came out into a large earthen room.

Michael held the torch high, illuminating an enormous cavern of stone. Natural steam baths of superheated mud bubbled in pools along the wall, the smell of their sulfur heavy in the air, their temperature enough to boil a man alive.

A voice echoed, its direction lost in the great space. Michael turned about, looking for its source. It was a whisper, the words indiscernible. He eyed the guards, who appeared unaware.

Michael shook it off and walked deeper into the cavern. Torches protruded at forty-five-degree angles from the wall. He lit them in succession, eight in all—though there were far more that continued along the never-ending space—and the lost world was brought into the orange glow of twilight, the light of the flames dancing and flickering, casting animate shadows about.

The ceiling was uneven and craggy, dotted with stalactites, some of which had long since connected with their stalagmite partners to form dozens of thick calcite columns that appeared to be holding up the world.

A gasp erupted from Silviu, and Michael spun to find the large man recoiling from a heavy shadow that flickered along the near wall. Michael walked closer, unconsciously holding his breath.

Lying on the ground was a skeleton, its head tilted back, its jaw wide open in a death scream. Protruding from its left eye socket was the hilt of a knife, clutched tightly in a death grip of white bone. Whoever it was had killed himself in the most hideous of fashions. Michael leaned over the corpse, surprised to find it lying upon a tattered leather blanket. Michael reached out, and as he touched it he realized his mistake. It wasn't made of leather, or wool, or cloth. It was human skin—the person's skin that had fallen from his body. Michael examined the corpse up close. With the heat of the cavern and the rate of natural decay, there should be no remains. Insects and bugs should have laid waste to the body after its own internal decay process had begun. In this warm, humid atmosphere there should have been nothing left after only a few days. But this body was old, centuries old. Its cotton shirt was wide open, mottled and stained with death. Its tattered gray pants were loose-fitting and thick, though their woolen material should have also disintegrated over time.

Michael realized he was looking at one of Kemal Reis's men, a corsair, a man of the sea who couldn't be farther from his aquatic home, a man who was devoted to his admiral until his last breath.

And it occurred to Michael that there was no life down here, no bugs or insects to eat the flesh, to promote decay. Bacteria, flies, ants, worms, and vermin exist miles down in the earth, and all of them would have feasted on this body, yet here there was no life.

As Michael stood, he saw Gianni shining his light on more skeletons. Some had been run through, grasping their own swords in a seppuku fashion. Others held rudimentary flint pistols, their skulls half missing.

"Why did they kill themselves?" Silviu blurted out in accented English.

"These are Turkish corsairs," Michael said. "Some of history's toughest men, they were pirates, men of the sea, unafraid to face their demons, yet down here . . ." Michael let his words hang as they looked at the bodies.

"What is down here?" Silviu asked.

"Didn't Iblis tell you?"

Gianni finally spoke. "He said money and books."

"Really." Michael couldn't help laughing. "Do either of you speak Arabic?"

"I'm Italian, for God's sake! Why ask such a stupid question?"

Silviu merely shook his head.

Michael nodded.

And Michael heard the voice again, this time louder, sending an icy chill through his heart.

"What is that?" Silviu said as he spun about, his gun held high, searching for a target.

"That's the sound of madness, the sound of evil," Michael whispered.

Michael's eyes fell on the stone wall to the rear of the stairs they had descended, and he spied a large wooden door. It was black as night, made of polished ebony that shimmered under the torchlight's glow. It was strapped along its base, crown, and center with iron bands for support. A large, tarnished gold ring dangled upon a heavy hasp anchored in the door. Its frame and seams were sealed and coated with pitch. The black tarlike substance not only provided fuel for torches but was the initial moisture barrier used in ships and barrels to keep out all forms of water. Made from a dry distillation of wood and resin, it was what allowed the initial seafarers of the world to travel far and wide.

"Hold this," Michael said, handing Silviu the torch. He grasped the golden handle and tugged. The door didn't budge, the heat having swollen the wood into the frame. Michael raised his right foot, placing it against the wall, and with enormous force, ripped the door open.

Michael gazed into the room, his shadow dancing in the de minimis torchlight that washed into the dark space. He took a tentative step into the room, pausing to allow his eyes to adjust. The air was dry and odorless compared to that of the humid cavern behind him. He could make out piles of metal, their sheen refracting the little light that fell upon them into twinkling stars. Skeletal bodies scattered the ground, ancient and shattered. The crewmen of Kemal Reis had killed one another and killed themselves; they lay with sabers in hand, strewn about the earthen floor.

As Michael headed deeper into the shadows, the cloak of darkness enveloping him, the voices began: soft, a murmur at first, sounding like a distant party, no words discernible, no tone sounding human.

And as the voices grew, they tugged at his sanity. Michael tried to keep his mind balanced, holding the voices at bay, but no matter what he thought about, no matter how he tried to clear his mind, the voices increased.

"Michael . . . remember me?" a malevolent voice whispered. *"Years ago you thought you could rid the world of me, buried me, hid me away in the German forest, but I can never be destroyed."*

Michael longed for a light, the torch, anything that would drive the darkness away. He felt like a child terrified of what lurked behind the dark. He felt the primordial fear rising, like an instinct telling him to run. He understood full well the monk's words of warning about remaining in the light, about the power of darkness.

"Michael," a new voice cried. He hadn't heard it in several years. It was a voice that used to bring comfort but now sounded angry, resentful.

"I die and you replace me with a new father," the voice of his adopted father, Alec St. Pierre, cried. *"You destroy my memory in hopes of creating a better one. Mary died and now you are burying her memory, replacing her like you did me."*

And Michael suddenly knew the voices were but a lie; they tapped into and manifested his fears, they were his unconscious screaming for release from the bonds of rationality, trying to suffuse his mind with guilt and shame, to plant seeds of paranoia that would consume his intellect. But no matter how he fought himself, the voices would not diminish. His psyche felt as if it had become an asylum run amok.

But then, finally, he focused on the one thing that brought peace to his mind; the one thing that could overcome his deteriorating balance rose from within him.

His heart.

KC had awakened it, had filled it with her own heart. Michael allowed that warmth to pour into his mind, into his soul, washing away the voices, balancing the fragility of his thoughts. He allowed KC's image to fill his mind; he held tight to the shine of her long blonde hair, to her eyes, which echoed the purity of her soul. He buried himself in the thought of their embrace, of making love, of her soft skin and tender touch.

Still the voices grew louder, on the verge of maddening screams, fighting against the balance that KC had brought to Michael's conscience.

But Michael knew how to defeat the exploding madness that blossomed in his head. He held tight to KC's image; he reached into his pocket and grasped the locket that she had returned to him with her letter. He seized it in his palm and began to step back from the room, heading away from the shadows that danced about, heading back toward the light. He crushed his fingers around the locket, willing KC to be the only thought and image before him. His departure was far more difficult than his casual entrance. His body struggled as his mind fought not to come apart at the seams; all that held him together was the thought of KC.

He finally turned and made his way back into the light, out through the ebony doorway. The voices died away as if they had never been there, as if his mind had slipped into a pool of insanity only to emerge dry as a bone with no recollection.

"What's in there?" Gianni demanded, stepping forward.

Michael looked at the two guards, wondering if either could survive a minute in the dark, within the godforsaken room.

Silviu took a step back while Gianni took a step forward

and shone his light inside to reveal a hoard of gold and jewels piled upon one another, spilling against the walls, their golden hue refracting the beam of light. Piles upon piles of coins and goblets, ingots, cups, and armor, chests of jewels and boxes of gems. A virtual ship's worth of treasure that had somehow been stolen from this place and traveled the high seas only to be returned here to this hidden cavity high upon the earth by Kemal Reis and his men.

There were several enormous tarps, gray and tattered, folded up, stacked high against the wall, seeming incongruous with the treasure in the room. Michael finally realized what they were: sails, enormous canvas sails, gray, torn, and aged.

Michael wondered what the nautical items were doing so far from the sea, but as he looked upon them he realized they were what Kemal and his men had used to carry the gold up the mountain and through the temple and caverns.

And, finally, in the corner, were the books, scrolls, parchments, and tablets, sitting upon a wooden pallet, dust-covered and hidden from the world—hundreds of documents rendered in the respective mediums of their times: animal hide, vellum, stone, leather, and paper. The purpose of the pitch that had been used to seal the door became obvious; it kept out moisture and protected the paper, protected the skins and hides from deteriorating, preserving them by creating a dry environment away from the humid hell outside. Michael didn't need to examine the documents up close to know what they were. He had read the tags upstairs in the library where these items had once been kept; he knew what they spoke of, what they revealed.

Michael understood the wealth of this room was not in the precious metals and exquisite jewels that captivated the guards but in words and information, an accumulation of knowledge that would lay bare the mysteries of darkness, its power and capabilities, its sources and secrets.

"Oh, my God," Gianni muttered, his eyes upon the piles of gold and gems.

Michael took the torch from the guard, resolving to go nowhere in these subterranean confines without illumination.

"I think it's safe to say God has nothing to do with this." Michael paused. "You can tell Venue we found what he's looking for."

CHAPTER 56

Gianni disappeared up the stairs to get Venue, leaving Silviu guarding Michael.

"Do you want to take a look?" Michael asked, pointing at the room filled with treasure.

Silviu held tight to his Heckler & Koch MP7 rifle and ignored the question. He had no desire to enter the room. He suspected the room was the root of the evil that permeated this underworld. He knew what this place was—it had filled him with fear since the moment they began their descent— but he wasn't about to show that fear to Michael. Silviu had grown up in Romania, and despite his life of crime and lack of Sunday observance, he still clung to his Catholic roots. The image of this cavern before him reflected his childhood image of hell, its reddish walls dancing with firelight, wisps of steam floating up from pools of molten earth. Though he knew in his rational mind that he stood on earth and not in some spiritual realm, he couldn't shake the feeling of evil in the air. It was in the shadows, lurking just beyond the throw of light as if waiting for him, like a wild animal in the bush stalking its prey.

As he watched Michael walk back into the room of books and treasure, he felt the world closing in on him, as if the cavern finally knew he was alone. He turned about, flicking on his flashlight as if it would somehow protect him, somehow hold the evil at bay.

He longed for Gianni to return with Venue; he prayed that his mounting paranoia would subside. Time seemed to drag, his isolation like a weight that grew heavier by the moment, until finally, the pain of solitude outweighed the fear of the room that Michael had walked into.

Silviu looked tentatively at the room; he couldn't be alone any longer.

He stepped through the doorway, his right hand wrapped about his rifle, his finger on the trigger. In his left he held his flashlight, an item he thought of as a weapon equal to or greater than his gun.

He shone his light about, looking for Michael, but his eyes were immediately captivated by the piles of gold. He had never seen such a trove of wealth: A handful alone would set him up for life. The momentary greed purged his mind of its fear, but it also purged it of its caution.

With a sudden realization, he knew the distraction had cost him his life. The blade plunged into his chest as his rifle was ripped from his hands. Despite the agony of his mortal injury, Silviu drew back his fist and hit Michael in the side of the head, sending him tumbling to the floor.

But that would be his last deed. As he took a step forward, he collapsed. He rolled onto his back and stared down in amazement at the jewel-encrusted dagger that protruded from his sternum. He felt the sudden chill pour over his body as his fear returned. He didn't want to die and, of all places, he didn't want to die here, where he knew evil lurked just beyond the shadows, waiting for his soul to leave his body.

As his lungs filled, drowning him in his own blood, Silviu couldn't pull his eyes from the ornamental weapon of death that protruded from his chest. He longed for Romania, he longed for life, for a second chance. And as death finally washed over his eyes, he thought he saw the shadows move, thought he saw them come alive.

MICHAEL TOOK SILVIU by the feet and dragged his body deeper into the room. He stripped him of his rifle and pistol and found four ammo clips, a knife, a cigarette lighter, and a cell phone.

Michael knew his worth to Venue had evaporated. While he had possessed the rod, he had value; as he searched the cavern, he had value; but now . . . he had nothing to offer but a threat to Venue and his endeavors, and they would kill him upon their return.

He walked out into the main cavern and looked at the rocky stairs that rose from the depths to freedom. Gianni would be back any second with Venue and who knew who else. A firefight without the higher ground was unwinnable. Michael's mind began spinning, thinking of alternatives. He thought on the assets he had just stolen from Silviu; he thought of the world he stood within.

He was almost out of time when a plan coalesced in his mind.

Michael ran back into the room filled with gold and set to work.

CHAPTER 57

Busch stood in the shadows of a stone archway, peering forty yards down the dark hall at the two guards who flanked a door. He could hear their murmur, as they were lost in conversation, unaware of the intruder in their midst. Intermittent torches glowed along the wall, casting undulating shadows that writhed along the floor. Busch felt as if he were looking back in time down some medieval tunnel, but he knew that this place, this impossible temple, was far, far older.

Busch glanced over his shoulder, saw no one there; he lifted the silencer-equipped sniper rifle off his back, quietly bringing it forward, flipping out its bipod V-legs under the front of the barrel. He silently got to his knees and slid onto his stomach. He peered through the gun sight at the two faces lit by dancing firelight; he could see their lips moving, absorbed by some story, unconcerned with whomever they were guarding. They were dressed in black, each with a holstered sidearm, clutching imposing-looking Heckler & Koch submachine guns against their chests.

Busch recognized the thin guard with the bony face and black hair; he had followed them to the airport and watched as the jet supposedly took Michael into the sky. There was no question these men had nothing to do with the temple. They were Iblis's men and as such deserved their fate.

With no time for a conscience, Busch lined up the cross hairs, swept the rifle between the two men, and flexed his neck and trigger finger. He took a slow, steady breath, exhaled, and pulled the trigger twice in quick succession. The rifle kicked hard against his shoulder with two gaseous *pops*, and the heads of both men exploded onto the stone wall.

Busch was up and running before the echoes of the muffled gunshots had died out. He ran to the door, stepping over the dead guards, but did not find what he expected. The room was filled with men of the cloth of varying religions, each sitting silently, unconcerned with the two dead bodies.

Busch was surprised at the sight, expecting Michael or at least Cindy. He had anticipated bald Oriental men in saffron gowns, not the host of nationalities and faiths before him.

He found two Sherpas, their traditional climbing attire in sharp contrast to the dress of the men around them. Busch drew his knife and turned to the older one, whose eyes were wise with no hint of fear.

"English?" Busch asked the older Sherpa as he cut the zip-tie binds from his hands.

"Yeah." Kunchen nodded as he rubbed his now-free wrists. Busch handed him the knife and pointed at everyone else. "After you cut them loose, stay in here until I come back."

"We can help," the younger Sherpa said as Kunchen cut him free.

"Yeah, you can." Busch grabbed one of the guards by the

legs and dragged his dead body into the room. He stripped the man of his rifle and passed it to the young Sherpa.

"I'm Sonam," the young man said.

"Sonam." Busch smiled. "Keep everyone in here."

"Where you going?" Sonam asked.

"I've got a date with a devil."

CHAPTER 58

KC found Cindy lying on the ground in a small, cold anteroom off the central corridor, her hand wrapped in a blood-soaked shirt. Her eyes were glassy and she stared at the wall, her body trembling from shock.

"Cindy," KC whispered as she crouched next to her. She rubbed her hand over her forehead and through her auburn hair as if she were a child.

Cindy slowly turned to her, her eyes gradually coming to the realization that her sister was there.

"He . . ." Cindy sputtered as she clutched her hand tighter. "He's my father, how could he . . . ?"

KC didn't know what to say in response to the disillusionment in her sister's voice.

"I'm sorry," Cindy said.

"No, I'm sorry," KC said softly.

"He left me in here to die, KC. He's our father." Tears finally poured from Cindy's eyes.

"I'll get you out of here."

"No." Cindy shook her head. "Find Michael; they're going to kill him."

"I'm going to get you out of here," KC said as she looked at her sister, at her blood loss, her pale skin.

"I'm sorry for judging you, for what you did to take care of me." Cindy's voice was weak. "You gave up everything for me. Don't give up Michael, too."

"Shhh," KC hushed her as she had when they were younger, when their mother was ripped from their young lives, leaving them alone. She pulled her close and that's when she saw the wound in her stomach. She wasn't dying from the blood loss from her missing fingers, but from internal bleeding.

Cindy fell unconscious into her arms. KC held her close, rocking her, hushing her. Everything was on the verge of slipping away, Cindy, Michael—

"Hey."

KC turned to see Busch standing in the doorway, his face sympathetic at seeing Cindy. He approached and knelt beside them. Their eyes met.

"I'm going to get Michael," Busch whispered.

"No," KC abruptly said. "It's my father. I need to do this—"

"Can't let you do that; you need to take care of your sister."

"There's nothing I can do for her." KC's words quivered as she spoke. She took a moment gathering herself. "Iblis will kill you on sight; I can get close. Paul"—KC's eyes pleaded—"I need to do this."

"You can't do this alone."

"Take care of her," KC said as she offered her sister's unconscious body to Busch.

Busch took a deep breath and finally exhaled. He gently

took Cindy from KC's arms and stood. He looked down on Cindy's sedate, childlike face and back at KC. "You get him, and you get back up here, or I'm coming after you."

"Thank you, Paul." KC kissed her sister's forehead and disappeared out the door.

CHAPTER 59

Hemi Masko rounded the corner on the first level, the cold finally beginning to shake from his bones. He was never one for winter weather, preferring the beach above all. He had, in fact, been in the snow only three times in his life, and he always said that was enough.

At five-nine with 220 pounds of muscle, Hemi was as wide as he was tall. His life hadn't taken the path he had intended. He had been a Grecian wrestler, but his career collapsed at the age of nineteen when his shoulder was torn out of its socket. As the years went on he found the remuneration for his fighting skills was far greater in the back alleys of Istanbul than it ever would have been on a wrestling mat.

He had worked for Iblis on and off for two years as a driver, a lookout, and a backup, but in all the jobs he had never been in a situation like this one, climbing up a frozen mountain like a Sherpa, wandering around a treasure-filled temple out of a folk tale. He had never been one for superstition or religion, but after seeing the rooms filled with gold and silver, after seeing an impossible land of greenery in the midst of a blizzard-encased mountain pass, he would be thinking twice about his faith, about what existed in the world beyond the reality he had grown accustomed to.

As he rounded the corner he saw the woman clinging tight to the shadows of the first hallway leading off the central mandala vestibule. Venue's daughter had returned, this time clutching a gun.

Hemi fell into a crouch, and he raised his pistol, drawing a bead on the blonde woman's forehead . . . It had been a while since he had taken a life; he had looked upon it as neither thrilling nor deplorable, equating it to smashing a bug on the wall. He closed his left eye and lined up his sight.

A sound came from behind him. He spun about, gun raised, but lowered his defenses when he saw it was only Iblis approaching. Turning back to his target, Hemi realigned his gun sight on KC. He flexed his trigger finger and gently began to pull . . .

And his body went limp. He fell backward, no longer able to control his legs, his arms; his entire body had gone numb. He tried to breathe but it was as if his lungs no longer listened to his brain, and he slowly began to suffocate. He tried to scream, but the only sound was the terror-filled shriek in his mind.

All his senses were gone but for his sight, and as he looked up his mind spun out of control. For looking down upon him was KC's savior, his killer, the man who had plucked him off the streets and employed him all these years, the last person he would have expected to sever his spinal cord.

CHAPTER 60

Gianni emerged from the stone stairway, Karl, the twenty-year-old neophyte guard, right behind him. Bendi and Thut, the brothers, came next, and behind them was Venue, who walked like a victorious king about to examine his new realm.

They emerged into the cavern and found it eerily dark. Only two torches that sat fifty yards away were lit. Where ten minutes earlier the cavern had been aglow in firelight, now it was heavy with shadows that danced among the stalactites and stalagmites, creating the appearances of black ghosts flitting about. The guards seemed to tighten up at the hellish sight, but it had no effect on Venue. He felt like he was home.

"Where's Michael?" Venue said, looking around.

"Where's Silviu?" Gianni responded with concern for his friend.

All eyes searched. Gianni and Karl flanked Venue. "You need to go back upstairs," Gianni said.

"Not with him loose down here," Venue said. "You find him and kill him, now."

The four guards huddled around Venue were all ready to take a bullet for their leader, as if he were the president.

Gianni led the way to the black door, the group moving en masse. He shone his light into the chamber to find only one torch lit and no sign of Michael or Silviu.

"I really think you need to go upstairs until we find him," Gianni said to Venue.

"Funny, I thought I was in charge." Venue cast a withering look at the guard. "You take a man and go search the cavern, leave two with me in this room."

Gianni held his resistance in check, turned to Karl, and nodded, the silent command given. Bendi and Thut flanked Venue and entered the room filled with gold as Gianni and Karl headed toward the two distant torches.

They both turned off their flashlights, so as not to be targets, and headed in opposite directions. The cavern was impossibly large, its calcite columns and lime deposits fragmenting the enormous space, creating pockets and obstacles where someone could hide without detection. The temperature had to be at least a hundred degrees and the sweat slid down Gianni's back, pooling at the waistband of his pants.

Gianni held his rifle high as his eyes scanned the darkness; he moved along the wall, using the stalagmites for cover. The two burning torches were thirty yards off. He worked his way toward them, using the glow of their dancing light to search for any movement, any sign of Michael. He didn't bother looking for Silviu; there was no question he was dead. The Romanian was his friend; they had both worked for Iblis for several years, slipping around the Istanbul underworld and sharing too many drinks together. Gianni promised himself he would toast his dead friend as soon as he dispatched his American killer.

The torches were twenty yards off now, with no sign of

Michael, when Gianni suddenly caught motion out of the corner of his left eye. He froze in place; there was no mistaking the movement ten yards to his left, shielded by the rocks and lime deposits.

And then he heard an odd noise, like a distant crowd, a buzzing in his ear that slipped ice into his veins. He had never heard anything like it and wondered where it was coming from. He strained his vision to see the man lurking not far away but knew he couldn't attribute the voices to just one man.

The man stopped. Gianni raised his rifle as the voices grew louder. He felt the fear wash over him, the dark creating a terror in him such as he hadn't felt since he was a child. It drove rational thinking from his mind, and he began to see things.

He remembered at the age of ten seeing the animals within the puffy clouds that floated through the blue sky, and when he went to bed at night, his imagination turned upside down. Where he saw animals in inanimate objects in daylight, the shadows cast about his room at night became everything that scared him: monsters and wild dogs, burglars and beasts, all seeming to lurk in the shadows waiting to snatch him from his bed. His nights were filled with frequent terror and restlessness that had been vanquished only by the logic of adulthood.

But now, with the voices in his ears, he reverted to adolescence, his fears growing anew—the only difference was that the something lurking in the shadows wasn't his imagination. It was Michael St. Pierre.

Gianni raised his rifle; he would kill the American with a single shot and get back to the stairs and to safety.

He watched through the near darkness as Michael

skirted one large rock and froze in place, unaware of the gun pointed his way.

Gianni held the rifle tight in his hands; he lined up the sight and took a single shot, the crack of his rifle shattering the silence, crashing his ears. He hit Michael square in the back of the head, dropping him where he stood.

Gianni raced to Michael's body, thankful that he would toast Silviu's memory before the day was done. Gianni pulled out his flashlight as he arrived and stood over the body. Michael was lying facedown, the blood pooling and haloing what was left of his skull. Gianni dug the tip of his boot under Michael's chest and rolled him over . . . and the voices grew louder. His rage mixed with fear as he looked at what was left of Karl's head.

Gianni spun about, furious at his stupidity, at his paranoia. He had killed Karl. Though they weren't friends, they were on the same side.

Gianni looked around. As he stood under the glow of the two torches, the voices seemed to fade away, a trick of the mind, the overwhelming pressure of being surrounded with death. He ascribed the voices to the altitude, to the diminished oxygen warping his mind. He refocused. He would find Michael and kill him.

And this time he saw him, there was no question. Gianni recognized his face, without doubt. He was moving among the rocks, by a group of stalagmites just beyond the second torch.

Gianni moved along the wall, the heat of the cavern rising the deeper he went, bearing down on him; it had to be over 120 now.

He saw him again. Michael was moving away from him, darting in and out among the rocks and limestone deposits.

Gianni threw caution to the wind and, holding his rifle up and ready like a commando, gave chase, running as fast as he could.

And then he had him in his sights. It was a clear shot, as Michael was out in the open, no rocks to hide behind, no outcroppings to duck under. Gianni took aim, slipped his finger around the trigger, and . . .

Suddenly the floor gave way, as if the bottom had just dropped out of the earth. Before he could scream, he sank into the earth, encased in a canvas skin that he realized was a piece of sail. The mud instantly scalded his skin and, as he sank deeper, the sail parted, the mud pouring in around him, filling his mouth, scorching his throat, cooking him from the inside out. Boiling him alive.

Michael walked to the pool of boiling mud. A piece of the sail cloth had caught on the rock but otherwise there was no sign of any disturbance; Gianni was gone.

Michael hadn't known how many guards there would be and wanted to conserve his ammo and not draw attention with gunfire. He had watched them come into the cavern and split up. He had stayed under the light of the second torch, avoiding the shadows, avoiding the fragility that would seep into his mind if he hid in the dark.

The sail had been ideal. Its tattered gray matched the stony ground perfectly; the piece he had cut off covered the pool of superheated mud, masking its deadly presence.

He wasted no more time. He headed back to the cavern's center, to the room where Venue was. It was time to end this.

CHAPTER 61

K C stood in the middle of the mandala foyer, her mind momentarily lost in the infinite design upon the floor, wondering whether if she stared at it long enough, she could truly see heaven, as legend said.

But her mind quickly rebounded; she felt a presence and spun about, her gun at the ready. Iblis stood there watching her, his arms hanging at his sides, his hands empty, no weapons visible.

"Why did you come back?" Iblis said.

"Did you kill my sister?" KC asked, her controlled voice ready to erupt.

Iblis remained silent.

"Did you do it?" KC's voice focused, filled with contained rage.

"No," Iblis finally said. "It was Venue; he called it his parting gift."

KC stared a moment, and they held each other's eyes, until she saw the motionless legs of one of the guards upon the floor. There was no question; Iblis had killed one of his own men.

"I came for Michael." KC raised her pistol, aiming at

Iblis. "Not that you could ever understand what it's like to love someone."

Iblis stepped forward without regard for the gun pointed at his head. He looked at KC, holding her eye, his perfect face relaxing, and for the briefest of moments she saw past his dark soul, deep into his heart, and what she saw frightened her more than death, more than anything they could find in this temple.

She saw his love for her. And for a short instant, it was as if she were a child again, when he had swooped in out of nowhere to rescue her, to teach her, to care for her and Cindy, to save them from their cruel fate.

But just as quickly the memories of Iblis's true self rose to the fore, his callous disregard for life, his brutal killings for pleasure and in the service of her father. She could not understand how such a being could even exist within his own head. He had a true detachment from reality.

"Michael's sacrifice is but a waste now," Iblis said. "We gave you the opportunity to live."

"You gave me the opportunity to live?" KC said, her voice filled with irony.

Two guards approached, their HK MP7s held high, aimed at KC.

"How could you possibly think you'd get past us?" Iblis said softly. "To get in and out?"

KC stepped into Iblis's space, uncomfortably close, and softly whispered, "Let him go, Chris."

Iblis looked at her in shock at the revelation that she knew his true name.

"He's all I want," KC said, hoping to plead to what little

conscience he might possess. "For all these years . . . it's the only thing I have ever wanted for myself. Please . . ."

Iblis stared at KC, his face a mask.

KC stared back, the moment hanging on until . . .

Iblis looked at his two men; they moved in on KC and snatched her gun away.

CHAPTER 62

Venue walked into the torchlit room, the glow of the flame refracting off the treasure. His smile could not have been broader. He walked to one of the mounds of treasure and ran his hands through it: jewelry, coins, weapons, holy crosses, utensils. He picked up a bejeweled chalice, its gold thick and heavy. He examined it up close, marveling at its craftsmanship, its sheer beauty. He looked out over the mounds, haphazardly strewn about the floor in three-foot piles. An entire ship's worth. He walked around the hoard like a man assessing his felled quarry; his mind's calculations of worth stopped after he exceeded three billion.

And then his eyes fell upon the bodies. Venue crouched over the skeletal remains of a corsair, his long cobweblike hair matted to his yellowed skull. He clutched a long saber, its honed edge stained black with blood. A dagger protruded from his bony chest; the hilt was leather-bound, accented with emeralds along its pommel. Venue clutched it and tore it out, shattering the man's rib cage into a pile of brittle bone. He examined the blade closely, admiring its balance, its still-honed edge. Venue wondered who the man before him was, whether it was Kemal Reis or just one of his many underlings who had ventured on a never-ending journey up rivers, through unknown lands, finally scaling a mountain to find the place where he would die.

As Venue looked upon the vast amount of treasure, he marveled at the fact that Kemal and his men had carried it all up the mountain, through the narrow passage, a journey that must have taken nine months of sailing, trekking, and exhaustion.

Venue finally turned to the stacks of books and scrolls, the true object of his desire. He approached them as if approaching heaven. They were stacked on the floor. There were stone tablets, etched in a language he didn't recognize, scrolls and parchments in Chinese, animal skins in Aramaic. It was a collection of writings and prayers, insights on and accounts of the primordial darkness, the evil that has been a part of existence since before the world began. There were maps leading to lost cracks in the earth, to the true location of Eden, to axis mundi that reached not only to heaven but also to hell.

He had read of this trove of literature back in his seminary days; it had been sought by Aleister Crowley, Heinrich Himmler, and Rudolph Hess, though the rumors of its existence were thought to be only the ramblings of insane minds. As Venue looked at them in their physical form he smiled; he had found that a grain of truth, no matter how minute, always existed in the heart of a rumor or myth.

Venue picked up a book. It was in Latin, a language he was more than familiar with from his days as a priest. Its leather cover was made of human flesh, a practice quite common centuries ago. Many times books on notorious individuals were bound in that person's own skin. Called anthropodermic bibliopegy, it was found in many libraries, including those of most of the Ivy League schools of America. Often were stories told of the flesh owners' ghostly faces materializing in the tanned and aged dermis, their souls trapped within the binding.

Written by an excommunicated priest, Jacarlo Jabad, in 1511, this was a treatise on evil, the fallen angels, and the suppression of all things incongruous with the Roman Church. It was said to speak of his encounters with the underworld, much as people of faith spoke of miracles. Bound in the former priest's skin at his own request, it was, Venue thought, a fitting book to start with.

He looked about the cavern, filled with riches that far exceeded his former net worth, but its value was nothing compared to that of the library before him. Sitting under the warm glow of the firelight, Venue gently opened the tanned flesh cover and began to read.

BENDI AND THUT stood back to back in the doorway of the gold chamber, one facing out, the other facing in, eyes alert, guns raised, guarding Venue as instructed.

They had swept the cavern with the gold in search of Michael, finding it hard to concentrate with such enormous wealth before them. They had found no sign of Michael or Silviu and assumed them to be somewhere out in the darkened cavern awaiting Gianni and Karl.

No one knew much about the two men, where they came from, their nationality, their last name, other than that they were brothers. In fact, that one assumed piece of information wasn't even true. They had been friends since they were five back in Spain and had begun calling themselves brothers in their early teens as a joke. Bendi had followed Thut into petty larceny and trailed him through

Europe. They had only done odd jobs for Iblis, but the offer of fifty thousand dollars to travel to India for a few days was tempting. They could take the next six months off and finally enjoy a vacation without having to finance it through picking pockets and stickups. It would be a nice break of bright sun and sand after traveling through the bitter cold and ending up in this dark place.

But the vacation would never happen.

The fusillade of bullets came without warning; the two "brothers" sailed back into the room, their bullet-riddled heads spilling blood upon the treasure. They never heard Michael's approach; they never got off a single shot.

MICHAEL STEPPED INTO the room, the butt of the MP7 rifle held tight against his cheek, smoke still pouring from the barrel. He lowered the rifle to find Venue engrossed in a book under the firelight of the lone flaming torch. He hadn't reacted to the violent deaths directly behind him, nor did he react to Michael's entrance now.

Michael pulled out and shone his flashlight about the room, ensuring no one else was there, flicked it off, and clipped it to his belt.

"Where better to hide gold and jewels than with the demons of the world," Venue said without rising, without looking at Michael. "And the books and scrolls, the secrets of man, the secrets of gods and demons . . . Where better to hide them than hell."

Michael looked at the stacks of scrolls and books, the various parchments that had survived time.

"This all about books?"

Venue slowly closed Jabad's treatise but didn't turn. "This is about far more than your feeble mind could imagine."

"You know, when someone is holding a gun to your head, particularly someone who has reason to kill you, you should choose your words more carefully."

Venue turned and rose to full height. "Do you know what fear is?"

"Yes, as a matter of fact, quite well. But I don't think you have truly tasted it."

"You believe in God, Michael?" Venue asked.

"More than you know." Michael nodded, confident that he had the upper hand as he held the gun on the man.

"Man embraces him in all forms: Jesus, Yahweh, Allah, Buddha, Vishnu. Man reveres him, places him upon a mountain to be worshipped. Yet here on earth we all seek freedom from rulers, freedom to follow our own paths. The days of absolute kings, monarchies, dictators are but a memory. We rebel against authority, against being told what to do, except in the Church. 'Follow the prescribed path written by men and thou shalt spend eternity in the warm embrace of the Lord, where we shalt spend a peaceful eternity in his worship.'

"There are other things out there, Michael. Man closes his mind to them, afraid of what he doesn't understand. There are alternatives to God.

"These books were hidden away to hide that truth. To hide what lies in the shadows, to hide what lies in our subconscious. Who are the monks of this place to judge what man should and shouldn't know?"

"And you're worthy of making those decisions on behalf of the world?"

"I will be the teacher, I will be a resource for the curious about what lies beyond the shadows, beyond the hidden doors. It is time."

"A twisted benevolent act? You're so full of shit."

"Do you know what this place is? Do you know what lies above us? It's Shambhala, Michael. A convergence."

"That's a name ascribed to it by men. An ideal, a Buddhist myth."

"Which you deny even after seeing it, even after standing in it."

"Enough." Michael waved the rifle at Venue, motioning him to walk out of the room. "You're the last person to try to convince me of anything."

"Call it what you will."

Venue laid down Jabad's book and walked through the room, past the piles of gold, and out into the main cavern. Michael followed right behind him, the gun aimed squarely at the man's back.

"You've seen the wealth here—"

"Which you were planning to steal—"

"I don't deny that, but what good is wealth, what good is all this knowledge and power if you're dead." Venue paused. "You still don't see it, do you?"

Michael looked at Venue as they walked through the main cavern toward the only exit.

"You did not see those that live here, those that visit. They do not age. And with all of this knowledge, all these years of philosophical debate, they have yet to share any of it with the world. From upon this mountain one could rule the world."

Michael broke out in a huge smile. "Do you hear yourself?"

They arrived at and stood before the rocky stairs that rose out of the cavern.

"You sent KC to die, you son of a bitch, you sent her to

prison to be executed, knowing she was your daughter. A man like you isn't fit to rule even himself. Get your ass to the door," Michael said, waving his gun at Venue.

Venue remained motionless. "If you're going to kill me, I suggest you do it now," Venue said. "Because if you don't, I promise it will be a mistake you will regret for the rest of your short life."

"You're my passport, for lack of a better word, out of here."

"Do you think there is anywhere you can go in this world where I can't reach into your life and destroy it, destroy everything you care about?" Venue paused. Hate filled his eyes as he looked down at Michael. "Do you really think I'll let KC live knowing how much you care for her?"

Michael smiled.

"Something humorous?"

"I said you were my ticket out of this temple; I never said anything about letting you live."

Venue took a step onto the first stair but abruptly stopped.

"No more talking. I'll shoot you where you stand."

"That would not be a good idea," a voice said from deep within the stairwell.

Michael instantly dove for cover, his gun raised in a two-handed grip, aiming at the dark-shrouded stairs.

"That would be an even worse idea," the voice said. "You don't want to hit KC, now, do you?"

Two rifles emerged from the darkened stairs, trained on Michael; the two guards approached, poised and ready to shoot, awaiting the order of their leader. Iblis came down the stairs behind them, KC at his side. He nodded at Venue as he passed.

Iblis's face was devoid of emotion as he pulled KC by the shoulder toward Michael.

KC and Michael locked eyes, pain-filled and heavy with regret.

The two guards approached Michael and tore the gun from his hand. They spun him around, zip-tied his wrists together, and shoved him back to the room of gold and books as everyone followed.

"You came back for him?" Venue looked at KC and shook his head in disappointment. "For what, something romantic like love? What a waste." Venue turned his attention back to Michael. "I told you, you should have killed me when you had the chance."

And with a sudden burst of violence, Venue drove his foot into Michael's back, kicking him to the ground. "Now, who do we kill first and who's the lucky one that gets to watch?"

CHAPTER 63

Busch carried Cindy into the room where the monks stood. The group parted and guided him to a prayer mat where he laid her down. The blood was everywhere, coming from the wound in her stomach, the shirt around her fingers. Her breathing was shallow, her skin beyond pale as the life seeped away.

Busch looked about the room and turned to Kunchen, who stood in the doorway holding the rifle.

"Where's your friend?" Busch asked.

"He went with one of the monks."

"What?"

"They said they had to go downstairs . . ."

Busch never heard the last of his words as he took off at a full tilt out of the room, running down the hall. He made it to the mandala vestibule and charged down the stairs, coming out in a dark foyer to find a tall monk. His skin was deep brown and weathered; he wore a simple blue robe, and he grasped a heinously evil-looking door, pushing it closed. Sonam stood there confused as Busch charged into the room and grabbed the man, fiercely pulling him back.

"We must close this," the man said in broken English. His voice was calm but firm.

"My friends are down there," Busch growled, ready to kill.

"You don't understand." The man stared at Busch with fear in his eyes. "There are things down there."

"I don't care what's down there, monsters, murderers, or boogeymen, you're not closing this door. Now, get back upstairs," Busch yelled, raising his rifle, pointing at the monk's head. "Before I shoot your ass."

CHAPTER 64

Michael sat on the floor, his back against the wall, under the lone torch that lit the piles of gold and stacks of books. His hands were trussed behind his back, as he constantly struggled to free himself. Venue, Iblis, and KC stood staring at one another.

"I don't have time to deal with you," Venue said to KC in a dismissive tone. "You're as stupid as your mother; you could have lived, but you came back. For that?" Venue pointed to Michael on the ground.

"My mother was far from stupid; she hated you."

"I know." Venue smiled coldly. "Do you know why?"

KC remained silent.

"She hated me because of what I was, a criminal; she couldn't handle the fact that she loved me in spite of that. She was so worried about the influence I would have on you. Ironic, isn't it?"

KC closed her eyes, hoping to block out his words.

"What do you suppose your mother would think of what you've become, darling?"

"She never loved you," KC said painfully.

"Parents rarely speak to their children of their own hearts, of what they truly feel."

"She wanted nothing to do with you."

"Actually, your mother chose me, pursued me. You can't handle that. Her mind was fragile, KC. I never really loved her; how could I? She was just a great fuck, that's where you came from. You were just a by-product of a drunken tumble in the hay. Did she ever tell you that?"

KC's eyes filled with pain.

"I figured as much. Hell, I only married her after I went to prison. And only then for conjugal visits."

"You're a despicable human being," KC finally exploded. "I'm ashamed that your blood flows in my veins."

Venue's words came slow and angry. "I'd be happy to remedy that."

"Thank God she thought you were dead."

"Actually, she was one of the few people to figure out I was still alive. Your mother found out I escaped from prison behind the ruse of death, substituting another body in place of mine. She knew I was alive, she saw my picture, somehow she recognized me, came to me for money, told me she would expose me if I didn't pay her. So I paid her a visit." Venue paused, taking a moment to build up her fear. "She didn't jump off that building, KC, I threw her. But before I did, before she sailed seventy-five feet to her death, I told her the one thing that I hoped would scare her even after death. I told her someday I would kill her daughters, our daughters." Venue paused, taking pleasure in his story. "Then, after she died, I thought of something better. What if I were to turn you into what she hated most? The irony of that would be just too good. I hope she knows that you turned out to be everything she loathed, that you turned out to be a criminal just like me."

KC's eyes filled with tears of rage. This man, this thing

before her, had killed her mother, taken everything from them. He had created her. Everything about her life was the result of Venue's actions: the loss of her mother, the loss of her childhood, the loss of her sister. And just as Michael was about to right her world, he was about to take it all away again.

Venue walked to Iblis and took his pistol from his shoulder holster. He raised the gun and pointed it at KC's head.

"You've taken everything else from me," KC shouted in challenge. "Take my life."

"Goddammit," Michael screamed. "Leave her alone!"

Venue stood there a moment, his mind spinning. And then he smiled. He turned the gun on Michael. "I haven't taken everything from you, KC . . . yet."

KC stepped in front of Michael. "Don't you dare," KC screamed. "This is between us."

"Exactly. You thought to rob me of my desires; I'll rob you of yours."

Iblis stood next to Venue, watching the battle of wills, his eyes flitting between KC and Venue.

"KC. No!" Michael yelled, struggling against his bonds, kicking and writhing on the floor. "You son of a bitch, you can't kill your own daughter."

"You don't think I would shoot my own daughter? You're mistaken."

Venue aimed the gun at KC's heart and pulled the trigger.

Iblis dove at Venue as the report of the gun exploded, echoing and amplified by the cavern.

KC's eyes went wide as Iblis snatched the gun from Venue's hands, tossing it into the darkness of the cavern . . . and collapsed. And as Iblis hit the ground, the blood began to blossom on his shirt.

To everyone's shock—Michael's, KC's, Venue's—Iblis had taken the bullet meant for KC.

Venue stared down at his partner, his underling, his personal assassin, his confusion finally erupting in a laugh.

Iblis stared up at him with his pale, hate-filled eyes.

"You fell in love with her," Venue said as he leaned forward. "Didn't you? When I sent you to teach her all those years ago, when you trained her . . ." Venue couldn't help laughing, but then his humor dissipated as a thought washed through his eyes. "It was you who tipped off the Vatican; that's how St. Pierre knew where she was, how she escaped from prison."

Iblis remained silent as he stared up at Venue.

"You love her . . . You truly are insane if you think someone like her could ever love you," Venue taunted, "that anyone could ever love someone like you."

KC stared at Iblis, backing up as he cast his dying eyes toward her. She slowly fell to her knees, their eyes fixed on each other. The shock of Iblis's feelings being verbalized as he lay dying numbed her. And as he stared at her, she finally leaned against Michael, the simple act of their touching conveying her love for him and the impossibility of her ever having feelings for Iblis.

"And you gave your life for her?" Venue continued. "Did you think that through? She's still going to die." Venue took a moment, watching as the life poured out of Iblis's chest. "You're going to die before I have a chance to punish you for this betrayal."

Iblis's two men stood there paralyzed as their leader lay dying, their eyes filled with confusion. They both suddenly raised their rifles at Venue.

"See this gold?" Venue said, looking back and forth

between them. "Keep me alive, you get to keep Iblis's portion."

Both men's loyalty was easily bought, their smiles reflecting their greed and agreement as they lowered their guns.

Venue looked about the cavern, his eyes finally falling on the bubbling pools just outside the door, and he smiled. "I have the perfect going-away gift."

Venue picked up the golden chalice and walked out the door to the pool of superheated water and clay. He dipped the goblet in, careful to hold only the bejeweled stem, and filled the goblet to the rim.

"Fitting where we are. Before you die," Venue walked back in and stood over Iblis, holding the chalice high. "I baptize you in the name of darkness, in the name of pain, for that is all you will know for eternity."

And Venue poured the boiling muck upon Iblis's face. It hit the left side, sizzling upon contact with his perfect skin, steaming, oozing down, the gray muck coating the side of his face, the smell of boiling flesh filling the air.

Iblis's eyes widened in a silent scream as he writhed upon the ground, his hands clawing at his melting flesh.

"Let your last moments of life be pure agony."

And then, with a sudden sharp jolt, Iblis stiffened and fell motionless.

Venue turned to Michael and KC, who lay against the wall under the lone torch, its wash of flame the only thing lighting the carnage and wealth in the room.

"No more screwing around," Venue said as he turned back to the guards and pointed at Michael and KC. "Kill them both now."

* * *

IN ALL THE confusion of Iblis's being shot, no one saw Michael pull the lighter from his back pocket, Silviu's lighter, a ninety-nine-cent Bic that Michael now held in his restrained hands behind his back. Nor did anyone notice the thin gray strip of sailcloth that blended with the earthen wall and ran straight up to the torch above their heads.

Michael flicked the Bic behind his back and leaned back against the wall.

The small flame hit the base of the makeshift fuse and instantly raced up the strip of cloth, up the wall, up the shaft of the torch, and with a loud crack the head of the torch exploded, extinguishing the flame in the same way Red Adair used to put out oil fires.

The room fell into total darkness, a pitch-black shroud that covered everyone, leaving them disoriented and shocked.

Michael had cut the strip of the sail, poured the gunpowder from twelve bullets along its length, and twisted it up, making a fuse. He had sealed it with dabs of pitch from the torches and used it to affix the makeshift fuse to the wall and the torch. He ran it along the shaft, terminating it at the small charge made from six bullets just below the torch flame.

KC fumbled for the flashlight on Michael's belt.

"No lights," Michael said as he stayed her hand.

"But—"

"Hold on to me," Michael whispered in her ear.

"Why?" KC said.

"Don't listen to the voices."

"What . . . ?" KC's whisper was filled with confusion.

AS MUCH AS KC tried to hide her childhood phobia, her fear of the dark, the fear she had felt back in the cistern in

Istanbul was back. She buried her head in Michael's shoulder and wrapped her arms about him.

As the darkness swallowed KC, her mind lost focus. The voices whispered in her ear; they were primal, filled with malice. The dark that she had always feared in her childhood, that she had struggled to overcome, had returned with a vengeance. But this time, it wasn't her imagination that was running; it was the shadows, the darkness, that was alive.

Michael could feel her beginning to tremble.

"Oh, God," KC said, her voice quivering in fear.

Michael knew the feeling of madness that was upon her.

"KC, don't listen with your mind, listen with your heart," Michael whispered. "You are what saved me, and I promise I will save you."

And then the voices started in Michael's head, and he could hear them himself. They began as a hiss, breathy and biting, like nails on a chalkboard. They filled his mind as he fought to hold on to KC, as he buried his head in her hair, her smell filling him with calm, and the voices began to fade. He could feel their hearts beating as one.

But then the voices became shouts, cries for mercy, cries of delusional rage brought on by terror. But these screams weren't imagined, they weren't in Michael's mind; they were real, coming from the guards, who were dealing with their own fragile sanity.

Suddenly gunfire erupted, deafening in the confined space. Michael rolled atop KC, shielding her, pressing her against the wall, his body tense, waiting to absorb the bullets.

The shots were followed by the sickening sound of bullets hitting flesh, wet and muffled, in quick succession, ending with bodies hitting the ground.

KC pulled the flashlight from Michael's hip and flipped it on to see the two guards lying dead in pools of blood, each having killed the other. She scrambled to her feet and grabbed a pistol off one of the guards' bodies. She spun about, gun at the ready, flashlight glowing, looking for her father. He hadn't made a sound; no fear had erupted from his lips as it had from the guards'. She found him lying atop the books, protecting them from the gunfire as if they were children.

KC grabbed a dagger from the pile of gold and sliced the restraints from Michael's wrists. Michael stood up, flicked the Bic, and relit the torch. The room slipped back into focus.

Michael and KC took a moment, gathering their wits. Michael took the guns off the dead guards and passed one to KC as he took back his flashlight, affixing it to his belt.

"What do you want to do with him?" Michael said, pointing at Venue.

"I'd like to kill him," KC said, "but then I'd truly be him."

"You already are me," Venue sneered. "I live inside you, KC. You said it, my blood runs through your veins."

KC eyes burned bright with rage as she stared at him.

Michael finally laid a hand on her shoulder. "Whatever you choose, I'm with you."

"He killed Cindy."

"I know; I'm sorry," Michael said softly. "And he tried to kill you."

"She'd be alive now, KC," Venue said, "if you'd just stayed away."

"Don't listen to him," Michael said. "He can't face the fact that he has lost everything; he's nothing but a worthless street hood who failed at everything he's ever touched." Michael's voice grew accusatory. "Thrown out of the Church, thrown in jail. Fools the world building up an empire only to lose it; finds the location of one of history's greatest places and chooses to ignore it in favor of all this," Michael said as he pointed at the gold and books. "Let him die down here, alone, in the dark, with his precious gold and books."

KC nodded at Michael. She turned to Venue, her father, her last living relative, sitting there, his bald head shining in the glow of firelight. He was everything she hated in the world: greed and avarice, malice and hate. He held no respect for human life; his heart was dark and without love. In this godforsaken crack in the earth, he was truly where he belonged.

Venue stared back at her, defiant and angry, their eyes locked in mutual revulsion and disgust.

"He wanted this," KC said to Michael, though her eyes remained fixed on Venue. "Let's just leave him here."

Michael removed his flashlight from his belt, flicked it on, and handed it to KC. They both walked out the door toward the stairs.

"Wait here a second," Michael said as he turned and walked back into the chamber.

Michael briefly looked at Venue, who sat by his precious books and parchments with rage-filled eyes, refusing to acknowledge defeat, refusing to plead for his life.

Michael lifted the torch out of the wall sconce, the shadows seeming to jump with renewed life. "I need a little extra light."

Michael looked about the cavern at the empty sconces high on the walls. He crouched to the pile of Kemal Reis's sails and tore off a jagged section.

"Between you and me, and as much as KC hates you, I don't want to leave you all alone in the dark," Michael said as he pulled out Silviu's lighter. He wrapped the gray sail-cloth around it several times, dropped it on the floor, and crushed it with his foot.

"My advice; use whatever you have to keep the room lit, because once the lights go out . . ."

Michael picked up the crushed lighter; the smell of leaking butane filled his nostrils as it soaked into the cotton sailcloth. Without hesitation, Michael touched it to the torch, igniting a fireball, and tossed the makeshift torch high in the air.

Venue watched, confused, as it soared over his head, missing his precious books, which were as dry as a desert wind and as flammable as tinder, landing ten feet behind them in a glow of orange flame. The parchment, paper, and skins had survived the ages in this airtight room that lacked the moisture of the main chamber. They had been blessed by the absence of bugs and insects, rats and mice, vermin that would have decimated this evil library centuries ago.

From beyond the documents, Michael's ball of flame cast a new light about the room, a growing light of intense orange. Venue stared, confused, and then his eyes ran to the walls, the empty sconces . . . And he realized.

The pitch-soaked torches lay scattered beyond the piles of parchment and books, the scrolls, animal skins, and hides. The ancient torches were as flammable as the day they were made and instantly caught. Their flame quickly spread, running along the floor. Venue stood and saw that Michael had laid a section of sailcloth along the floor, spread out behind and under his precious find. The dry cotton material encouraged a conflagration, and within seconds the fire jumped to the first scroll, a two-thousand-year-old prayer to Satan.

Venue scrambled about like a confused child as his world began to burn around him; flares and sparks leaped to the more recent texts and to thousand-year-old parchments. Flames licked the air as black and gray smoke curled up into thick clouds that hugged the ceiling. Venue slapped the dancing fire, pulling away as many books as he could before they were all lost.

Michael took one last look at the room, at the piles of gold and precious gems, the ingots, the golden artwork, artifacts, and treasure, their bright metal aglow in firelight. It was a treasure that would never again see the light of day. A hoard worth billions, amassed through history by nameless men and stolen to end up on the high seas. Kemal Reis, a feared corsair, a renowned admiral of the Turkish navy, gave his life in returning it and many of the dark texts that sat within the growing flame; Michael would make sure his sacrifice was not a wasted one.

As Michael looked about, he suddenly realized something was missing. He quickly ran from the room and closed the door on Venue. He grabbed KC by the hand and charged up the stairs.

MICHAEL AND KC emerged through the dark doorway winded and gasping from the three-minute climb. They took hold of the enormous black door and, putting all of their weight into it, shoved it closed. It hit the frame with a deep, slow thud, sealing Venue and this dark part of the world away.

Michael grabbed the snake-wrapped shaft that sat in the center of the door, the sultan's staff, and pulled on it until it finally tore free in his hands. As the locks fell into place, the door hissed with a mechanical rasp and then fell into a deathly silence. Michael looked at the door, at its hideous depiction of death and of man at his worst, of dark-shadowed beasts and of the suffering of the people who lay in its depths. And he finally understood the door was not a glorification of evil and death, but a warning of what lay beyond.

Michael grabbed the leather tube off the ground where he had left it and stuffed the rod back inside, turning the hasp and sealing it up. He took KC by the hand. They climbed the stairs to the mandala room to find Busch at the top, his gun propped up in his lap and aimed at any intruder, his face awash in sudden relief.

"Thank God. Are you guys all right?"

They both nodded as their minds struggled to cope with their ordeal.

"Venue?" Busch asked.

Michael shook his head, not wanting to speak of the end of KC's father. Though she hated him, though he deserved his fate, he didn't want to refer to Venue's demise in front of her.

"What about Iblis?" Busch said as they began walking down the corridor.

"Dead," KC said, but didn't continue.

Michael knew her thoughts had shifted to her sister, to her death and the emptiness it would fill her with. He briefly turned to Busch and slowed as KC headed out of the corridor. "Did you see anyone come out of here, out of there?" Michael pointed back at the stairs that went down.

"No," Busch said, tilting his head in confusion. "Who are we talking about?"

Michael shook his head.

Michael had seen him hit the floor, had seen the bullet wound as it blossomed red on his chest, had watched as Venue poured the boiling mud upon his face. Michael had seen the small dark man's body spasm in death.

But as Michael had turned to leave the room filled with gold, as he had lit the books and parchment on fire, there was no sign of him.

Iblis's body was gone.

MICHAEL AND KC walked up the hallway with Busch to see Kunchen and Sonam standing with rifles, guarding the door, making sure no one went in . . . or out. The monks were inside, milling about the room, their arms free of their restraints but unable to leave.

"Paul?" Michael looked at him with questioning eyes.

"Everything's fine now." Busch nodded to the Sherpas, who laid their guns down and walked back into the room.

KC followed them in. There was a group of monks, ten of them, their eyes soft and wise; their countenances gave the impression they were the senior of the group of forty. Three were crouched on the floor as seven stood over them.

As KC approached, they parted to reveal Cindy lying upon several prayer rugs. Scores of small candles were strewn around her and incense burned upon small hollowed stones, its tranquil odor heavy in the air.

KC crouched next to her sister's body, her eyes filling with tears.

Michael took a step toward her—

"Wait," Busch whispered, placing his hand on his chest, holding him back.

KC brushed the auburn hair off Cindy's childlike face, so innocent and pure. She lay there covered in a blanket, the monks kneeling at her side. A stillness, a peace floated about. It was the antithesis of what she had felt in the cavern deep below this place. It filled her with a warmth and serenity such as she had never known, feelings incompatible with the death of a loved one.

She looked at the three kneeling monks; their faces were calm and ageless. They were the essence of peace, their legs tucked under them, their hands folded upon their laps. They looked upon her without emotion, without sympathy, holding her eyes for the longest of moments before they turned their gaze upon her sister.

And as KC followed their look, to her shock and utter joy, Cindy opened her eyes and smiled.

Michael looked at Busch.

"Seems these guys know more than just gods and religion," Busch said with a smile.

CHAPTER 65

Venue sat on the floor, much of his collection destroyed, lying in piles of smoldering ash. He had managed to save fourteen pieces in addition to the stone tablets, which were thick with scorch marks.

Venue read as fast as he could, lost in the Latin text, the book bound in skin upon his lap under the lone torch. He read as if seeking the answer to survival, as if the words before him would somehow set him free. The wealth of kings lay behind him and the knowledge of darkness before him. He knew he would somehow escape the confines of this place. He had ventured up the stairs to find the door secured, but he knew there were always alternatives; he had never known failure, he had never feared it. He would find a way to survive and he knew the answer lay in the books before him.

But then the firelight of the torch began to fade, its pitch exhausted. The other torches had long since burned out. There was nothing that could be used as fuel. The sails would burn quickly and be devoured in minutes without the sustenance of a thick fuel upon them.

As the flame fell to but a wisp, the shadows grew longer and deeper, darting in and out at him, flitting about as if alive. There was a subtle sound, muddled and distant, as if from the corner of his mind. It was scratching, its pitch modulating from high to low like the Doppler effect of a passing train. Its volume grew distracting, pulling him from his reading, from his concentration.

The sounds began to grow distinct, separating into voices, voices that he knew, voices that erupted in pain and rage, stabbing at his mind in anger: Jennifer Ryan, the woman whose love he had exploited, who had borne KC and Cindy, the woman he viciously threw from a rooftop; Jean-Paul, the young employee whom he had so ruthlessly murdered. All the people he had killed directly or indirectly: Father Oswyn and the six priests who had excommunicated him, his competitors in business, his underlings who underperformed. Each of the people whom he had destroyed railed against him, chipping away at his sanity until he saw their faces in the shadows, waiting, watching . . .

And as the torch fell to an ember, its flame diminished to sputtering sparks, the shadows moved in, overcoming him in darkness, and Philippe Venue's mind finally crumbled in fear.

CHAPTER 66

A refined man, his salt-and-pepper hair perfectly cut, his blue eyes piercing the morning air, stood on the front porch of the large ranch-style house in Byram Hills. He watched as the limo drove up the drive and came to a halt.

Hawk, Raven, and the younger Bear came barreling out of the house, barking and jumping in anticipation of their master's return.

Michael emerged from the limo and took KC's hand, helping her out. From the other side Simon and Busch came. They carried nothing but exhaustion.

"Stephen," Simon said as he shook the refined man's hand. "I owe you—"

Stephen Kelley held up his hands, halting Simon in mid-sentence. "Good to see you."

Busch walked over and looked down at the tall man. "Hey, Steve." Busch smiled. "You really need a better choice of beer in your jet."

Stephen laughed as Simon and Busch let themselves into the house.

"Hey, Dad," Michael said as he warmly shook his father's hand.

"KC," Michael said, turning to her, "I'd like you to meet my father, Stephen Kelley."

"It's such a pleasure." KC smiled.

"Not half as much as mine. I hear you and Michael have a lot in common."

KC turned to Michael and grinned.

"I told him he needed to find an athletic woman. I hear you humbled him in basketball," Stephen said with a smile.

"Among other things." KC laughed as she jabbed Michael with her elbow before turning back to Stephen. "Thank you for the jet."

"You're very welcome."

"Yeah," Michael said. "Thanks."

"Just wait until you get the bill for the fuel."

KC WALKED INTO Michael's study. She was showered and wore a pair of Levi's and a white cashmere sweater; her blonde hair was brushed out, falling long down her back; her green eyes sparkled with a light that brought a smile to Michael's face.

She looked about his sanctuary, at his golf clubs in the corner, the picture above his fireplace of a 1920s leatherhead football team awaiting the snap, at his overflowing shelves. She glanced at books on everything from magic to safes, chemistry to boats, music to art. She turned back to Michael, who was lost in the map on his desk.

"What are you going to do with that?" KC asked. "Don't you think you should burn it or something?"

Michael looked at the five-hundred-year-old chart drawn by Piri Reis; its detail and insight spoke of more than just the mountain Kanchenjunga. It was a chart that revealed much of the world that still remained hidden.

"Maybe you should give it to Simon," she said.

"He has the rod, he tucked it away somewhere only he knows. We agreed I would do the same. Keep the two items as far apart as possible, with no one other than us knowing their whereabouts or existence."

Michael rolled up the chart, tucked it into the tube, and slipped it into his golf bag next to his nine iron.

He walked over to KC, stepping close to her; he could smell a hint of her perfume, subtle, unmistakably her. He reached into his pocket and pulled out the silver Tiffany necklace. He leaned forward and gently strung it about KC's neck, brushing aside her blonde hair, his heart jumping as his fingers brushed the skin of her neck. He straightened the locket so it fell centered just below her neck and finally looked at the engraving: *There's always tomorrow*. He had been thinking only of sports and rematches when he bought it, but the simple words of hope were much more prophetic and meaningful now as he looked into KC's green eyes.

He reached out and drew his hand down her soft cheek; their eyes held each other as a comfort filled them, as a warmth rose from within places it had been buried away in both of them for so long.

EPILOGUE

The Bay of Bengal was a deep blue, mirroring the bright, clear morning sky. The sixty-foot yacht drifted through the harbor, arriving at the public dock. Its captain threw a mooring line to the shirtless, dark-skinned boy who stood on the deck. He caught it and secured it to the open mooring post. He followed suit with two more lines, helping to secure the boat tightly to the gray, weathered dock.

The man stepped to the yacht's edge and passed a handful of bills to the boy. The skinny child gladly took the large tip, but as he looked up he jumped in sudden fear. He stared for a moment, unable to tear himself from the man's image. He finally averted his eyes, nodded in thanks, and ran off.

The captain paid the boy no mind, walked along the deck of the yacht, and went below. He stepped over the woman's body as if she were a sleeping pet; he had thrown her husband overboard three hours earlier in the middle of the sea with an anchor tied about his feet and his belly slit wide open in invitation to the ocean's carnivores.

The man's face had begun to heal, but the scarring was nothing short of terrifying; children gasped as he walked by, women did everything not to shriek. He was like a monster that had arisen from the grave, out of the depths and darkness of the earth. His left eye was milky white, the pale blue iris seemingly dissolved. The skin from the top left of his forehead down along his cheek, over his chin and down his neck appeared to have melted like wax into a rippled, scarred mass of flesh. He walked with his body slightly askew, twisted to the left as if carrying a heavy weight. The bullet had remained lodged in the bone of his fifth left rib, its pain a constant reminder of his near-death experience.

He took down the framed picture of the husband and wife from the wall, removed the back, and tore out the photo. He pulled out and looked at the dog-eared picture. It was his favorite, the way the sun reflected off her blonde hair, her eyes as green as priceless emeralds. He slid it into the frame, placed the picture back on the wall, and stood back. The subtle rock of the boat made her almost seem alive before him and his heart smiled. She was the only thing he loved in this world. As far as he was concerned the rest of the world could burn.

ACKNOWLEDGMENTS

Life is far more enjoyable when you work with people you like and respect. I would personally like to thank:

Gene and Wanda Sgarlata, the owners of Womrath Bookshop in Bronxville, N.Y., for their continued support and friendship.

Peter Borland, for your encouragement, insight, and that amazing ability to figure out what I'm trying to say. I'm truly blessed to not only have you as my editor but as my friend. Judith Curr, the most forward-thinking professional in the publishing world, and Louise Burke, for her unwavering support and belief. I could not be in better hands. Nick Simonds, for keeping it all together; Dave Brown, for getting people to sit up and take notice; Joel Gotler, my Obi Wan guide in the West Coast world.

And heads and shoulders above all, Cynthia Manson. First and foremost, for your continued friendship—it is something I truly treasure. Thank you for your innovative thinking, your continued faith in the face of adversity, and unlimited tenacity. Your inspiration, guidance, and business acumen are exceeded by no one.

Thank you to my family:

My children, you are the best part of my life. Richard,

you are my mind, your brilliance and creativity know no bounds; Marguerite, you are my heart, constantly reminding me of what is important in life—your style, grace under pressure, and sense of humor are an example to all. Isabelle, you are my soul—your laughter and inquisitive mind keep my eyes open to the magic of this world we live in.

Dad, for always being my dad and the voice of wisdom that forever rings in my ear. Mom, you were always my champion on terra firma and you no doubt still are—how else can I explain my good fortune since your passing?

Most important, thank you, Virginia, for your patience with my unconventional life. My heart still skips a beat when you walk into the room with those dancer legs and deep brown eyes. No matter how dark the day, how high the mountain, or how difficult the task, when we are wrapped in each other's arms, the world fails silent and nothing is impossible. Thank you for our life, thank you for our children, thank you for your love.

Finally, thank you to you, the reader, for taking the time to read my stories, for reaching out through your notes, letters, and emails. Your kind words inspire me and fill me with the responsibility to never let you down.

Please turn the page for a look at
Richard Doetsch's mesmerizing thriller

THE 13TH HOUR

Now in paperback from Pocket Books

THE DARK-HAIRED MAN SLID the exotic, custom-made Peacemaker across the table. With a frame of polished bronze with gold accents, its ivory grip inlaid with precious stones, it was unlike any other weapon produced in the nineteenth century, a six-shooter crafted in 1872 that had been lost to time, forgotten by history, spoken of in collectors' circles as myth.

As with many of the finest pistols of the day, intricate etchings appeared along the stock and seven-and-a-half-inch barrel. But these etchings were unique—religious texts drawn from the Bible, the Koran, and the Torah, expertly rendered in an elegant calligraphy: *The gate that leads to damnation is wide—To hell you shall be gathered together—Yet ye bring wrath—Darkness which may be felt—Whoever offers violence to you, offer you the like violence to him.* The sayings were rendered in English, Latin, and Arabic, as if the gun were a weapon of God designed to strike down the sinner.

Crafted for Murad V, the thirty-seventh sultan of the

Ottoman Empire, it had supposedly disappeared from existence in August 1876 when he was deposed for insanity after only ninety-three days of rule.

"Dual action," the man said as he picked up the weapon in his gloved hand. "You don't see many like this. In fact, I would dare to say this is one of a kind."

Ethan Dance handled the gun with reverence, as if it were a newborn baby. His sleepy, bloodshot eyes scanned the intricacies of the weapon, his latex-encased finger running about the gunmetal and gold in appreciation of the Colt pistol's craftsmanship. He finally laid it down and reached into the pocket of his wrinkled blue blazer.

"Looks like the same religious fervor was scratched into the ammunition." Dance laid a bullet on the table, silver, forty-five caliber. It, too, was etched, the casing wrapped in a flowing Arabic script. "There were five left in the cylinder. They're silver, you know, not sure why, it's not like there were werewolves running around Istanbul in 1876. Then again, the pistol was designed for a madman."

Nicholas Quinn sat across from Dance, silently looking at the weapon. He could smell the fresh oil on its workings, a hint of sulfur residue in its chamber.

"What does something like this cost? Fifty, one hundred thousand?" Dance picked it up again, rolled out the cylinder, spinning it like a western lawman. "This gun was just a rumor, no record of ownership for 130 years. Where do you find something like this? On the antique market, black market, the hush-hush just-between-us market?"

Nick sat there in silence, his mind spinning.

The door opened, and a gray-haired man in a blue suit poked his head in. "Need you for a second, Dance."

Dance threw up his hands. "Kind of got some stuff going on."

"Well, life sucks out loud. With the plane crash, it's the two of us, Shannon, and Manz for the whole place. So unless you want to get back down to that field and start sorting through mangled bodies of women and children, you'll get your ass out here."

Dance slammed the cylinder back up into the gun, spun it once for effect, and held it up, looking down the barrel as if he were aiming at an imaginary target.

He laid the gun back in front of Nick and looked at him a moment before grabbing the lone silver bullet.

"Don't go away," Dance said as he walked out, closing the steel door behind him.

Nicholas Quinn finally inhaled, as if he were taking his first breath in three hours. He did everything he could to hold back his emotions, tucking the news in the farthest corner of his mind, knowing that if he let it run about it would eat him from the inside out.

He was dressed in the muted blue and gray Zegna sport jacket Julia had given him two weeks earlier for his thirty-second birthday, freshly pressed, looking as if it had just come from the tailor. He wore it over a light green polo shirt with his jeans, pretty much his uniform for casual Friday. Nick's dark blond hair was on the long side, in need of a cut, one that he had been promising Julia he would get for the last three weeks. His strong face was handsome and unreadable, a trait that had proven invaluable in business and poker. No one could see through his eyes to the truth in his heart, except for Julia, who could always read his thoughts from just the curve of his lip.

Nick looked around the small, confined room, a space clearly designed for the purpose of creating anxiety. There was the single metal table, the ornate, bejeweled gun upon its lime-green Formica surface; four extremely uncomfortable thick metal chairs, his ass already numb after fifteen minutes; a white wire-caged clock hung by the door, the time approaching 9:30. The walls were bare but for a giant white board on the near wall, three colored markers hanging from a tattered shoelace off a corner. On the opposite side of the room sat a two-way mirror, which not only allowed observation by whoever stood on the other side but also created a feeling of paranoia for whoever sat in this room wondering how many people were watching, assessing, convicting you before a plea had even been entered.

An intense agony began to strangle Nick's heart. Everything in his world had stopped. His emotions had been wrung dry over the two hours before he got here. A swirl of questions and confusion dominated his thoughts.

For the briefest of seconds, he thought he could smell her, Julia's essence, as if it somehow lingered upon his soul.

Nick had gotten home at three this morning after a four-day whirlwind business trip around the Southwest, so exhausted he didn't even remember getting into bed. But he did remember waking up.

As he had drifted into consciousness, he looked directly into Julia's blue eyes, which were filled with love. She had been gently kissing him, drawing him up from whatever dream held him tight, coaxing him back into the world.

She wore nothing but an Eric Clapton T-shirt, which remained on for only three more seconds, tossed to the floor to reveal a perfect body. She was nearly as fit at thirty-one as she had been at sixteen, her breasts firm, her belly tight with just a hint of a six-pack. Her forever long legs were tan and lithe. She was of Spanish, Irish, and Scottish descent, and there was a classic beauty to her face, her high cheekbones and full lips turning the heads of most men when she walked into a room. Her large blue eyes always grew more alluring during the summer when her skin tanned to a light golden hue, with a hint of freckles rising up on her nose.

Julia straddled Nick, leaning down to lightly kiss his lips awake. Becoming lost in her tangle of long blond hair, the smell of lavender and her natural essence filling his mind, Nick's dream of moments earlier was coming to life.

They made love with the heat and excitement of first love, lost in each other's arms, hands roaming each other's bodies, kisses and warm breaths trailing skin. Their passion had rarely waned, even after sixteen years. And it was never merely sex, despite the preternatural lust they felt for each other, there was always the selfless abandonment, each delaying fulfillment in deference to the other, each concerned with the other's pleasure above his or her own, it was always making love.

And as they lay entwined, in the afterglow of the moment, the sheets in a ball at their feet, they both lost sense of time, of where they were, of whatever worries they faced in the coming day, taking comfort in each other's embrace.

With the sunlight dancing upon the white pillows, Nick finally rose from the bed, stretching his toned body to full alertness, and caught sight of the small table on their porch.

Despite her own lack of sleep from too many hours at the office, Julia had risen to prepare breakfast and set the wrought-iron table on the private, second-floor deck just off the sitting room. There was bacon, eggs, fresh-squeezed orange juice, and skillet cake, all fixed and silently carried up from the kitchen as he'd slept.

In nothing but underwear and T-shirts they ate as the sun began its climb in the summer morning sky.

"Special occasion?" Nick asked, alluding to the meal.

"Can't I just welcome you home?"

Nick smiled. "After that first course, a dry bagel would have been more than enough."

Julia smiled back, her look warm and caring, but there was something else there, a hesitation in her eyes.

"What did you do?" Nick asked with a chuckle.

"Nothing." But her voice and the slight dimple rising on her cheek said otherwise.

"Julia . . . ?"

"We have dinner with the Mullers tonight at Valhalla," Julia said quickly.

Nick stopped eating as he looked up. "I thought we agreed we were staying home."

"They're not so horrible." Julia smiled a disarming smile. "I really like Fran. And come on, Tom's not that bad."

"When he stops talking about himself. If I hear one more word about how much money he makes, or what kind of car he just bought—"

"—He's just insecure. Think of it as a compliment."

"How could I possibly think of his yammering as a compliment?"

"He's trying to impress you; he obviously cares about your opinion."

"All he cares about is himself." Nick cleared his plate, placing it on the large serving tray. Julia grabbed the remaining dishes, stacking them atop his.

"I thought we made plans together, not for each other," Nick said.

"Nick." Julia grimaced. "We couldn't get reservations until 9:00."

The moment was suddenly lost as a tension grew between them.

Julia picked up the tray and walked to the door. "It's Friday night; I just wanted to go out."

And she slipped back inside the house, leaving Nick standing there alone.

Nick walked inside, through the sitting room and into his bathroom, shutting the door, turning on the shower. He stepped in, hoping the cool water would wash away his suddenly foul mood. He hated wasting time with superficial friends, those whose thoughts never ran deeper than the menu.

Fifteen minutes later he was dressed in his favorite Levi's and a polo shirt and walked back into the room to find Julia dressed and heading for the door. She had transformed from his sexy wife to a businesswoman in a black skirt, Tory Burch shoes, and a white silk blouse. She picked up her purse, throwing it on her shoulder, and looked at him.

"I think we should cancel," Nick said calmly, in an almost pleading voice. "I really just want to be home."

"You'll be home all day," she said.

"Yeah, in my office working, trying to finish my report," Nick said a little too quickly.

"Why don't you work out? Go for a run. Relieve some of that stress. I really want to go out tonight. It will only be two hours, we can even skip dessert."

"Like that will make the evening any more bearable." His dismissive tone came out as a challenge.

"Just do it for me," Julia said as she walked to the door. "You never know, it might turn out to be a good time."

"What about me? I've been on too many planes to count, and we both know how much I love flying. I'm lucky to know what state I'm in."

"Nine o'clock."

"I don't want to."

"Nine o'clock." The anger was beginning to show in her voice as she walked out. "I'm late for work."

"Fine," Nick exploded, his voice echoing through the room and down the hall.

Her only response came ten seconds later with the slamming of the back door, the thud shaking the whole house.

It was the first time in months that a morning had ended badly. The days were always supposed to start with hope and optimism before being pulled into an abyss by the trials and tribulations of work.

And all at once he regretted his rage, regretted parting at odds over something so trivial as a dinner date. There was always tomorrow, there was always Sunday. He tried her on her cell phone but there was no answer, and rightly so.

• • •

The lights of the interrogation room flickered on and off, the windowless space falling in and out of a pitch-black dark before the overhead fluorescent light settled back into its pale dim glow.

"Sorry about that," Dance said. "The generator's been running over nine hours now. It's seen better days."

He settled back in his chair and tilted his head. "You a Yankees or Mets fan?"

Nick just stared at him, amazed that he would ask such a question, considering everything going on.

"Jeter just hit a grand slam in the bottom of the ninth to beat the Red Sox, six to five." Dance shook his head, seeing Nick's lack of interest, and reached into his pocket.

A second man had joined them and had yet to say a word. His chair was tipped back against the wall as he pushed a few strands of out-of-place hair from his face. Detective Robert Shannon was an unfortunate stereotype, his muscled body crammed into a black short-sleeved shirt two sizes too small, accentuating his arms and chest. His black Irish hair was slicked back, and there was a small scar on his chin. His slate-blue eyes were angry, accusatory. He was spinning an old-fashioned billy club in his hand, tossing it back and forth like a miniature baseball bat, as if he were some beat cop out of 1950s New York. Nick couldn't help thinking the guy was already convinced of his guilt.

Dance pulled a small Dictaphone from his pocket, held it out, and hit play.

"Nine-one-one emergency?" a woman's voice sang out.

"My name is Julia Quinn," Julia's whispered voice said. "Five Townsend Court, Byram Hills. You have to hurry, my husband and—"

The phone clicked off. "Hello," the operator said. "Hello, ma'am?"

And Dance clicked off the recorder.

"She made that call at 6:42," Dance said. "May I ask where you were?"

Nick remained silent. Not out of defensiveness but because he was afraid that if he spoke he would break down. Hearing Julia's voice only magnified his pain, the suffering that infused his heart.

He knew exactly where he'd been at 6:42; he was still in his library working, he had been there most of the day except for grabbing a few Cokes and Oreos from the kitchen.

The gunshot had startled him from his concentration, his hearing grew suddenly acute, and, as if he had been on some delay, he finally bolted up from his chair. He ran out through the living room, through the kitchen, to the mudroom, where the back door to the garage hung wide open.

He couldn't understand why Julia had left the door open again. He saw her purse on the floor by the coat hooks where it usually hung, its contents scattered on the floor. And as he crouched to pick it up he finally saw the blood dripping down the white wainscoting, his eyes trailing it down to see her black skirt, her long leg, her foot in its yellow Tory Burch shoe sticking out by the back stairs, her body, her face concealed by the lowest steps.

And in that moment, all the air left his lungs as he collapsed to the floor. Shaking uncontrollably, he rubbed her leg, calling to her, whispering her name, knowing she would never answer him again.

After a minute, his heart all but dead, he finally looked up, to see his best friend standing over them with tear-streaked eyes. Nick released her leg and rose to his feet. Marcus laid his hands upon Nick's shoulders, holding him back from advancing toward Julia's upper body, putting all 220 pounds of what was once muscle into keeping him from a sight that would haunt him till the end of days.

As Nick fought his best friend to get near his wife, a scream of anguish finally poured forth, filling the small room before dissolving to silent tears, the sounds of the world falling away to nothing as the reality of the moment set in.

They waited at Marcus's house next door, silently sitting on the front steps for over an hour before they heard the sirens announcing to the neighborhood that something horrible had happened. It was a sound that would be with Nick forever, for it was the sound track to his tragic loss and the prelude to the unthinkable nightmare of accusations that were about to begin.

The gray-haired man stuck his head into the room, again. "His attorney's here."

"That was fast," Dance said.

"The wealthy don't wait," Shannon said, speaking for the first time, as he tipped his chair forward and stood up. His eyes bore into Nick as he headed for the door.

"Let's go." The gray-haired man waved his hand, ushering the two policemen out.

The door closed with a loud clang behind them but reopened not thirty seconds later; Nick's heart hadn't even had a moment to slow.

The man walked in as if he owned the room, tall, polished, with an air of wisdom and calm that displaced some of the terror that had enveloped Nick for much of the last several hours. His hair was dark, flecked with gray, silver highlights at the temple; his eyes were sharp and focused. His face was weathered from life, character lines etching the tanned skin about his eyes and forehead. He was dressed in a double-breasted blue blazer and sharply creased linen pants, his yellow silk tie set off against a pale blue shirt, all of it combining to display a man of refinement and taste. He even smelled rich.

"They already took most of you, eh?" the man said in a deep European-sounding voice as he pulled out a metal chair and took a seat across from Nick.

Nick stared at the man, confusion filling his eyes.

"Your wallet, keys, cell phone, even your watch," the man said, looking at the pale stripe on Nick's bare wrist. "They slowly strip your identity, then they take away your heart, and finally your soul, until you'll say whatever they want you to say."

"Who are you?" Nick asked, the first words he had spoken inside the confines of these walls. "Did Mitch send you?"

"No." The man paused, looking about the room, assessing it and Nick at the same time. "With the case they have against you, an attorney is the last thing you need. He'll charge six hundred an hour, give you a bill for half a million, and make you feel like you owe him as you sit in your prison cell doing twenty-five to life."

Nick stared at the elegant man, even more confused. "Mitch is on his way. I've got nothing to say to you."

The man nodded, exuding calm, as he laid his arms upon the table and leaned forward.

"I understand the crippling grief you must be feeling. It's horrible that they don't even allow you a moment of mourning before they start trying to steer you into a confession." The man paused. "When did justice start to become about winning and losing, an us-against-them mentality, instead of the revelation and uncovering of truth?"

Nick looked the man up and down.

"Have you seen the file on you, their case?" the man said. "It's detailed; I doubt they'll even offer you a plea deal."

"I didn't kill my wife," Nick finally said.

"I know, but that's not how they see it. They see motive, the weapon," the man said, casting his eyes at the gun sitting in the middle of the table. "They're hoping for a confession to avoid the extra paperwork."

"How do you know?"

"They'll spend twelve hours slowly wearing you down getting you to confess to avoid the weeks of meeting with the DA for months of trial preparation." The man paused. "You'll be convicted, spend the rest of your days in prison, mourning the death of your wife, always wondering what really happened."

"So, if you're not an attorney, why are you here?"

The man's warm eyes remained fixed on Nick as he took a deep breath, his chest expanding before finally exhaling.

"You can still save her."

Nick stared back at the man, the words not making sense. He leaned closer for clarity. "What?"

"If you could get out of here, if you could save her, would you?"

"She's dead," Nick said with confusion, as if the man were unaware of the fact.

"Are you sure?" the man said, looking more closely at Nick. "Things aren't always what they seem."

"Are you saying my wife is alive?" Nick's voice cracked. "How? I saw—"

The man reached into the inner breast pocket of his Ralph Lauren jacket, pulled out a sealed letter, and slid it across the table to Nick.

Nick looked at the two-way mirror.

"Don't worry." The man smiled. "No one is watching."

"How do you know?"

"They're busy with the plane crash. Two hundred and twelve dead. This town, like your life, has been turned on its head."

Nick felt his world spinning, as if he were in that twilight between waking and sleep where the mind is peppered with incongruous images and thoughts that desperately try to coalesce into a coherent notion.

He looked down at the envelope and slid his finger under the glue flap—

"Don't open that now." The man laid his hand upon Nick's.

"Why?"

"Wait until you're out of here." The man withdrew his hand as he leaned back in the chair.

"Out of here?"

"You've got twelve hours."

Nick looked at the clock on the wall: it was 9:51. "Twelve hours for what?"

The man pulled a gold pocket watch from within his jacket and flipped it open to reveal an old-fashioned clock face. "Time is not something to waste, a particularly true statement in your case." The man closed the watch and handed it to Nick. "Seeing you're short one timepiece, and the pressure you're under, you'd best hold on to that and keep an eye on the hour hand."

"Who are you?"

"Everything you need to know is in that letter. But as I said, don't open it until you're out of here."

Nick looked around the room, at the two-way glass, at the decrepit steel door. "How the hell am I supposed to get out of here?"

"You can't save her life if you're in here."

"What are you saying? I don't understand, where is she?"

The man looked at the clock on the wall as he stood up. "You better start thinking how you're getting out; you've only got nine minutes."

"Wait—"

"Good luck." The man tapped the door twice. "Keep an eye on that watch. You have twelve hours. In the thirteenth hour all will be lost, her fate, your fate will be sealed. And she'll have died a far worse death than you already think."

The door opened and the man slipped out, leaving Nick sitting alone. He stared at the envelope, tempted to open it. But he quickly tucked it, along with the gold watch, into the breast pocket of his jacket, knowing that if they were found he would never know what the man was talking about.

The man had offered no other information, no name, no explanation for how Julia could be alive.

Nick had seen her body, though he had not looked upon her face, as Marcus had held him back, protecting him from her image, her beauty stolen by the gunshot that ended her life. But he had held her leg, seen the clothes she'd worn when she left for work this morning.

There was no question it was Julia. She had called to him when she'd arrived home, but she didn't enter the library where he worked, knowing not to disturb him, knowing he was trying to finish a major acquisition analysis stemming from his week's travels and that if he didn't finish before they went out for dinner, he would be working the weekend.

He could still hear her voice; it was the last time she called his name. And the guilt rained down on him: He had ignored her not just because he was immersed in work but because he was still angry about having to go out for dinner.

Nick reached into his pocket and drew the letter halfway out, but the words of warning echoed in his head. He tucked it away and thought of the man's eyes, filled with such conviction, such honesty, such sense of purpose.

Where all hope had been wiped from the world, this man had reignited it. Nick couldn't imagine how Julia could be alive but . . . if there was even a glimmer of hope. If there was any chance of saving her . . .

. . . he would have to find a way out of this locked room and station.

Grief and confusion had been replaced with possibility and purpose. Escaping from an interrogation room, a police station, was an inconceivable, improbable, foolhardy task, but . . .

Not impossible.

Nick looked at the door, two inches thick, a heavy dead bolt as a lock. There were no windows or other doors. He looked at the white board, the clock on the wall ticking toward 10:00 P.M., and then his eyes fell on the ominous two-way mirror. He stared at his reflection sitting alone in the bleak, humid room in the uncomfortable metal chair, the deadly Colt Peacemaker in the center of the table, and he smiled . . .

The window was made of glass . . .